THE BANKER'S GREED

To: E.D. + SONIA

T.R... (signature)

2011

THE BANKER'S GREED
by
p.m.terrell
and
T. Randy Stevens

Published by
Drake Valley Press
USA

ISBN 978-0-9728186-9-8 (Soft cover)
ISBN 978-1-935970-02-6 (eBook)

Library of Congress Cataloging-in-Publication Data applied for

Printed in the United States of America

10 9 8 7 6 5 4 3 2 1

Authors' websites: www.pmterrell.com and www.trandystevens.com

ACKNOWLEDGEMENTS

The technical, grammatical and editorial accuracy of this book would not have been possible without the assistance and input of many people who were gracious enough to lend their time and efforts to this project, including (in alphabetical order):

Kayla M. DeWire with First Farmers and Merchants Bank, for the cover photograph;

Rebecca S. Fua for the photography used in the book trailer and marketing campaigns;

Pamela June Kimmell, for her editorial expertise;

Suspense/thriller expert Karen Luffred;

Martha McKennon, who was patient with Randy as she typed from his handwritten pages;

Retired FBI Special Agent John W. Neelley, Sr., for his technical expertise regarding FBI procedures;

Branson J. Stevens, for developing the book trailer used in the promotional campaign for *The Banker's Greed*;

Richard Taylor, for his expertise in antique cars;

Barry B. White, Esq., for his legal and courtroom expertise and advice regarding the investigation and prosecution;

Real estate agent Kay Kay Williams in Columbia, TN, for the use of her name in the book.

A VERY SPECIAL THANKS

From T. Randy Stevens to Leesa Morrow Stevens, who was a great critic and cheerleader as he wrote the original story. Her editing was a major part of the success of the manuscript and her influence on Randy continues to be a major element of his success in life. And from p.m.terrell to Leesa, for her constant devotion to the project, her willingness to help whenever needed, and her undying support. This book would not have been written without her.

From p.m.terrell to Randy Stevens, who originally conceived of the plot and the cast of characters; for being an absolute joy to work with from start to finish; for his talent and vision and positive attitude.

And from T. Randy Stevens to p.m.terrell, with gratitude for her work on this book. As an extremely talented and creative author of suspense thrillers and historical fiction, she is a great teacher and motivator. The Stevens family is honored to call her their friend.

1

Jessie couldn't shake the feeling of dread that was sweeping over her.

There was no reason why she should feel this way, she told herself nervously. She glanced at the group of law students who'd gathered at Vanderbilt University's Blackacre courtyard. She had been at Vanderbilt for seven years now; first earning an undergraduate degree and now she was within sight of graduating from law school. She was accustomed to the laughter and polite conversation with premier law firms who courted Vanderbilt's graduating classes. There was a gathering just like this every Friday night; it was a chance to grab a sandwich and chips, maybe a beer or two, catch up with classmates, and participate in impromptu interviews.

But tonight felt different. Jessie pulled her jacket collar closer to her neck and studied the sky. It was the last Friday before Christmas break and there was a chill in the air. She wondered if snow was forecast, but she quickly determined that her anxiety was not weather-related. It was something else; something she just couldn't put her finger on.

"It's not like you to be a wallflower. Care to tango?"

She recognized the voice before she turned to face Nick Rhodes. It was the voice she loved to hear more than anyone else's. It was gentle and soft, although he was over six feet tall and could easily have been a star quarterback. The moon caught his warm brown hair, casting strands of it into shades of deep auburn. His skin was darker than most, perhaps a testament to the Cherokee blood his mother insisted was in them, even if it was six generations deep. But his blue eyes were vivid and sharp, appearing understanding and probing all at once.

"I don't hear any music," she teased. "What would we dance to?"

"The beating of our hearts," he whispered, sitting beside her. He leaned in, planting a kiss just below her ear before his lips unhurriedly followed the line of her cheekbone.

She fought the impulse to turn to him as her eyes panned the students and potential employers. It wouldn't do for her to fall into his dizzying embrace just now, she thought.

But they reached for each other's hands simultaneously, each chuckling when they noticed the other's movements. She dipped her hands into his jacket pocket. It was nice and warm, and she inched closer to him.

"You're freezing," he said.

"I've been out here too long."

He wrapped his arm around her and they sat quietly watching the crowd dwindle down and any remaining warmth sneak away.

"You're still leaving tomorrow morning to go home, Jess?"

She peeked at him out of the corner of her eye. For some reason, just the thought of leaving caused her heart to sink. "You know I have to."

"Are you going to tell them?"

Jessie didn't answer, though she knew what he was referring to. They'd been dating for almost four years now, and her parents were no closer to knowing about Nick than the day she met him. "It's complicated," she said.

"Jess," he said, squeezing her hand, "are you ever gonna tell them?"

"Yes." She turned to look him square in the eyes. It was a mistake, she realized instantly; his eyes were dark and tortured.

"Yes, I am." She snuggled closer to him in an effort to block out the cold. "You know my dad's reputation. I have to find the right time."

"I know." His voice was soft, but she wondered if he truly understood.

Jessica Palmer was an only child, born to a privileged family that the locals referred to as "old money." Nick was everything her parents would have wanted for her, she thought: a kind, gentle soul with intellect, ambition and striking good looks— but he was dirt poor. He'd entered Vanderbilt's journalism curriculum on a scholarship; and what it didn't cover, he'd made up for by working part-time for *The Tennessean* newspaper. His mother had "mental issues," as he kindly put it, and he'd never known his father.

"Abby going with you?"

"Of course! I'd never leave my dog behind." She shivered. "You want to keep her here, don't you?"

He shrugged. "She'd make a warm body to wake up to Christmas morning."

"Oh!" she groaned, ribbing him. "I'll only be an hour away. And we have plans to get together Christmas Day."

He didn't answer, and after a moment of silence, she said, "Gotta get going. I need to get to my condo and let Abby out." As they stood, she reluctantly removed her hands from Nick's pocket and hunched her shoulders against the cold. She retrieved her half-eaten sandwich from the bench where she'd been sitting, and carefully returned it to its wrapper. Abby, her golden retriever, would enjoy it.

It was a short walk to the condominium her father had purchased for her several years ago, but now as they walked away from the others, it appeared darker than usual.

"Bet most everybody has already left for the holidays," she said.

"Yep."

Her heart felt heavy as they continued walking. Nick had been there for her every Friday night, waiting to walk her home. He'd been there every time she'd needed him. Why was it so difficult for her to tell her parents about him? It bothered her to think that he had nowhere to go on Christmas break; that he would remain in his rented apartment just two blocks from her condo, awakening to a neighborhood that was deserted as students fled the campus for the holidays.

"Got any job offers?" he asked.

"A couple."

"Seems to me, you'd go into your daddy's business."

"Oh? Why's that?"

"Oh, him owning that big old bank and all....and being an only child, seems like you'd want to keep the bank in the family."

Jessie shrugged. "Maybe. I'm debating whether to work at the bank or take a job with a law firm. I've been getting some great offers."

"Bet you have." He nodded back toward the party. "You haven't missed a chance to network."

"Neither have you."

They stopped at an intersection and waited for the light to turn, though the streets were almost deserted. As she stood there, moving from foot to foot in an effort to keep warm, a beige sedan whipped around the corner and stopped in front of them.

"Nick!" the driver called out as he rolled down his window.

"It's Aubrey Shippman, from *The Tennessean*," Nick said. "Yo!" he called louder.

"Boss wants to talk to you," Aubrey yelled. "Been trying to reach you. Your cell phone dead?"

Nick grabbed Jessie's hand and they crossed into the intersection, stopping next to the sedan. "What's up?"

"Big story. He wants you to cover it. You're goin' full-time, partner."

Nick's face was a myriad of emotions. He appeared ready to jump into Aubrey's car and take off for the newspaper building, but his eyes shifted back to Jessie. "I've got to take my girl home first," he said. "Then I'll get up with you."

"Big stories don't wait."

"Go on," Jessie said.

"No," Nick answered. "I always walk you home. Always."

Aubrey thumped the steering wheel with obvious impatience.

"I'm a block away," Jessie said. "Look, I can see the lights in my condo from here." She pointed. "I insist. Go."

Nick appeared to hesitate and Aubrey stepped on the gas, moving the car forward by a few feet. "Fate don't wait for no man," he called, rolling up his window.

"Go. I mean it," Jessie said, pushing Nick toward the car.

"You sure?"

"Go!"

Nick bounded around the car as Aubrey stepped on the gas again. "I'll call you!" he managed to say as he slipped into the sedan. The car sped off with Nick's door still open.

As Jessie stepped into the empty street, she felt a wave of apprehension return. "I've walked this way countless times," she said out loud, "and it's never been a problem." Though she thought the sound of her own voice would bolster her confidence, it had the opposite effect. As she reached the sidewalk on the opposite side of the street, she felt an eerie sensation building inside her, as if her gut was telling her to turn around and rush back to Blackacre. Instead, she focused her attention on the condominium building just up ahead. As it came into view, her eyes wandered to the brightly lit window on the second floor behind which Abby would be waiting for her.

It was completely silent. A street light was out near her condo, throwing the sidewalk into blackness. She shivered now as much from the feeling she couldn't shake as from the cold night air. She glanced behind her, almost expecting someone to be following her, but the sidewalk was empty.

Her mouth was dry and her heart began to race. This is so silly, she thought, half-irritated with herself. There were only two more buildings to pass before she would be safely inside her lobby. She inched closer to the street as she began to pass some ancient boxwood. She was halfway past them when a rustling caught her attention and her heart began to pound furiously. Two squirrels bounded out from under the bushes, and she chastised herself for being so jumpy.

But as she reached her building and took the short flight of steps up to the front door, she realized her hands were shaking so fiercely that she was unable to get the key in the lock. Calm down, she told herself. She stared through the glass in the door at the pristine foyer. On the opposite side of the foyer was a wide mirror, and she caught her reflection. Slim. Her dark blond hair crossed over her shoulders and caressed her neck. People had always commented about her high cheekbones, but now, staring at herself in the mirror, she appeared gaunt. Her eyes were hazel, just like her father's—which meant they always appeared to be changing colors—from emerald green to vivid blue and everything in between. Now they appeared dark, almost brown, and wide.

Just get the key in the lock. You'll be inside in a second with the door closed behind you, she thought. One flight up was her condo, and behind that door was Abby. She would feel safe with her.

The key slid into the lock. As she began to turn it, she heard the sound of rapid footsteps behind her. She quickly turned the key and threw the door open. It banged against the inside wall and she rushed inside just as an arm cloaked in black reached toward her.

She whipped around. He towered over her, his broad shoulders extending the width of the doorway. And as she looked upward at his face, she realized in horror that he was covered completely in black from head to toe. A ski mask covered his face and only his eyes were visible—narrow, black eyes that matched his clothing.

She screamed and grabbed the door, ramming it against him. He stumbled in the doorway and as she tried to slam the door shut, his arm caught in the opening. She threw her body against the door, smashing his arm between the door and the jamb. Somewhere in the back of her mind, she knew Abby was barking ferociously; she wished somehow the dog could break through the condo door and bound down those stairs—the glass in the door cracked against her weight and the man's beefy hand grasped for her. She slammed the door against him again and again, his wounded cry strengthening her resolve to fight him off.

Why wasn't anyone coming? She thought frantically. "Call the police!" she managed to scream. "Somebody help me!"

The door was thrown open with such force that it hurled her against a condo door on the opposite side of the foyer. As he crossed the marble floor, she banged on the door. "Help me!" she screamed as Abby's barking intensified. "Help me!" She turned, flattening her back against the condo door. Instinctively, she balled her hands into fists. Her mind raced; she had no weapon—no mace, nothing. Only Abby's doggie bag, a five dollar bill in her pocket and the keys that still dangled from the doorknob.

He approached slowly, without speaking.

She threw the sandwich at him but he easily ducked.

"I have five dollars," she said, yanking the bill out of her pocket. She tossed it on the floor away from her as she inched along the wall toward the open foyer door. "It's all I've got."

He paid no attention as he reached into his own pocket. He withdrew a sandwich bag not unlike the one she'd just flung at him. As she moved closer to the door ever so slowly, he opened it and quietly removed a handkerchief.

The odor reached her nostrils almost instantly, and she screamed again as she threw herself toward the open door.

He caught her and pitched her back into the foyer, throwing her to the floor. She screamed again and again as she fought him tooth and nail. Her fists pounded against him as he knelt on top of her.

"God, no!" she screamed. "No!"

She tightened her thighs against each other and grabbed his ski mask, poking her finger into his eye as she scraped her nails across his bare skin. The ski mask was askew now, and his wounded eye was tearing. She could hear his breathing as well as she could hear her own, and she redoubled her efforts.

But in an instant, his knees had her pinned to the floor and as he knelt over her, she saw the handkerchief nearing her face, the stench of ether so strong that she held her breath. She shook her head, trying to avoid the handkerchief, but as his hand drew closer, she suddenly turned and bit into him as fiercely as a snapping turtle. She held on for dear life as he yelled in pain. She would lose every tooth in her head before she let go, she thought frantically.

She briefly saw his free arm as it sailed through the air and pounded against her jaw, knocking her mouth free from his other hand. And then the world began to spin as the handkerchief was rammed against her nose and mouth. It was covered in blood, she thought. Is it his blood or mine?

Then Abby's barking sounded as though it was a mile away, and the foyer spun into shades of brown and then black.

2

Detective Scott Capps pulled his patrol car past the throngs of onlookers and double-parked in front of the condominium building. He took his time before turning off the engine, his expert eyes scanning the crowd, the building and the police officers. When he finally exited the vehicle, his movements were laborious, his 250-pound gelatinous frame sounding like an ancient, creaking building. He hadn't always been this way; he'd once been a trim, athletic rookie but thirty years and a lifetime of tragedies had taken its toll.

He absent-mindedly brushed the front of his beige trench coat, but it did nothing to flatten the wrinkles that had been there for months. He approached the battleground of yellow crime scene tape as casually as if he were standing in line at McDonald's and watched Larry Johns, a fellow Metro police officer, secure the foyer.

Scott pulled out a cigarette and left it dangling unlit from the corner of his mouth. "Who's the new guy?" he asked.

"Roy Whitten," Larry answered. "Rookie. Told him to rope off a semi-circle around the entrance. You got mustard on your coat," he added as if it was an afterthought.

Scott ignored his comment. "And who's she?" he said, nodding toward a young woman who stood a few yards away.

"Name's Ingrid Karin. Lives downstairs. She discovered the crime scene."

"Best I go speak to her then, hey?"

Without waiting for an answer, he arduously climbed back down the short flight of steps to the front lawn and made his way to the young girl. College student, he thought as he neared her. He'd seen enough of them; they all looked so fresh-faced, so unaffected were they by Life's trials. But as he drew closer, he spotted wide streaks from tears that had been pouring down her face. Her nose was red and slightly swollen and she hugged herself in the cold air.

"Ms. Karin?"

"Yes, sir."

"Detective Capps. I understand you called the police?"

"Yes, sir."

"Why don't you tell me what happened?"

"I—I just got home and found the foyer like—" she nodded toward the building "—like *that*."

"Where were you?"

"Where was I when?"

"Right before you got home."

Her eyes widened. "About a block away. Having dinner."

Scott pulled out his small notebook and began to write. "Anybody with you?"

"Am I a suspect?"

"No. Just routine questions."

"I was with a group of friends—classmates."

"Ah-ha. So you had dinner and you drove home?"

"Walked home. I was only a block away."

"And you live here?"

"Downstairs."

"And what did you discover when you got home?"

"Well, the door was open. It's never open. We're all real careful to keep it closed, and it locks automatically."

"Ah-ha… So you called the police?"

"Well, not right away. I walked up to the door and I noticed a lamp that always sits on the entryway table was on the floor. It's broken..." She began to tear up and Scott looked away while she dabbed at her eyes.

After a moment, he said, "So the lamp was on the floor, broken. Anything else?"

"The foyer was a mess. It's never a mess—"

"Anything else?"

"Yes. Jessie Palmer's keys were still in the door."

Scott's head jerked up. "Jessie Palmer? Not *the Jessica* Palmer—"

"She lives upstairs from me. That's her dog that keeps barking."

Scott turned and looked back at the building as if he could see the dog whose barking filled the air. With the mention of Jessie's name, the case had begun to take on a more serious dimension. "How do you know they were Jessie's keys?"

"Her dad had just given her a Mercedes for her birthday. She was so proud of it—" She began to cry again and Scott waited rather impatiently for her to continue. "It's a silver Mercedes Benz key ring. If you flip it over, it has her name etched on the back."

"Ah-ha. So you called the police?"

"I ran up to her condo and pounded on her door, but she didn't answer. And her dog was barking so ferociously—I didn't know if the attacker was still around, so I ran back downstairs to my condo and called the police."

"Her *attacker?*" Scott probed. "Why do you assume she was attacked?"

She stumbled on her words. "Why, just look at the foyer!" she finally managed to say.

Scott closed his notebook and returned it to the inside pocket of his jacket.

"I know something is wrong!" Ingrid cried. "Something has happened to Jessie!"

"Let's just calm down here," Scott said in what he hoped was a bored tone. "Do you have a key to her condo?"

"No—but her dad does."

Scott pulled out his cell phone.

"I can get his number for you—"

"No need," he said. He used speed dial to call the dispatcher. "Judy, can you get Vincent Palmer on the line for me?"

"*The* Vincent Palmer? The banker?"

"You heard me."

"Hold on."

A moment later, Judy said, "Go ahead."

"Mr. Palmer?"

"Yes. Who is this?"

"Detective Capps of the Metro Nashville Police Department."

"The police department?" he said haltingly.

"We need for you to come to your daughter's condo in Nashville."

"What's wrong?" his voice bellowed through the phone.

Scott held the phone away from his ear for a moment before responding. "Mr. Palmer, you need to stay calm. We don't know if anything is wrong yet. We just need for you to open Jessie's door so we can have a look around."

"You think I was born yesterday? Tell me what's wrong!"

"One of her roommates found her keys in the foyer and we can't get into her unit to check on her. Now, how long will it take for you to get here?"

"What is it?" came a shrill voice in the background. "What is it?"

"I live in Columbia," Vincent Palmer answered. The phone sounded as though it was being jostled, as if someone else was trying to grab it. "I'll leave right away."

Before Scott could respond, he heard him continue in a slightly muffled voice, "Meg, get hold of yourself. It's the police. I'm going to Jessie's condo."

"What happened?" the woman screeched. "What's happened to Jessie?"

"Mr. Palmer," Scott said, "We need you to hurry."

"Where's my coat?" the woman was exclaiming. "Where's my coat?"

"You're not going with me," Vincent said. "Stay here. Jessie might try to call."

"Mr. Palmer—"

"I'm leaving right now."

Before Scott could reply, he hung up.

Scott flipped his cell phone closed. Turning away from Ingrid, he made his way back to the foyer. "Get forensics here to collect this blood," he ordered Larry, pointing to a few drops of blood that lay drying on the floor.

"They're on their way."

He carefully stepped around the door and studied the key ring without touching it. "This, too," he said.

He then turned his attention to a large piece of broken lamp. Poking out from underneath it was a crumpled five dollar bill. Even partially hidden, he could see fresh specks of blood on it. He knew forensics would take pictures of it from every angle before removing it and cataloguing it. Within hours, it would be on its way to the crime lab.

He wandered around the small foyer and up the stairs, carefully noting the lack of blood or other evidence on the stairs or second floor landing. Whoever had attacked Jessie Palmer obviously had not gotten past the front foyer, he thought as he neared her condo door. Why didn't this dog shut up? Was it barking because of all the strange voices downstairs, or trying to tell them Jessie was inside and needed help?

It was almost an hour before he heard sirens approaching in the distance. He made his way downstairs and was just stepping onto the front stoop when a highway patrolman arrived at the complex. Behind him was a shiny black Porsche Cayenne. Before the officer could exit his vehicle, the door to the Porsche flew open and Vincent Palmer was storming across the lawn, his coat flying open as if it were a cape. He was a large man who towered over the others, his wide shoulders appearing even broader under his stiff overcoat. He cut a formidable figure of a man who demanded respect and commanded attention.

"Who is that?" Larry breathed.

"Vincent Palmer," Scott answered calmly.

"*The* Vincent Palmer?"

"Yep."

"The guy who runs Maury County?"

"Tries to. My cousin used to be sheriff there. It's because of the Palmer family that he lost his job."

"Yeah; I heard he was a piece of work."

Vincent took the steps two at a time.

"Mr. Palmer," Scott said, "I'm Detective Scott Capps."

He brushed past him.

"Mr. Palmer," Scott said, his voice growing louder as he followed him up the stairs to Jessie's condo, "I'm the one who called you. I need for you to wait and let the police enter the unit first."

From the foyer below, he heard the highway patrolman speaking to Larry. "I clocked that guy going 114 miles an hour. He didn't want to stop; I was getting ready to radio for backup when he slams on his brakes and stops right in the middle of the street. Tells me he doesn't have time for me; his daughter is in trouble—he *demanded* I escort him here!"

"You follow citizens' demands, do ya?" Larry answered.

"When they got the Governor on speed dial, I do!"

Scott could hear Larry chuckling.

"He's yours," the patrolman said, "Good riddance."

"Mr. Palmer," Scott called out again, "we've got procedures here. Please wait for me—"

Scott was gasping for air as he neared the top step. But before he could join Vincent at the door, he'd opened it and stepped inside. A blur of light golden fur flew past Scott, almost knocking him off his feet as it bounded down the stairs.

"Close the door!" he bellowed. "Don't let the dog out!"

He grasped the railing and peered downstairs. But the dog stopped cold in the foyer and began to sniff around. "Somebody get that dog!" he yelled. "She's disturbing the crime scene!" When he turned back around, the door to Jessie's condo was open and Vincent was nowhere to be seen.

"Mr. Palmer!" he shouted as he rushed to join him. "You cannot come in here! We have police procedures!"

"Don't tell me what I can't do!"

Scott swore under his breath.

He was sweating profusely as he entered the condo. In contrast with the scene below, Jessie's unit appeared pristine, even tranquil. He walked through the living room and dining area, noting the upscale furniture. It wasn't cheap stuff, he noted.

He found Vincent in the bedroom.

"Anything missing?" Scott said, taking in the flat screen TV on the wall, the laptop and accessories on the desk, and the crisply made bed.

"I don't think so," Vincent said.

"Mr. Palmer—"

"Where's Jessie?"

"We don't know."

"What do you mean, you don't know?"

"Come downstairs with me, and I'll fill you in on all the details."

"You'll fill me in right here, right now."

"Actually, Mr. Palmer, I won't." With that, Scott turned and made his way back through the dining area. He glanced into the kitchen, where state of the art appliances gleamed in the overhead light. As he approached the door to the condo, he stopped. He'd been in such a hurry to catch up with Jessie's father, he hadn't noticed the pile of wood shavings on the floor. With one finger, he pushed the door almost closed. The back of the door was scratched and scuffed—the signs of a dog frantic to get out, he thought. That dog knows what happened.

As Scott suspected, Vincent followed him downstairs. The dog was placed into the back seat of the Porsche, where her nose remained plastered against the window. Eventually, the windows fogged up and all Scott could see were smeared nose prints all over the glass. Despite himself, he smirked at the sight.

He was just finishing up explaining the situation to an increasingly impatient Vincent Palmer when he caught sight of the rookie cop trying to get the crowd to move on. There was something about one of the bystanders that caused him to pause and watch. He couldn't quite put his finger on it—not yet, anyway—but through the past thirty years, if there was one thing he'd learned, it was to follow his hunches.

He crossed to the edge of the crime scene tape and stood in front of the young man.

"You know Jessica Palmer?" Scott asked him.

The man's eyes shifted toward Ingrid Karin before answering. "We both go to Vanderbilt."

"Then you *do* know her."

He squeezed his lips together as if he were biting the inside of his upper lip. His eyes shifted toward Vincent before he answered, "We share a class."

"That right?" Scott said, raising the crime scene tape. "Come on over here. Let's talk."

As the young man knelt under the tape, Scott continued, "What's your name again, son?"

"Nick. Nick Rhodes."

"You live in this building?"

"No." This time the response was immediate. "I rent a place couple blocks away."

"So when was the last time you saw her, Nick?"

He had a pained look on his face as he answered, "Maybe an hour ago. Maybe two."

"Where?"

"Blackacre. We left together; I walked with her to that traffic light," he said as he pointed down the street.

"Why'd you stop at the traffic light?"

He didn't look at the officer but continued staring at the intersection where they'd parted. Scott thought he saw a tear in the young man's eye and he maneuvered closer so he could see it more clearly, but Nick looked down at his shoes. "A—friend—stopped me. Told me I was wanted at work."

"And where's work?"

"*The Tennessean.*"

"So if I call *The Tennessean*, they'll tell me you were there tonight?"

"Ah-ha."

"It's the truth," Nick said, bristling.

"So you left her in the middle of the intersection to get home by herself." Before Nick could respond, he added, "Why are you here now?"

"I can see her place from my apartment window. I saw the crowd over here and the cop cars and came to see what was happening... What is happening? Is Jessie okay?"

"Detective?"

Scott turned to look at the rookie.

"What do you want me to do with this?" He held up a plastic pouch.

Before Scott could respond, Vincent marched up from behind and grabbed the pouch out of his hand. In one swift movement, he emptied the contents into his palm. "It's Jessie's key ring! Where did you get this?"

"You idiot!" Scott blasted. "That key ring is evidence! Get your fingers off it." He swore as he grabbed the key ring with the plastic pouch and shook it back into the bag. "This could have fingerprints on it. You may have just destroyed evidence!"

"This is preposterous!" Vincent roared. "You handed me the pouch and it was unzipped. If you knew what you were doing, you would have had it secured and protected!"

"Nobody handed you that pouch!"

From over his shoulder, Scott heard the dog barking and snarling as she tried vainly to get out of the car. He could only hope the dog had torn Palmer's leather seats to shreds.

Vincent's cell phone began to ring. Frustrated, Scott returned the pouch to the rookie. "What's your name again?"

"Roy Whitten."

"Listen, *Roy Whitten*, you'd better put this right back where forensics left it and get out of my crime scene. You got that?"

"What? Who is this?"

At the sound of Vincent's voice, Scott turned back to him. His face was becoming ashen and his jaw had gone slack. Scott stepped closer to him and placed his hand on top of Vincent's as he held the phone. Oddly, Vincent did not attempt to wrench it away from him.

The volume was turned up on the phone so Scott could hear it without having to wrestle with Vincent for it. The voice on the phone was husky—too husky, Scott thought, as if the caller was speaking through a cloth laid over the mouthpiece. "If you want to see Jessie alive," he was saying, "it'll cost you five mil. Got it?"

"Let me talk to her!" Vincent demanded.

"Get the money. Then you can talk to her." With that, the caller hung up.

"Give me the phone," Scott said. He flipped through the Caller ID. *Anonymous.* He used his own cell phone to call his office. "Put a trace on the last call placed to—what's your phone number?"

Vincent answered robotically and Scott repeated it.

"Who's your carrier?"

As Scott relayed the information to his office, Vincent began to sway.

"You okay?" Scott said, hanging up.

"My cell phone number is private."

"How'd they get your number then?"

"I—I don't know." As he stared at Vincent, his eyes became larger. "Get her back!" he insisted. But his voice had lost its authority, the words tumbling out as more of a plea than a demand.

"This is out of my hands now," Scott said, almost apologetically.

"What do you mean, out of your hands?" Vincent's spine snapped to attention.

"We're looking at a kidnapping case, Mr. Palmer. I'm going to have to call my supervisor."

"Your—?"

"I'm going to have to ask you to stay right here. He'll want to speak to you."

Scott turned his back to Vincent. Forgetting Nick, he dialed his office. But before he could advise them of the situation, he heard tires screeching behind him. He turned just in time to see the sleek black Porsche pulling away from the curb and barreling down the street.

3

Jessie couldn't remember the last time she'd slept in such an awkward position. But as she attempted to roll over and stretch, she realized she was not in her familiar, cozy bed at home but in the confines of a vehicle that jostled her relentlessly as it placed miles behind them.

She struggled to open her eyes through a dizzy haze that threatened to engulf her. In the back of her mind, she knew her survival could depend on her ability to break through the grogginess, while another part of her wanted nothing more than to fall back asleep.

The vehicle lurched and her head bounced off the door, causing her eyes to jerk open.

She was in the back seat of an aging vehicle with stark metal doors, Spartan seats with imprints where the springs had long ago given way under heavy bodies, and the rancid stench of old food.

She struggled to move but her wrists and ankles were bound with duct tape that threatened to rip the hairs from her skin with every movement.

As the vehicle continued to bounce her unceremoniously around the back seat and she began to regain full consciousness, pure panic swept over her. She tried to open her mouth to scream, to call for help—but her lips were wrapped around a filthy cloth that had been jammed into her mouth. Efforts to spit it out only resulted in a caustic taste that almost caused her to pass out once again. With a sinking heart, she realized it was covered with another cloth that had been tied around her head. And with each minute that passed, she was being taken further and further away from Nashville.

How long have I been out? She wondered. As she looked upward through the windows, she realized it was still dark; she might have been unconscious for a few minutes or a few hours. And as a steady light sped through the vehicle, she recognized the regular rhythm of the Interstate's street lights as they passed under each one in turn.

She inched her way onto one elbow. There were two people in the front seat and for a fleeting moment, she considered kicking the back of their seat with enough force to throw them into the dashboard and run the vehicle off the road. But as she struggled to gather momentum, she realized she had no more control over her legs than she had over her voice or her wrists. She was, she realized, at the mercy of these thugs.

She fought the panic that threatened to overwhelm her. I must stay calm, she told herself over and over again. But the constant refrain did nothing to dispel her rising terror. And after a few moments, she tried instead to focus on her surroundings, to memorize this vehicle, this stench, the two people who sat only inches away from her but appeared oblivious to her awakening.

As her eyes adjusted to the streaks from the Interstate lights followed by brief periods of darkness, she searched for anything that would help her describe the vehicle to the police—because, she told herself with more conviction than she felt, she *would* get out of this alive. And the scum in the front seat would pay for what they'd put her through.

As her eyes surveyed the back seat and what she could see of the front, she realized she was not in a car but in a truck with an extended cab. From the constant rattling of the engine, she realized it was straining at the faster highway speed; perhaps, she thought, this was more of a farm vehicle, unaccustomed to being driven on public roads. As her mind began to focus on more details, she began to feel a calmness sweep over her. It was slow at first and almost imperceptible, but then her heart stopped its rapid-fire thumping and her breathing ceased to cause her chest to heave with its exertion.

"That's it," one of the people in the front seat said. It was a male voice, muffled and low.

As she labored to move into a seated position, the vehicle slowed with such instant deceleration that it almost tossed her onto the floor. Then they were whizzing around an off-ramp, heading under the Interstate and onto another road.

She was able to maneuver close enough to the side door to prop her elbow onto the armrest and haul herself closer to an upright position. She glimpsed the neon lights of aging motels, a restaurant name with half its lights out and the other half flickering, and a gasoline station with old-fashioned pumps. The sign by the road read "Gulf Oil" and the price was seventy-nine cents.

She tried to think back to all the times she'd driven home from Nashville, all the occasions when she'd visited friends. But these remnants of yesteryear did nothing to stir feelings of familiarity within her. And as the vehicle bounced and jostled her, she realized they were moving further from civilization and deep into a rustic countryside where time appeared to have stood still.

I have to escape, she thought, her eyes darting wildly from one man to the other. But how?

The driver took a cigarette out of his shirt pocket. She watched him through the rearview mirror as he lit it, his hands slow and steady. She tried to see his face, to memorize his features, to view anything that could help her identify her kidnappers later—but he wore a golf cap with a brim set low on his forehead, casting his face in shadow. As he took his first puff, Jessie took a deep breath and allowed her lungs to fill with stale air.

She felt a surge of adrenaline as she slammed her bound fists against the driver's head, pushing him forward with such force that the sound of his head hitting the steering wheel reverberated over the engine. Out of the corner of her eye, she caught a glimpse of the other man's wide eyes and open mouth. He lunged for her but the driver's frantic efforts at regaining control of the steering wheel caused the vehicle to swerve, sliding the other man across the seat and slamming him into the passenger door.

Instinctively, she wrapped her arms over the driver's head, cramming the golf cap across his face, until she felt his throat beneath her skin. Then with all the strength she could muster, she squeezed with the power of a boa constrictor. If she could only snap his neck, she thought in a growing rage borne of panic— She felt the tension growing as she tightened her hold on his throat, his Adam's apple collapsing into a slow-motion bob.

She caught a glimpse of herself in the rearview mirror, her eyes wild and animalistic, the pure terror mixed with determination frightening her even further. And as the vehicle careened out of control, she glimpsed the golf cap against the driver's face like a grotesque mask. In the middle of the cap, her eyes rested on an oval, multi-colored shark logo. She'd seen that emblem somewhere before, she thought, her eyes riveted on it.

Then the vehicle swerved and the man in the passenger seat sprang back into action. He moved like a wild man as he struggled to regain command of the out-of-control vehicle while simultaneously fighting to free the driver from Jessie's grasp. But her bound wrists were now so close around his neck that the duct tape was adhering to his skin. The golf cap collapsed as his nostrils fought for air; then the imprint of his mouth appeared as he gasped.

Even as the vehicle bounced and veered from one side of the road to the other, careening along the shoulder and tossing gravel into the air, her arms remained fixed around his neck. Blood began to spurt onto the golf cap in the vicinity of his mouth and throat and Jessie closed her eyes.

I've never killed a man before, she thought, fleetingly considering whether to relax her grip on him. But in the next

instant, she knew she couldn't dare relinquish her deadly grasp—
to do so could sign her own death warrant.

The stench of smoke and fire spread upward through her
nostrils and she shook her head, trying to clear her nose. The
cigarette had fallen and was beginning to burn through the front
seat. In an instant, she realized the old vehicle's stuffing was visible
through the cracked, aged leather and now it was igniting with
frightening speed.

Unable to gain control of the vehicle, it began to spin
dizzyingly. Jessie closed her eyes as the neon lights from a nearby
motel spun past her three and then four times. The other man
fought to steer the vehicle back into the roadway but the driver's
foot had slammed the gas pedal to the floorboard.

As they crisscrossed the road, she felt a rising sensation in
the pit of her stomach, as if they were becoming airborne. Then
they slammed into a ditch with such speed that the man fighting
for control of the vehicle hit the windshield with so much force
that it cracked the glass. The driver's head collided against the
steering wheel and lolled forward, pulling Jessie's arms with him.
She found herself straddling the headrest, her abdomen jammed
against the back of the seat with such pressure that she was
unable to catch her breath. Gasping desperately for air, her arms
now flailed helplessly as the vehicle went airborne once again.

The windshield was filled with the sight of pine trees as the
vehicle sheered through them. As if the world had slowed around
her, Jessie stared at the needles that remained stuck in the cracked
windshield and the pine cones that seemed to turn into grenades.

When the truck came to a stop, they were surrounded by a
grove of trees. The vehicle swayed first to one side and then to
the other, as if the only thing holding it up were the bent trunks
of trees too small and too weak to support them for more than
a moment.

The driver remained slumped over the steering wheel. Jessie
wrestled with the duct tape that was glued both to her wrists
and to his neck.

The passenger looked like a madman. His sandy hair, long
and unkempt, stuck out in every direction. As he turned to her,
the moonlight caught his eyes, causing them to appear wide,

glazed and otherworldly. His mouth was moving, his teeth yellowed and uneven. Somewhere in the haze that was taking over her mind, she realized he was shouting obscenities at her but his voice seemed to fade into the air before it reached her.

Liquid was running down her face and she wiped her eyes with the back of her arm. When she pulled it away, her arm was bloodied. Her head was beginning to loll and she realized she was in danger of losing consciousness.

Before she could rally her strength, she felt the full force of his fist between her eyes. As her head jerked backward, she heard a snap so thunderous that she wondered if her neck had broken. Funny, she thought, I don't feel anything...

Then the passenger was pulling a ski mask over his face, hiding all but his blazing eyes and the tip of his nose. It was scarred, she thought as she stared at it. Viciously, he tore her wrists from the neck of his accomplice and jerked them over the unconscious man's head. With the sudden movement came a searing pain that ripped through her body like a bolt of lightning.

Then she was struck again against the side of her head, causing her body to thrust backward as the vehicle teetered precariously. The last thing she remembered before all went black were the trees swaying against the windows, their fragile branches screeching with every move. And as her eyes closed and she slumped backward, something deep inside her told her: it wasn't the branches that were screeching; it was her own voice.

4

It was a small office with an odd mixture of aging file cabinets filled with the distinctive odor of old paper and desks crammed with desktop computers, the wires forming unbridled spaghetti that snaked across the office as though they were alive. The windows were large, their sheer size a problem when the sun rose and bore down on the busy group of employees. But now, they seemed almost asleep, the full moon shining in a cloudless sky, millions of miles away but seemingly within his grasp.

FBI Special Agent Grant Bailey rubbed his eyes and glanced at the window closest to him. His reflection stared back at him, and for a brief moment, he didn't recognize himself. His features had once been described as chiseled, his jaw firm, his green eyes intense, his hair thick. He'd prided himself on his six-pack abs and muscled arms, his easy gait a reflection of his inner strength and confidence. Now the eyes that stared back at him were weary and rimmed with red. Bags formed underneath them, exposing his chronic lack of sleep. There were jowls beneath his jaw, and his thick brown hair had been replaced with thinning salt and pepper strands. His white shirt seemed huge as it was reflected in the window; he couldn't be that large, he thought as he stared at the way it widened as it reached his middle. He subconsciously reached for his belt, realizing it was hidden beneath an expanding midriff.

He forced himself to look away from his reflection and stare downward at Nashville's downtown, where the neon lights flashed and the faint sound of country music wafted upward from the bars below. When he gazed downward, the city came alive and his heart for the briefest of moments quickened its pace.

Then he turned back to his desk and the half-eaten sandwich that rested off to the side, the constant hum of voices lulling him back into complacency. It was just another Friday night in the office, a Friday night that began what he dreaded most: a weekend off.

He drummed his fingers on the top of his desk and stared at the mounting paperwork. It was never-ending. He was glad for the work, as it kept him busy, too busy for the memories to come racing back. They came on the weekends, at the oddest of times: when he was standing over the stove, heating a can of Spaghetti-O's, or as he glimpsed his reflection in the bathroom mirror, or when he passed *her* bedroom, the room with the white furniture and pink ruffled bedspread…

"You gonna finish that?"

The voice startled him back to the present. He glanced up to see his partner, Agent Ivory Lang, pointing at the half-eaten sandwich.

"Go ahead," he said.

She picked it up and bit into it, her eyes rolling back for a moment as she enjoyed it. He studied her mahogany complexion as she ate. She was frequently the butt of jokes because her name didn't match her appearance, but her response was always rapid-fire and no-nonsense: "My teeth are ivory. What's your problem?"

She was in her late twenties. She was rail thin with a metabolism he envied. She was tall enough to be considered statuesque but she could never have been considered model material, he thought. Her lips were too full, her eyes too wide set, and her dark skin showed permanent acne damage. He enjoyed working with her, even if she didn't have the years of experience he had. But then, he reasoned, she was fresh and daring, where he… he was tired.

The phone rang and she reached across his desk to grab it, wiping the back of her hand across her lips.

"If this is another bank robbery—" he began but didn't finish the sentence as she answered the phone. He sighed and looked again at the mound of paperwork. Bank robberies were his specialty, and he had plenty to keep him busy.

Ivory was looking at him. "Can I tell him who's—?"

He could hear a voice on the other end of the line, cutting her off. It was male; brusque and rude.

She held the phone out to him. "It's for you." Her lips were pursed and she tilted her head. He'd seen that tilt before; it was the kind of gesture that was usually followed up with a wisecrack.

He took the phone and mouthed, "Who is it?"

"Vincent Palmer," she mouthed back, leaning over the desk to gauge his reaction.

He felt his cheeks flush. He held the phone against his chest and whispered, "Why's he calling me?"

"Why don't you ask him?" she said slowly, her lips smacking with the last word. Another line began to ring, and she moved back to her own desk to answer it.

"Yes, Mr. Palmer," Grant said, "what can I—"

"Be at my home in thirty minutes."

"Excuse me?"

"I'll meet you there. I'm on my way."

"On your way from where? Mr. Palmer, what's going on?" He felt his face grow hotter. He really had to watch it or his blood pressure was going to spike, he thought. "I can't just drop—"

"It's Jessie. She's been kidnapped."

Grant gasped, despite himself.

"And my wife and I want you to handle it. You—you would understand."

Ivory was staring at him from her desk as she listened intently to the caller on the other line. "Mr. Palmer," he said, his words measured, "I do understand. But I can't take instructions from civilians. I need my supervisor—"

Ivory shook the receiver in the air a couple of times, and Grant frowned.

"Your supervisor will approve it," Vincent said. "Be there."

Before Grant could respond, he was met with a dial tone. He let the receiver dangle from the cord as he glared at Ivory. "What?"

She continued to shake her own receiver. "The man's got friends in high places."

"What are you talking about?"

"That was the boss. Mr. Palmer's already been on the phone with the attorney general. The case has been bumped to the FBI… and you've just been assigned the case."

The drive from Nashville to the Maury County line was a blur, both agonizingly slow and gone in a flash. Though Grant was driving, he didn't remember turning onto Highway 43 nor did he recall the turnoff near the Maury County line. Though his unblinking eyes were focused ahead, his mind was miles—and years—behind him. It was as if it was happening all over again; only it was happening to *him*… And there was still a chance of saving *her*.

"You okay?"

The voice startled him and as he glanced at Ivory in the passenger seat, her eyes were wide and concerned.

"Don't you worry 'bout me," he said grimly as he slowed the vehicle.

"You don't look okay."

He turned left between two overgrown bushes that almost completely obscured a narrow driveway. As the headlights caught the gravel, it revealed two narrow ruts with a grassy strip in between that snaked its way around overbearing evergreens that raked the roof of the car.

"This can't be it," Ivory said.

"Oh, it's it, alright."

"How can you be sure?"

"Been here plenty of times when I was a kid—back when the home was open every year to the school field trips."

"You're kidding me."

He almost slowed to a stop to round a hairpin curve. "Yep. Then Old Man Palmer—Vincent's father—had the National Historic Landmark sign removed. Never came back after that."

"What'd he do that for?" Ivory asked as she involuntarily ducked. A giant branch scraped the windshield, creating a piercing sound akin to fingernails on a blackboard.

"Said the sign violated his privacy. Same year, the schools were told this place was off limits."

"I don't know what I'm most surprised about—the fact that the Society allowed it, or that he did an about-face on the school visits."

"Money talks," Grant stated flatly.

"You sure know a lot about this Palmer guy."

"Never met him."

The trees seemed to close in around them like a dense forest coming alive; even in December, the woods were flush with thick green boughs. Grant's mind registered the overgrowth of evergreens as he continued to navigate the narrow, meandering driveway. Without even a mail box at the main road, anyone venturing this far would assume they'd made a wrong turn. As if in response to his thoughts, there was a clearing that appeared out of nowhere; a clearing just large enough for a car to turn around and head back to civilization.

As he passed by the clearing, the road narrowed further, the trees becoming so impenetrable that they blocked the moon's meager light. An owl hooted in the distance. He could feel Ivory's body tensing beside him.

Then around another hairpin turn, they came to an abrupt stop.

They sat for a moment without speaking. Grant took in the massive iron gate that blocked their path, the twelve foot brick wall that joined it on either side only to disappear within the folds of the thick woods, and the security system that provided both a camera view of their vehicle and a speaker that rose out of the underbrush like a black serpent.

He rolled down his window and leaned toward the speaker. But before he could press the button to speak, the gates came alive with an agonizing wail, spreading wide to allow their entry.

He glanced at Ivory just as her Adam's apple bobbed with a giant swallow.

"This reminds me of a prison," Ivory said, her voice barely above a whisper. Catching his eye, she forced a chuckle. "You sure we'll be able to get back out?"

Grant hit the button to roll his window back up. "Count on it," he said gruffly. "He's an eccentric and he's paranoid. And he doesn't like company."

Once through the gate, the road widened to smooth asphalt. The woods were replaced with a rolling lawn that remained green even in winter. Grant took in a swath of bright yellow and purple pansies transforming the landscape into something akin to a Monet. Full-time landscapers, he thought wryly.

Then they rounded a gentle curve and a massive mansion atop a hill seemed to appear out of nowhere. Strategically placed in the landscape were brilliant floodlights that shone on the structure, illuminating eight immense stark white columns that rose from the ground to the roofline far above them, like a miniature version of the Acropolis.

Ivory gasped.

"Hundred and fifty years old," Grant said, grudgingly admiring it. "If Old Man Palmer had won a 'certain election', he could have boasted that a Governor of Tennessee once lived here."

He navigated the car along the semi-circle that wound its way in front of the mansion. When he stopped parallel to a set of massive stone steps, the headlights illuminated a lake just in front of them, set at the base of the hill. The water appeared black and unwelcoming. As if in answer to his darkening mood, he noticed stark white slabs rising from the ground just to the left of the lake.

"Tombstones." Ivory's voice was a husky whisper. "I don't care too much for dead folks." She shivered and grabbed the door handle. "We gonna stay out here all night or get this over with?"

Grant glanced at his partner as the enormous double doors at the top of the steps just beyond the car parted. He turned off the engine. "Looks like we've got company."

5

Jessie awakened to the sound of a low, muffled moaning. It came to her through a blackness like she'd never experienced before; a blackness so complete that she touched her eyelids to make certain her eyes were actually open.

As she came to, she realized the moaning had come from her own parched lips. As she began to reposition herself, a searing pain shot through her head. She felt her face in the darkness, using hands bound together at the wrists to feel each feature as though she were blind. At her temple, her fingers found a large lump that caused her to cry out in pain as she touched it.

I must stay focused, she told herself as she tried to calm her frantically beating heart. I must stay calm.

As she felt the lump, she realized nothing had broken the skin; and as she groped her way around her body, she decided there had been no bleeding.

The drone of the vehicle continued at an uneven pace and she began to bounce around the small enclosure. A lump formed in her throat, threatening to cut off any oxygen as she realized she could no longer see a window.

Am I blind? She thought, panicked.

Then as the vehicle continued its jerky movement, she tried to grasp hold of anything that could steady her. As she felt her way around, she realized she was no longer in the back seat but in an enclosed area, like a trunk. But how could I be in a trunk, she thought wildly, when I was in a truck?

She tried to feel above her but her movements were cut short by a firm, metal ceiling only three feet from where she lay. She *was* in the back of the truck, she thought—in the bed and locked in by some sort of a cargo cover.

Then the truck came to such an abrupt halt that it caused her to roll from one side to the other like a can of biscuits rolling out of a grocery bag.

She wanted to cry out for help but her lips were covered in duct tape. She rested her fingers on the edge of the tape, debating whether to tear it loose and scream for help. But before she could decide her next course of action, the sound of two doors opening and closing reached her ears. She held her breath as she listened to the male voices; it seemed as if they were on opposite sides of the vehicle, talking as they approached the rear.

Then a swath of light jabbed her in the eyes as a tiny door was opened. Her first thought was that she had been in a coffin of some sort, but as they dragged her out by her hair through the small opening, she discovered it was a dog box. She had been inside a truck all along, she realized; a truck with an extended cab. And in the truck bed was a metal box; the type used to transport hunting dogs.

The men wore ski masks that obscured everything but their eyes. One still wore the golf cap with its distinctive shark emblem, only now it was speckled with blood. His ski mask also had blood around the nose and mouth. She had certainly left her mark. She didn't know whether to be proud of her work or to fear retribution, but instinctively she felt her chin lift proudly. She tried to focus on their eyes or their hands or anything she could use later to describe her attackers—but the muted light peeking over the distant horizon was too weak.

The man covered in blood closed the door to the dog box while the other man unceremoniously set her on her feet. She almost collapsed but he caught her with strong, capable arms. Her ankles were bound together with duct tape, and her feet had the prickly sensation she normally experienced when her feet were asleep.

She watched as the moon rose ever so slowly through a forest of trees and undergrowth, like a wild animal's eye attempting to sneak a peek at the intruders. She forced her mind to focus on her surroundings, to rise above the frantic beat of her heart and her awkward, labored breathing.

They stood in a forest of pine trees. The truck had stopped on what was barely more than a dirt path, certainly not a driveway of any type but more of an infrequently used logging road. A small yellow bug light caught her eye and as she focused on it, she realized they were a short distance from a tiny rustic cabin with a weathered front porch. It was unpainted, its wood weathered into a blotched gray. As her eyes moved upward, she caught sight of a chimney and an old metal roof.

The man covered in blood was moving away from the truck and toward the cabin, his heavy boots almost echoing in the eerie silence as he climbed three short steps onto the porch. Her eyes reluctantly moved from the cabin to her other surroundings; surroundings, she thought, that could make the difference between life and death.

There was a pond adjacent to the cabin; so close, in fact, that she wondered if rains ever caused the small dwelling to flood. But now the water lay dormant and still, covered in dark green moss. A mosquito pond is what her mother would call it, she thought, fighting off the urge to cry at the thought of her mother and father.

As if it felt her confusion and yearning to be home, a dog began to bark in the distance, perhaps two or three hollows away…A mile, she thought. Can I be hearing something a mile away? She wondered if the dog was running free or if its master was close by. Would they hear me if I screamed? She thought frantically. But screaming was not an option, she reminded herself as the duct tape pinched her lips.

She was mentally and physically exhausted. Her stomach churned and growled in hunger, but the mere thought of food nauseated her. Every inch of her body ached, and her head felt as if she'd been in a prize fight and lost. Her jaw and her temple throbbed with pain.

Then, she gasped, as the man standing beside her grabbed her hair by the fistful.

"Move!" he barked as he pushed her toward the rustic cabin.

6

Grant stood before the massive bookcases, his eyes wandering from one shelf to the next. The room seemed dimly lit, although now he noticed each bookshelf contained its own targeted light strip. Out of the corner of his eye, he realized the lamps on every table were also turned on. Interesting, he thought. Maybe they're just low wattage.

Or maybe it was the colors, he decided as he continued to study the room. The bookcases were made of black walnut, the shelves lined with dark leather covers that spoke of old books with yellowed pages. The heavy draperies were crimson, drawn back with ornate tiebacks that dropped weighty tassels toward the dark hardwood floors. The room was wallpapered in the same crimson but interspersed with gold fleur-de-lis.

His eyes rested on a black-and-white photograph of a young football star, one knee on the ground while the other was used to prop up a helmet. The jersey was emblazoned with the number "11", above which the young man's wide grin appeared infectious. It was obviously Vincent Palmer, he thought as he studied the eyes, the bone structure, and the physique. Much younger, to be sure; but it was definitely him, perhaps on the eve of setting a new record.

Further down, there were more pictures—of Vincent on the field, of him accepting honors and awards… of him standing in front of his family's bank, perhaps on his first day at work. There were other pictures taken on later dates as a heavier but still fit Vincent looked at the camera, his eyes morphing from those of an optimistic youth to the serious and sometimes sad eyes of one in middle age.

One picture in particular caught his eye: one of Vincent standing next to a fallen deer, one hand holding up the deer's head by its ample rack, its eyes open and wide, even in death. Vincent was dressed not in his customary business attire but in a dark pullover sweater and camouflage overalls. Behind him, some distance away, was a decrepit-looking log cabin, the porch tilting as though its underpinnings were about to give way. Perhaps it was the shock of seeing such a powerful man in such uncharacteristic attire and surroundings that drew his attention to the picture, and he stood for a moment staring into Vincent's expressionless face as he held his trophy.

A soft cough behind him brought him back to the present and he turned to face Mrs. Palmer, who sat on the sofa. A former beauty queen, he had seen many pictures of her on the society pages of local newspapers, but she was even more ravishing in person. Though she was reported to be in her late forties, she could easily have given any top model a run for their money. She was tall and while she leaned toward the slender side, she was curvy as well. Her blond hair was straight and long, cascading over her shoulder to a point just past her breastbone. Her eyes were blue-green, like the waters of the Mediterranean. Her skin was flawless, the skin of a woman who could afford any efforts to keep her face wrinkle-free.

But now her hands were held out in front of her as if her wrists had been pulled up by a puppeteer. They waved about like a limp-wristed wringing; she was clearly unable to stop them. She's a nervous wreck, he thought as he watched her. Just the movement was enough to make his own nerves reach the edge. When they'd been introduced, she'd looked him square in the eyes, seemingly unaware of her jerking hands. Her face had been starkly white, as it appeared now: the face of a woman in shock.

"I want you involved in this right from the start," Vincent was saying in his deep, authoritative voice as he stopped at the entrance to the library. He motioned for another man to enter the room.

Grant recognized the second man as Dalton Mitchell, the famed Nashville attorney whose legendary prowess in the courtroom had spawned a movie and several documentaries. His fees were reported to be more than eight hundred dollars an hour, and his client list was impressive—primarily corporate law, but every now and then, his clients found themselves in undesirable situations that almost inevitably led to paparazzi fodder.

As he moved past Vincent into the room, Grant was struck at the difference in size and demeanor: Vincent appeared much taller, his shoulders broad and imposing, his movements fluid. In contrast, Dalton was a smaller man, thin and reedy, his actions almost jerky. His hair was the color of maple sugar and brushed past his collar in rebellious curls. His gold-framed glasses made him appear more like a college professor than an attorney, and certainly not the former Green Beret and war hero that Grant had read so much about.

"Grant Bailey," Grant said, holding out his hand to Dalton. The attorney's hand was small but his shake so firm that it caught Grant off guard.

Ivory introduced herself and then Dalton moved to Mrs. Palmer's side. "Meg," he said gently, "we're going to do everything we can to find her."

Grant took a step into the center of the room. "Mr. Palmer has already filled us in on his daughter's disappearance—"

"Please, call me Vincent. And my wife is Meg."

"Yes, sir." He cleared his throat. "Now, you said that you received a call on your cell phone."

"That's right."

"And cell phone numbers are not published anywhere."

Vincent's face grew ruddy and his eyes remained fixed on Grant's for a long moment. When he broke his stare, Grant's eyes moved to Meg, whose hands were moving even faster.

"I need to know—"

"I know what you need. You need the names of every person who has my cell phone number. And that's impossible." He crossed to the bar and poured himself a drink. Whiskey, Grant noted. After downing it, he added, "I'm involved in a lot of activities—you know I'm the Chairman and CEO. I also serve on numerous banking committees, non-profit boards… There must be hundreds who have my number. And who knows who they've given it to."

"The point is, Mr.—Vincent, whoever called you has to know you personally, or at least know someone who knows you. Knows you well enough to have your cell phone number."

"Your point?" Dalton asked, settling into an overstuffed armchair.

"His point," Vincent barked, "is *I* know who called me."

"Not necessarily," Grant said, glancing sideways at Ivory. "Let's not jump to conclusions here. Just take a step back—"

"Don't tell me to 'take a step back' when my daughter is missing!"

Grant waited for Dalton or Meg to assume the voice of reason but neither spoke up. Dalton simply gazed at Grant blankly like a dutiful employee. Meg's hands were wringing so fretfully that Grant wondered if they needed to call a doctor to give her something to calm her nerves. The little wife, Grant thought, was clearly overshadowed by her husband's stronger personality.

"Do either of you have any enemies?" Grant asked after a moment of awkward silence.

"Of course I have enemies. All bankers have them," Vincent stated flatly.

Grant moved to the chair opposite the sofa and the other armchair. Once he settled in, he noticed Ivory had taken his cue and was seated across the room in a high-back chair. Good place to observe all the parties, he thought. "Why do bankers have enemies?" he asked, his voice a bit more casual than he intended.

"When we don't make a loan, a customer may go broke. Or maybe we've given them a loan and they've defaulted. They lose their business; sometimes they lose their spouse and family; sometimes their house and their car… the list goes on. Sometimes they blame themselves and sometimes they blame the bank. It's a whole lot easier to blame the bank."

"When they 'blame the bank', do they blame you personally or are there others in between you and the customer?"

Vincent shrugged. "A little of both, I suppose." He tilted his head back as though he was peering at Grant through the lower half of bifocals, though he wore no glasses. "I don't waste my time thinking about it."

"Maybe you should." Before Vincent could retort, he held up his hand and continued, "Maybe your daughter was kidnapped because someone wants to get back at you. Maybe there's somebody out there carrying a grudge. And our best chance of getting your daughter back unharmed is to run down every lead we can. Starting with your biggest enemies."

Vincent poured himself another glass of whiskey. "Care for any?"

"No, sir," Grant answered. Ivory's voice echoed Grant's.

Vincent poured a glass of sherry and handed it to Meg. Dalton opted for a rum and coke.

Meg managed to stop one hand from shaking while she downed the liquid, but the other continued. First time I've ever seen a person wring their hands with one hand, Grant thought as he watched.

Vincent sat on the arm of the sofa and stared at Meg's hands for a moment before speaking. His face was dispassionate as if Meg's obvious distress was not registering with him. "You know about my cousin, James Palmer."

"Why don't you tell me?" Grant prompted Vincent.

"He was an alcoholic. Demanded that I make him a loan. He drank up all his profits and his farm was about to be foreclosed upon. I refused to authorize the loan… you read the papers; you know what happened next."

Ivory spoke up. "James got drunk, went to his barn, and committed suicide."

"So that's one potential enemy that can't exactly kidnap your daughter now, can he?" Grant chided.

"His son Thomas found him. Told several people that he blamed me for James' death. Said he'd get even with me."

Grant pulled a small notebook out of the inside pocket of his jacket and scrawled the name on the lined paper, though he was certain it was a name he wouldn't forget. "Any more?" he asked.

"Joe Jackson."

"Tell me about him."

"My grandfather shot and killed his grandfather. It was a fair fight; occurred more than fifty years ago."

"That's a long time to hold a grudge."

Vincent shrugged. "After that, the Jackson family struggled financially… Went down a path that just got increasingly more difficult. Anyway, Joe lost his business and his wife recently divorced him. He wanted one more loan to keep the business going and the bank turned him down. He now blames the bank, and specifically me, for his failed business and marriage." He sipped his drink with a complete lack of emotion. "As I said, it's easier to blame the bank than yourself."

"Do you think Thomas or Joe would kidnap your daughter?" Grant asked.

"That's your job." Vincent's eyes met Grant's across the room. They were unblinking, Grant thought, unflinching. The eyes of a man who makes tough decisions every day and never looks back.

Grant looked around the room. "We're going to set up here. We'll start with taps on your phone, tracing devices. Including your cell phone. When he calls back—and he will— you're to keep him on the phone as long as possible. The longer the conversation, the more likely we are to trace it to the exact location."

"My house is yours." Vincent rose and deposited his empty glass on the table. "Meanwhile, I'll call the bank and have someone deliver five million in cash to me."

Grant almost gasped. "That might not be necessary." Then despite himself, he asked, "You've got that kind of money immediately available?"

"The bank has a five million dollar insurance policy."

"What kind of insurance policy?"

"In the event a bank employee's family is kidnapped."

"When was it purchased?"

"Years ago."

"Who knows about it?"

"I suppose you're going to want that list, too."

"I suppose I do," Grant answered, rising from his chair. "I suppose I do."

7

Grant watched Shannon Wells as he finished connecting the monitors and wiretaps to the Palmers' house phone. An MIT graduate and a technology whiz kid, he'd been with the FBI for more than eleven years. Grant had recruited him while Shannon was still in college. He was lean and trim as only a track athlete could be. His above-average height was accentuated by shiny, blue-black hair that flowed halfway down his back as though he was an ancient Native American in contemporary clothing. Grant took in his faded jeans with the hole in one knee, the long-sleeved black tee shirt, and the worn sneakers; being a techie and not an agent allowed him to appear much more like a hippie and an unlikely FBI employee, which came in handy on more than one occasion.

"You're not done yet?" Grant teased, though he looked nervously at his watch as he spoke.

"A work of art takes time," Shannon said smoothly, glancing over his shoulder at Grant.

Jessie's golden retriever, Abby, nuzzled against Shannon's hand and the technician stopped what he was doing to rub her muzzle. "How you doin', girl?" he said softly.

Grant glanced across the room at Vincent, who was perched on the arm of an overstuffed leather chair, sipping another drink. He'd been drinking all evening, Grant noted; he'd become increasingly more quiet and more withdrawn, though it was difficult for him to assess whether the alcohol was causing his sudden reclusiveness or the fact that his daughter was missing. As Shannon continued to pet the dog fondly, Grant noticed Vincent's expression beginning to perk up, his eyes riveted on the dog; then slowly, a fog seemed to wash over him. His eyes lost their luster and he returned to staring at the amber liquid in his glass.

Meg was an enigma, Grant thought as his eyes wandered from Vincent to his wife. He longed to get her away from Vincent, to talk to her privately. Perhaps he could explain to her that he understood what she was going through, as no one else could…

He thought of how he'd acted that day so long ago. It had been different then. Halfway around the globe and a world away. The Mediterranean had glistened in a mosaic of cobalt, celestial blue, and crystal as the pristine Turkish sands wound their way to the water. A tranquil setting, he thought, where countless tourists had found their solace but where he had lost that which he had loved the most…

"I'm finished," Shannon said, abruptly bringing Grant back to the present.

He sighed. "Now we wait."

"That's it? We wait?" Vincent growled, a dark scowl creeping over his face.

"It's not easy," Grant said, realizing as he said it that he was stating the obvious.

"You would know, wouldn't you?" Vincent snapped.

Grant felt his stomach constricting as if he'd been punched in the gut. He fell silent, choosing instead to inspect the wires and monitor the equipment Shannon had installed. The moments passed and the shadows lengthened in the room. Vincent paced, alternately parting the heavy draperies to peer outside into the darkness and perching on the edge of the chair while he swirled his drink and watched it like a fortune teller reading tea leaves.

In contrast, Meg leaned into the sofa, her eyes closed as if she was asleep. She might have appeared like an alabaster statue if her hands were able to stop moving.

Quite some time had passed before Grant realized that neither Shannon nor Ivory were in the room. Puzzled, he left the library quietly and made his way around the serpentine hallway until he spotted them in the vast kitchen with its soaring walnut cabinets and marbled granite countertops. They were standing with their backs to the door, dipping their fingers into an inviting bowl of M&M's in the center island.

"Don't you know about the Mediterranean event?" Shannon was whispering conspiratorially.

"No. What's that all about?" Ivory asked.

Shannon popped another handful of M&M's into his mouth. "That's when Grant's life turned upside down."

"Yeah? What happened?"

"His daughter. She was only six—"

They were interrupted by a burst of animated barking. They both turned toward the open doorway. Grant's eyes met theirs for the briefest of moments. Shannon looked away, his cheeks turning crimson, but Ivory's eyes did not waver from Grant's. Her brow was furrowed and her eyes dark and he wondered if they were the slightest bit moist or if the light was playing games.

After a moment, Grant turned and followed the sound of Abby's barking. As he approached the front hallway, he could barely make out the sound of the doorbell chiming. Abby was feverishly raking the inside of the door as if she was trying to open it to the person on the other side.

"What is this, Grand Central Station?" Vincent roared as he joined them.

Grant extended his arm in front of him, blocking his entry into the hallway. "Did she act like this when we showed up?" he asked.

"No," Vincent answered. "She didn't make a sound."

"Stay back," he said. He caught sight of Meg's drawn face just beyond Vincent's shoulder. Then, eyeing Abby, he added, "Vincent, get the dog. Then get in another room and close the door." He signaled to Ivory, who had pushed back her jacket and was gripping her pistol as it peeked from her holster.

As the dog was dragged from the massive foyer, its rear claws raking the marble floor, Ivory took up her post on the hinged side of the door as Grant grabbed the doorknob.

8

If there was one thing Grant despised, it was for a scene to fall into chaos. He liked order, and he liked everything to move forward in a methodical, precise fashion. He didn't like chaos and he didn't like surprises.

Now he stood in the center of the foyer with both arms spread wide. One hand pointed at Vincent, who had opened the door and was dangerously close to allowing Abby to escape from the den. The other hand was pointed at the young man who stood defiantly at the opened front door.

"No press," he said, his eyes glaring at the press pass the young man continued to hold up as if it were a magic key.

"You can't stop me from covering the news," the man answered smoothly. "I won't get in your way."

"You're already in my way," Grant growled.

Vincent opened the door from the den wider.

"Stay where you are," Grant ordered.

Vincent ignored him, striding into the foyer with his eyes narrowed. At the sight of the man, Abby tore away from him and bounded into the visitor's arms. The man knelt to the ground, holding and hugging the dog as if she were his own. Abby responded by licking his face and wagging her tail. It was obvious,

Grant thought, that they knew each other. And knew each other well.

As if reading Grant's mind, Vincent barked, "Do I know you?"

"Name's Nick," he answered, stepping inside and holding out his hand. "Nick Rhodes. I'm a friend of Jessie's."

Meg peeked into the foyer next. Grant noticed her face seemed to lose some of its color and her eyes narrowed to the point where he could no longer observe them. It was as if a veil of some sort had been thrown over them, closing them off from the rest of the world, a veil epitomized by her long lashes shielding her.

"Stop right there," Grant said. "Are you here in the capacity of a reporter or a friend?"

"Friend."

"Then why'd you show the press pass?"

Nick shrugged. "Opens doors." He managed a grin but his eyes were somber. "Opened this one."

"I know all of Jessie's friends," Vincent said, pointedly ignoring Nick's extended hand. "And I don't know you."

"It's entirely too crowded in this room," Grant said, stepping in between the two men. He watched the dog pawing at Nick as if demanding his attention. "Everybody in the den. *Now.*"

A moment later, they had fallen silent as they took their places in the den. Vincent's attorney, Dalton, had not moved a muscle from his original location. Vincent had returned to his perch beside the bar; Grant noted his face was crimson and he suspected if he were to touch it, it would feel feverishly hot. Ivory stood at the door to the den like a guard watching over inmates. Shannon had retreated altogether, possibly back to the kitchen.

Only Meg had not returned to her former spot. She was now perched toward the edge of the sofa, her hands so frenetic that it was difficult to look at her without staring at them. She was watching the intruder with a great deal of interest—interest that her narrowed eyes attempted to mask, Grant noted. Her lips were thin and held in a completely straight line.

Grant turned his attention to Nick, who was standing in the middle of the room, one hand wrapped through Abby's fur, massaging her.

"Why are you here?" Grant asked.

"I heard about Jessie, and I came to offer assistance."

"What about Jessie?"

Vincent made a move to retort but Grant held up his hand, cutting off his words. "What about Jessie?" Grant repeated, his voice deeper and slower.

"She's been kidnapped," Nick answered incredulously.

"How do *you* know?"

Nick's eyes widened.

"I have already told Officer Whitten and Detective Capps everything I know," Nick answered.

"So you're the kid who was with Jessie an hour before her abduction," Grant asked.

"Yes sir," Nick answered.

"Well….good. This is good timing," Grant said. "Instead of us trying to find you, you've found us. We have several questions for you, but the first one is how did you know we were here?"

"Police scanner," Nick said. "It's in my car. You can check it. I listened to the dispatches—"

"Ambulance chaser," Vincent interrupted.

"Vincent," Grant said, his eyes not wavering from Nick's, "do you know this young man?"

"No. He's not one of Jessie's friends. I'd know him if he were."

"Meg?"

She looked startled that she'd been called upon, and for a moment Grant wondered if she planned to respond to him. Then she said, "No. Never seen him before."

Grant glanced at Ivory and their eyes met for the briefest of moments across the room. It didn't add up, he thought.

"So tell me about your 'friendship'," Grant said. He positioned his feet far apart and crossed his arms in front of his chest.

"I just go to college with her. Earlier this evening, we were hanging out at the Blackacre gathering."

"Yeah, well, we've got this covered, Son," Vincent said, moving toward the door as if he was going to escort him outside. "We don't need any 'friends' here, with or without a press pass."

"Just a minute," Grant said, blocking Nick's exit. "How well do you know Jessie?"

Though he attempted to disguise it, Nick's eyes moved to Vincent before he answered. His voice was soft and hesitant. "Like I said, I go to the same college."

Before Grant could stop him, Vincent had bounded off his chair and in two swift steps, was in the boy's face, his hands wrapped around his neck. "What are you hiding?" he bellowed. "What did you do with my daughter?"

There were times when Grant felt as though everything happened in the briefest of instants, and if one blinked they could miss every piece of the action. Then there were times like this when all of his senses snapped to attention and he could feel the room pulsing with each movement, no matter how slight. Everyone appeared to move in slow motion.

Dalton, the bespectacled lawyer, had moved like the swiftest of hawks from his comfortable seat to the middle of the room, where his hands grasped Vincent's and sought to pull him off the boy. Abby was in the middle, barking ferociously at Vincent as she leaned her body against Nick's legs. Ivory's eyes met Grant's with an imploring look that begged for instruction but she remained rooted at the door. Now Shannon's face popped into the doorway, his brows furrowed as his eyes took in the commotion.

Only Meg remained silent. Her face appeared to relax, her lips almost turning up at the corners, and she sank deeper into the cushions.

"What have you done with my daughter?" Vincent continued to roar as Nick fought off his attack.

In the next instant, Grant was upon them, simultaneously pushing Nick away from Vincent as he fought alongside Dalton to loosen the man's grip on the boy's throat. When they had finally separated them, Ivory was there, pulling Nick further from the angry father as he rubbed his throat and felt his Adam's apple. Abby followed Nick, pawing at him once again as if seeking reassurance that he was alright.

Dalton continued to pull Vincent back across the room until the older man and the younger man were at opposite ends.

"Nick," Grant said, watching the dog, "I'm going to ask you to come to my office."

"Am I under arrest?"

"No. I just have a few questions and I think it would be better to ask them there."

"Then ask them here."

"I'm going to talk to you whenever and wherever I choose," Grant answered. "And you can choose to do this the easy way… or the hard way."

Their eyes locked.

Then the silence was broken with the rude sound of a cell phone's incessant ring.

"Get him out of here," Grant ordered. His words had barely left his tongue before Ivory had stepped forward to grasp Nick and escort him briskly out of the room. He knew he'd see him next in the back of his bureau car en route to his office. But for now, he had more pressing matters.

He signaled to Shannon, who was already manning the equipment and giving Grant the nod he needed.

Vincent's hand was on the cell phone. "Anonymous caller," he said, reading the small screen.

"Not for long," Shannon said smoothly.

"Keep him on the phone as long as you can," Grant ordered.

Then he picked up an ear bud as Vincent pressed a button and placed the cell phone next to his ear.

"And it's show time," Shannon whispered.

9

Jessie bolted upright, her heart racing, as the sudden sound of the heavy wood door slamming shut resonated through the darkness, the impact so great that the rusty metal hinges rang like a high note on a baby grand piano. She strained to hear the sound of footsteps leaving the isolated cabin in a vain attempt to determine whether only one or both of her kidnappers were leaving. But the hoot of an owl and the distant howl of a coyote drowned out any sounds their shoes might have made in the pine-covered yard.

Then the old farm truck roared to life. Jessie struggled to control her breathing as she listened, trying to memorize the sound of the truck—a sound that made her recall old farm trucks with mufflers that had rotted out over decades. It was a sound that was only too familiar in farm country; a sound she knew could never lead the police back to her abductors.

She listened as fallen pine cones were crunched under the tires and in a few short moments, the sound of the truck faded in the distance.

She tried holding her breath as she listened to the old cabin, but it was eerily silent. She thought of screaming for help but caught herself; she'd seen with her own eyes how secluded she was here. There was little or no chance of anyone hearing her cries for help—anyone except the kidnappers. And though the house remained silent as a tomb, she knew one of them was still there. She could feel him.

She squinted and tried to adjust to the darkness; tried to get her bearings even though panic threatened to sweep over her. She was handcuffed to a heavy chain approximately ten feet long, which in turn was secured to an antiquated wood-burning stove. As her eyes slowly adjusted, she realized the cabin was comprised of only one room and the stove was centrally located in the middle of it. This meant the chain was long enough for her to make her way around the cabin. With her heart beating rapidly and her breath coming in short, sporadic bursts, she unsteadily rose to her feet. Clasping the chain with her free hand to reduce the weight on her bound wrist, she shuffled around the small room, her feet kicking up dust.

Her arms were bound to her body at her elbows with a generous mountain of duct tape, as if the kidnappers had rolled her up like a mummy. But from her elbows to her fingers, she was free from the bonds. Her hands shakily found her face, and as her fingers crawled over her features like a blind woman's, she realized they had placed a black cotton ski cap over her head. She felt the ribbing in the knit fabric and gave it a firm tug, but it was held in place by duct tape. Only her nose protruded from the fabric.

As her hands found their way down the length of her torso, she realized her ankles were also duct taped together, but the men had left enough space between her feet to allow her to take tiny baby steps around the small cabin.

As she stumbled around the room, she found an old sofa which reeked of mold; when she pressed down on it, she determined it was most likely made of cheap foam. Shakily, she attempted to sit on it but halfway down, hampered by her bonds, she fell onto it, kicking up a cloud of dust and decay.

She struggled against the panic that threatened to overwhelm her. I have to remain calm, she thought, even while her heart beat so wildly that she had difficulty catching her breath. *Be calm.*

She labored with the mask. It was as if they'd placed it on her head backwards so the eye holes were taped against the back of her head. But they had cut a hole to allow her to breathe, and the hole had continued to grow like a run in a stocking until one eye was able to see through the torn fabric; the rest still held in place by the duct tape that had been so zealously applied.

With the limited scope of her vision, she peered around the interior. The walls were rough-hewn, as though tree trunks had been hastily hacked length-wise and erected without the slightest bit of sanding. She wondered if the same wood extended all the way to the exterior, but as she felt her way along the wall beside the sofa, she thought there had to be at least two layers between her and freedom.

She unsteadily came to her feet and used her feet to feel the floor beneath her. It was uneven, rough. But it was definitely wood and not dirt.

She determined the cabin was probably sixteen feet square with a low ceiling—perhaps eight feet or less. A single bulb extended from the ceiling by a flimsy wire, and now as she struggled to move the mask further from her one unobstructed eye, she realized it was turned on but the bulb was probably no brighter than twenty-five watts.

On one side of the cabin was something akin to a kitchen sink; it was porcelain and so old that it was pockmarked with chips half the size of her fist. Above the sink was a cloudy window that she quickly determined was not large enough for her to crawl through, even if she were able to escape from the handcuffs and duct tape. Though she struggled to see outside, the dim light from the quarter moon threw the surrounding trees into shadowy figures that swayed in the wind like murky figures that blocked out any detail she might have been able to glimpse.

Turning back to her prison, she noted a table a few feet away: a tiny, primitive, unbalanced wood structure that was obviously handmade. Two crooked stools sat forlornly on either side.

A minuscule bathroom was located on the far side of the room. The toilet stank with rancid water that had almost evaporated, leaving behind a thick yellow stain that she could detect even in the dim light. A sink barely large enough for a pair of hands protruded from the wall beside it, and on the other side of the toilet was a shower stall scarcely wide enough for an adult to stand in, the shower nozzle hardly five feet above the uneven floor. Just above the stall was another window, this one smaller than the first and most likely used only for a useless attempt at ventilation. A bright yellow orb spider dangled on the other side, its elaborate web evidence that the window had gone undisturbed in recent days. There was no door, only a gap in the wall that separated the two rooms.

She retraced her steps until she had come full circle, and then focused her attention on the only door. It was obviously handmade and comprised of two-by-four lumber with two additional pieces of lumber marking an X across its center, giving it strength and stability. The door knob and the door hinges appeared aged, the metal rusting with humidity and the elements that seemed to defy the tiny confines of the cabin.

She wanted nothing better than to rip the duct tape from her body, even if it meant her hands would be bloodied with the effort; to tear the mask from her face and leave it in a pile of threads on the floor; to throw open that door and run into the darkness, hoping the trees would envelop her in their branches and obscure her escape.

But it was useless. All she had right now, at this one moment, was her presence of mind. And though she felt as if she were teetering on the edge of an insane situation, she knew she had to keep her wits about her. She had to memorize everything, no matter how small or how seemingly insignificant.

She painstakingly made her way back to the decrepit sofa and fell backwards on it as her breath whooshed out of her. She was scared, hungry, thirsty… and sapped.

She tried to calm her nerves by convincing herself that her father would rally everyone from the FBI to the local sheriff's department and certainly they would be searching for her.

If they knew she was missing.

They had to know, she told herself. Someone would have to come home to the apartment building; someone would have to find her things there—unless the men took everything. Could they have cleaned up the foyer to make it look as if nothing had happened?

Nick would telephone. Certainly he would have expected to have seen her again the following morning, before she left for her parents' estate. When she didn't answer her phone, he would show up at her condo, find her car still there, and know something had happened to her.

What about Abby?

Her heart began beating out of control as she worried about her cooped up in the apartment. How long would her water and food last? She wondered. But Nick would feed her. Nick had a spare key to the condo; he wouldn't let her suffer. He would take care of her.

I'm driving myself crazy, she thought. They've discovered I'm missing by now. Or have they?

She hadn't realized she'd fallen asleep until the door was thrown open with such force that the knob bounced off the wall behind it as it swung a full one hundred and eighty degrees.

Her mask had fallen askew in her sleep and was now obscuring her vision once more. She resisted the temptation to right it but peered hazily between the threads at the two shadowy images who stood silently in the doorway.

"I'll give you anything—" she began to say, her voice muffled beneath the material and the duct tape.

"Shut up."

The voice was venomous, deep, and final.

"Tape her yapper."

Jessie braced herself as the brawnier of the two men grabbed the roll of duct tape off the table and approached her.

He knelt before her and yanked at her mask. "Looks like she tried to take this thing off."

Jessie heard footsteps that were heavy but fast. A moment later, she felt more than saw the other kidnapper's head peering over the shoulder of the first man.

"Wrap her up good." Then louder, he warned, "Try that again and we'll tape your nose, too. See how long you can last without oxygen." He cackled before moving off.

Two men, Jessie thought as the duct tape was placed across the mask, securing the fabric to her skin so solidly that she could taste the thread. Two men: one older and in charge; the other younger and... and what? She wondered. Why two? One to give the orders and the other to take them?

She could hear the sound of footsteps as one of the men retreated through the door and slammed it behind him. One was still left inside with her and she tilted her head as she tried to peer through the threads to see where he had gone.

A moment later, she heard a voice. It was the older man, the brains, she thought. Mr. Brainiac. Who was he talking to?

"Listen closely," he was saying.

There was a brief pause and then he shouted, "Don't interrupt me again!"

The phone, she thought. He's on the phone. To Daddy?

"I know you have the FBI involved. Get rid of them. This is about you and me." There was an accent in his voice, one she couldn't quite identify. Then she realized he was attempting to obscure his natural, southern accent with a foreign one that really didn't reflect any legitimate region.

The voice stopped and a long moment of silence enveloped the cabin. She could almost hear the man breathing on the other side of the room. Then he rose from the kitchen stool and strode to the front door.

"That it?" he asked in a puzzled voice as he opened the door and stuck his head out.

"Is that it?" the other man mimicked. "You dimwit. They're tracing the calls." His normal voice was back. He was a Tennessean, of that she was sure.

"Then how—?"

"Close the door and shut up."

Brutus retreated through the door onto the front porch and closed the door behind him. Somehow it felt comforting to name them, she thought. Brainiac and Brutus. Couldn't be more appropriate.

And the phone call. That meant someone knew she was missing, and that someone had notified the FBI. And the kidnapper believed the FBI was so involved that they were tracing the call. Her heart quickened again but with hopefulness. They were coming to get her, she thought.

She heard muffled voices from the other side of the door: Brutus seemed to be questioning while Brainiac was impatient and quick-tempered.

Then Brainiac's voice was louder and sounded different, more authoritative. He was on the phone again. How much time had elapsed, she wondered? Half an hour? An hour?

"Five mil in a duffle bag. Chickasaw Park. Be there in one hour. Alone."

Then there was silence. And as the minutes ticked slowly past, Jessie realized the phone call was over. Her eyes wandered around the tiny cabin once more, encumbered by the mask that allowed only thin swaths of light to penetrate. She felt a tear stinging her eye and wondered when this would all be over.

Or if it ever would be.

10

Shannon shook his head, his eyes fixated on the equipment in Vincent Palmer's den. "The first call was six seconds. Second one was two." He turned toward Grant. "This guy's a pro."

Grant rubbed his chin. "Okay," he said, speaking more to himself than anyone else in the room, "the kidnapping was planned out. We're dealing with a professional and he knows we're here... He knows we're tracing the calls and he knows how much time we need to pinpoint his location."

He turned back to Shannon. "What about caller i.d.?"

Shannon shook his head once more. "Out of area. But I'm on it," he added, placing a headset over his ears, "we'll get the phone company involved and get the number. It's undoubtedly a cell phone; the system picked up some static. Once we get the number, we can pick up a ping—GPS—and zero in on the location."

"We're wasting time." The voice was husky and strained. Grant turned toward the other side of the room, where Vincent was pacing impatiently. "I don't give a goat's hair whether this guy is a professional or a paranoid lunatic. All I care about is my daughter."

"That's who we all care about," Grant said calmly.

"While you guys are discussing the latest technology," Vincent continued, his voice growing louder, "the clock is ticking. We have—" he raised his watch and looked at the dial "—precisely fifty-four minutes. We're wasting precious time."

Grant raised his hand. "I understand what you're going through. You know I do." He cleared his throat. "But let me give you some statistics about kidnappings."

"I couldn't care less about your statistics. This is my daughter we're talking about; not a statistic." He grabbed a coat from the back of a chair. As he hurriedly slid his arms into it, he said, "I'm going to the bank. Getting the money, giving it to the kidnappers. I'm bringing my daughter home. And I'm doing it without you— just as the man on the phone directed."

Grant's eyes met Ivory's. She had returned from escorting Nick to their car, and was standing in the doorway. The look in her eyes told him that it hadn't been lost on her, either, that the kidnappers had demanded the exact amount Vincent had been prepared to remove from the bank—*before* their call. "Are you telling me," Grant said, "you can waltz into your bank at this hour and pull out five million dollars? Just like that?"

"Just like that," Vincent replied.

The room fell silent.

"Look," Vincent said, "as I told you before, the bank keeps a five million dollar insurance policy, precisely for kidnapping and ransom protection."

"*Precisely* five million dollars? The exact amount the kidnappers want—what a coincidence."

Vincent's face paled. "Several years ago, my father instituted a one million dollar kidnapping and ransom insurance policy— approved by the bank board, of course. He knew if an employee's child was kidnapped, they'd do anything to get them back, including borrowing the money—or just taking it. Over the years, it's been increased—nothing underhanded; it's always been approved by the board."

"And right now, it stands at five mil."

"That's right."

Grant's eyes met Ivory's once again.

"We're wasting time!" Vincent shouted. "Don't you understand—Jessie's life is at stake here. If anyone would understand," he added, pointedly staring at Grant, "I thought you would!"

"You're going to get that five mil," Grant said evenly. "But I'm going with you. You'll be alone in your car, but I'll be a decent distance behind you."

Ivory raised one eyebrow.

"Ivory, you stay here," Grant continued. "Dalton," he said, turning to Vincent's attorney, "you're staying with Ivory and Meg. Only Vincent and I are leaving."

"What about Nick?" Ivory whispered as Grant neared her. "He's in the car."

"Then he's along for the ride. It'll give us a chance to chat."

Vincent was halfway through the foyer when Grant caught up with him. "Where are you going? Which branch?" Grant asked.

"The main office."

Grant nodded. "Don't try to lose me."

Vincent nodded.

Grant grabbed his arm. Vincent turned around, his face reddening with anger.

"Don't try to lose me," Grant said again, his voice slow and deliberate.

Instead of retorting, Vincent nodded again silently, his anger appearing to have subsided.

"Understood?"

Vincent nodded. "Understood."

As Vincent hurried through the door, Grant turned to Ivory.

"What are you doing?" Ivory asked.

"You know as well as I do that more than eighty percent of the kidnappings in this country are committed by family members."

"Yes, but—"

"And this is an inside job."

Ivory only stared at Grant, her eyes wide. "I know."

"He isn't getting out of my sight. I'll see to it. But while I'm gone, I want Dalton to give you the name of every board member; every person who knows about this insurance policy. We're going to talk to every single one of them."

Ivory nodded. "What about *her*?" She tilted her head toward Meg.

"Find out what makes her tick," Grant said. "Without Vincent around, maybe she'll open up to you. Something's not right here." He raised his voice. "Shannon, I want that phone number."

"Working on it now," he said without turning around.

"You know where I'll be," Grant said as he hurried out the door. "The bank's main office and Chickasaw Park."

"You be careful," Ivory said.

Grant stopped for a brief moment and looked back at her. "I always am." Then he was hurrying to his bureau car as Vincent's tires squealed, the Porsche careening out of its parking spot and racing down the driveway toward the road.

11

The first pellet of snow hit Grant's windshield shortly after leaving Vincent's driveway. It struck with a tinny sound akin to a needle striking the glass, and he realized with a sinking heart that it was snow mixed with sleet. Always a dicey combination on the best of days, it was particularly troublesome tonight; between the darkness and the decreased visibility, it would take all his concentration to stay on Vincent's heels.

And Vincent was driving like a madman. He drove well above the speed limit, Grant noted as he glanced at his own speedometer, and he was weaving in and out of traffic like a criminal attempting to evade police. Why? He wondered as he zigzagged his own vehicle in an attempt to stay on him.

The pellets grew larger and he turned on his windshield wipers. Some of the flakes were large blobs of wet snow, which quickly melted when they struck the glass, while others were icy tablets that accumulated on the wipers themselves, further hindering his view.

His car swerved on the slick pavement and he corrected; then slowed his vehicle to a more manageable pace. He kept his eyes riveted on the tail lights of Vincent's Porsche Cayenne but every vehicle on the road seemed to be an SUV and soon he was wondering if he was still focused on the correct one. It was either four-wheel drive or all-wheel, Grant deduced, and his bureau car was neither. It slid like a knife on butter while Vincent continued to pull away effortlessly.

Grant's cell phone rang and he hit the speaker button before rapidly returning both hands to the steering wheel. "This had better be important," he said in lieu of a greeting.

"Might be," Shannon's voice rang out. "Vincent's on his phone; has been since he left here."

"Who's he calling?"

"Edward Buchanan mean anything to you?"

Grant shook his head, though he knew Shannon was unable to see his gesture. "Wait a minute," he said, "doesn't he work at the bank?"

"He's the bank president," Nick said in a stage whisper from the back seat.

Grant almost recoiled from the sudden voice. Nick had been so silent that he'd forgotten he'd been along for the ride.

"Right…" Shannon's voice faded before returning. "He's right, Grant."

"He's lining up the insurance money?" Grant pondered out loud.

"Could be."

"He's the only one he called?"

"Nope. One other. Phone's registered to William Woody."

"Name's not familiar."

Nick leaned forward once more. "Maybe he called his wife, Pam."

Grant glanced into the rearview mirror. Nick's unblinking vivid blue eyes stared back at him.

"What do you know about his wife?"

Nick shrugged. "Just that she's the bank's chief financial officer."

Grant nodded. He barely missed grazing a vehicle that changed lanes too abruptly, and he returned his attention to the road. "Anything else?" he asked Shannon.

"That's it. Cell phone's quiet, for now."

"Stay on it."

"You got it."

Grant hit the disconnect key. He hadn't realized how tightly he'd been gripping the wheel until he removed his hand to turn off the cell phone. Now he flexed his hand in an attempt to loosen the muscles.

Vincent careened onto a side street, and seconds later, Grant followed. He watched as Vincent ran the first red light on the deserted street and after glancing both ways, Grant followed suit.

Vincent pulled in front of the bank's headquarters. He left the Porsche running and the door open as he slipped and slid toward the front doors. Grant caught his shadowy figure in his headlights as he attempted to pull alongside the Porsche but his car began to weave on the icy road. Grasping the wheel again, he maneuvered out of a spin and came to rest with one front wheel over the curb.

Vincent disappeared into the building as an older gentleman in a security uniform held the door for him.

"Stay here," Grant ordered as he jumped out of the vehicle. Within seconds, he was at the front door of the bank building.

"I'm sorry—" the guard said, starting to wave him away.

"FBI," Grant said, flourishing his badge as he pushed past him into the building. "Where did Mr. Palmer go?"

"I don't know, sir."

"Which direction?" Grant barked.

The guard gestured toward the elevators. "His office is on the top floor."

"I figured as much," Grant mumbled to himself as he raced to the elevator. "Come on, come on," he urged as the elevator doors closed and he was whisked all too slowly upward.

When the doors reopened, Grant found himself in an expansive lobby decorated with cherry furniture, plush carpet, and paintings illuminated by specially placed spotlights. It was silent; eerily so, he thought. He stepped out of the elevator and eyed his surroundings. The lobby was dimly lit, the desks empty, the phones hushed.

He made his way down a wide hall bordered on both sides by photographs of past and present bank officials, until he glimpsed a thin ray of light peeking from behind a partially closed door.

He could hear the voices before he reached the doorway. "Are you sure there's five million in here?" Vincent was saying. "Positive." The voice was female.

Grant eased the door open as Vincent glanced up from behind his desk. On top of the heavy mahogany desk was a duffle bag. As he entered the room, he saw Vincent holding up a wad of bills.

"Unmarked," Vincent was saying.

"No," Grant interrupted. The woman turned toward him. She was younger than he would have imagined a chief financial officer. She couldn't have weighed more than a hundred pounds, he deduced, as his eyes moved swiftly from her small feet to her deep, reddish-brown mop of curls. Between her petite stature and her wild hair, he might have been tempted to underestimate her—were it not for the round gold-rimmed glasses that stood out from her lightly freckled, fair skin; in contrast, they made her appear more like a brilliant professor. "FBI," he said before she could question him. He waved his badge in front of her before returning it to his inside coat pocket. "The bills must be marked."

"We don't have five million in marked bills," Pam said.

"There's no time," Vincent said, his voice strained. "I have less than half an hour to get to Chickasaw Park."

Grant hesitated. It was happening too fast—the phone call, the time limit. It prevented a methodical approach, and he realized the kidnappers had planned it this way. This was a professional hit, he thought, and they had an inside man.

"Then let's get going," Grant said. He turned toward the doorway and almost bumped into another man.

"Who—?"

"FBI," Grant said, pulling out his credentials for a third time. "Who are you?"

"Edward Buchanan, bank—"

"President," Grant finished. He studied his face carefully. If this is an inside job, every person in the room is suspect, he thought. Buchanan's eyes were round—almost too round, he thought—and were the color of a midnight blue sky. Hard to read, but the dark circles under them spoke of sleepless nights and less than stellar health. He was shorter than Grant but stockier.

His neck was short and thick, giving him the appearance of a fireplug. His nose was crooked, as if it had once been broken and heeled improperly, and his graying temples seemed premature against the otherwise dark brown hair. But what stood out most prominently was his chin; there was something about it, Grant thought, that didn't seem quite right.

When he began to speak, Grant realized only one side of his face moved, as if he'd been stricken with a stroke that had left one side of his face immobile. "Mr. Palmer," Edward said, looking over Grant's shoulder at Vincent, "I'll have to contact the insurance company."

"Then do it." Vincent closed the duffle bag and groaned as he raised the heavy bag from the table.

"What about the cash on hand to reopen Monday?" Pam asked.

"What about it?" Vincent snapped as he moved swiftly toward the door.

"We need to account for this money," she said, her voice becoming shrill. "And we need cash for the tellers—"

Vincent whirled on her, swearing in her face. She recoiled, her eyes wide, her face white.

"Do what you have to do," Vincent snarled. "Don't bother me with it."

He pushed past them. Grant hesitated only briefly to look purposely at Pam and then at Edward. Their expressions were etched on his brain; expressions, he knew, that he would have to analyze later.

But for now, Vincent was leaving for Chickasaw Park and he needed to stick with him like a tick on a hound dog.

As Grant burst through the front doors, he caught a glimpse of Vincent slipping and sliding to his waiting car. Before he could reach his own vehicle, Vincent was gone, his SUV careening down West Fifth Street and around a curve.

"He went thataway," Nick said as Grant slipped into the front seat.

Grant rolled his eyes. "Thanks," he said sarcastically.

Then he was off with a lurch, his car sliding through the slippery streets like an ice skater out of control. Once or twice, he thought he spotted Vincent's tail lights but as soon as he'd glimpsed them, they were gone again, disappearing around a curve or over a hill; and once Grant had turned that same corner or crested that same hill, he was nowhere in sight.

The snow and sleet were coming down in earnest now, the windshield wipers so caked with ice that with each swipe, it simply served to blanket the glass with a frosty blotch that further impeded his vision.

When he finally reached Chickasaw Park, he turned off his headlights and slowed to a crawl. He rolled down the window and tried to peer outside, to catch a glimpse of Vincent and his vehicle, but the night sky was as black as pitch. He stopped the car and listened, his head partway out of the window, but all he heard was the sound of sleet hitting the metal side of the vehicle. There were no headlights and now as he placed the car in park and stepped outside, he realized there were no tire tracks.

He whirled in one direction and then in another. How many entrances, he thought wildly, how many entrances to Chickasaw Park?

He involuntarily shook with the chill of ice striking the back of his neck. With snow beginning to accumulate on the shoulders of his dark trench coat, he could feel his jaw stiffening and his hands balling into fists. He'd lost him, he thought as an unbridled ire caused his face to grow heated. And losing him was not an option.

12

Jessie awakened with the violent jerk of a fitful sleep, her heart pounding so loudly that it threatened to obscure any other sound. Her head ached with a monstrous headache that was both throbbing and jabbing, and she realized in addition to the blows she'd taken during her abduction that she was fighting for oxygen. Painstakingly, she moved the ski mask as best she could to provide more airflow, but it was scanty at best. Any air that made its way through was permeated with the stench of moldy fabric.

Her hands slowly felt their way over the sofa as she tried to recall the position of the furniture in the room and other surroundings that might mean the difference between captivity or escape... life or death.

The rapid clatter of tiny feet above her caused her to peer upward, even as the ski mask blocked all sight except the thinnest ray of light emitted from the low wattage bulb overhead. Squirrels, she thought, listening. Squirrels on a tin roof. It was comforting in an odd sort of way, to think of a family of small rodents with bushy tails rushing about, gathering nuts for the winter. It meant the roof must be located directly below the trees, she thought, trying to picture it in her mind's eye. It had been too dark for her to see much detail when she had arrived here, but now she pictured trees with branches reaching over the cabin like caressing arms, the squirrels scampering from branch to branch, onto the rooftop and back, dashing about as if their only mission on earth was to survive the night.

Just like her, she thought with a sinking heart.

Somewhere in the distance, she heard the sound of a coyote howling, followed immediately by the distinct baying of beagles and hounds. There had to be a hunting lodge out there somewhere, she thought; a cabin larger than this one, a place that housed dogs—and several of them, judging by the sound. She listened for the telltale sound of the hounds running through woods or across the hills, but as the baying continued, she realized they were remaining fixed in one location—the sure sign, she thought, that there were kennels somewhere within hollering distance.

She struggled to rise out of the fog her brain seemed enmeshed within. But she was exhausted beyond words; the ordeal and the spotty sleep she'd grabbed were taking their toll.

She shook involuntarily. The fire in the wood-burning stove barely took the chill off the room and she wondered where the kidnappers were.

She sank fitfully into another bout of sleep. When she awakened again, it was not the sound of the squirrels or the hounds that forced her from her restless slumber, but Brainiac's impatient voice. As she struggled to fully awaken, she realized he was not in the room with her, but somewhere outside.

She could no longer see the embers from the stove and realized it had died down completely. She rose to an awkward seated position on the sofa and cocked her head. He was on the front porch, just outside the door.

"The project's completed," Brainiac was saying. His voice had an air of authority, a matter-of-factness that felt as even as if he were standing in an office.

"It did not go as smoothly as I wanted," a second voice replied.

Jessie gasped. It was her father's voice, she thought as her heart raced out of control. No, she thought, digging her fingers into her skin to bring her back to reality. It couldn't be.

"You know this was a major job. It's completed, it's done satisfactorily, and I want to be compensated as you promised," Brainiac replied.

"But as I said, the results were not exactly as I wanted. Do you think you should be fully compensated?"

Jessie fought back tears that threatened to explode from her. It was her father's voice; there was no mistaking it. She would know that voice anywhere.

"Yes, I do," Brainiac was saying. "You knew it was a complicated project, and we agreed you'd pay me accordingly."

"I know what our deal was," her father answered. "You'd make a one-time bonus. And in return, I'd make a lot more."

"And the bottom line is, I did what you wanted, the job is over, and we both profit."

There was a pause. Jessie thought she heard another voice but she couldn't be certain. She cocked her head further toward the door as she strained to listen.

"Okay," her father's voice came at last, "I'll pay you what we agreed."

She felt her face become flushed and she fought the urge to be overcome with emotion. Her father was outside the door—of that there was no doubt—but was he paying her ransom? Would she soon be set free? There was something in her father's voice—the total lack of emotion, as if he were discussing a simple business transaction—that swept over her like a wave, threatening to disarm any remaining self-control she possessed. If only they hadn't taped her mouth, she thought frantically. If only she could call out to him!

She kicked at the sofa in panic and when the dull thud permeated the air, she realized she might not be able to speak but she could make other noise. She struggled up from the sofa and began banging her arms through the room, rattling the chain that bound her to the stove against anything within reach. She thought of kicking the stove with enough force to overturn it; certainly if the cabin went up in flames, her father would see it! But she thought better of the idea as the voices abruptly stopped; if she caught the cabin on fire and no one came to her aid, the outcome was unthinkable.

She waited for him to come charging through the door, to unwrap her from her ridiculous bondage, to whisk her away, back to the safety of their home, to Abby, and to Nick—

But he didn't come.

No one came.

The voices were silent. Her father did not burst through the door. Brainiac was no longer speaking. Yet there were no sounds of a car starting, no crunch of the tires on the fallen pine cones or gravel, no footsteps on the wood porch.

There was nothing. Nothing but the final embers dying in the stove, the last rays of light vanishing along with it, casting the cabin into blackness.

13

The frigid air was soaking into Grant's bones, causing him to shiver involuntarily. As he climbed back into his vehicle, he tried to kick the ice and snow from his shoes, but it stubbornly clung to them. He banged the door shut behind him, causing an avalanche to cascade down the side of the car. His foot slipped on the brake as he prepared to engage the gear shift and he slammed his foot onto the floorboard in another effort to break the ice from the sole of his shoe.

He swore under his breath as he called Shannon. When the technician answered, he didn't bother with niceties. "Is there another entrance to this park?"

"Hold on," Shannon said. Grant could hear the clacking of the keyboard on the other end of the line. Within seconds, Shannon was back. "No. There's nothing on the map to indicate more than one entrance."

"I'm going in," Grant said. He placed the car into third gear. The tires spun for a brief moment before the car began to slide to the left. He corrected it with the calmness of a man acting from instinct, but inside he was beginning to boil.

He passed a sign that read "Open. 15 mph" and despite himself, he chuckled. There was little chance of him driving much faster than that, he thought as the freshly fallen sleet and snow crunched under his tires.

A movement caught his eye and he almost slammed on the brakes as a deer broke from the nearby woods and raced through the park, its slender legs sinking into the snow with every step. He followed its progress, his eyes raking the wood line, searching for anything out of the ordinary.

As his eyes cut to the right, he spotted a tiny log cabin sitting forlornly at the top of a small hill. He stopped the car, his foot sliding from the gas pedal to the brake like a skier out of control. He found himself grabbing the steering wheel with both hands as he attempted to find the brake with both feet. When at last the car rolled to a stop, he peered downward to the floorboard. The heat was melting the snow and ice and now it was forming a dangerous puddle just below the pedals.

He returned his attention to the log cabin. It was made of logs that had weathered into shades of gray that blended almost seamlessly with the surrounding woods. The roof, however, was red and stood out like a beacon. The park lighting and the full moon combined to illuminate the structure, exposing two stately rock chimneys. A wood sign erected next to the driveway stated: Derryberry Log Cabin.

He placed the car into a lower gear and prepared to drive up the driveway. It was difficult to see the edges of the driveway now that the snow was falling more earnestly than before. He could only hope there were no soft shoulders on either side of the drive, shoulders that could easily suck his car downward and leave him trapped in a snow bank.

"I guess getting out here isn't an option, is it?" Nick quipped from the back seat.

Grant didn't respond but grasped the wheel even tighter as his tires spun on the slick drive. There were no tire tracks before him, no sign that anyone had come up this drive; but he couldn't see behind the cabin and didn't know if there was another entrance to it.

He felt one of the tires slide off the roadway, and his heart sank as the car began to tip to the left. As he struggled to right it, his cell phone began ringing.

It rang incessantly as he tried to maintain control of the vehicle. When he finally was able to relinquish his grip on the steering wheel, he flipped open the phone and spoke through the speakerphone. "Yeah?"

"Vincent didn't turn into Chickasaw Park," Shannon said, his voice fast and breathless.

"Oh?" Grant placed his foot on the brake pedal once more.

"He continued down the road another mile. Turned into Darks Mill Road."

"How—?"

"Ivory planted a Live-Wire FastTrac GPS tracing device in Vincent's car."

Grant placed the phone on the seat beside him and began backing down the drive. "Stay on the phone," he ordered Shannon.

"Not going anywhere."

He came to a stop at the bottom of the drive and turned the car toward the entrance. He left a huge swath in the middle of the entrance where he had pulled around. For some reason, it made him think of making angels in the snow. He shook the thought out of his head and returned to the main road.

"We're still tracing his calls," Shannon was saying. "About the time he should have been turning into Chickasaw Park, he got a phone call."

"The kidnapper?"

"We're tracing it now. We're going on the assumption that the kidnapper redirected him to Darks Mill Road."

"I'm approaching it now. What's next?"

"Vincent's on the Nashville Highway traveling south."

Grant's mind raced.

"Turn right on Carter's Creek Pike; that'll get you to the highway," Shannon said as if reading his mind.

"Turning now," Grant said. He glanced into his rearview mirror. Other than Nick's wide eyes staring back at him, there was no one behind them; the road remained deserted.

"Turning left on Bear Creek Pike," Shannon continued. "Where are you now?"

"Nashville Highway," Grant replied.

"You might be about 2½ miles behind him. Be careful. Radar tells me the white stuff is more ice than snow….He's turning right on Tom Hitch Parkway."

"I'm gaining on him," Grant said, speeding up despite Shannon's warning.

A couple of minutes later, Shannon continued, "He drove about a mile and a half. Turned left on Iron Bridge Road. Immediate sharp right turn."

Grant turned onto Tom Hitch Parkway and glanced at his odometer. A mile passed, and he began to slow.

"He's stopped," Shannon's voice crackled over the cell phone. "He's next to the Duck River."

Grant turned left onto Iron Bridge Road. The tracks were evident in the pristine snow, making a hard right turn. One set of tracks, he noted. One.

"I'm on him," Grant said.

"He's moving again." There was a brief pause. "He's turning around—"

"I got him," Grant interrupted. "I see him."

"He's traveling west on Iron Bridge Road."

Grant pulled to the boat ramp and struggled to turn around. These bureau cars were not designed for this slick ice, he thought. He could see Vincent hunched over the steering wheel, intent on leaving, driving past him as though he didn't exist. Grant hit the steering wheel as his tires lost traction on the ice. He punched the gas pedal but the car began to swerve out of control and he found himself circling dangerously near the boat ramp.

"Ooooohhhhhhh," Nick's voice echoed through the car as they spun.

Grant swore again as he struggled to right the vehicle and get back on Vincent's trail.

"He's headed for downtown Columbia," Shannon's voice continued. A moment later, "He's turning right on South Garden Street."

"Don't lose him."

"No chance of that," Shannon said, a hint of glee in his voice.

Grant pulled the car out of the spin and headed back to Iron Bridge Road. A drop of perspiration fell onto his brow but he didn't remove his hands from the steering wheel.

"He's traveling north on Highway 31."

Grant didn't respond. Despite the road conditions, he sped up, his car fishtailing as he struggled to reach Vincent.

"He's getting another call."

Grant grunted.

"First trace is in. It's coming from a cell phone – one of those that you pay up front for the minutes. We're running a trace now on the owner."

"Do you know—?"

"Not yet, but we will."

"He's turning left on Theta Pike."

Grant finally wiped the perspiration from his brow. His forehead was covered in sweat. "They're taking him in circles," he said gruffly.

"They're taking *you* in circles," Shannon answered.

"Trying to shake us," Grant said. "And they might have done it, had Ivory not put that tracking device on his car."

"Vincent's crossed over Highway 43. Staying on Theta Pike."

Grant struggled to catch up with him.

"He's getting another call… Second trace is in. Each call is coming from a different cell phone."

"The kidnapper's a professional," Grant said. "He's keeping each call short; always using a different number."

"He's turning left."

"Left where? What road?"

"Don't know. It's not marked."

"I'm two minutes behind him."

"Slow down; he's stopping. Look for the tracks. There's no road name on this map."

Grant's heart was racing as he turned left on Theta Pike and crossed over the intersection of Highway 43. After a mile, he slowed the car despite his longing to keep going, to catch Vincent before he sped off again. He used the search light in the bureau car to illuminate the sides of the road, where ghostly signs began to come into view: NO HUNTING NO FISHING NO TRESPASSING.

"There they are," he said as he spotted the tire tracks in the snow. Slowing further, he turned left onto a narrow roadway. There was an entrance gate here and another sign; this one proclaimed: OxyChem Park Facility. A chain and commercial blue lock securing the double wire security gate had been cut. The chain was dangling on the gate and the blue lock was still secure.

"Hey," Nick said from the back seat, "this place is owned by Occidental Chemical Company. I was here once for a Christmas party."

"Yeah?" Grant said without much interest.

"Yeah. There's a recreational lodge on the back of the property," Nick answered.

Grant hesitated and peered at him through the rearview mirror. "This the only way in and out?" Grant asked.

"I think so. At least by car… There's a boat ramp about 200 feet behind the lodge."

Grant turned off the search light and slowed to a crawl. As he neared the lodge, he spotted Vincent's Porsche. His eyes swept the terrain but there were no other vehicles. As he pulled alongside the SUV, he noted it was empty. One set of footprints snaked from the vehicle toward the water.

He parked behind Vincent's SUV, pulling his vehicle at an angle in order to block him in. As he opened the door, he said to Nick, "Stay here."

"Don't worry," Nick answered as the door was closing, "I've got your back."

Grant barely heard him as he followed the lone set of footprints from Vincent's SUV. They led down a meandering path; as Grant slipped and slid on the mixture of ice and snow, he wondered if the path itself was straight and the terrain had caused them both to wander like drunkards along the slippery slope. His ears were pricked to catch any sound, no matter how slight, but all he heard was his own breathing, which was more labored and hoarse than he would have wanted it to be.

Then he spotted the boat ramp and the Duck River.

About fifty feet from the water's edge stood Vincent. His back was to the water and he faced Grant with an immobile expression.

As he neared him, he shone his flashlight in Vincent's face. He winced slightly at the harshness of the light, but his lips were set. He moved the light away from him, down his rigid body and toward the boat ramp and the water's edge.

Three inches of snow had fallen on the ramp. It was pristine, like the frosting on a European cake—except for a sudden indenture the size of a duffle bag. The bag was gone and as Grant shone the light toward the Duck River, he saw a wake in the water caused by the departure of a boat.

The boat was nowhere in sight.

14

Grant sighed deeply as he opened the pantry door. His small house was cold, the contents sparse, and it reeked of emptiness. He stared at the shelves, his eyes barely registering two cans of soup and a half-empty roll of crackers, the wax paper neatly folded back and secured with a clothespin. Beneath the shelves were a half dozen bottles of wine. Now he leaned down, grasped one and with an audible sigh, placed it on the counter beside the pantry door.

The corkscrew was already there on the counter, as it always was, and he took a moment to disengage the last cork from it before he began to peel the foil from the new bottle. He stopped for a moment and tilted the bottle as if viewing the label for the first time. It was Chilean; a blend of Cabernet Sauvignon and Merlot with just a hint of Cabernet Franc. It was from Casablanca, a region rich with grapes that served up a hearty, warming blend of red wines.

He always drank Chilean wines. Well, not always. There was a time when he preferred those from the Mediterranean. But that was before. Now the mere thought of anything from that region sank him into a deep depression filled with thoughts of love lost forever.

He shook his head as if to clear his thoughts and popped the cork with the finesse of one accustomed to the action. He grabbed a whiskey glass and poured the wine into it as if it were water. He chugged it down, refilled the glass and carried it in one hand and the bottle in the other to the kitchen table, where after depositing them on the contemporary granite, he pulled up a chair and sat in front of them like a student studying a textbook.

He tried to keep his eyes open but his eyelids were heavy. He fought for a few moments but as the warmth of the wine sank into his bones, he rested his chin on his chest and allowed his eyes to close. He felt a twinge of pain as his mind's eye envisioned Linda, his beautiful wife. Linda, with her statuesque figure, the olive skin glowing in the candlelight of his dreams. Linda, with her long, silky black hair, so shiny that he often teased that it reflected his own image as though it were a mirror. Linda, with her enormous chocolate brown eyes. Eyes that looked to him for comfort, eyes that counted on him to take care of her—and their daughter, Julia.

Julia had been a carbon copy of her mother. He used to hold her in his arms and envision his wife as a little girl, until the images became fused into one. Immense brown eyes that appeared so trusting, so innocent. Eyes that seemed to worship her father. Tiny hands that grasped his finger, hands that were so small that even as she grew, she could only hold onto his thumb when they walked together. Little arms that surrounded his neck and sweet lips that kissed his cheek as her diminutive voice whispered, "I love you, Daddy…"

He'd been in the Air Force then, stationed in Incirlik, Turkey. It had been a beautiful day, the kind of day best captured on postcards. They'd decided on the spur of the moment to visit Kusadasi, a stunning island whose name meant "Bird Island" in English. They'd sung songs as he'd driven them across the causeway; he remembered gazing out at the sparkling blue waters of the Aegean Sea and the dazzling white beaches, past the largest marina he'd ever seen—a marina that must have contained upwards of five hundred boats ranging from speed boats to luxurious yachts.

He remembered thinking that Life couldn't get any better.

They'd parked in the downtown region of Kusadasi. The area was alive with the bustling sounds of thousands of tourists haggling over souvenir prices, the numerous ferries dropping them off from nearby Ephesus and other shopping and tourist meccas. The shops went on as far as the eye could see; those with permanent structures had inexpensive souvenirs stacked from the street floor to tables overflowing with merchandise; beside them the vendors shouted to the crowds, cajoling them into stepping inside, where the more expensive commodities were sold.

The streets were laid out in a square; why Grant remembered this fact more than many others was beyond him. But he did remember them: the streets running east to west and the cross streets from north to south. They were laid out very neatly, almost rhythmically; ancient streets that had been there thousands of years, streets that had been bustling with activity when North America was still centuries away from being discovered.

They wandered along one of the main thoroughfares; Julia was holding onto his thumb and he clasped Linda's hand in his other, strong hand. The sound was deafening; the vendors aggressively competing against one another for each tourist's attention. They looked to Grant like gypsies, their skin dark, their eyes black, as if they all belonged to one large family.

One stepped in front of Linda, attempting to entice her with a brightly colored silk scarf. Another flattered her in a vain attempt to persuade her into a clothing shop. Still another tried to coax him into a flower shop with calls of "don't you love her?" as he held out brilliantly colored flowers.

Each step seemed to grow more difficult as they sidestepped insistent vendors. Linda grasped his hand even tighter as the crowd grew heavier.

And then it happened.

She was there one moment, holding onto his thumb; his six-year-old little girl who pressed against him. A tear escaped his eye and ran down his cheek now as he thought about it, thought about the tiny creature that looked to him for protection and security.

And in the next instant, she was gone. He knew the moment she lost her grip on him, and he turned quickly, expecting to see her inches away from him. But she wasn't there. There wasn't even an empty spot where she might have stood; there were only vendors and tourists pressing in, their bodies becoming as one, and a desperate air of claustrophobia arising within him as he pushed against them like a fish trying to swim upstream.

"Julia!" he hollered, the intensity of his voice startling even him.

But though the people continued pressing in, there was no response from the tiny girl. There was no scream. No cry for her father. No sound from her at all. It had been as if she had never been there at all.

A second tear ran down his cheek and then a third. He tried to drown out his sorrow with massive gulps of the deep red wine, but he felt pulled downward into a nightmare he could never quite awaken from: a nightmare filled with running down one street and then another, of crying out for his daughter, of begging the vendors who had just accosted him with their wares now turning away from him, focusing their attention on fat tourists with fatter wallets.

The streets ran east and west. North to south. It was a fact he always remembered, though he didn't quite know why...

A sob escaped from him and he bent his head over the kitchen table until his forehead rested upon it and he cried as though his heart would break in two.

The first rays of morning light were muted as if the sun couldn't quite find him there in Nashville; as if the winter clouds had descended upon them like a blanket, shutting out all else.

He stirred slightly, slowly feeling his cheek against the cold granite, gradually realizing his toes were near freezing in the small, chilly kitchen. His fingertips were frigid as they touched his forehead, which oddly felt as if it was burning, his peppered locks of hair wet against his skin.

He groaned as he struggled to sit erect in the hard kitchen chair, his backbone stiffened into the slumped position he'd assumed for half the night. He rubbed his eyes until the bottle came into view. Then he grasped the neck of the bottle and tilted it, noting only mere drops existed at the bottom. He stared into the narrow opening, smelled the stale smell of spent wine, and thought of the secrets that were now stored inside that bottle... Secrets of a little girl who was there one minute and gone the next, vanished without a trace...

He groaned again as he rose unsteadily and strode to the waste can that sat at the far end of the kitchen, where he deposited the empty bottle alongside the others. Then he half-shuffled down the hallway to the bathroom to begin his day as he did all the others.

15

Jessie awoke from a fitful sleep. Her bones and muscles ached as much from the cold as the cramped position in which she was forced to lie. The cabin was permeated with the pungent odor of burning wood, though the stove had long since died down. And with the waning of the flames, the heat was quickly replaced with a chilling draft that caused her to shiver uncontrollably.

Her head was pounding. She tried to remember the last time it had hurt so badly that she was almost seeing double, but couldn't. The pain was too intense for her to focus. The hood over her face scratched at her skin, but she was actually grateful for the little bit of fabric that protected her nose from the overpowering stench of burnt wood.

Her stomach growled so loudly that she might have been embarrassed had she not been alone. She struggled to come to a seated position on the damp, moldy couch; tried to see through the tiny holes in the hood as she took in her surroundings.

It was impossible to determine how much time had passed. It was still dark outside, a blackness that seemed as solid as a living, breathing being. She remembered a verse from a song—*it was always darkest just before dawn*—and struggled to remember the rest of the lyrics. But though she knew she needed to remain alert, she couldn't. With her head pounding, her lips cracked and dry, her muscles aching, and her stomach growling, it was all she could do to hang on to any semblance of hope.

A coyote howled a mournful, elongated howl that didn't seem as if it would ever end. She tried to calculate the distance, but it was impossible. It could have been yards from the cabin or a half mile away. She shivered again, as much now from fear as the cold, as her situation sank in ever deeper, threatening to overcome her emotions. She tried to focus on the sound of flying squirrels scampering on the tin roof, tried to concentrate on their mundane task of finding nuts or making nests, anything that had any resemblance to normalcy.

From off in the distance, she heard the faint sound of a vehicle with a muffler too loud to ignore and as she tilted her head and listened, it grew stronger as it approached. It was the old farm truck, the one that had brought her here. How quickly she'd come to recognize the distinct sound of that muffler with its odd misfiring, as though it was long overdue for a tune-up. She thought of Abby and how alert she was to the sound of differing vehicles, knowing when her father was pulling up in front or when to ignore the vehicles parking so near to their condo. She squeezed her eyes to stop the tears when she thought of her, telling herself that Nick had certainly found her by now, and she was not alone.

Now the tires were crunching along the gravel. There had been another sound, too, she remembered as she heard the truck approach: sometime during the night, it had rained. And perhaps that rain had turned to ice or sleet; she recalled now hearing the drops hitting the tin roof as she struggled between wakefulness and sleep. Now the sound of the tires was slightly different, and she wondered if they were crunching over ice as they approached.

It seemed to stop just beyond the cabin. The engine continued to run and she listened to that sound for what seemed like an excruciatingly long time. She didn't know much about engines, but she recalled as a young girl, her father had purchased an old Hudson and had hired someone to overhaul the engine and bring it to showroom condition. He'd taken her to their massive garage on the Palmer estate one day to watch it being worked on. She remembered standing on a crate, peering over the expansive hood, staring into the cavern that housed the engine. And how the mechanic spoke of spark plugs and how he could tell which ones were fouled by the way the engine coughed and sputtered.

Why she would remember that now, of all times, she struggled to figure out even as she realized the truck outside had a similar sputter, one she knew she could never forget.

The engine abruptly died and the truck door opened with a creaking groan before slamming shut. A second door opened and slammed more forcefully.

Brainiac and Brutus were back.

She heard their footsteps approaching, the thud of their heavy boots on the wood steps, and the sound of the boards creaking on the porch as they neared the front door. With an abrupt movement that startled her, the door flew open. Snow swirled around them as they strode wordlessly into the cabin, and suddenly the tiny building seemed dwarfed by their presence.

She peered through the fibers in the hood as Brainiac lit a cigarette. He still wore the cap she'd seen in the truck; a cap that successfully hid his face in the bill's shadows.

Brutus approached the cold stove, opened the door, and forcefully tossed in wood chips. When they began to smolder and burn, he added two more logs. Soon the cabin was again overcome with the stench of too much wood burning, but in contrast, the warmth began to permeate her clothing.

Brainiac approached her and stood wordlessly in front of her. He seemed to be staring her down, she thought, as she looked back at him through the fabric. She wondered if he could see her eyes or if the hood successfully obscured them.

He blew smoke from his cigarette into her face. She turned her head away as he chuckled. His voice was low, his chuckle barely audible, and something about it caused her to freeze.

Behind him, Brutus had picked up an axe and was pushing the wood around inside the stove, causing the flames to reach ever higher. When he finished, he propped the axe against the door frame and vigorously rubbed his hands together near the wood stove.

Brainiac continued to stare at her and she began to feel a lump growing in her throat. Is this how it will all end? She thought as a fresh wave of panic began to sweep over her. Here alone in this cabin with these two thugs, isolated from everyone else? Will the end come swiftly and mercifully or will I linger on in horrific pain?

She squeezed her eyes to fight back the tears that threatened to overwhelm her, but they rushed down her cheeks unchecked. I have to fight, she thought, even as she knew with her bonds it would be impossible. I must find the strength somewhere, somehow.

Brutus was at the kitchen table now, leaning over it with both palms resting on the tabletop. Through her tears and the rough fabric, Jessie could barely make out a small bottle. But even before she saw the cotton balls Brutus retrieved unceremoniously from a plastic bag beside it, she detected the strong odor of ether.

She pulled at her bonds, but she was securely tied. Her mind raced as she struggled to come up with a plan as Brutus approached her.

Brainiac stepped back, his cigarette still glowing as he watched her. Then Brutus was coming up from behind him, and he stepped to the side to allow him to pass. It was all too silent, she thought. Not a word was spoken between the two men; they each seemed to know exactly what to do.

Brutus was only a step away from her now, and the reek of ether was so strong that she wondered how he could avoid inhaling the toxic fumes. Brianiac moved behind him, his progress slow and methodical. And although Brutus was closer and the cotton was mere inches away from her, she found her attention riveted to Brainiac.

Brutus reached toward her, pulling the hood off her head in a sudden jerk that caused the duct tape to rip away from her, and she screamed out in pain. The hood was hanging now near the back of her head, and her nose and mouth were uncovered, vulnerable and helpless against the ether.

Brutus stepped forward but as he did so, she saw the gleam of the axe behind him as Brainiac raised it high above his head. Then it came back down with a force so great that when it hit the back of Brutus' head, Jessie heard a crack that echoed through the tiny cabin. Then Brutus was falling forward, his body landing across her own, the axe still embedded in the back of his head. The room swirled around her. The stench of wood now mingled with the reek of blood. The bulb swung overhead and then it was gone, leaving her drowning in the stench of ether.

16

Grant heard Ivory's voice before he was halfway through the door.

"Well, I would have thought you'd look a little more rested than that," she said.

He caught her out of the corner of his eye, pouring two cups of coffee as he made his way to his desk. With a heavy sigh, he removed his overcoat and draped it over the back of his chair.

"Thanks," he said as he took the cup she offered him.

"Didn't sleep?"

"Not a wink." He sipped the coffee, closing his eyes momentarily while he savored the feel of the hot liquid cascading down his throat. Then he eyed the bulletins that had been placed on his desk, as they always were first thing in the morning. "You?"

"I need to be headed home soon or I'm likely to collapse right here," Ivory said. "Spent the rest of the night at the Palmer house."

"Give me an update." He sat on the edge of his desk and waited for her to continue.

"It appears Vincent came straight home after dropping off the money. Shannon kept the GPS going—"

"No more detours?"

"No more detours. He fell asleep in the den where we had all the equipment set up. Woke up around dawn and went back upstairs."

"Did he have his cell phone with him?"

"Yes." Grant opened his mouth to speak but Ivory interrupted him, "No calls. He didn't make any; didn't receive any."

"What about the home phone?"

"Nothing."

Grant sipped the coffee thoughtfully. "What about Meg?"

"Upstairs all night."

"Are we tracking her cell phone?"

"Yes. All the calls have been placed to Vincent's." She pulled up a chair but instead of sitting in it, she placed her foot on the seat and leaned into the chair back. "Vincent told us that Meg was so distraught, she took sleeping pills and went to bed. Still there when I left shortly after dawn."

"You see her?"

"Didn't have to. Maid confirmed it."

Grant glanced at his watch. It was shortly after eight o'clock. "Any word from either of them this morning?"

"Not yet."

"Hhmm." He closed his eyes tightly, trying to rid his mind of the images that threatened to invade it: of Linda running with him all over Kusadasi. Of pounding on the gates at the American Embassy, of begging the Marine on guard to let them in. Of discovering the Ambassador was out of the country, and of their frustration at having to deal with a lower-ranking person who didn't seem to work fast enough or efficiently enough.

Of driving to the police station, speaking to anyone and everyone. Calling the media and trying to get national and then international attention.

They were frantic, he thought as he sipped his coffee again. They probably didn't sleep for a good three days after that. And even then, they never slept as they had before.

Linda hadn't returned to the military base and taken a sleeping pill. He hadn't returned home and dozed in the chair and then retired to his bedroom. Of course, their situation had been so different. They'd been in a foreign country and the ransom call had never come—

"Are you listening to me?"

"Yeah," he said, shaking himself back to reality.

"So he was here this morning when I arrived," she was saying.

"Vincent?"

"Nick. You weren't listening."

He waved his hand as if to dismiss her comment. "Just trying to think ten steps ahead of the kidnappers."

"Well, while you were thinking, I was telling you that Nick was here first thing. Said you dropped him off at his apartment and told him to be here when the office opened. And he was here." She dropped a file on his desk. "Also received this fax a few minutes ago. Jessica Palmer's curriculum at Vanderbilt."

Grant handed Nick a cup of coffee before sitting down across from him. The room was cold, as if the heat in the building wasn't able to reach it. The table was metal and contained multiple chips along the edges, most likely from careless movers. The chairs were aluminum and as Grant leaned back in his, the chill was intensified by the cold metal.

He stifled the impulse to lean forward, choosing instead to pointedly stare at Nick for a long moment.

Nick sipped on his coffee, lingering over the steam. He held the cup with both hands; perhaps for warmth, Grant thought as he watched, but just as likely as a crutch to keep his hands from shaking. The young man didn't appear to have gotten much sleep. His hair was still rumpled, his clothes wrinkled, and he had dark bags under his eyes. Grant hoped he didn't look as bad.

"So," Grant said after what he hoped had been an awkward silence, "tell me about your relationship with Jessica Palmer."

Nick's eyes shot up in surprise. They lingered on Grant for a moment before focusing on the coffee cup.

"I'm waiting," Grant said.

Nick chewed his lower lip for a moment. "We're both enrolled at Vanderbilt."

"You in law school, too?"

"Journalism."

"That's right," Grant said in a hoarse whisper. "*The Tennessean.*"

"I work there."

"So, what classes are you taking with Jessie?"

Nick hesitated.

Grant opened a stack of papers in front of him and rifled through them until he came to her curriculum. "So," he said, trying to sound casual, "you're taking the Cecil D. Branstetter Litigation and Dispute Resolution Program?"

"No."

"No? But that might come in handy for a journalism major, don't you think?"

Nick didn't respond, but kept his eyes focused on his coffee.

"Law and Business?"

"No."

"Well, how about this course—Law and Economics, the Ph.D. Program?"

"No."

Grant leaned forward. "Why don't we stop wasting time, young man?" His voice had a hoarse edge to it. "You and I both know you're not enrolled in any of the same courses as Jessica Palmer."

Nick looked up from his coffee. He didn't respond, but Grant thought his eyes appeared tortured.

"Don't tell me you've seen her around the campus, either, and that's the extent of your relationship."

Nick swallowed.

"You and I both know you two are close. Closer than two students who just happen to be attending the same university." Grant paused for effect.

After a lengthy silence, Nick nodded. His lips appeared dry, almost cracking.

"So why don't you tell me how you know her." After a moment, he added, "I'll find out. If I find out from you, you could get off looking better than if I have to waste my time hunting down the facts from someone else. But I *will* find out the truth."

Nick swirled his coffee around his cup for a moment and then set it down on the table. He leaned back and dug his hands into his pockets. "We've been dating for some time."

"Is it serious?"

"Yes."

"Why are you keeping it secret from her parents?"

Nick's face was flushed. "I don't come from the best of families." He seemed to be searching for the right words. "Jessie promised she'd tell her folks, but… The timing was never right."

Grant nodded. "Is the relationship monogamous?"

He didn't hesitate. "Yes."

"Did you have a little spat, the night she disappeared?"

"No!" Nick's eyes were wide and incredulous. "Absolutely not. Look, I was walking her home from Blackacre—like I do every Friday night, ask anybody—and Aubrey Shippman, from *The Tennessean*, stopped his car right in the middle of the road and told me the editor wanted to see me, pronto. Jessie insisted that I go. We could see her condo from the intersection—" He burst into tears.

Grant was caught off guard. He watched silently as Nick bawled in front of him.

"I knew I shouldn't 've left her," Nick continued when he'd regained enough control to continue. "I didn't want to. But we could see her condo— there was nobody else out. The building was less than a block away. I should have walked her home. If I'd have walked her home, she'd be here today—"

Grant wrote on the manila folder on top of his paperwork. "So this Aubrey Shippman," he said, trying to keep his voice curt, "he'll confirm you were with him last evening?"

Nick nodded. Though he wiped his eyes, it was futile; the tears kept pouring. "And the editor."

"Ah, yes. Your meeting. How did it go?"

"I'm being transitioned to full-time," he said. He sighed heavily. "I—we should have been celebrating. But I'd rather be with Jessie right now than…" His voice faded.

"And the editor's name?"

Nick provided the name, and Grant wrote it down matter-of-factly. He waited until Nick had regained his composure somewhat before continuing.

"What did you do after the meeting?"

"Aubrey drove me back home. I went upstairs." His voice cracked.

Grant thought the young man would begin crying again and wondered if he should go to his desk and retrieve a box of tissues.

"My window looks toward Jessie's condo. I—I was gonna call her and look at her condo at the same time. She usually comes to the window, and we look across at each other while we're talking." He burst into tears again.

Grant waited patiently for him to continue.

After a long, agonized moment, Nick said, "I looked out the window and saw all the cop cars. And I ran downstairs. Ran to her condo—"

As he continued crying, Grant got up and walked quietly to his desk, where he retrieved the box of tissues. He hesitated momentarily, wiping away a single tear that threatened to form at the edge of his eye. It was Julia all over again. If he'd only done this. If he'd only been on the left side and not the right side. If only. He should've been there. He would've been there. The torture was never-ending.

17

Jessie groaned as her head was flung against the edge of the truck bed, the sound of the impact echoing through the mist. It took a superhuman effort to keep her eyes closed and feign unconsciousness, even as she felt the trickle of blood seeping through her hair. It was only after Brainiac flung her legs into the confined space and slammed the door, locking her into the enclosed truck bed, that she allowed the tears to escape from her.

She could smell the now-familiar odor of ether and she tilted her head back, trying to find the most oxygen in the tiny space. It seemed air-tight and she fought the impulse to panic. He wouldn't leave her in here, she thought as the engine started up. Or would he? Would he take her to another location where he would dump both her and the truck, leaving her to suffocate?

She squeezed her eyes and tried to maintain her focus. She couldn't panic now. Not after all she'd been through.

Brainiac might have been the brains of the kidnapping and ransom scheme, but he didn't have the street smarts of Brutus, that was certain. After he'd embedded the axe in Brutus' skull and the brawnier man had fallen across her body and the sofa, Brainac had struggled to move the body onto the floor. He'd huffed and puffed as he tried lifting a leg or an arm and by the time the body had fallen to the floor with a resounding thud, blood was splattered all over her, the sofa, Brutus and Brainiac. She'd heard Brutus groan more than once. Each time she tried not to envision him rising from the floor with the axe still embedded in his head like something out of a horror film. What steadied her nerves was the thought that his focus would not be on her but on his partner—and if they destroyed each other, there had to be a chance that she could escape.

Brainiac had gone in search of the ether-stained cotton balls, which he found on the floor near the sofa. Jessie had allowed the hood to slide back down over her face. The thick threads had served as a barrier between her nostrils and the cotton. Somehow, from the time Brutus had soaked the cotton to the time Brainiac had located it, it had lost some of its strength. She had steeled herself and as he approached, she had sucked in her breath. Now, as she lay in the bed of the truck as it bumped along the gravel driveway, listening to the misfiring of the spark plugs and the engine coughing, she realized Brainiac was so inept that he'd barely given her enough ether to even cause the slightest wooziness.

The truck moved slowly and she tried to gauge the distance they'd traveled. It wasn't long before the vehicle stopped and the door was opened with the creaking sound of rusty hinges. But the door wasn't closed as she might have anticipated and the engine continued to sputter as it idled. She heard the muffled noise of another sound—perhaps of chains clanking—and she braced herself. He wouldn't wrap her in chains and toss her into a river, would he? She struggled against the ropes that bound her, but they were too tight to free herself.

After a moment, the truck door slammed shut and the truck lurched into gear. It traveled only a few feet before it stopped again, and the sounds were repeated: the door opened but did not close, the chains rattled again—this time closer to the back of the truck than to the front as it had before—and the door was shut once more. As it lurched forward once again, stopping briefly before turning abruptly to the right onto a road that was far less noisy than the first, she pieced together what was happening. They had come to the end of the road leading to the cabin, where a gate of some sort blocked it from casual visitors. Brainiac had exited the truck, removed a chain that was perhaps padlocked to the gate, opened it, drove through it, and stopped to secure it once more.

She wondered briefly how long Brutus' body would remain in the cabin before it was found. How long it would take for him to bleed to death or die from his injuries. Then abruptly, she realized each sound was a clue—a clue that could help her lead the authorities back to her captors. She felt her heart surge as she thought of arriving safely in her own home, and then serving as a level-headed witness and assisting the police in finding her captors.

She became acutely more aware of the sounds around her, trying to memorize everything as best she could. The driveway to the cabin was gravel or rocks, but the road they traveled now was neither. However, the truck was still maintaining a slow speed—while it was faster than the bouncing and bumping along she experienced on the cabin road, it was not traveling along an Interstate.

The truck came to a stop. She heard the sound of other vehicles before they began to speed up once more, the engine straining as they gathered speed. This, she realized, was the Interstate. It was smooth, even for the clunky truck, and the minutes became monotonous.

She was sleep-deprived and wanted nothing more than to fall asleep and wake up to find this had all been a horrible dream. But she had to remain awake and alert, she told herself. She had to. If the roads held clues to the location of the cabin, every detail she remembered about her captors would help in their apprehension. But she'd never actually seen Brainiac's face, she realized as she closed her eyes and tried to visualize it. He'd always worn the cap with the long bill and his face had always managed to remain in the shadows… The shadows of the night; the shadows of the cap. Except—

Her eyes flew open. Except when he leaned toward her with the ether-soaked cotton. Just before she'd closed her eyes and held her breath. She'd caught a glimpse of his chin. It was angular and had dimpling in it, like the cellulite on a woman's thigh.

He reeked of smoke. But not just any kind of cigarette, she realized. Though she'd only seen him smoking cigarettes, there was another distinct tobacco odor about him. She sucked in her breath as she realized it was a pipe. It was almost like the Cavendish tobacco flavored with cherry that her grandfather used to smoke in his unique ivory pipe shaped like a man's head, a man with flowing hair that turned shades of brown through years of use. She hadn't thought of that pipe in years.

So, Brainiac smoked a pipe and had cellulite on his chin.

It was scant information to give to the police.

As she wracked her brain for more clues, she realized his physical fitness—or lack of it—also told her a lot about the man. When she feigned unconsciousness and he tried to lift her, he was clumsy, his flesh doughy. He was a man out of shape, a man who huffed and puffed while carrying her, a man who had to lean her against a tree at one point to keep from dropping her. A man unaccustomed to physical fitness.

The truck was cold. Even though her space was small and confined, her body heat did nothing to warm it up. The metal was freezing, the chill reaching through to her bones even through her layers of clothing. She could almost detect the scent of snow in the air, and she wondered if it had snowed while she'd remained in the cabin. If it had, she thought, there would be fresh tracks leading from the road past the locked gate.

An hour might have gone by when they began to slow and she felt her body slide across the truck bed as if the vehicle was traveling around a cloverleaf. The engine strained as it down-shifted, eventually coming to a brief stop before lurching forward and turning.

This road was paved but she arrived at the conclusion that it was a secondary road. There were too many curves in the road, too many times where the truck slowed to a near stop, for it to be an Interstate.

They stopped again a few minutes later and sat for a moment longer, as if Brainiac was in doubt as to which direction to go— or he was sitting at a red light, waiting for it to turn. When they started again, their pace was slower and felt more uncertain.

They came to a sudden stop, throwing Jessie against the far wheel well. Then, it was backing up before the gears changed and it turned once more.

She was bounced unceremoniously around the truck bed, but unlike the cabin road, she did not detect the sound of rocks or gravel crunching under the tires. She sank more than once and she realized they must have been traveling along a dirt road that was poorly maintained. The wheels were sinking into potholes before rising again and continuing the journey.

They turned yet again, and she heard the sound of branches scraping against the metal sides. Eventually, it came to a stop. As she lay motionless in the truck bed, the engine was turned off and she was surrounded by total silence. It was, she thought as she fought to remain calm, a silence more terrifying than the cabin itself or the sight of Brutus' body crashing on top of her, the axe embedded in his skull. It was a silence that spoke of the end of the journey. Despite her efforts to remain calm, she felt a rising panic as she realized the journey might not be the only thing that was about to end.

18

Grant could hear the dog barking before he'd even pushed the doorbell. He listened carefully to the flurry of footsteps inside the home. He'd heard that flurry only too many times before, but they were usually rushing in the opposite direction—a fugitive racing to a back window or trying to slip out a back door while he was at the front, or attempting to find a hiding place when the FBI inevitably entered.

This time, it was obvious the footsteps were attempting to answer the door and hold back the animal at the same time. When it was finally opened, it was a stout black woman who stood at the door. She held herself erect, her chin tilted slightly upward, but her eyes were red and puffy as if she'd been crying. She wore a deep blue dress with a lace-trimmed apron over it which reminded Grant of maids from a bygone era. As his eyes swept downward, he noticed worn blue shoes, the shoes of a working woman.

"It's alright, Heddy," Vincent said as he moved into the foyer. He let go of the golden retriever, who bounded to Grant's side to sniff him. "This is FBI Agent Grant Bailey. He's going to get Jessie back for us. Aren't you?"

"Oh, Lawd," Heddy said, grasping Grant's hand and shaking it with the strength of a bodybuilder, "Thank you so much. Thank you. Thank you."

"I haven't done anything yet," Grant replied, feeling a bit sheepish. "But I'm working on it." He turned to Vincent. "Shannon here?"

Vincent said something that was barely audible as he turned his head back toward the den. A second later, Shannon popped his head into the hallway.

"Have you got something?"

Grant ignored him and nodded his head toward the door. Wordlessly, he stepped onto the front porch with Shannon.

"Have you heard—Jessie's not—?"

"No," Grant said, turning back toward the foyer. "We've heard nothing. I'll just be a minute." Before Vincent could respond, he closed the massive door behind him.

"Tell me what happened after I left."

Shannon's eyes cut toward the windows, as if he were concerned someone could be lurking just on the other side, listening. When he spoke, his voice was low. "Mrs. Palmer—she's—I can't tell whether the stress is getting to her or if she's kinda slightly off center, if you know what I mean."

"What happened?"

"Soon as you left, she poured a tall glass with gin and a couple of ice cubes. Seemed like I'd turned around for a minute and when I glanced back, the glass was empty."

Grant nodded. "Calming her nerves?" he surmised.

"Yeah, well, then she reached for a bottle of prescription pills."

"You know what they were?"

"Nope. But she took a handful before anybody could stop her. If it hadn't happened right in front of everybody, I'd have thought it was a suicide attempt."

"Was Dalton still here?"

"Sat right there and watched her. Didn't seem to faze him. So I'm thinkin' she's like that all the time."

"Did they knock her out?"

"She seemed kind of loopy. Kept nodding off and when she'd wake up, she'd pour another drink. She got real unsteady. Eventually, Dalton half-carried her upstairs."

"He didn't think her behavior was alarming?"

"Nope. Gave me the impression this wasn't the first time. So maybe the pills weren't so strong."

"I'd like to see that pill bottle."

"Should still be on the coffee table. Unless the maid moved it. I haven't exactly been watching it."

"So, what happened after Dalton took her upstairs?"

Shannon's face became flushed. "Well, I didn't mean to be spying—"

"Sure you did," Grant said with a wry smile.

"From the doorway downstairs, you can kinda see straight up that massive staircase. It kind of winds up and there's this banister overlooking the downstairs—"

"You trying to sell me a house or tell me what happened?"

"Yeah, well, I guess it was the bedroom door where Dalton led her. He brought her inside, I heard something like springs, and then he was back at the door. It was just enough time for him to plop her onto the bed and leave her that way."

"I guess it's not in his job description to take her shoes off and get her in a nightie." When Shannon didn't respond, Grant continued, "So then what happened?"

He shrugged. "Dalton came back downstairs. Looked like he was kind of resting his eyes until Vincent returned—wasn't asleep. Ivory almost pounced on Vincent when he walked in and Dalton went into lawyer-defense-mode."

"What do you mean?"

"Hey, I'm just the tech guy. You know? I've got my back to them and I'm tinkering with the equipment—"

"And listening."

"You can't close your ears."

"Yeah, right." The drapes were pulled back overlooking the porch and they waited for a moment. It was Heddy. When she saw them, she quickly finished adjusting them before moving away from the window. "So what'd you hear?"

"Ivory was pretty hot about Vincent losing you."

"So was I."

"She demanded to know what he was doing."

"And?"

"He said he was following orders, trying to get his daughter back."

Grant nodded.

"Then Ivory asked him about that insurance policy."

Grant raised an eyebrow.

"Vincent reviews it personally once a year. It's his decision to raise it, lower it, leave it, or discontinue it."

"Who else knows about it?"

"Board of directors. And the way Vincent was spouting off, I got the impression he told everybody at the bank about it, too."

"Why would he go and do a thing like that?"

"Makes him look like a big man?"

"Or so he thinks. He may as well have put a target on his family."

Shannon nodded. "Awfully coincidental."

"Isn't it, though."

"Let's just hope Jessie is more balanced than her momma."

"That's a broad statement."

"She gives me the impression she's a bit unbalanced," Shannon said, his voice barely above a whisper.

"Might serve her well right now."

"Why do you say that?" Shannon asked.

"You know the stats. Eighty percent of all kidnappings are committed by family members. I'm looking at the possibility of this being an inside job—"

"You don't think Vincent—"

Grant shrugged. "Somebody knows how this bank operates. Not only how much the insurance policy was for, but how much time to allow—or not allow—to force Vincent to get the money in unmarked bills. They knew the bank would have that much on hand."

"Still, that doesn't mean Vincent—"

"Everybody's a suspect. *Everybody.*"

Shannon was silent for a moment. "Well, I think you can cross Mrs. Palmer off your list. She's reclusive. Socially withdrawn."

"You a shrink now?"

"All I'm saying is, we don't need to spend any time watching her. All she does is drink and sleep."

"Maybe. But she gets sober enough, long enough, to get her photo taken for the Society pages, if you know what I mean."

The front door opened. As Grant turned, he came face to face with Vincent, who was staring at him as if he was trying to read his mind. Beside him was the golden retriever. He was no longer holding her back, but she stood perfectly still, her eyes the only movement as they moved back and forth between Grant and Shannon. A witness, Grant thought. A witness who tried to claw her way out of the condo to rescue her owner. He knelt down and scratched her under her chin. Her fur was soft and silky, her eyes large and inquisitive. Her muzzle was turning white.

"Why don't you tell me what happened?" Grant said, his eyes still on the dog.

"You were there," Vincent answered flatly.

"No," Grant said, raising his head to look him in the eye, "I wasn't."

"Look, they knew you were on the case. I think they had me drive in circles, just to get rid of you."

"You think that, do you?"

"Well, it didn't work. You stayed right on me the whole time."

Grant's eyes didn't waver from his. He doesn't know about the tracking device, he thought as he stared at him. He has no clue how close he came to completely losing me. "I wasn't 'right on you' or I'd have seen what happened at the lake. Why don't you enlighten me?"

"It happened so quickly. He called me on my cell, told me where to go, and to leave the money on the boat ramp. He told me to turn my back to the water or I'd die and Jessie would, too. Then you got there and when I turned back around, the money was gone."

"And you didn't hear a thing."

"Nothing."

"Not even a boat engine."

Vincent stared back at him. "Not even a boat engine."

Grant nodded.

"I did what he told me to do," Vincent said, his voice rising. "Now where's my baby?"

"If they're going to let her go, they'll do it within the next eight hours."

"If—if—" Vincent stammered, his face reddening.

"There's a good chance they'll let her go. There's no more reason to keep her. They've got the money."

"Then why not release her immediately? Why didn't they let her out at the boat ramp?"

"Because she wasn't there."

"You saw them?"

"No. But they're not usually with the person picking up the cash. They're released later, after the kidnappers have a chance to get away."

"So what do we do now?"

Vincent's face had become ashen and it occurred to Grant that this could be the first time in his life that he wasn't in complete control of a situation. "We run down leads," Grant said, hoping his voice sounded confident. "In rare cases, they ask for more money."

"What do you mean, ask for more money? They kidnapped her, they asked for a ransom, I paid it. Now she comes home. End of story."

"Tell me, Mr. Palmer, what if they'd asked for ten million?"

"Then I'd have given them ten million."

"Your bank keep ten million lying around?"

"No," Vincent said, his voice softer. "We barely keep five million."

"So, how would you get ten million?"

"This is ridiculous," Vincent snapped. "You should be looking for my daughter instead of asking all these hypotheticals. They didn't ask for ten, they asked for five."

"They did, didn't they?"

"I don't know what your game is, but if I don't get my daughter back—and get her back soon—I'm calling the Governor, the Attorney General—hell, I'm calling Washington—until every law enforcement man in the country is looking for her. You understand me?"

Before Grant could respond, the phone began ringing inside the house.

Shannon pushed past them in a rush to get inside. "Showtime, everybody," he called out as he disappeared into the den.

19

Her body trembled with a fear more intense than anything she'd ever experienced. Even the time she'd spent in the decrepit cabin seemed tame compared to what she felt was now inevitable. Oddly, it wasn't the sounds around her that caused her blood to run cold, but the quietness, the deliberate softness, as though Brainiac was intentionally attempting to avoid any unnecessary noise.

She tried to feign sleep as she listened to the truck door close so gently that it was obvious he had barely latched it. She tried to stop her breath from convulsing as she held her hands over her face. If he believed she was still out from the ether, perhaps he wouldn't—he wouldn't kill her. There, I considered it, Jessie thought. Considered the inevitable. But with the mere thought came a wave of emotions—everything from wanting more than anything to fight to stay alive, to wishing he would simply get it over quickly so she wouldn't suffer.

She squeezed her eyes and tried not to think of the man in the cabin, of the cold-bloodedness Brainiac displayed when he sunk the axe deep into his skull.

His footsteps were slow and calculated. A noise above her head made her visualize his hands grasping the edge of the truck, as if steadying himself as he moved toward the truck bed. Then he was around the back. She could feel him, even if she couldn't see him. He was there, standing silently for what seemed an eternity.

When he opened the door to the dog cage she was in, it happened so suddenly that she jumped before she could restrain herself.

"Get out," he said.

His voice was husky. Strained.

"Get out!" he hissed again. He grabbed her ankle and pulled her unceremoniously through the cage. She fought the urge to dig her nails in; whatever awaited her outside the truck could be delayed, perhaps, but not avoided.

Her thoughts swam in every direction at once, from appealing to him, begging for mercy, kicking him, fighting to the last breath she had—but she was almost paralyzed from her bonds and could do little more than bump through the truck bed like a sack of potatoes before being dumped onto the ground.

It was daylight, she thought suddenly, as though the muted rays of light that found their way through the face mask could perhaps, in some way, save her.

He stood inches from her. His shoes were expensive, she realized with a start. Why she thought that, she didn't know. She couldn't see them clearly. But they were not the hunting boots she'd imagined he would wear. They weren't grimy and worn. She fixated on them but she was unable to see the details. Then it dawned on her: she could smell the shoe polish. Funny, how she'd think of something like that at a time like this—

He yanked her to her feet but the tape around her ankles made it difficult for her to stand. He steadied her but Jessie got the impression it was borne more from the need to move her to another location than from any act of chivalry.

"Move," he said. His voice was low and threatening but as he spoke, his head jerked around, as if he was making sure they were not spotted.

We have to be close to someone, Jessie thought as she stumbled across the uneven ground. If we were in the middle of nowhere, it wouldn't matter how loud he talked. The thought of being so close to others—others who could possibly rescue her—was enough to bolster her spirits somewhat as she alternately lurched and faltered. The only thing that kept her from falling was Brainiac's hands grasping each bicep and keeping her erect.

It was only twenty feet from the truck to a building, Jessie calculated. The building itself was large and imposing with an unusual structure in the front. As she tried to peer upward, she caught a glimpse of the sky behind it, which meant the structure itself was taller than the building behind it. She tried to search her memory of such a place but knew she had never been here before.

She was pushed and prodded around the building until they came to a stop about ten feet behind it. Had Brainiac not kept her under his control, she might have stumbled into an open pit but he halted her at the top of it. A grave? She thought. An image flashed through her mind of a documentary she'd once seen where people were marched into open graves and then shot, and she tried to turn and run but her bound feet and her captor's hands stopped her cold.

He appeared to hesitate. "Sit down," he ordered.

Painstakingly, she crouched on the ground. He grabbed her feet and swung them into the pit. She was surprised to find her feet touching something solid. She placed her hands on the ground beside her and felt concrete beneath her. She was sitting at the top of some steps.

Brainiac stepped around her and began to walk into the chasm. He grabbed her feet and pulled them onto the next step. "Push yourself down," he said. Each step seemed slow and arduous. If she could only speak, she would beg him to remove the bondages from her ankles—presumably so she could navigate the stairwell easier. But, she knew she would have been far more likely to turn and race up the stairs than continue down—and she was confident he knew it, too.

She counted twelve steps. And though each one brought her further from the sunlight and deeper into the pit, she knew it was no grave. That fact alone helped to keep her sane.

Finally, they had reached the bottom.

"Sit down," he directed.

She was already in a seated position, and she didn't understand at first. But he grabbed her arms and pulled her to the side, away from the entrance.

Once he let go of her, she kept her hands on the floor. It was cold and had a layer of dirt over it, but whether a concrete floor existed underneath, she couldn't tell. Even through the fabric that surrounded her face, she detected the dank stench of mildew. It was impossible to see and the uncertainty caused sweat to pop out across her forehead and her skin to grow hot, though it was so cold that she began to shiver.

Brainiac leaned so close to her that his lips brushed the fabric around one ear. "Your father knows exactly where you are," he said.

Her heart skipped a beat and she almost began to cry tears of joy.

"He just might want you to suffer awhile before he releases you."

She jerked her head in his direction, almost striking him. Then with every ounce of strength she had left in her, she swung her arms across his face, sending his cap flying off his head. He grabbed at his nose as he howled in pain. She struck him again and heard a crack resound through the small room.

Then, he was stumbling away from her and up the steps.

She waited for a door to slam shut, sealing her inside this underground tomb, but once his shadowy figure left the entrance, it was replaced instead with a glimpse of muted sunlight.

It seemed like an eternity passed as she sat there, working her arms back and forth, trying to break free. Then a voice stopped her cold.

"We need to get rid of her." The voice was Brainiac's.

"I disagree."

Jessie sucked in her breath. It was her father's voice.

"If we get rid of her now, she can't cause any more problems," Brainiac was saying.

"We're not getting rid of her. That's final," her father responded.

Jessie felt the tears stinging against the outer corner of her eyes. She longed to call out to him, to beg him to help her, but her mouth was covered so tightly, she could barely create an audible moan.

"You're making a big mistake," Brainiac stated firmly.

"The only mistake I've made is letting you take care of it." It was definitely Daddy's voice, she thought. It was strained as though he was holding his temper barely in check.

She heard footsteps moving away from the entrance. A few moments later, she heard the truck door open and shut and the engine started up with a sputter and cough.

Daddy? She thought. Daddy?

But no one appeared in the entrance. The sound of the truck died away and she was left alone, the only hint of civilization the sun rising ever higher to shine a hopeful swath of light across the entrance to this new dungeon.

20

Everyone was on their feet as Shannon counted the rings like a television news director counting down the seconds to show time. On the third ring, he pushed the speakerphone button.

"Hello?" Vincent said, his eyes riveted on Grant's.

"It's Agent Lang." Ivory's voice was clear and strong. "I need to speak to Agent Bailey."

Grant grabbed the receiver. "Take her off speaker."

"No," Vincent said, taking a step toward Shannon. "I want to hear what she's got to say."

"Take her off speaker," Grant repeated, each word sounding slow and forced. His eyes locked onto Vincent's like a father struggling for dominance over a misbehaving teen.

Shannon pushed a button and nodded silently.

"Why didn't you call my cell?" Grant asked, lowering his voice.

"You checked it lately?" Ivory asked. "I'm getting your voice mail on the first ring."

He slipped his cell phone out of his jacket pocket. "It's dead." He put it back in his pocket. "What've you got?"

"We've got a crew at the boat ramp where the money was left. No tire marks except those that can be traced to you and Vincent. We're positive the kidnappers came by boat."

"Tell me something I don't know."

"We've got a set of footprints. Started from the water's edge, walked in a few yards, turned and walked back. The return prints are deeper."

"Like they're carrying the weight of five million dollars," Grant finished wryly.

"You got it."

"Check all boat rentals—"

"Already on it. I should have more by the end of the day."

"Anything else?"

"Crime scene techs still processing evidence taken at Jessie's condo."

"And?"

"Lots of fingerprints. But no leads."

"What does that mean?" Vincent had leaned close to the receiver.

"They don't match up with any on file," Grant said cautiously. When Vincent simply stared back at him, he added, "It means whoever kidnapped Jessie either wore gloves or their fingerprints are not catalogued."

"If they're not catalogued, it means they've never been arrested," Vincent stated.

"Not necessarily. We don't have a central databank with every criminal's prints."

"That's preposterous!"

"Grant, I'm still here," Ivory's voice sounded impatient on the other end of the line.

Grant turned his back to Vincent. "Okay."

"You planning the next phase?"

"Yep."

"What's the next phase?" Vincent said, almost brushing against Grant as he tried to listen in on the conversation.

"Head back here," Grant said. He hung up the phone and turned to Vincent. "We have three possible outcomes."

Vincent stiffened.

"You know the first one," Grant said. "I'm not going to sugarcoat it."

Vincent held up his hand. "Jessie's still alive. I know it. I can feel it."

Grant nodded. "The second is, the kidnappers contact us and let us know where to find Jessie. They've played this game successfully so far," he added as he watched Vincent's eyes carefully, "so there's all indications they'll continue the same way."

"Which means?"

"Which means they'll wait until they're safe before they call us."

"Until *they're* safe?"

"Out of the area. Far enough away that they think we won't be hot on their trail."

Vincent nodded. Grant felt his body steeling itself for the next question. When it came, it was exactly what he had anticipated.

"And if they don't call?"

"We're already investigating two crime scenes—Jessie's condo building and the money drop. We'll know who the kidnappers are and we'll track them down."

"How will you know?"

Vincent's eyes had narrowed to the point that Grant could no longer read any expression in them. It was the kind of response a law enforcement officer has when they want to maintain a veil of secrecy between themselves and the public, he thought. "We'll know," Grant answered.

The phone rang again, causing them both to start.

Shannon held up his hand, counting off the rings with his fingers. On the third ring, Vincent answered as Shannon simultaneously pressed the speaker button.

"Vincent Palmer?" the voice on the other end of the line asked.

"Yes." Vincent's eyes met Grant's.

"This is Sheriff George Howell in Giles County. By any chance, is there an Agent Grant Bailey at your house?"

"Right here," Grant said before Vincent could answer. He grabbed the receiver. Without any instruction, Shannon cut off the speakerphone.

"This is Agent Bailey. What have you got?"

"We got a call short time ago from a farmer on Rolin Hollow Road. You know where that is?"

"Tell me."

"Right near the Alabama line. Not too far from the interstate, but it's rural."

"Go on."

"Seems he was leaving his barn and saw some suspicious activity in his field. The way he described it, a man was walking around an old beat-up truck, dousing it with gasoline. He started yelling, running across the field."

Grant could feel Vincent crowding him as he strained to eavesdrop. "He scare him off?"

"No, but his dogs did."

"He set the truck on fire?"

"No. Farmer got there before he did."

"You got the man in custody?"

"Negative. By the time the farmer got back to his house and called us, the man had took off. We're searching for him now."

"Why'd you call me?" Grant said.

"That kidnapping case, Jessica Palmer. You're the agent in charge of that?"

"That's right."

"Well, when we got to the scene and took a look at the truck, we found some things that made it look like somebody'd been bound up."

"Like what?"

"Duct tape. Rope. Ether… blood."

"Give me the address."

After Grant wrote down the address, he said, "I'm on my way."

"I'm going with you," Vincent stated in a no-nonsense tone of voice.

"Jessie's not there," Grant said. "You need to be here to wait for the kidnapper's call."

"I said—"

"Look," Grant said, placing one hand on Vincent's shoulder, "the kidnapper is not in custody. He's either got Jessie or he knows where she is. If he tries to reach you and can't…"

Vincent nodded.

Grant started toward the door.

"Take Abby."

"What?" He stopped and looked back at him.

"Abby. She'll know if Jessie was in that truck."

Grant hesitated. "She got a leash?"

"Yes, but she won't need one. Just talk to her like you would if she was a person. She'll understand."

Grant nodded though he wasn't entirely convinced. "Come on, Abby." The dog followed him eagerly out the door and to his bureau car. He opened the back door. She hopped in and he shut the door behind her. But as he opened his driver's side door, he found her already sitting in the front passenger seat. He climbed in and connected his cell phone to the car charger. Then he used the radio to contact Shannon.

"You just left," Shannon said in lieu of a greeting.

"Let me know if Vincent leaves."

"Will do."

Grant started up the car. Vincent hadn't put up an argument when he'd directed him to stay home to wait for the kidnapper's call. But it hadn't escaped him that the only way the kidnapper had contacted Vincent was through his cell phone. Grant put the car in gear. Nope, he thought, it hadn't escaped him at all.

21

The minutes ticked by as Jessie began to shiver uncontrollably in the cold, dank confines of the cellar. The winter sun rose slowly, its subdued rays stretching like cautious fingers into the open doorway, casting freckled lights across the cobwebbed walls, as if its rays had to thread their way through branches of emaciated trees before reaching her.

And as the gentle light touched her feet and climbed ever more slowly up her torso, she felt a strength beginning to rise within her.

She listened intently but heard nothing more than the distant sound of birds too hardy or foolish to have migrated south for the winter. There were no sounds of engines, tires crunching across graveled roads, or footsteps approaching.

As the minutes crept by and the sound of her own breathing began to fill the stale air, she managed to raise her hands to her face. Her fingers stroked the fabric that bound her face, her fingertips, numb from the cold, finding the duct tape and searching for the end. She struggled to grasp the tape but her fingers were like sausages in a freezer and she had to stop several times and rub them between her thighs or try to blow on them through the coarse fabric to warm them. Then the sun found her neck, her face, and the top of her head and she breathed in its soothing rays, trying to convince herself that the light was enough to thaw her fingers.

At last, she found the tape's end at the back of her head and she began to pick and pull at it in an arduously slow process. Her arms were bound and her wrists stuck together, making every movement excruciating. She stopped more than once to let her muscles rest while she listened carefully for any sounds that her captor was returning.

Oddly, it was the memory of her father's voice that kept her going, that gave her the strength to work at the tape relentlessly, to convince herself that she would escape—and she would face her kidnappers in a courtroom and watch them led off to their own captivity.

Kidnappers. There were three of them, though she'd seen only two. One was dead. One was out there somewhere, perhaps escaping. And the third…

Her fingers grasped hold of the tape and yanked it around her head until she felt it pulling away from her face. Minute by agonizing minute passed until at last the tape was balled up and tossed at her feet.

She ripped the fabric away from her eyes, her nose and her mouth. She touched her cheeks and rubbed her jaw, where it felt bruised and battered.

Then she quickly peered around her. Her body was still bound, and if she was ever going to get away from here, she had to work quickly.

The duct tape was wrapped tightly around her wrists, almost threatening to cut off blood circulation. She had to find something to cut the tape, to free her hands enough to liberate the rest of her body.

Painstakingly, she rolled onto her side and then onto her knees. She had to crawl on the fronts of her shins and her forearms. The cellar floor had probably been poured cement at one time, but now it was coated with so much dirt that she wondered if it had been abandoned for decades. She glanced at the open door several times as she struggled to free herself before Brainiac returned; she could see the hinges but the door had been removed. She envisioned Brainiac and perhaps Brutus visiting this site days or weeks ago, as they'd planned her capture. They'd no doubt removed the door, though she couldn't imagine why; if they'd left it intact and even secured it from the outside, it would have become her tomb. She shuddered at the vision of someone finding her skeleton years after she'd died and decayed. The mere thought spurred her on.

She reached one wall, her fingers finding bookcases that sent up plumes of powdery dust when she touched the books still held on the shelves. The second wall had only a wheelbarrow, propped against the wall as though it awaited the return of a gardener at any moment.

As the sun began to bathe the room in its light, she realized the two remaining walls were bare.

She fought a despair that threatened to overwhelm her, as she realized she had no chance of climbing up those steps wrapped up as she was. She thought of screaming, crying out for help—but she was more frightened of alerting Brainiac to the fact that her face was now free than she was hopeful that she would be rescued.

No, she thought, squeezing her eyes to fight back the tears that threatened to unnerve her, she had to rescue herself. She had to find the strength. Somewhere, somehow, she had to believe with all her heart that she would get out of here and get to safety.

But the minutes were ticking past and with each one, she worried more than ever that Brainiac would return and seal her inside forever. Perhaps he'd gone to find a tool with which to reposition the door in its frame. Or perhaps he went for a weapon, a knife to slit her throat, or—

She had to get out.

She turned her attention to the bookcase. Slowly, she made her way back to it. Once there, she tried to use her elbows to push her body up. Then she painstakingly transferred her weight from her elbows to her wrists. She could hear her labored breathing as she fought against the pain of using her bound wrists to provide the leverage she needed to push up her body. Finally, she reached a squatting position. She remained there for a minute as her muscles shook with her exertion. Then she gradually straightened her spine until her knees raised off the floor and she came unsteadily to her feet.

She was now face to face with the bookcase. The shelves were metal, and she began to run her fingers along them, hoping and praying she would find a jagged edge. The first shelf was smooth. The second was flawless.

She felt more precious time slipping away from her as she fought the fear and panic that threatened to overcome her. Then her fingers found a metal support bracket. It was sharp, its edge almost a full inch beyond the shelf. It was the closest thing to a knife she would be likely to find.

As she began to move the duct tape that bound her wrists over the bracket, moving slowly at first and then quickening her efforts, she realized it was covered in rust. As she moved, the pieces fell off in chunks, revealing a sharper edge than before.

When she'd sawed through the first layer of duct tape, she felt a sense of satisfaction stronger than anything she'd ever known. It bolstered her and her wrists moved faster and faster, until the second layer was torn apart and then a third.

Finally, she could stretch her wrists apart and feel the tape fall from one side. She stretched her fingers unnaturally to grasp the ends and clumsily flung the tape away from her, tearing off the fine hairs from her skin as she did so.

Then she was ripping off the duct tape from the rest of her body, rending through it like a madman. She could feel her freedom now; she could taste it.

She was already moving toward the doorway as she peeled the rest of the tape from around her ankles. Though her body was exhausted, her mind was sharp. Now was her chance to escape. And it might be her only chance.

Before she reached the doorway, she could feel the chill from a winter breeze. When she moved up the steps to the entrance, she was surprised to see snow blanketing the ground. Two sets of footprints had made their way to the entrance; one was walking and the other dragging. She flashed back to Brainiac forcing her to the cellar, but then she quickly pushed it from her mind.

She took a step forward and slipped. She caught herself on the door frame, her open palm finding the hinge. She cried out with the pain as it sliced through her hand, and she struggled to keep herself from crashing down the steps and back into the cellar.

Her other hand found the door jamb and steadied her. She wiped her bleeding palm against her pants and looked toward the ground.

It was a glove. She'd tripped on a leather glove. She almost laughed at the lunacy after all she'd been through. And how a simple leather glove could have caused her to fall backward onto the concrete, crushing her skull and leaving her helpless in her prison.

She realized the glove could be wrapped around her bleeding palm, serving as a bandage. She reached down and grabbed it, dusting the snowflakes from its cold leather. Her blood froze and she felt immobilized as though an invisible vise had her in its grasp.

Against the black leather was an embroidered "P" in an elaborate scroll. She held it in her hand, oblivious now of the pain in her other hand. This was her father's glove.

She had ordered it herself for his last birthday.

It had been custom made; she'd selected the font from a long list and even the placement of the letter on the back of the glove, nearest the wrist. There could not be another like it. She was positive of that.

She was wasting time.

She grasped the glove in her offended hand, barely noticing her blood seeping across the embroidered letter as she stepped onto the snow outside the cellar.

She made her way a few feet from the entrance, feeling stronger that her escape would be successful as she put ground between herself and the cellar. In the distance, she saw a church steeple and she slipped and slid along the ground as she made her way toward it. The sun and the rising temperature were melting the snow so she felt as though she was sliding on gelatin. But even the rising temperature was not enough to take the chill from her bones. By the time she'd reached the church, the snow had soaked through her shoes and left her toes freezing and trembling.

The church was vacant. As she made her way around it, her heart sank. The plants that lined its brick walls were old, dying and crumbling. This church had been unoccupied for years.

The road leading to the church was visible only because of the set of tire tracks: one leading inward and another leading out. Afraid Brainiac would use the same entrance when he returned, she slipped and slid to the edge of some woods and made her way parallel to the driveway in search of a road.

The going was steep and arduous. She felt her strength sapped from her; the hours she'd remained awake through the long night, the stress of her abduction, the painful way in which she'd been trussed up. Every muscle in her body ached and yet she knew she had to press on. She glanced behind her once and gasped at the line of visible prints in the snow. When Brainiac returned, it would be simple for him to track her down. The sight spurred her onward even faster as her body began to shake violently with the winter chill.

At last, she had reached the top of a hill. She grabbed hold of a tree and steadied herself against the trunk as her knees began to shake, threatening to give way beneath her.

She was near a road; a paved road. It might not have been plowed, she reasoned, but it had been driven, the tracks of multiple vehicles flattening the snow and causing it to melt ever faster.

And just over the hill in the valley below, she could see smoke curling from a chimney. It was a farmhouse.

As her eyes searched the terrain for signs of Brainiac, they came to rest on a set of vehicles in a field on the other side of the farmhouse. She shielded her eyes against the sun. One was a white car; she was sure of it.

Her heart quickened as she strained to see it more clearly. She was afraid to hope it was a sheriff's car, but the longer she stared at it, the more convinced she became.

Her eyes moved backward now, along the path between the cars and the farmhouse and the hill and valley that lay between her and safety. Her knees were shaking violently and with her first steps away from the tree, they threatened to give way beneath her. But she kept her eyes focused on the cars. Mindlessly now, almost robotically, she moved forward. She had to reach them. She had to.

22

As soon as Grant opened the door, Abby leapt across him and into the field. He swore under his breath. Whatever had compelled him to bring a dog to a crime scene? He wondered as he got out of the car. His mind flashed forward to the paperwork he'd have to file to explain his decision.

"You Sheriff Howell?" he asked as he approached a man in uniform.

He nodded. "You must be Agent Bailey." He was a tall man, almost as tall as Grant's six-foot-two. His hair was grayish-white with wavy curls that were slightly longer than he'd have expected on a law enforcement officer. But he was distinguished looking, possibly in his early sixties. As Grant shook his hand, he noticed twin dimples the size of marbles on his sunken cheeks.

"Call me Grant." He stood a few feet from the truck. "Chevy Tahoe," he said.

Sheriff Howell nodded. "1992."

It was a two-toned truck, Grant noted as he walked around it. The bottom half was probably silver at one time but now it was a dull gray, as though it had been exposed to years of acid rain. The top half was turquoise, but one of the truck panels had been replaced with a part from a red vehicle. It was scratched almost from one end to the other, as though it had been used primarily off-road.

"Four wheel drive?" he asked.

"You got it."

He stopped along the driver's side. The door was bent, almost as if the truck had once been wrapped around a tree, but it wasn't recent. There was too much rust. His eyes wandered down the side of the truck. The undercarriage was pockmarked.

"Listen, I've got—"

Abby began barking ferociously, drowning out the sheriff's voice.

Grant followed the sound of the dog until he was at the rear of the truck. She was furiously trying to get inside the truck bed, but it was covered with an after-market hinged tonneau cover.

"Have you—?"

Sheriff Howell stepped to the back of the truck and gingerly raised the cover. "First thing we checked. When we saw the paraphernalia in the truck, we thought…" His voice drifted off as he opened it. "But it's empty."

Grant stared inside at two low-lying aluminum dog boxes. Together, they covered the entire truck bed. Though the end facing the rear of the truck had plenty of air holes, he was hard-pressed to figure out how a dog could breathe in there with the tonneau cover down.

"Listen, Agent—Grant, there's something—"

Abby began barking once again, her voice gaining in excitement. "She must smell other dogs," Grant said, shaking his head. "I should have known better than to bring her here."

He noted two crime scene technicians dusting the vehicle. Usually, local law enforcement would have secured the scene but waited for the FBI technicians to process it. But he knew why Sheriff Howell didn't wait. It was Vincent Palmer's daughter, one of the most influential families in the state. What a feather that would be in his cap, he thought as he walked back to the driver's side door. Extended cab, he thought, peaking into the back seat.

When he opened the door, it groaned as metal met metal. He stood outside and pushed the door back and forth for a moment. The groan was caused by the old dent; every time the door was opened, more rust appeared to fall off.

"No prints," the crime scene technician said, stepping out from the passenger side.

"What do you mean?"

"It's been wiped clean." The technician was young and fit. He wore a close crew cut and Grant could see his scalp. It was bronzed, as though it was mid-summer. "Already dusted the dash, the vinyl seats, the doors… Haven't come up with anything. Not even a partial print."

Professionals, Grant thought, down to the very last detail. Well, not quite, he added as he sniffed the gasoline in the air.

"Done the door handles yet?"

"First thing," the technician answered. "You can open it."

Grant held the door in his hands and decided not to mention that he'd already opened it, though a glance at the sheriff's face made him feel foolish. Sheriff Howell appeared to be ready to say something, but Grant hopped into the front seat.

It was smoky smelling, he thought. Not like gasoline and a lit match. Something else. He closed his eyes and inhaled. Stale cigarette smoke. Lots of it. And something else. Cigar? Maybe. Something flavored.

"No prints, huh?" he said.

The technician remained outside the passenger door. "Not a one. I'm getting ready to process the truck bed, but if there's nothing in here—"

"There's likely not going to be anything back there," Grant finished.

"No, sir."

Grant nodded as the technician went around to the back of the truck. He could see Abby in his rear-view mirror, her head bobbing above the tonneau cover as she jumped onto the tail gate. She was still barking, and it was beginning to annoy him. He couldn't think with that incessant noise.

The dash had once been coated with dust and dirt. He was sure of it. Now he could clearly see tracks caused by material that had wiped over every inch. It hadn't completely cleared away the dirt, just smeared it around. The individual had even crammed it into the dashboard, wiping the speedometer and gauges. Only in the tiniest pockets could he see the dirt built up. It was the kind of dirt that didn't happen overnight and not on a truck with the windows rolled up, he thought. This was a hunter's truck. No doubt about it. He could picture the windows rolled down, some bubba dressed in camouflage rolling past trees without regard to branches swiping at the paint, a cigarette dangling from the corner of his mouth while he talked.

As he sat there, the sun made its way through the open field, finding the truck and shining its winter brilliance onto the dull hood. Grant stared at it for a moment before the sun began to blind him.

Sheriff Howell cleared his throat. "I don't know quite how to tell you this, but—"

Grant glanced at the visor above his head. "Get your technician," he said abruptly.

"Chip!" Sheriff Howell called out.

Grant continued to stare at the visor.

"Yes, sir?" The young man now filled the door.

"You dust this visor?"

His eyes widened. "No, sir."

Grant clambered out of the truck. "Do it."

Grant stepped away from the truck while the technician took his place. A moment later, he shouted, "Bingo!"

Grant nodded, a smile spreading across his tired face.

"I'm sorry I keep interrupting you, but—" Sheriff Howell's voice was drowned out by Abby's barking.

Grant swore under his breath before taking wide steps toward the back of the truck. It was a mistake to bring this dog to a crime scene, he thought, more irritated with himself than with the dog. But he'd take care of this. That dog was going back into the bureau car.

When he reached the back of the truck, he found Abby clawing at the door to one of the dog boxes. He grabbed her by the collar but he couldn't bring himself to yank her away with the ill temper he felt. Instead, he lifted her off the tail gate and deposited all four feet on the ground. But before he could disengage his hand from her collar, she'd leapt back onto the tail gate and was pawing at the dog box again.

"What the—?"

Grant leaned toward the box and pushed Abby away. He stared inside for a moment. When he pulled himself away, he was surprised to find Sheriff Howell watching him. "I want this dog box processed. Look for hairs, skin… I want DNA."

"You think you found something?"

"No." Grant glanced at Abby, her golden fur quivering in her excitement. "But she has."

Sheriff Howell called to Chip. "Get this dog box processed. Every inch." He turned back to Grant. "I need to tell you—"

"This truck's got a license plate on it," Grant exclaimed.

"That's what I've been trying to tell you."

"Have you run the plates?"

"First thing."

Grant stared at him. His face was weathered and the dimples appeared to stand out more than ever. "Well?"

"The truck's registered to Vincent Palmer."

23

The steps leading up to the farmhouse door seemed uneven, the wood worn and rotting, with one end sinking into the soft dirt. Jessie tried to steady herself with the handrail. The steps blurred in front of her as though she was surfing on a robust sea; they dipped to the left and then to the right in a constant wave that made her nauseous.

She had come so far. Down the hill, navigating through overgrown brambles that were thick with snow and ice in the heavily shaded woods. But when she reached the sunlight, her travels were no better; the sun had melted the snow until it became a slippery slope that threatened to prevent her from reaching her destination.

She had lost sight of the vehicles long ago and had walked blindly forward, hoping she was continuing to move in the right direction. What she saw from the top of the hill had appeared so near. Now, as she used every ounce of strength that was left inside her, it seemed with every step she took, an unseen force moved the farmhouse that much further away.

She wondered more than once whether she'd been asleep on her feet. She couldn't remember crossing the road but she found herself at the base of a hill. She didn't remember starting down a winding road barely wide enough for two vehicles to pass one another, and yet there she was, moving forward one step at a time, right in the middle of it.

And when she reached the mailbox with its slipcover of poinsettias painted on the side, she walked almost like a zombie past it, her mind numb and her feet moving forward like a wind-up doll winding down.

And as she'd walked up the driveway, she knew the rock beneath her feet was trying to chip through the soles of her shoes, but she could no longer feel it. She tried to focus her eyes on the front door of the farmhouse that looked to be so far removed from the mailbox. But her head wanted to loll forward like a bowling ball that her neck could no longer support and she found her eyes staring instead at the ground moving slowly past under her feet.

But somehow, the minutes ticked past and she found herself holding onto the handrail, hoisting herself up one step at a time, her palm bleeding even while it held the glove firmly in its grasp, her arms and legs aching with a tiredness she'd never known before.

And when she finally reached the top step, she stood shakily on the old porch, not knowing if she had the strength left to take the two steps that remained to reach the doorbell. She waited there, her breath hurting her lungs and her chest, her nose frozen from the cold air, her toes and her fingers numb.

When she tried to take another step, her foot shuffled forward instead like a woman ready to collapse into her grave.

Somehow, she managed to reach the door. The sound of the television reached her ears, along with the sound of a woman humming amid the clank of pots and pans.

She raised her finger to the doorbell but collapsed in a heap onto the porch.

She tried to open her eyes. The doorbell swam above her. She tried to call for help, but her throat was parched and only a whisper escaped her. As blackness threatened to overtake her, she wondered if she'd ever rung the doorbell.

* * * * *

Jessie sat next to an aging wood stove. She was wrapped in an old quilt that felt comforting to her somehow, as if she'd traveled to her grandmother's house. Her head barely peeked out from the top, and her hands were covered up to the wrists. Only her fingers protruded outside the quilt, just far enough to grasp a large mug of hot coffee.

The bleeding on her palm had stopped, or at least had been wrapped tight enough to prevent the blood from oozing out onto the patch-worked material. Her nose was beginning to thaw as she held it over the steaming hot liquid. But as the feeling returned to her extremities, it brought with it searing pain.

Her hands shook and the old woman reached over to steady her. "Let me take that," she said with the confidence of one who had raised many a child.

"My mother?" Jessie managed to say. She looked up but the woman's face was hidden in shadows as the sun poured into the window behind her. The sun. It had led her here, she thought, like a beacon.

The old woman held the mug in her hands now, and Jessie found herself staring at it. It was deep royal blue with strong white letters that spelled out *First Palmer Bank*. Jessie would have chuckled if she'd had the strength. The irony of her rescuers having one of the bank's give-away mugs, she thought.

There were others in the room, she realized suddenly. She tried to turn her head but the quilt was confining. "Mother?" she repeated.

"She's been called," a male voice answered. Then a face came into view: a worn face surrounded by short, salt and pepper hair. Twin lines between his brows were deep and the flesh along his lower eyes were rimmed in red, as though it had been a long time since he'd had a restful night's sleep. "Special Agent Grant Bailey," he said. "FBI."

FBI, she thought. She wanted to believe at the mere mention of his introduction that she was safe. But even as she tried to manage a slight smile, she couldn't push the thought of Brainiac barging in through the door behind him and sinking an axe into his head.

"You were kidnapped last night," he was saying softly.

"Last night," she repeated robotically. Had only one night slipped past?

"Your father paid the ransom—"

"My father—"

"—and we've been looking for you. You'll be okay now. We won't let you out of our sight."

She thought she detected a tear forming in the innermost corner of his eye, but he looked down and wiped his cheek briskly.

"We've called for an ambulance," he continued.

"I don't need an ambulance," she managed to say. "I want to go home."

"You will. You will," he attempted to reassure her. "But you've been—battered a bit—and we just want to get you checked out. Don't worry," he hastily added, "your mother will be there with you."

She nodded and leaned back. Her eyes closed but she thought she would never be able to sleep again. Each time she closed her eyes, she saw Brainiac, the cap covering his facial features, the axe in his hands.

"I know you're exhausted," Grant was saying, "but I need to know where you've been and how you got here, to this house."

"I don't know where I was," she said. The old woman handed her the cup again and she swallowed another unsteady swig of coffee. "I felt like I was in the middle of nowhere."

"Did they tie you up in the woods?" he asked, looking pointedly at her wrists. She followed his gaze and stared at the marks the tight duct tape had made.

"In a cabin. Like a hunting lodge or something. It was one room, plus a bathroom."

"How far did you have to walk until you got here?"

She looked him straight in the eyes. They were sad eyes, she thought, cheerless but kind. They were hazel, and the outer corners sank downward beneath sagging lids. "They moved me sometime during the night to a basement, or an underground storm cellar. I managed to escape after the kidnapper left."

"So there was only one?"

"Two... One of them," she swallowed hard, "killed the other."

The air changed in the small farmhouse as the screen door opened and slammed shut. Jessie heard a flurry of footsteps rushing through the house, and she steeled herself, her hands wrapping so tightly against the mug that she knew she had to relax her grip or she'd risk breaking it.

But it wasn't Brainiac rushing through with the axe in his hands. Her mother's face filled the doorway, her eyes appearing like two full moons drawn against her pale skin. "Jessie!" she exclaimed, dashing toward her.

"I asked you to meet us at the hospital," Grant said, rising to his feet.

"Ambulance is here," Sheriff Howell announced before Meg could respond.

"What are you doing, interrogating my daughter?" Vincent demanded.

Grant whipped around to face him, and as she fell into her mother's arms, Jessie's eyes turned toward the two men.

"Interrogating?" Grant said.

"You can't question my daughter without her attorney present!" Vincent shouted, his face red and swollen.

"Your daughter," Grant responded, his voice low but commanding, "is not a suspect. She's a victim. You want us to catch the kidnappers, don't you? *Don't you?*"

Jessie gently but firmly pushed her mother away from her. Out of the corner of her eye, she could feel her mother's gaze on her, her eyes still wide and incredulous. She felt as though she was in the middle of a bad dream, as if she was watching herself from outside herself, as she stepped forward.

The quilt fell away from her and her mother and the old woman scurried to grab it before she tripped on it. But Jessie's eyes never wavered from Vincent's face.

He turned toward her. His face was red with anger but when his eyes met hers, the color appeared to fade. His narrowed eyes became wider and he looked almost stupefied.

It might have been only a few minutes ago that she wondered if she could reach the porch, or ring the bell, or hold her own coffee cup. But now she moved with complete assurance.

She stepped around Meg and strode across the small kitchen. Then with every ounce of strength she had left in her body, she pulled her arm back and slapped Vincent's face with such force that it knocked him backward against the wall.

24

Grant stood at the entrance to the cellar and peered into the tiny room that had served as Jessie's prison cell. It hadn't been difficult to find; from the field by the truck, they could see the hill upon which Jessie had stood watching them from afar, and from her description of the walk from the church, the farmer had known immediately where she'd been taken.

The place had been vacant for years. A church stood at one end of the property and adjacent to it was another building that had served as a private school in years past. The cellar might have been built to store food, but instead they had moved unused books into it. The door had been removed and was found propped against the side of the building.

The room was flooded in light from the forensic team's lamps. They had explicit instructions to search every inch and process every clue. The door had already been dusted for fingerprints, and Grant hoped to find the matching glove to the one Jessie had given him. He could still see her firm, square jaw as she told him where she'd found it. Her eyes had been steely and emotionless, though he'd detected a slight quiver in her lip.

She'd been transported to the hospital by ambulance. Sheriff Howell had accompanied her and would remain with her until they had someone assigned to guard her.

He glanced over his shoulder at Ivory, who had roped off the entire driveway with crime scene tape from the road all the way to the church. Following his instructions, she'd included about twenty-five feet on either side of the drive as well, which necessitated her walking through the church cemetery.

He smiled now as he watched her. She was terrified of graveyards, though he'd tried to convince her that the residents were the best neighbors in the world. Always nice and quiet, never complained... But she hadn't bought it. Especially this one.

The grounds were overgrown to the point that gravestones were teetering in one direction or the other. The earth had shifted in places so some gravesites appeared to have collapsed in on themselves while others had shifted upwards, almost as if the inhabitant had tried to escape. Landscaping, that at one time might have been beautiful, was now out of control. In some areas, the bushes were so overgrown they had taken over the plots, while in other places, they were reduced to dying brambles that appeared to him like skeletal fingers stretching across the ground.

Now, as Ivory searched the area inside the crime scene tape, she appeared to tip-toe on the graves, her shoulders hunched forward as if she could make herself smaller and less detectable. When she stepped on a twig, she jumped as though someone was rising from the grave. Even in broad daylight with the area swarming with law enforcement, she appeared apt to run back to the car and roll up the windows.

Turning back to the cellar, he watched as one of the crime scene technicians processed the duct tape on the floor, photographing it from every angle. He hoped they'd be able to get prints off it, prints from the man who had bound up Jessie and left her here.

He wondered why they had chosen to remove the door. They could have closed it, sealing her inside like a tomb. No, he thought, shaking his head. They wanted her to live.

But why remove the door? Why not just leave it open, or cracked a bit, or even closed but possible for her to open? And if they intended for her to live, why keep her trussed up like a Thanksgiving turkey?

Unless they planned to call Vincent with directions on where to find her.

He almost snickered. No. Vincent knew where she would be, he was sure of it. He didn't want her harmed or killed. He just wanted the insurance money.

He called Shannon and instructed him to remove the monitoring equipment from the house. It would no longer be needed. He could get the records from Vincent's cell phone. He had no doubt he would find calls from the kidnappers days or even weeks before the attack, and probably after Jessie had been left here as well.

"Tape's got some hairs on it," the crime scene technician announced.

Grant made his way down the steps and knelt beside the technician.

"Right there. Three gray hairs."

"Jessie's hair isn't gray."

The technician raised an eyebrow.

"Good job." Grant stood up. "You're going to process the mask and all the duct tape, aren't you?"

"Prints and DNA. Standard procedure."

Grant knew he wouldn't have to instruct him to look for every piece of evidence possible, no matter how minute. The technicians would do it automatically. This was a high profile case that was already making its way into the headlines. They would all have to make sure not to leave one stone unturned.

He walked to the bureau car as Ivory was returning from the driveway.

"Any luck?"

"Footprints," she said. "I've already alerted the techs. I think they're Jessie's—they go from the driveway into the woods, following the path she told us about. I suspect they'll lead to the top of the hill and down the other side toward the farmhouse."

"Anything else?"

"Tire tracks. One vehicle. I bet they'll match the tread on that truck."

"Vincent's truck." Grant opened the back door to the bureau car. "He's not the professional he thinks he is."

"What do you mean?"

"He thought he was being smart—the five million insurance policy, getting the money so quickly we couldn't mark it, trying to lose me to deliver the money. But we're good," he said, grabbing an evidence bag from the floorboard. "We're good."

"What's that?"

He held it up for Ivory to peer through the clear plastic bag at the Waterford whiskey glass inside.

"You didn't."

"I did." He tilted it so the letter "P" was clearly visible. He closed the door and started toward the cellar.

"What're you doing with that?" Ivory called out as she followed him.

"Taking it to the technicians," he answered smoothly. "I want to know if any fingerprints or DNA match Vincent's."

"But we could have required—"

"With his lawyer?" Grant stopped and looked at her. "He's going to stonewall us at every step. You saw Vincent demanding his daughter—the *victim*, for Christ's sake—have a lawyer present before she could even talk to us. He knows he's guilty. But we're gonna get him. There's nothing more despicable than a man willing to torment his own child—for any reason." He turned back toward the cellar. "We'll get him. We just have to be smarter than he is."

25

J essie stared at the huge bouquet of flowers. Her hospital bed was partially raised so she only had to look past her feet to the opposite wall, where the peppermint striped Asiatic lilies, hot pink roses, and white cremons stood tall and majestic in a white vase with an enormous red bow. The colors served as a reminder that Christmas was right around the corner, which felt somehow surreal to her now. In her hand, she still held the note card: it bore the logo of her father's bank but was signed personally by Edward Buchanan, the bank president, along with a notation to "get well soon." She'd heard rumors her whole life that he was somewhat of an ambulance chaser, but she was intrigued at how quickly he'd known she'd been found. The flowers had been waiting in her room before she'd even arrived at the hospital.

She'd been whisked past photographers and a swarm of reporters calling out questions as she'd been taken from the ambulance into the hospital. But once inside, the atmosphere was one of calm and order. She'd been spirited past the emergency room, where throngs of people with varying ailments waited to be seen, had efficiently bypassed registration and was taken directly upstairs to her room. Within five minutes, Dr. William Fua, the Palmer's personal physician, was there.

He'd greeted Jessie with only a hint of an Asian accent that still lingered even after more than twenty years in the Nashville area. While Meg produced an insurance card and answered questions of the registration representative who had come to the room to process Jessie's intake, Jessie succumbed to a thorough examination and responded to questions concerning the bruises on her head and body.

She struggled to remain awake as Dr. Fua questioned her. "Twice," she remembered saying in response to one of his questions, "I was hit on the jaw. I think I was hit between my eyes." Her lids were heavy and she wished they would leave her alone.

"You were only hit twice?" Dr. Fua said. His voice was gentle but firm with the confidence of a man who'd graduated at the top of his class and had remained at the top echelons of the medical field. "I think you were hit more. Perhaps you were in a scuffle—or two?"

"Maybe," she said, closing her eyes and trying to nestle down beneath the sheet even as a nurse assisted her mother with removing her clothing, replacing it with a crisp green hospital gown.

"I can't believe they hit you," her mother said. Jessie opened her eyes long enough to see Meg's ashen face above her, her eyes filled with tears. As she pulled a blanket up to her daughter's neck, Meg's hands shook.

"They will pay for this," Vincent said, his voice strong and stormy. "I swear to everyone in this room: they will pay for this."

Dr. Fua glanced at Vincent, looked back toward Jessie, and then turned abruptly to face Vincent again. "What happened to you?"

"What do you mean?" Vincent demanded.

"Jessie slapped him," Meg said. "At the farmhouse, when she first saw us."

Dr. Fua shook his head. "You hadn't said anything to her?"

"No; of course not. I rushed to her side and—" Vincent stopped and rubbed his cheek.

"She's in shock," the doctor said. "She probably thought you were one of the kidnappers." He turned to the nurse. "We're going to schedule her for a full battery of tests."

"Can't you see she's exhausted?" Vincent said incredulously.

"Mr. Palmer," Dr. Fua said calmly, "she may have a concussion. Or worse. I know she's tired. Anybody would be, after the ordeal she's been through. But you want me to find out what her injuries are, don't you? She could have bleeding on the brain—"

"Oh, my God!" Meg exclaimed. "They hit you! They hit you!" She kept repeating the words, as if she couldn't quite believe it.

"I'm not saying she is bleeding internally," Dr. Fua continued evenly. "But we want to make sure she doesn't have any internal injuries." He turned again to the nurse. "Schedule an MRI immediately. Let's look at her jaw, her brain, her entire head in fact—and her neck."

"Could she have permanent damage?" Vincent said, his voice now hushed.

"Oh, my God," Meg exclaimed again. "I can't believe they hit you!"

"Nurse, help Mrs. Palmer to a seat."

With Jessie's clothing now changed, she closed her eyes once more and scrunched the blanket around her neck, only to have it removed immediately by Dr. Fua. She attempted to voice a feeble objection but he interrupted her.

"You have low grade frostbite," he said. His voice became louder. "Nurse, we're going to treat her for hypothermia and frostbite here—" he touched her toes "—on both feet."

"My hand—"

"That's just the tube for the IV," Dr. Fua said. "We're giving you something now to help you sleep."

A knock interrupted them. Dr. Fua hesitated momentarily while he scanned her body for other injuries. Then he pulled the sheet and blanket over Jessie as a uniformed officer entered the room.

"I've been assigned to guard Miss Palmer," the officer announced.

"Who ordered that?" Vincent demanded.

"FBI. Agent Bailey."

"You're not with—"

"No, sir. I'm a police officer. Name's Skipper. Officer Skipper."

"Well, Officer Skipper," Vincent said, "only four people can enter this room. Her mother—" he gestured toward Meg "—myself, Dr. Fua, and this nurse here, Rebecca. You understand?"

"Yes, sir."

Vincent made eye contact with Dr. Fua. "I want a nurse in this room 24/7."

"Done," Dr. Fua answered. He turned back to Jessie. "Get some rest, young lady. Rebecca will escort you for some tests once we get everything set up."

With that, he was gone.

Jessie tiredly looked around the room. There was the police officer, moving to the doorway. Her mother sat in a chair by the window, staring outside. Her hands continued to wring as if she was conducting an internal monologue that was seeping outward through her hands. Rebecca, whom Jessie had known since pre-school, pulled another chair beside the bed and dutifully straightened the blanket before sitting down within arm's reach. And Vincent—Jessie struggled to look away from him lest she spit in his direction—Vincent was standing in the center of the room as if he didn't have a clue what to do next.

"I'll turn on some TV for you," Rebecca whispered. "Oh, no," she said suddenly.

Jessie looked first at Rebecca and then followed her gaze to the television screen mounted on the wall. Her picture was flashed across the screen with the caption: "Jessica Palmer: KIDNAPPED AND SAFELY FOUND."

"He knows," she said. Her voice came hoarsely, as if she was fighting some unseen force of wind.

"Who knows?" Rebecca said. She shook her head at Vincent's silent questioning and Jessie saw her mouth the single word "concussion."

"The man who kidnapped me," Jessie forced herself to say. "He knows I escaped."

"It's okay, honey," Rebecca said. "You're safe here. There's a police officer right outside your door." She turned the channel.

As sounds from an old episode of *I Love Lucy* drifted through the room, Jessie struggled to keep her eyes open. I can't sleep now, she thought frantically. If he comes for me, I can't be asleep. I have to be ready.

Then she thought of her father standing in the middle of the room. Her hand began to squeeze shut just as it had when she'd walked down that hill to the farmhouse in the valley. And though the glove with his initial was gone, she could still feel it; she would always feel it. She murmured something to Rebecca; she had to warn her. If Vincent was in the room, he could order the police officer away. He could open the door to Brainiac— he could—

"What did you say, Jessie?" Rebecca leaned in close. "I can't understand you."

The IV, she thought dreamily. They've given me something to sleep. But I can't sleep. Not now. I'm not safe yet—

She reached for the tubing as if to pull it from the back of her hand, but she could no longer feel her extremities. She couldn't feel anything at all. And though she tried to keep her eyes focused on Vincent, he began to blur and weave until he became part of the wall and the room and the voices around her droned into the distance.

I'm not safe, she tried to tell them. I'll never be safe again.

26

She awakened with a start. "Rebecca?"

"Right here, Jessie."

Jessie leaned back against the hospital bed. It was still raised on an incline, as if she'd been watching television all this time. Groggily, she looked around the room but they were the only ones there.

"Where's Daddy?"

"He said something about a phone call. He'll be back."

"I don't want him back."

Rebecca's voice became softer and lower. "You don't mean that, Jessie."

Before she could answer, there was a soft knock at the door. Rebecca patted her hand a couple of times. "I'll find out who it is," she said before leaving Jessie's side to cross the room.

Jessie heard a few low mumblings before Rebecca turned around. "She's decent," she said before opening the door wider.

A man in a black trench coat stepped inside. "Jessie," he said as the door closed behind him, "Don't know if you remember me—"

"Of course I do," Jessie interrupted. "You're the FBI Agent."

He nodded. "Grant Bailey."

She smiled mischievously. "Daddy left instructions that only four people could enter this room. And you're not one of the four."

"Your father always get his way?"

"Always."

He pulled up a chair. "Then his luck just changed."

She felt the smile fade even as her heart began to beat faster. But before she could respond, he continued, "I have a few questions to ask you."

"Questions?"

"I'll try to make this brief." He pulled a small spiral pad from his jacket's inside pocket. "I need you to tell me exactly what happened. No matter how insignificant. How many people, where they took you—everything."

Jessie glanced sideways at Rebecca.

Grant followed her gaze. "Would you feel more comfortable if she wasn't here?"

"I'm sorry, Rebecca—"

"No need to be." Rebecca quickly crossed the room. "I'll be right outside."

Jessie waited until the door had closed behind her before she began to speak. She told of the man in the lobby and her struggle to break free, interrupting herself to inquire about Abby.

"She's fine," Grant said, a slow smile crossing his face. "She misses you. But your father had her within an hour of your neighbor calling the police. She's at his house now."

Jessie leaned back and gave a sigh of relief.

"So they drugged you," Grant said, taking some notes. He glanced up at Jessie. "When you woke up, where were you?"

He had hazel eyes, she thought. They were kind eyes. Sad, but kind. For some reason, she glanced at his hands. He wore a gold wedding band. "In the truck." She described the ordeal as they drove further from Nashville, including the aging buildings and signs that seemed as though she'd been driven off the highway into the 1950's.

Grant slipped his hand back to an inside coat pocket. "This truck look familiar?" he asked, handing her a photograph.

She held it in her hands for a long time. She could feel him staring at her, almost as if he was analyzing her reaction. She thought she would know the truck anywhere; she thought she had memorized it, that it was etched on her brain forever. She closed her eyes, remembering the smell of the old upholstery, heard the distinct sound of the engine misfiring, could still see her face in the rear-view mirror as she sought to overtake Brainiac behind the wheel. But when she opened her eyes, she saw a truck from the outside; a banged-up, old truck.

"I don't know," she said at last.

He didn't move to take the photograph from her.

She continued staring at it.

"It might be," she said. "I was in a truck with an extended cab—like this one. It was old; the engine misfired like spark plugs needed cleaning. I would know the sound of it anywhere. And when we left the cabin, he put me in a dog kennel in the truck bed. But there was a top over the bed, not like a regular cap but—"

He produced another photograph. "Like this?"

Her hand was shaking as she took the picture from him. It was taken from the rear of the vehicle. The top was up, exposing two dog kennels in the back. She tried to speak but the words wouldn't come.

"Jessie?" his voice sounded soft, patient—and a hundred miles away.

She glanced up. "This is it. I know this is it."

He took the two pictures from her. "Have you ever seen the truck before you were abducted?"

"No. Why would I?"

He returned them to his coat pocket. "No reason. Tell me about the cabin."

She continued haltingly, stopping several times to dab at her eyes or take a sip of water before continuing. She wanted more than anything to forget everything, to wipe it from her mind forever—and yet she knew as she continued looking into Grant Bailey's eyes, he needed the information. And she also knew she could never forget it.

When she came to the part about Brainiac sinking the axe into Brutus' head, she felt nauseous. And when he asked for a description of Brutus, she was surprised to find that she no longer remembered his facial features; she could only describe the way the axe appeared sticking out of the back of his skull. And how red the blood was, and how quickly it flowed out of him.

She shook her head.

"So," Grant said softly, "the one you call 'Brainiac', he's the guy who survived."

"Yes. He's the one who took me to the cellar where I escaped."

"You remember what color hair he had?"

She sucked in her breath. "No. Though I think it was dark." She noticed a puzzled look on Grant's face. "He always wore a ball cap. It had an oval logo with a shark. Seemed like every time I looked at him, that's all I saw."

"So, his age?"

"Haven't a clue."

"Any habits?"

"He smoked."

"Cigarettes."

"Sometimes. Also, he smelled like a pipe. I can't place the kind of tobacco, but it was—I don't know, flavored somehow."

Grant made a few notes on his pad.

Jessie tried to laugh but it got stuck in her throat. "And he should have a bruised Adam's apple."

Grant smiled. "Any other injuries?"

"His forehead might be bruised. I don't know if he was hurt in any other way when we ran off the road."

"You're doing good, Jessie. Real good. Now, just try to think back. He wore a cap and his hair was dark. He smoked. You could smell the pipe…"

"And his shoes."

"What about them?"

"It was interesting. I don't usually smell shoes."

"But his, you did?" Now it was Grant's turn to laugh, though it sounded forced. "Are you telling me his feet stink?"

Jessie laughed a good, hearty laugh like she thought she'd never be able to do again. "No, it wasn't his feet. His shoes had a really strong odor of shoe polish. Made my eyes water, actually."

He scribbled on his note pad.

"And he had a strange kind of face, something of a scar on his chin."

Grant looked up quickly.

"Right here." Jessie pointed toward the center of her chin, but then moved her finger toward one side. "Like his chin was lop-sided. That make sense?" She stroked her chin almost as if she could feel it.

He shrugged. "It could. Now for the toughest question. I need a promise you won't repeat it. Okay?"

Jessie could feel her body growing tense. But after a moment, she nodded.

"Promise?"

"I promise."

"Does your dad ever—" he shrugged "—oh, I don't know, maybe—go hunting?"

She could feel her eyes widening. "Why, yes. Especially deer hunting."

His eyes locked onto hers. "So, where does he usually go?"

She knew he was trying to make the questions sound casual, but she began to hear her father's voice at the cabin and then again at the cellar. "Are you trying to tell me—?"

"I'm not trying to tell you anything. I'm asking; that's all."

"On the Alabama-Tennessee border."

He waited. When she didn't continue, he said, "What about the border?"

"He owns a lot of land. I think he sells the timber."

"He have a cabin on that land, Jessie?"

She stared at him, at those hazel eyes with the downturned outer edges, at the folds of skin that showed years of squinting into the sun, at the bags that spoke of sleepless nights. "He was there."

"Who was where?"

She thought the color had drained out of his face. She knew what she wanted to tell him, what she needed to tell him, but now that the time had come, the words were failing her.

Then she heard her father's voice yelling at Rebecca, demanding to know why she wasn't in Jessie's room.

"Don't let him in here," she hissed at Grant.

He stood up. His broad shoulders completely obscured the door behind him.

"Why not?" he said.

"Because he was there," she said, her voice coming fast and breathless. "He was there at the cabin—and at the cellar. And if you leave me alone with him, I'm afraid—I'm afraid he'll kill me."

27

Before he became an FBI Agent, Grant often wondered why suspects were not immediately apprehended. It just seemed like plain common sense if you knew who committed the crime to simply take him off the streets and lock him up. Now that he was on the other side of the desk, he felt the same amount of frustration even if he understood the reasoning behind it. He had to build his case. And with a high profile arrest, it had better be a good one.

He pulled out of the parking lot at Maury Regional Medical Center and onto the bypass that circled behind it. Needing some time to organize his thoughts, he'd decided on taking the long route to BD's Title and Escrow Company.

As he drove, he thought of the look of sheer terror on Jessie's face as Vincent had burst through the door. It had taken some fast thinking and good acting to immediately announce that she was scheduled for an MRI, which would take some time. Rebecca had looked at him quizzically but fallen right into the act, expertly wheeling Jessie's hospital bed through the corridors en route to Radiology.

He'd left Ivory with her as well. Between the two women and the police officer, she was safe. He'd barely made it out of the hospital before Ivory was texting him: *What's up?*

He'd texted back: *Do not leave her alone with Vincent. Stall.* Then he'd gone straight to his car, made some phone calls to the staff in the Bureau office, and arranged to meet Branson DuBois, the owner of BD's, at his main office. Only minutes later, he was pulling onto West 7th Street. He glanced to his left at the stately two story stone courthouse with its majestic steeple and impressive clock. By the time he'd passed the ancestral home of James K. Polk, he'd begun to slow down.

The title company was located in a beautiful two story Victorian home. As Grant pulled into the back parking lot and parked beside a white SUV, he glanced at the aged white structure. He figured it had been built over a hundred years ago but it had been fairly recently restored to mint condition. Everything from the white clapboard to the freshly painted gray trim and black shutters were flawless.

Branson DuBois was waiting for him on the front steps. He was a rotund man about as big around as he was tall, with large, thick hands and a ruddy complexion. He was obviously ill at ease, his thick fingers fumbling with the keys as he tried to open the door. Grant introduced himself and then waited patiently as he stared at *BD's Title and Escrow Company* etched in the glass of the double oak doors. To the right was a bronze plaque stating *DuBois-Grace House 1895*.

"You're not under any type of investigation," Grant said as the silence grew awkward.

Branson dropped the keys on the porch.

Grant bent down, immediately sweeping them up before Branson could react. "This the one?" he asked, holding up one of the larger keys.

Branson nodded.

Grant slid the key into the lock. The door opened easily, and the two men stepped inside.

"Then—?" Branson paused awkwardly.

"I need information on some land," Grant said. "I understand you can get that for me."

"Well, yes, but wouldn't the Register of Deeds be a better place to go?"

"May we sit down, Mr. DuBois?"

"Branson," he corrected. He walked down a short hall and slid his hand inside the door to turn on the light. "Our conference room."

The two men stepped inside. Grant perched on the edge of the conference table. He tried to appear casual. He could see Branson beginning to sweat and he wondered if the man was that intimidated or if his weight or health caused the excess perspiration.

"Branson, I know the Register of Deeds in each county keeps records on land ownership."

"That's right."

"But I don't know what county I need to be searching."

"Ah-ha."

"My office tells me that your title company can access the records throughout the state."

"Well, not the whole state." He pulled a handkerchief out of his pocket and swabbed at his forehead. "Mostly middle Tennessee. You see, most of the Register of Deeds offices have computerized records. I pay a monthly fee to each county for access to their private databases." His voice began to gain confidence as he spoke. "I pay for eight counties, which represents about ninety-five percent of all my research."

"What about northern Alabama?" Grant asked.

"Parts of it."

"Mr. DuBois—"

"Branson. Please."

"Branson. I need to inform you that the information I'm about to request must be kept confidential. You understand?"

"Yes, sir."

"I need information on every piece of property Vincent Palmer owns."

Branson's face grew white. "Does this have anything to do with the Jessica Palmer kidnapping?"

"I'm not at liberty to discuss that," Grant said. "Can you get me the information?"

Branson rubbed his chin. "Only those in the eight counties I subscribe to. Would that help?"

"It might." Grant glanced around the conference room. "Where do we need to go to get that?"

"My office," Branson said, immediately heading for the door. It might have been Grant's imagination, but he thought the man no longer appeared as nervous as he had originally. In fact, as he followed him down the corridor, he thought there was now an eager spring in his step.

"I've been in this business for twenty years," Branson said as he rolled his chair in front of the computer. The chair groaned with his weight as he lowered himself into it. Grant perched on the edge of Branson's desk, where he could look over his head at the computer screen.

"He owns several tracts of real estate," he was saying. "But no mortgages."

"None?"

"Ironic, isn't it, being a banker." He laughed but it sounded forced. "The Palmer family doesn't believe in debt. Never has."

"So they pay cash for everything?"

"I don't know all their financial dealings, of course, but all the real estate has either been passed down through the family or it's paid for in cash, yes."

Branson logged into the Maury County database and entered a few pieces of criteria. Within seconds, a long list of real estate holdings appeared. "They're all in Vincent's name only."

"You mean, jointly between Vincent and Margaret."

"No. Just Vincent's."

"Isn't that unusual?"

Branson glanced at him out of the corner of his eye. "The whole Palmer family is unusual, if you ask me." Then he leaned across the desk and flipped on the printer. "I assume you want this printed out?"

Grant nodded. A moment later, the printer began spitting out page after page.

"Is there any way I can see an aerial view of where these tracts are located?"

"Sure." Branson's fingers didn't seem so fat now, Grant thought as they whipped across the keyboard. In less than a minute, he was viewing an aerial map with tiny yellow balloons across it, as though they were pushpins on a bulletin board.

"When Vincent's daddy died, his will left all his real estate holdings to him." He beamed. "I helped him record the documents in order to settle the estate."

"Looks like I came to the right man, then."

"There's more."

Grant watched as Branson logged onto the surrounding county databases. The stack of pages being printed continued to grow, but as Grant peered at the aerial maps on the screen, he knew none of them fit the description he was looking for. There were commercial buildings, undeveloped but cleared land, apartment complexes—even the condominium in Nashville where Jessie had been abducted.

"Is this everything?" Grant said, trying to hide his disappointment.

"Everything in these parts. He's got some land a bit further away—"

"Where?"

Branson called up the information on the screen and hit the *print* button. "It's nothing much. Just mostly some wooded acreage close to the border of Alabama."

"In Tennessee? Or Alabama?"

"It straddles the line."

"Are there any structures there?"

"Structures? You mean, like housing? Buildings?" Branson chuckled. "I doubt it. It's so far away from everything, the land's pretty much worthless at this point. Maybe someday, a generation or two down the road, towns will have spread out in that direction. Right now, it's probably just used for hunting."

"Hunting."

"You know, like deer—oh," Branson interrupted himself. "I stand corrected. There is a structure there. Probably not much, but there's a tiny cabin. May not be habitable. It's just over the Alabama line."

Grant whipped the paper out of the printer before it had barely printed. "Old Scrouge Road."

"Not familiar with it?"

"Afraid not."

"Well, that's what they call it when you cross the Alabama border."

"And in Tennessee, it's—?"

"Rolin Hollow Road."

"Rolin Hollow Road?" Grant could feel his jaw dropping but he wasn't inclined to close his mouth.

"Two hundred, twenty-five acres."

"Is this everything?" Grant asked. His mouth felt dry.

"Everything I have access to."

Grant started down the hallway at a sprint. "Thank you, Branson," he called over his shoulder. "This is exactly what I needed." He stopped with his hand on the front doorknob. When he turned to face Branson, the large man had stopped in the hallway and was peering at him curiously. "Remember," Grant said as he turned the knob and stepped onto the front porch, "I was never here."

28

They were not expecting her in Radiology. But, as Ivory and Rebecca wheeled Jessie's bed into a waiting area and pulled the curtain behind them, she knew the MRI was not important. They were beyond Vincent's controlling grasp.

"You're okay, Jessie," Rebecca said, patting her hand. "We're not going to leave you alone."

She looked past Rebecca to Ivory, who appeared to be checking her text messages. "Agent Bailey—when will he be back?" Jessie asked.

Ivory glanced up, her ebony eyes veiled. "He's, uh, running down a lead on your kidnapper," she said, her eyes moving to a point around Jessie's chin. "He wants me to join him."

"You can't!" Jessie said, reaching across the bed to grab her. "Please!" She glanced at Rebecca. She'd known her since they were young, but this—this was a sensitive matter, a private matter. She couldn't simply blurt it out in front of her that she thought her own father had orchestrated her kidnapping.

"It's okay," Ivory said, stepping closer to the bed. "You'll be safe here with Rebecca."

"I—I don't want to seem ungrateful," Jessie said, glancing at her old friend, "but I need the FBI. Not a nurse. A nurse may not be able to help me—" She found her voice catching and she cleared her throat.

"Jessie," Ivory said, "Rebecca's not a nurse."

"Why, of course she is. I attended her graduation at Belmont. Everyone knew when she got her nursing degree." Jessie watched as Ivory's and Rebecca's eyes met over her. "What's going on?" she asked.

"You're right," Rebecca said. "I do have a nursing degree. But I have something else." She slipped her hand into her jacket and pulled out something that looked like a black leather wallet. Jessie gasped as she opened it to reveal her FBI identification.

"You're—?"

"Shhh," Rebecca warned. "No one should know."

"Does the hospital?"

"Only those who need to know."

Jessie leaned back. "Oh."

"Jessie," Ivory said, "I have to go. Grant—Agent Bailey—is waiting for me. We're running down some evidence. I promise you, I will be back. And so will he."

Jessie nodded. She was still feeling at a loss for words as Ivory said something softly to Rebecca. Then she slipped away, drawing the curtain taut around them.

A moment passed in awkward silence. Rebecca checked Jessie's pulse and made a notation in her chart.

"Rebecca," Jessie said. Her voice was softer than she would have preferred it.

"Yes?"

"I—I need to tell you something. Something that I was just beginning to tell Agent Bailey before he left."

"What is it?"

"I'm not safe here."

"Of course you are. I won't allow anything to happen to you."

"No, you don't understand. I have *two* threats—the first is the kidnapper, the one I called Brainiac. If he's seen the news, he knows I escaped. And he knows I'm here."

"But he can't get to you here. I'm here and right outside your room is a police officer."

"But I realize now that calling him Brainiac was giving him too much credit."

"What do you mean?" Rebecca's large green eyes stared at her, unblinking.

"He wasn't the brains of the operation. My father was. Is."

"What are you saying?"

"I'm saying my father was there—in both places. He was at the cabin where they kept me—"

"Did you actually see him?"

"I heard him."

Rebecca sighed.

"You don't think I'd know my own father's voice? If your father was speaking just on the other side of that curtain, you don't think you'd recognize it—beyond a shadow of a doubt?"

Rebecca blinked and then looked at Jessie's hands. "You're that sure?"

"I am that sure. I'd stake my life on it. And there's more—he was also at the cellar, where they took me just before I escaped."

"But you didn't see him there, either," she finished for her.

"No. But I heard him. And he dropped his glove there. I gave it to Agent Bailey at the farmhouse."

"Yes. Ivory told me."

"Rebecca," Jessie said, squeezing her hand, "do you understand what that means? My father did it. My own father arranged my kidnapping. He never expected me to escape. And he's here now, in this building. He's waiting, waiting for just the right opportunity."

"To do what? Kidnap you again?"

"Or kill me."

Rebecca shook her head.

"Think about it. He never expected me to escape," she repeated. "He has to know he's a suspect. He has to. What better way to get away with the crime than to kill me?"

"He wouldn't—"

"He wouldn't have to. He had two goons kidnap me, do his dirty work. What makes you think he wouldn't have one of them finish me off?"

"Miss Palmer," came a voice just beyond the curtain. The curtains were pulled apart to reveal a stout older woman in a nurse's uniform. She glanced at Rebecca. "We're ready for your MRI."

Before Jessie could object, they were wheeling the bed out of the room and down a short hallway where the MRI equipment waited in a stark, chilly room. A wheelchair was pushed against the far wall, as if left by a previous patient. A chair contained blankets, neatly folded.

"I'm Holly," the nurse announced. She had a permanent dimple on one cheek that made her appear as though she was always smiling.

As they neared the equipment, Jessie said, "I can get over there myself." She climbed out of the bed and walked the few remaining steps to the MRI. She stood for a moment staring at the equipment with its pristine, sanitized bed and its enclosed chamber.

"You're not claustrophobic, are you?" Holly asked.

Jessie glanced at Rebecca. "I didn't use to be."

"You have a call," another nurse announced, poking her head in the doorway.

"I'll be right back," Holly said. "Stay right there, and I'll get you situated in just a moment."

The two women watched her exit the room, her sneakers making a soft, padded sound as she moved away from them.

"Get in the wheelchair," Rebecca said suddenly.

Without a word, Jessie jumped into the wheelchair.

Rebecca threw a blanket to her. "Cover yourself."

Before Jessie could maneuver the blanket around her, Rebecca had wheeled her through a door on the opposite side of the room. Then she was rolling her at breakneck speed down a wide, empty hallway toward a set of gray double doors.

"Hold on," she said as they reached them. She whirled her around, pushed through the doors, and hesitated only briefly before she raced down the hallway toward the elevators. They had barely reached them before Rebecca began wildly pressing the elevator buttons.

Behind them, they heard Holly calling out. "Miss Palmer? Miss Palmer!"

As Rebecca continued to press the elevator call button, Holly opened a door at the far end of the hall. "Miss Palmer!"

"Come on, come on!" Jessie hissed under her breath.

Holly began trotting down the hallway, her face red and angry.

The elevator doors opened and Rebecca pushed Jessie inside, bumping her against a sole inhabitant. Then she raced in behind her and pushed the close button. Holly reached the elevator just as the doors closed.

"Going up?" came a pleasant voice behind them.

Jessie gasped. Behind her was a huge mass of flowers that almost completely obscured the man's head. He glanced from behind them and smiled.

"Nick!"

"You know him?" Rebecca said tensely.

"He's—a good friend," Jessie said.

"Well, we're going to find out how good a friend he is," Rebecca said. She pushed the button to halt the elevator before grabbing the flowers. "Take off your jacket and put it on Jessie."

"Yes, ma'am," he said. He looked at them both quizzically but complied. "Are you in some sort of trouble?" he said as he gently helped her into it.

"You could say that," Jessie said.

"Does your father know this guy?" Rebecca asked.

"Name's Nick," he said. "He kind of knows me."

"Does he know where you live?"

His eyes widened. "No. I don't think so."

Rebecca pushed the elevator button. It shuddered as it began to move again. "Where are you parked?"

"In the parking lot next door."

"Jessie, take these flowers," she said, shoving them into Jessie's hands. "Keep them in front of your face and stay in the wheelchair. When the elevator gets to the top, we're not getting off. We're going straight back down. You got that?"

Almost on cue, the elevator stopped at the floor where Jessie's room was located. But as the doors began to open, Rebecca pushed the button to close the doors. After opening a short distance during which Jessie held her breath and prayed her father wouldn't be on the opposite side, it began to close again. Then she pressed the button for the lobby.

"Listen to me," she hissed. "When we get to the lobby, get to your car immediately, you got that? Drive it up to the front of the hospital, under the canopy. I'll be right there with Jessie in the wheelchair. Happens all the time. No patient leaves this hospital until they're in a wheelchair and a nurse is with them. Be ready to get her in the car pronto. Got it?"

"Got it." Nick turned to Jessie. "Jessie, what's happening?"

"She can explain everything in the car," Rebecca said as the elevator reached the lobby. "Now go!"

As Nick sprinted through the lobby to the doors, Rebecca wheeled Jessie very slowly out of the elevator. As they approached the front doors, she leaned down toward her. "What is his address?"

Jessie whispered it to her.

"Have him drive you straight there, you understand?"

She nodded.

"You're not to leave. Either me or Ivory or Grant will come and get you. Nobody else."

Nick drove the car to the front doors and hopped out. Before he could reach the passenger door, Rebecca had Jessie inside. "Keep the flowers in front of your face," she said, "and be careful nobody sees you."

"But—where will you be?" Jessie asked.

Rebecca glanced back at the hospital. "I have some explaining to do," she said before slamming the door shut behind Jessie. A moment later, Nick was behind the wheel. Jessie glanced back as she saw Rebecca moving back inside the hospital, pushing an empty wheelchair.

29

The winter sun was unusually intense as Grant pulled the FBI car onto Interstate 65 and headed for the Alabama-Tennessee border. He flipped the sun visor down to shield his eyes, but the sun seemed insistent on peaking through the side window. After a moment, he flipped it back up.

"You okay?" Ivory asked from the passenger seat.

"I'm convinced Vincent masterminded this whole thing," he said, ignoring her question.

Ivory let out a short whistle. "Vincent Palmer arrested for his own daughter's kidnapping? We'd better have some solid evidence before going to the US Attorney with that!"

"You think?" he answered. He glanced at the GPS and then at his watch. Forty-seven minutes from Maury Regional Hospital to Vincent's property along the Alabama border. Forty-seven minutes and already he wished he'd been there five minutes ago.

"So," Ivory was saying, "what's his motive?"

"Money."

She snickered. "Yeah. Right. I bet he's got more money than he knows what to do with."

"Maybe. Maybe not. Looks can be deceiving." He set the cruise control to 80 miles per hour. Sometimes it was nice driving a law enforcement vehicle. "Besides, money can be addictive. Even if he had enough for either of us, is it enough for him? Or would he always crave more?"

"Five mil tax-free…" Ivory said thoughtfully, "but how could he hide it?"

"Would he have to? He owns the bank."

"Still, a five million dollar deposit? Really."

Grant was silent. He watched the yellow stripe on the edge of the road whiz past him. An aging pickup truck was going slower than the speed limit, and he whipped into the next lane to avoid it.

"I've heard a lot of rumors about the Palmer family," Ivory said.

"Yeah? Like what?"

"Like murder."

Grant peered at her out of the corner of his eye.

"Vincent's grandfather. He shot and killed a man. Everybody knows it."

"The trial was the stuff of legends," Grant said as he impatiently slowed behind a line of vehicles. "You know Joe Jackson, the guy whose business went under around the corner from the FBI office?"

"Yeah. I used to grab lunch there a lot."

"Well, Old Man Palmer shot his grandfather—and there were plenty of witnesses. No jury, just the judge. He was found innocent."

"How could that be?"

Grant shrugged. "Rumor was, Vincent's daddy paid off the judge. But that's pure rumor."

"Of course."

Traffic began to pick up and Grant leaned heavily on the steering wheel as if he could force the cars out from in front of him with a cold stare. "Thing was, that was the old man's second murder."

"You serious?"

"Dead serious." He glanced at her. "No pun intended. But a year or two before, Old Man Palmer killed a man for stealing an apple from his store."

"You're kidding."

"Nope. One measly apple."

"What happened?"

"Never went to trial. They couldn't find a single witness who'd testify against him."

"Hhmm," Ivory said.

"Rumor has it, the store was full. Only one register and there was a line of people in it. Right there at the front door. The man walked right out with the apple in his pocket. Old Man Palmer was after him before he could step off the sidewalk; killed him right there." He peered at Ivory for a second before returning his gaze to the road. "And nobody saw a thing."

"That must have been one evil man," Ivory said.

"Evil. And greedy."

"I've heard the same about Vincent Palmer."

"Blood runs thick."

They were silent for a long moment as Grant maneuvered around the slower vehicles.

"What kind of a man would have his own daughter kidnapped?" he said suddenly.

Ivory's head whipped toward him so suddenly that he could see the rapid movement in his peripheral vision, even as he sought to concentrate on the road.

"You okay with this case?" Ivory asked.

"Why wouldn't I be?"

"Oh, I don't know," she said softly. "Maybe it reminds you too much of—of your own daughter. Maybe it's too personal."

He narrowed his eyes and ground his teeth.

"You're sure you're okay?"

"Julia would have been Jessie's age," he said, "had she lived."

Ivory was silent for a long moment and waited for him to continue. When he didn't, she said, "Did they ever catch the guys who took her?"

The road seemed to ripple in front of him and he self-consciously dabbed at the corner of his eye. "Allergies," he said.

"They never found her, did they?" Ivory asked.

He shook his head. "Nope."

"She just vanished."

"Into thin air. The Turkish government never found the first bit of evidence. Nothing."

"So no one was ever charged."

"Nope."

"But," Ivory said, "If they never found her, she could still be alive."

Grant gasped as if someone had punched him in the chest. "No. God, no—"

"But, don't you see—"

"Don't *you* see," he snapped. "She'd be better off dead, than—" His words abruptly stopped and seem to hang in mid-air. All of the things that could happen to a young girl flashed before his eyes even as he fought to push the images away.

"What about Linda—that was her name, right? Your wife?"

"What is this, you want to shine a bright light in my eyes while you're at it?"

Grant stared at the open road in front of him. The speedometer inched past eighty and then ninety. Exit 1, he reminded himself. After a moment, his voice became softer. "Linda left me. Said she never wanted to lay eyes on me again."

"I'm sorry."

"She blamed me for Julia's abduction. Said I was her father, and a father was supposed to protect his child. And I wasn't fit to be a father."

As his exit approached, he maneuvered into the turning lane and slowed down. "I can't change the past," he said as he took the turn. "But when a kidnapping happens on *my* turf, I can pull out all the stops to solve it."

"Vincent Palmer is a confident man."

"An arrogant man."

"You know the difference between confidence and arrogance?"

He glanced at her. "I'll bite."

"The degree to which you like the man."

He chuckled. He thought he saw Ivory relax, as though she'd been trying to break the serious mood. "Then how 'bout this—I can't stand the guy."

"Hey, check it out," Ivory said suddenly.

"What?" Grant slowed the car as he merged onto the rural road. "I see it."

"Neon lights."

"Just like Jessie remembered."

"See that restaurant? Half the lights are out."

"And look," he said excitedly, pointing. "Gulf Oil."

"This is it," Ivory said, her voice a mixture of excitement and awe. "This is where they took her."

"Pleasant Hill Road," he muttered. "In just a couple of minutes, we should see the turn-off for Rolin Hollow Road…"

"My God," Ivory breathed as they rounded a bend and turned left onto another rural road.

They drove silently for a few minutes until they spotted a locked gate at the end of a short stretch of driveway that faced the road. Grant stopped the sedan. He glanced in the rear-view mirror. Seeing the road behind him deserted, he backed up the car and swung into the driveway. They stared for a brief moment at the gate before wordlessly they both opened their doors and walked toward one side of the gate.

"Be careful," Grant said as he stepped through some thick brambles to get around the gate. Once on the other side, he turned and offered Ivory a hand, but she waved him away.

"I'm your partner, not your girlfriend."

He smiled wryly and turned his attention to the winding driveway. It was silent here, he thought; too silent. As he walked along the deserted drive, he realized there were no birds in the trees overhead. There were no sounds of dogs barking, of vehicles on the road behind them; nothing to remind them how close they actually were to civilization.

"Think someone would hear me scream out here?" Ivory said, as if reading his thoughts.

"I don't know," he answered. "Feel like screaming?"

Before she could answer, he stopped abruptly.

"What—?" she said as she almost bumped into him.

He pointed. About fifty yards in front of them was a small, rough-hewn cabin nestled among a grove of pine trees. "Smell that?"

Ivory took a deep breath. "Fireplace. Somebody's been burning wood."

"Pretty recently," he said. They stood there for a long moment. His eyes moved from the chimney to the weathered roof, down the crooked and aging four-by-fours that served as columns holding up the roof over a small, tilting porch. "I've seen this before," he said.

"You serious?"

He shook his head. "Just don't know when." He began walking slowly toward the small structure. As they neared, his gait slowed and he could feel Ivory slowing as well.

"You see this?" she asked.

"Yep." He stopped and looked at her. "Tire tracks."

"They look fresh."

He pulled out his cell phone. He hit speed dial and after a brief moment, he said, "I need crime scene techs." He glanced at Ivory as he gave the address. She had moved to the side of the driveway and was walking along an area that might have been grass in sunnier, warmer weather but was now a cushion of soggy brown vegetation. Once he finished his conversation, he followed behind her, his eyes riveted on the driveway.

Where the tire tracks ended, a set of footprints led to the porch. They wandered back and forth several times, as if the same person had come and gone multiple times. But in the midst of those footprints was a set of smaller ones that led only one way—toward the cabin. Interesting, he thought as he approached the porch. "She walked in," he said more to himself than to Ivory, "but she was carried out."

He felt his heart quicken as he realized the significance of his find. He smiled wryly. "Bingo."

30

Jessie could barely wait for Nick to close the door to his apartment before she was in his arms. The tears that she hadn't even realized were there, just under the surface, came pouring out of her like a dam bursting. She felt his muscular arms surround her, pulling her so close that she could hear his heart beating between her sobs.

She was grateful that he didn't try to quiet her, but allowed her to tremble in his arms with the weight of the events that had occurred over the past twenty-four hours. She felt her strength begin to leave, the strength that she'd manage to hold onto by a tenuous thread, the strength that now seemed to stream out of her in waves of tears that left his shirt wet.

She grabbed the shirt with her fist, her tears now turning to anger—fury at the man who had fought her in her apartment lobby, resentment toward Brainiac and his cruelty—and rage at her own father.

When her sobs finally left her and the rage had hardened into a knot of resolve in the pit of her stomach, she allowed herself to breathe in the aroma of Nick's shirt, that odd but intoxicating mingling of musk and men's soap and her own tears.

When she loosened her grasp, she was surprised to have learned how tightly she'd held him; how both of her fists had been intertwined in the material, how she had pulled on his shirt so strongly that it was gaping open to reveal reddened skin where she'd pressed her face so forcefully against him.

But, as she began to pull away, she felt his strong arms pulling her back to him. He was pressing against her now, a slow squeeze that made her feel as if she was safe in his arms. Her fingers left the entanglement of his shirt and grazed his ribs as they moved around to his back and then his shoulders. She felt his dark hair barely reaching past his shirt collar, one curl seeming to wrap around her finger on its own accord.

He pulled away from her for the briefest of moments, his cheek finding hers, his lips skimming her wet skin. Then he was squeezing her again, holding her ever closer, his mouth now next to her ear. His breath came smoothly, evenly, like a man who was sure of himself.

She didn't know how long they stood there. It was long enough for her face to dry against his shoulder. Long enough for her own breathing to return to normal. Long enough to realize she was pressed against the back of the door with his full weight against her. Long enough to become conscious of the fact that they swayed together almost as if they were engaged in a slow, romantic dance.

When at last he pulled back far enough to look her in the face, he gazed at her with vivid blue eyes that showed concern but not pity—and something else, she thought as she looked back at him. Something tender, something loving…

"Did they hurt you?" he whispered, breaking her train of thought.

"I fought with them, maybe a couple of times."

"No," he said, his voice slightly louder, "did they *hurt* you?"

She looked at him, surprised and at first not quite comprehending. When it occurred to her what he was asking, she pressed her face against his with an almost inaudible, "Oh."

He pulled gently but firmly away from her and held her chin in his hand until she looked him in the eyes. "Did they?"

"They didn't—rape me."

He exhaled as if the weight of the world had been lifted, but he continued peering into her eyes.

"When they took me," she said haltingly, "I—I fought the one man, who pushed his way into the lobby."

"I knew I should have walked you home."

"Don't do that to yourself."

He half-nodded and his eyes drifted to the outline of her cheek and chin.

"Then I tried to fight them again, in the truck—" she tried to laugh as she pointed at her face, but the laughter sounded more like a choking sound, "—and I got this." She felt him staring at her bruises for a long moment. Then he pulled her tight to him again.

"I swear I'll never let anything happen to you again."

She started to answer but thought better of it. Instead, she allowed her eyes to close and she stood there, breathing in his cologne and wishing the moment could last forever.

A short time later, Jessie leaned back against the brown leather couch and watched as Nick added pasta to boiling water. His apartment was smaller than her condominium. It consisted of an L-shaped room that served as a small living and dining area, as well as a kitchen that was separated only by an island that contained the stove he was laboring over now. He glanced up at her as he stirred the pot, his eyes moving from her wet hair to his shirt that appeared so oversized on her, to her bare legs that lay curled on the couch.

Only minutes before, she'd emerged from a hot shower that she wanted to remain in forever, one whose water seemed to cleanse the essence of Brainiac and Brutus from her, even as Nick's lips against hers made her feel as if she was awakening from a bad dream; a dream that felt more distant as each second passed.

Her eyes wandered from Nick to the short hallway that separated the living area from the bedroom. When she looked back at Nick, he was busy chopping tomatoes for the sauce.

"I have to admit," he said, smiling at her, "that shirt looks better on you than it does on me."

She laughed. "Sure beats the heck out of that hospital gown."

"What do you think they'll do when they realize you're gone?"

"I have no idea." She watched him cook for a long moment. "You know I'm going to need more clothes."

He drained the pasta before answering. "I figured as much. If you trust me to pick out clothes for you, I'll go to the mall and bring something back."

"Thanks. But what's the point of buying new stuff when I have plenty in my condo?"

"You can't go back there, Jess. It's too risky."

"I can't. But you can."

He stirred tomato sauce, tomatoes and chopped onion into the pasta.

"You okay with that?" she asked.

"I'd do anything for you, Jess. You know that. At least," he said, glancing up, "I hope you know that."

She watched him cook before answering. "Nick, I need to ask you something."

"Anything."

"Keep Daddy away from me."

This time when he looked at her, his eyes locked onto hers. "Why?"

"I—I don't know how to say it."

He waited so long for her to continue that the sauce began to bubble. "Just say it, Jess."

"I think—I think Daddy was the ringleader in my kidnapping."

"No."

She watched the sauce bubble over, and he grabbed the pot and removed it from the hot burner. When it had receded, he rested his palms on the countertop.

"Why would he do that?" he asked, his voice incredulous. "Jess, the reason we're not together more is—"

"I know," she interrupted, trying to keep her voice gentle. "Because of Daddy."

"He's always wanted the best for you."

She dabbed at her eye, but it was dry. I'm all cried out, she thought.

"I don't know," she said. "I can't tell you why he'd do it."

He set the pot on a cool burner as he came around the counter. When he sat down beside her, he calmly clasped both her hands in his. He kissed the open palm of one before staring at it for a long time. When he looked into her eyes, his were clouded with doubt.

"Why do you think he's involved?"

"I heard his voice."

"Jessie," he said, cocking his head, "are you sure?"

"I'd bet my life on it. I know the sound of my own father's voice."

"I didn't mean that, it's just—you were under a lot of stress—"

"It doesn't change the fact that he was there."

"Did you see him?"

She shook her head. "No. But I heard him talking to one of the kidnappers, right outside the door of the cabin. I was inside, bound and gagged—"

He squeezed her hands.

"I couldn't get to him. I thought he was there to rescue me. But after he left, I realized—I realized he was part of the plan."

He stared at her hands.

"Then, when I was in the cellar, I heard him again. And when I managed to escape—I—I found his glove." Her voice choked and she leaned her head against the back of the couch.

"Jessie," he said at last, "I don't know what to say." He hesitated only a moment before continuing, "Of course I'll keep him away from you. Whatever it takes."

She nodded.

"Did you tell the FBI?"

"Yes."

"Then—why haven't they arrested him?"

"I don't know." She straightened and felt her back stiffen. "Nick, don't you understand—I can't go back to my own place because *he* could be there. He's even got a key."

"You can stay here as long as you want."

She squeezed his hand, but he was looking at her so intently that she didn't know if he'd even felt it. "I know."

"But you can't stay here dressed like that," he said.

"You took the words right out of my mouth. As comfortable as this shirt is," she hastened to add.

"I'll go to your place as soon as I've fed you."

"Go now. Please."

He turned his head as though looking back at the kitchen. A long moment passed. She became acutely aware of a lone curl against his neck and the faintness of a five o'clock shadow.

"Okay." He rose slowly, leaning over her as he did, his lips brushing against hers. "I'll be right back."

"What will you say if—if he's there?"

"I'm there to see Ingrid, of course."

She nodded.

He strode to the kitchen counter, where he picked up his key ring. He flipped through them, finding the spare key to Jessie's condominium. Then he was gone, leaving through the same door that she'd been leaning against just a short time before. It seemed as if she was in a vacuum when he left, as though the very life of his apartment had gone with him, and she quickly jumped to her feet and rushed to the window.

A minute later, he was exiting the building just below her, his wavy, damp hair shining in the waning winter light. Though she could almost feel the chill against the windowpane, he strolled down the sidewalk wearing only his jeans, sneakers and a worn, red plaid shirt as though it was late spring. He stopped at the crosswalk as the busy traffic inched its way through the intersection. Almost as if he could feel her eyes on him, he turned and looked up at her.

Jessie felt her chest swell with pride and she quietly raised her hand for a half-wave.

He kept his hands by his side but she thought she detected a slight, conspiratorial grin. Then the light changed and he had his back to her as he walked toward her condominium.

Something glanced off her shin and she jumped. Then she giggled nervously as she realized it was only Nick's stunning white Persian. "JP," she said, scooping up the large cat in her arms. She buried her face in the cat's long fur and closed her eyes. She remembered the day he'd brought her home: she'd been run over by a car in front of his apartment. Her fur had been matted and brown and she'd been pregnant. He'd whisked her off to a local veterinarian, who set the broken hind leg in a cast. And he'd nursed her back to health, bathing her and working out all the mats. And when the kittens were born, it was Nick who was there to take care of them.

When she opened her eyes and peered out the window once more, he was gone and she found herself wondering how many times he'd stood at this very window and stared across the two blocks between them.

31

Grant stood in the middle of the cabin. Though the grove of pine trees outside provided very little shade, the cabin itself was bathed in shadows. If it weren't for the larger size, he would have felt as if he was entering a roughly constructed outhouse: the rough hewn logs were the same ones on the inside that he observed from the outside, without as much as a layer of insulation or drywall. In the center of the room stood an aging wood stove that still reeked of burnt firewood. And now as he opened the door and poked inside with a crooked metal poker, he could see dying embers still inside. The cabin had been occupied within the last twenty-four hours, he thought.

He watched the crime scene technicians as they photographed every inch of the room. Every inch would also be fingerprinted, especially the smoother surfaces like the refrigerator's door handle, the bathroom and kitchen faucet handles, the door knobs, and even the door to the wood stove.

A heavy chain was padlocked around the base of the wood stove, and he imagined Jessie in this tiny, dark room, chained in a way from which she would have certainly known she could not have escaped. He walked slowly to the couch with its sagging springs and envisioned the imprint on the cushion where Jessie might have spent the previous night, alone and afraid.

Terrified, he thought. Not knowing whether they would, at any moment, rape her, kill her, torture her. And here she was, inside this prison, breathing this stench, while her own father stood on that crooked porch and talked about her kidnapping.

And as he stared at that couch and breathed in the thick odor of wood, he wondered if half a world away, Julia had been confined in a place like this. A dark room, all alone, terrified of the next sound of footsteps approaching her, waiting for her father to rescue her. A father that would never arrive.

"You okay?"

The sound of Ivory's voice startled him back to the present.

"Just thinking."

"I can see that."

"I have the strangest feeling I've seen this cabin before," he continued.

"You think you've been here?"

"No. No, I'm sure I've never been here. And the inside isn't familiar. But the outside is."

"It's a hunting lodge—or shack. They must all look the same."

He walked to a grimy window and tried to peer outside. The filth prevented him from seeing more than swaying cobwebs nestled against the glass; cobwebs that occasionally ensnared another piece of debris from the air. "I can't picture Vincent Palmer in this place."

"I agree with you there," Ivory said.

As Grant turned back to look at her, his eyes dropped to the floor in front of her where a crime scene number was placed in front of a patch of dried blood. "Jessie would have been seated on that couch right there," he said thoughtfully, "gagged and bound, while one of the kidnappers killed the other in this very spot."

"Then after the kidnapper took Jessie to the cellar, he returned here and disposed of the body."

"That's what it looks like." He moved out of the way while the crime scene techs continued processing the area. "But why return? Why not take the body out first, while Jessie is already bound? Why take her miles away and then return here?"

"Maybe she forgot to tell us something?"

"I don't think so." He hesitated. "I specifically recall her telling us the body was on the floor when she was taken out. With an axe in the back of his skull."

Ivory looked around. "Where's the axe?"

"Maybe we'll find it outside. Tossed in the woods somewhere."

He finished walking around the tiny room, stopping to stare at the grimy toilet in a bathroom with no ventilation and again at the kitchen sink, where he tried to envision Vincent Palmer making dinner after a day of hunting. "I don't think Vincent ever stayed here," he said suddenly.

"Somebody has been. They've kept the electricity on."

"Electricity? Or a generator?" He pointed out the kitchen window. "There's a propane tank out there, and I bet if we look a bit further, we'll find a generator. This place is too far removed from anything to have electricity run to it. Besides," he said, leaning over the sink to peer outside, "there are no electric lines."

"I'm surprised it has plumbing."

"Might have a well and septic." He turned back to look at the technicians. "Let's get out of here."

They were silent on the drive back. When they reached the hospital, it felt as though they'd just left the cabin two minutes before. Grant's mind was racing; so many unanswered questions. But it was a puzzle, and he liked puzzles. And something told him he was going to enjoy putting Vincent Palmer and his arrogant attitude behind bars.

He pulled in front of the double doors and stopped just beyond the wheelchair ramp. As he started to get out of the vehicle, a security guard called out to him. Without missing a step, he flashed his FBI credentials and walked into the hospital and to the elevators.

The police officer was standing at the door to Jessie's room but he appeared ill. When he saw Grant and Ivory approaching, he let out an audible groan.

"What's happened?" Grant said before they'd even reached him.

The officer shook his head and pointed inside at Rebecca, who sat beside Jessie's bed. The bed was empty, the sheets rumpled. Grant looked toward the bathroom door.

"She's not in there," Rebecca said.

"You didn't lose her. Tell me you didn't lose her."

Rebecca held up a piece of paper. "She's not lost."

Grant grabbed the paper out of her hand. "What is this?" he said, staring at the address.

"She was convinced that Vincent Palmer was going to hurt her."

"Why? What happened?"

"Nothing that wasn't going on before you left," Rebecca said grimly. "He's a pompous, condescending man with a God complex. But I never saw him threaten Jessie or look as though he might harm her. Not in any way."

Grant felt his breathing begin to return to normal.

"But when he returned to her room this afternoon, she freaked."

"So you what, got her discharged?"

Rebecca raised one eyebrow. "I took her for the MRI. That took care of an hour or so, but she was adamant about not going back to this room. She wanted to go someplace where her father couldn't get to her."

Grant held up the paper. "I don't recognize this address as one of our safe houses."

"Her boyfriend showed up."

"Nick Rhodes."

"You know him?"

Grant nodded. "We've met."

"Well, he showed up just as I was getting her out of the hospital."

"That was convenient."

Rebecca shook her head. "Anyway, he took her to his place."

"And Vincent Palmer won't know where it is because he doesn't know who Nick Rhodes is," Grant finished.

"Other than an upstart newspaper reporter," Ivory finished.

"Why didn't you go with them?"

"I figured somebody needed to stay here and handle Vincent Palmer."

Grant smiled wryly. "And were you able to?"

Rebecca rolled her eyes. "Could you?"

He slid the paper into his pants pocket. He knew the address; he knew the exact location. It was only two blocks from Jessie's condominium. Two blocks from where she was brutally abducted. "Where's Vincent now?"

"He didn't exactly fill me in on his plans," Rebecca said. "But if I had to guess, I'd say he's looking for you."

He turned to Ivory. "Let him look," he said. Then over his shoulder, "we're on our way to Nick's. Get this room cleared. She won't be coming back here."

32

Jessie lay quietly between the light blue sheets. The room was dim; only the faintest bit of light crept between the slightly parted curtains in Nick's bedroom. The door wasn't quite closed, and she could hear the faint sound of the television down the hall. She lay on her back and stared at the ceiling as though she was studying the stippled texture.

She'd been trying to sleep for more than an hour. She had a stomach full of pasta and hadn't slept the night before, but though she should have been conked out, she found herself wide awake.

It wasn't fear, she thought. She felt perfectly safe with Nick in the next room. He'd done an excellent job of retrieving plenty of her clothes as well as other items he thought she might want—her hairbrush, cosmetics, and even her slippers. Her father would never suspect that she was there with him. And from the windows in Nick's living room, he would be able to see if her father came back to her condo.

She listened to the television. It must have been the nightly news, she thought. And she would no doubt be on it. It might have been why Nick was watching it.

She sat up in bed and stared at the bedroom door, then laid back down and pulled the sheet up to her neck. She lay on one side and closed her eyes, and when that didn't work, she turned to the other side.

Finally, she sat up once more. With a heavy sigh, she pushed back the covers and slipped her legs over the side of the bed. Her feet found the soft comfort of her slippers easily, and she padded down the hallway toward the television.

The living room was empty, the television broadcasting information about an impending storm. A sound behind her caused her to jump.

"You should be sleeping," Nick said.

She turned toward the kitchen to see him drying the spaghetti pot. The kitchen was spotless, right down to the sauce that had spilled onto the burner. "Couldn't sleep."

"You want a sleeping pill?"

"You got one?" Then before he could answer, she said, "No. I don't want to be incapacitated."

He finished drying the pot and placed it back in the cabinet beneath the counter. "You don't have to stay awake, you know. I'm awake and I swear to you, I won't let anything happen to you."

"I know." She walked to the island. "I've just been doing a lot of thinking."

He smiled. His face always looked different when he smiled, she thought. As if smiling didn't quite come naturally to him, and he was a bit embarrassed about it.

"I've seen that look before," he said.

She nodded. "I've got to go."

"You're not leaving without me."

"Didn't plan to."

He tossed the dish towel onto the counter. "So, where are we going?"

The Federal Building appeared imposing with its oversized limestone block and formal architecture. Two massive oak trees framed either side, casting it in muted shadows as the naked branches appeared to be reaching for the structure like aged fingers.

She felt as though her breath was caught in her throat as Nick ushered her through the massive front doors with their heavy, impenetrable glass. They stopped briefly in the colossal foyer.

It was dark, the marble floor with its diamond-shaped pattern of light and dark appearing cold and forbidding. It must have had a twenty foot ceiling, Jessie thought as she glanced upward. It might have been white at one time or another, but now the ceiling was gray pockmarked with mold and for some strange reason, she thought of asbestos. The walls were cracked and the foyer gave the overall appearance of having been vacated decades before. It even had the kind of musty odor of a furnace with a mildew-infested filter.

"So this is our Federal Building," Nick said. His voice echoed through the massive chamber.

"Over there," Jessie said, pointing toward an elevator.

Their footsteps echoed on the marble floor as if an army was crossing it instead of two lovers.

"First floor," Nick read aloud, "Courtroom. Second: Federal Home Loan Bank—"

"Third, IRS—there, fourth floor. FBI."

They entered the diminutive elevator that seemed in stark contrast to the massive proportions of the lobby. "Our tax dollars at work," Nick said as he punched the button for the fourth floor. The elevator creaked and moaned as it came to life. It seemed to labor as it rose and Jessie found herself holding onto the wall as though it could support her if the elevator were to collapse and career downward.

They heard her father's voice before they'd reached the fourth floor. It boomed as if it was everywhere at once—above them and below them, on the left and the right—and Nick's and Jessie's eyes met for a brief, panic-stricken moment as the elevator screeched to a halt and the doors prepared to open.

Nick grabbed Jessie's arm. "You're okay," he whispered to her.

"He can't know I'm here."

Nick pushed the button to keep the door from opening, but it began to open and shut with enough noise to wake the dead. He swore under his breath. "Stay here."

As the doors opened, Jessie pressed herself against the side wall of the elevator. She kept her eyes on Nick's profile as he leaned cautiously into the hallway. He looked toward the origin of Vincent's voice, and then in the opposite direction. Then he swiftly returned to Jessie and grabbed her hand. "Straight ahead," he ordered her as he pushed her out of the elevator.

In the briefest moment that she stood in the hallway, feeling naked and guilty, she could tell that she was in the center of a narrow, aged center hall. It had the same musty odor as the downstairs lobby but the dark walls appeared to close in around her. She felt her heart quicken and her toes tingled with the sudden urge to escape.

Then, Nick was rushing to the left and into a small alcove, pulling Jessie behind him. In an instant, they were standing next to an ancient pay telephone. She started to speak but Nick placed his hand over her mouth and nodded toward the end of the hall.

A shadow reached outside the door and her father's voice became louder and more belligerent.

"Do you know who I am?" he bellowed. "I'll have every one of your jobs!"

"You're welcome to it, Mr. Palmer," came a calm, male voice. "In the meantime, we'll let Agent Bailey know you're looking for him."

"What is your name?" he demanded.

Jessie could envision him standing in the doorway, his face reddened with anger, the vein pulsing and throbbing along the side of his neck as it always did when he became angry. She turned and rested her face against Nick's chest, but a moment later, she was peeking back down the hallway.

"Take my card," the male voice answered.

"My daughter's missing!" he shouted. "Why aren't every one of you out there looking for her?"

When there was no answer, he continued, "I pay your salaries!"

"Then, I'd like a raise, Mr. Palmer."

What followed was a stream of expletives that caused Jessie to blush. She wanted to apologize to Nick, who stood transfixed listening, but when she started to speak, he clamped his hand tighter over her mouth.

The cursing continued to grow in intensity as the shadow turned into her father's figure. She thought she was going to faint as he started down the hallway in their direction. She buried her face back into Nick's chest and felt him wrap his arms around her so strongly that if she could have disappeared within his grasp, she would have. She heard the footsteps marching down the hallway, growing louder with every step. The floor seemed to reverberate with his anger.

He reached the elevator. She could hear him punching the button and when the elevator didn't immediately open its doors, he rammed his fist into the steel. With the violent outburst, she felt her breath rushing from her. She wondered if she would have fainted had Nick not been there to hold her up.

No, she thought. I can't faint. If he turns around and sees me, I have to be brave. I have to be.

She pulled away from Nick, but he started to reel her back to him. She stopped and looked him dead in the eye. They stood there in utter silence, their eyes locked, as Vincent now stood silent and seething just six feet away from them.

33

Grant pushed the elevator button several times. "It's faster to take the stairs," he grumbled.

Ivory leaned toward the elevator door. "It's coming," she said.

Before he could take the few steps across the Federal Building lobby to the stairwell, he heard the elevator groan to a halt. "One of these days, this thing is going to die," he said as he stepped inside.

"Let's hope we're not on it when it does."

Ivory pressed the button for the fourth floor. As it began to creak and moan, she turned to Grant. "She did what she had to do."

"Rebecca? Yeah, I know… I just don't understand why they weren't at Nick's apartment. They said they were going there; they even gave her the address. So what happened?"

"They went out for pizza?" Ivory quipped.

Grant stared her in the eye. "Funny," he said. "Very funny. We've got a kidnap victim running around Nashville and you're making jokes."

"You're right," she said as the elevator crept upward, "it's not a laughing matter."

"We lost her," Grant said. His voice caught in his throat and Ivory jerked her head toward him.

"We'll find her," she said, her voice suddenly hushed.

He didn't answer but stared back at her with tortured eyes. "We'll find her."

The elevator ground to a halt and seemed to hang in mid-air for a long time.

"You're going to have to face Vincent sooner or later," Ivory said.

"In time." He ground his teeth.

The doors opened with a sound that was almost painful to hear. Ivory started to step out of the elevator and then she abruptly stopped and turned back to Grant. "Your time just ran out."

"What?" He looked past her into the hallway. Standing in front of him with a face filled with fury was Vincent Palmer. And just beyond his shoulder was Jessie, her back to her father, her face buried against Nick's chest. At the sound of the elevator door opening, Jessie turned toward the elevator and for a brief instant, her eyes met Grant's. Her face went white and she shook her head as she raised one finger to her lips.

"Mr. Palmer," Grant said, his voice sounding louder than normal. "We've been searching all over for you."

Vincent sputtered something. A fleck of saliva flew toward them.

"Jesus, he's rabid," Ivory said under her breath.

"Hurry up," Grant said, grabbing Vincent and pulling him unceremoniously inside the elevator.

"Get your hands off me!" Vincent demanded.

Ivory began pushing the button furiously for the first floor.

"Don't you want to see Jessie?" Grant said. He backed into the elevator so he was against the far wall, but he didn't let go of Vincent's jacket.

"Where is she?"

The doors remained open even as Ivory continued to push the button to close them. For an agonizingly long moment, Grant kept his eyes locked on Vincent's even as he watched Jessie and

Nick in his peripheral vision. "In a safe house—an FBI safe house."

"Why? Why did you take her without my permission?"

The doors finally began to close. Grant knew Jessie's face would remain etched on his mind forever—as white as if she were seeing a ghost, her eyes so large they almost looked alien.

As the elevator began the slow creep downward, Grant relaxed his hold on Vincent. He watched as Vincent brushed his jacket as though ridding it of germs.

"Answer me!" Vincent demanded.

"Jessica Palmer is an adult," Grant said, his voice level though he could feel his own sense of rage beginning to boil. "We didn't need your permission."

"Do you know who I am?" Vincent demanded.

Grant cocked his head. "I'm assuming that's a rhetorical question."

"Don't get smart with me."

"Mr. Palmer," Grant said, taking a step toward him, "Don't get smart with *me*. I'll arrest you for interfering with an investigation."

"I'll have the Governor—the President—down on you so fast, your head will swim."

The two men stared at each other, unblinking, as the elevator continued to inch its way downward.

As the elevator ground to a halt on the first floor, Vincent growled, "Take me to my daughter."

"Go home, Mr. Palmer," Grant said, stepping outside the elevator and holding the door for Vincent. "Your daughter is safe with us. I'll be in touch."

Vincent stepped out of the elevator and turned back to face Grant. "If anything happens to her—anything—"

"Is that a threat, Mr. Palmer?" Grant said evenly. Vincent's neck was throbbing and Grant felt the heat begin to rise in his own.

"I don't make threats," Vincent growled. "I make promises." He turned once more to go but turned back before Ivory could press the elevator button to whisk them back to the fourth floor. "And I don't get mad. I get even."

As he stormed across the lobby and the doors on the elevator began to close once more, Ivory breathed, "Sure looks like 'mad' to me."

"Mad?" Grant said. "Or insane?"

34

Grant stood just out of earshot, his eyes riveted on Jessie and Nick as he held a quiet conversation with Ivory. "I need you to do something for me," he said.

"Name it."

He studied Jessie as she sat in one of the aging metal chairs in the FBI office. Around her, phones were ringing and agents were talking on top of each other regarding various calls and cases. Yet, in the midst of the hubbub, she sat quietly, stoically, as though she was in a world of her own. His eyes wandered down her slender back to her arms, and as he followed the gentle curve of her bicep and her forearm, his eyes came to rest on her hands.

"I need to interview Meg," Grant said slowly, his eyes still on Jessie's hands.

"And you want me to—?"

"Stall Vincent. Make sure he doesn't go home." Jessie's hands were intertwined with Nick's. They looked small and white compared to Nick's larger, olive skin.

"Gotcha."

Grant tore his eyes away from Jessie to look at Ivory. "I need to—"

"—interview Meg without Vincent interfering," Ivory finished.

"You do this to your husband?"

"You know I'm not married."

"Someday you'll be married. And you'll do it to him."

"Someday I'll be married," Ivory said, moving toward the doorway, "and he'll need somebody to do it."

"We still talking about finishing each other's sentences?" Grant asked.

Ivory smiled and slapped the doorframe on her way out. "I'll text you when I can't detain him any longer," she said over her shoulder.

Grant watched her disappear around the corner of the door before turning back to Jessie. Though she was still facing away from him, Nick turned slightly and their eyes met. Nick raised one eyebrow and cocked his head slightly, as if silently questioning him. With a deep breath, Grant returned to his desk. His chair groaned as he sat in it and he struggled to make the chair roll forward to get closer to his desk. Someday he needed to oil this wretched chair.

"So, how are you doing?" he asked, forcing a small smile.

She shrugged and squeezed Nick's hands. "How would you be doing?"

Grant peered at her head, at the bruises that were turning shades of green and yellow at her hairline and on one cheekbone. It was a high cheekbone, like his wife's and daughter's. "I'd be recovering physically," he said quietly, pointedly looking at her bruises again, "but emotionally, it would take me longer."

"That's how I'm doing," Jessie answered.

He leaned forward. "So, why did you come here?" He glanced at Nick.

"I've got to tell you something," Jessie said.

Nick remained silent, but his eyes appeared tortured. Interesting, Grant thought. He looked back at their hands. "Does it have anything to do with you not wanting your dad to know you were here?"

Jessie sighed. "Thank you for not blowing our cover."

"Some cover," he answered.

"We didn't know he was here. Otherwise, we wouldn't have come. At least, not until later."

Grant slid his business card to her. "My cell phone's on the card. Call me next time. I'll make sure the coast is clear."

Jessie retrieved the card, stared at it for a moment and then slid it into her coat pocket.

A long moment elapsed. Grant no longer heard the hustle and bustle around him; it seemed as if everyone had disappeared, their voices only faint memories. "So," he said, "you've been kidnapped by two thugs. One of them is killed right before your eyes. Your only hope is for your father to pay the ransom. He does. And you manage to escape. Whether they would have eventually let you go is anybody's guess. Or maybe they transferred you to a place where they knew you could escape." Jessie opened her mouth to speak, but he held up his hand to silence her and continued, "Now you're free. And your own flesh-and-blood, the father who paid your ransom, is standing a few feet away from you. And you don't want him to know you exist. What's wrong with that picture?"

"Look, Mister—Agent—Bailey. I know this is going to be hard for you to believe, but…"

"Go on."

"I—I think Daddy arranged the kidnapping."

"I know."

"You know?"

"You told me about hearing his voice—not once but twice—while you were in captivity."

"Once at the cabin—"

"And again in the cellar."

"And the glove—"

"The glove has been entered as evidence."

"Evidence."

"Evidence that your father was there, speaking to one of the kidnappers while you were bound and gagged just a few feet from him."

"Then," Jessie said, looking at her hands and Nick's as if seeing them for the first time. She looked up suddenly, her eyes meeting Grant's. "Then, you know he arranged it."

"I know he was there. I don't know who did the arranging, who did the actual kidnapping, or who got the money."

"Look, Agent—"

"Grant. Call me Grant."

"Grant. I don't know how to say this exactly, but—" She stopped and looked at Nick as if beseeching him to find the words for her.

"She's afraid of her father," Nick said.

"I know."

"You know?" Jessie's lower lip quivered.

"I know you're afraid he's going to do something to you, now that you've escaped."

"Then why don't you arrest him?"

"On what evidence?"

"I heard his voice—twice. Doesn't that count for something?"

"Yes," Grant said. For some reason, a rubber band on his desk caught his eye and he fingered it for a moment.

"And the glove—it's physical evidence."

"Yes," he said again. He looked up at her. "But it's not enough."

"I—I don't know what to do."

"Jessie," Grant said, leaning over his desk, "I need you to trust me. I know your father was there. I know he's in on this somehow, someway. But I have to build a case. If I arrest him now, his attorney will just have him right back out on the street. Bail will be nothing to him. But they'll know that we have our suspicions. And that will give him an opportunity to try and hide his tracks."

"Then—what do I do?"

Grant looked at Nick. The younger man remained silent, his blue eyes appearing large and questioning. He looked again at their hands, so intertwined in each other's. "You go back to Nick's apartment," he said. "Your father doesn't know he's your boyfriend, does he?"

Jessie blushed. "No. He wouldn't approve."

Grant nodded slightly before turning to Nick. "You got anyplace you need to be, Son?"

Nick shook his head.

"Anything you got to do?"

"No."

"Then, can I trust you to stay with her? And to call me if anything—*anything*—out of the ordinary happens?"

"Absolutely."

"Take her straight to your place. Don't stop in some romantic restaurant, or catch a movie, or grab a quick drink. Go straight home. And don't allow her to leave again. You got that?"

"I got it." Nick stood.

"That's it?" Jessie said, standing. "I go back to his place for—what, a day, a week, a month?"

"A day. Maybe two. Maybe three. I'll be in touch. You can count on that."

"But—"

"Listen, Jessie," Grant said, standing. He became acutely aware of the other agents now and his voice became barely louder than a whisper. "We found the cabin."

"Where I was held?"

He nodded. "We're processing it now, gathering evidence."

"Oh." She looked down, but her eyes remained wide as though her brain was moving at a hundred miles an hour.

"Everything is just as you described it." He reached across his desk and patted her on the shoulder. "You did good," he said, managing a smile. "You kept your wits about you and you remembered everything. You helped lead us to the exact spot."

"I did?"

"All those things you remembered—the Gulf Oil sign, the neon lights, even the restaurant with half its lights out—it's all there. Exactly as you told us it would be."

"You went inside?" she said.

"Yes. We went inside."

She swallowed and appeared to hesitate. Grant didn't rush her. He watched her skin grow paler, her eyes squeeze shut as if she was trying to maintain her composure. When she spoke again, her voice was firm. "Then you found *him*."

"No. He was gone."

"But—but he was there."

"We know he was there. There was a pool of dried blood right in front of the couch, at the spot where you told us he was hit by the axe."

Jessie looked at him. Her eyes seemed to move from one eye to the other, as if searching for an answer. "But what happened to him?"

Grant shrugged. "He was moved. The other guy was trying to hide the body, probably."

"Then you may never find it."

"We're looking for it. We've got multiple agencies on this case. Dogs as well as people."

"Oh."

"When you managed to get to that farmhouse," Grant continued, "and I just happened to be in the farmer's field—I was investigating a truck left on his property." When Jessie didn't respond, he continued, "Somebody was getting ready to burn it. It was the truck you were taken in, Jessie."

"How do you know?"

"It matched the description you gave me. And your dog led me right to the cage you were transported in."

Jessie shivered. "Abby," she said suddenly. "Is she—?"

"She's fine. Your mom is taking good care of her."

"I want her back."

"You'll get her back," Grant said. "But for now, she's better off where she is. What would somebody think, seeing Nick here walking your dog?"

She nodded. "I suppose you're right."

"There's more," Grant said.

Jessie looked at him, her mouth slightly open, her lower lip no longer trembling. But she held onto Nick's hands so tightly that Grant wondered if the younger man was uncomfortable.

"We've identified the owner of the truck. And the cabin."

Jessie gulped so deeply that it was audible. "And?"

Grant walked around the desk and came face to face with her. Nick extricated one of his hands and placed his arm around her shoulder. Grant fixed his eyes on hers before he answered. "I think you know who owns them."

He waited. He reached across his desk and pulled a tissue from a box and offered it to her, but she shook her head and didn't take it.

"It's your father's cabin," Grant said. His voice seemed raspy, as if he was in need of a long drink of water. "And it's your father's truck."

35

Grant stood in the dimly lit Palmer den. It seemed as if ages had passed since he'd stood here last, peering at the books and photographs on the massive bookshelves. He had to remind himself that only a day had gone by. He glanced at his wristwatch. It had been an excruciatingly long day. He wondered where he might be able to stop between the Palmer estate and his small home to grab a drink—or two. No, he thought as he wandered along the seemingly endless shelves, it was better to drink at home. Alone.

"Agent Bailey."

The sound of Margaret Palmer's voice stirred him back to the present, and he tried to appear casual as he turned to greet her. "Mrs. Palmer."

"Meg," she corrected.

She crossed the expansive room, her small feet barely making a sound on the thick Oriental rugs. Her shoes were high, he thought, probably three inch heels or more. He couldn't imagine a woman walking in those shoes for any great distance, and now he wondered as he shook her hand how she spent her days and whether she whiled away the hours sitting in a comfortable, overstuffed chair with those high heels.

"I wasn't expecting you," she said, then quickly added, "but please. Sit down. Let me get you a drink."

His eyes wandered to the decanters but he shook his head. "Thank you, no. I'm here on business."

"Of course you are."

Her hand was soft and limp, the hand of a woman who didn't lift anything heavier than a dinner plate.

"Mind if I have one?" she asked.

"Go right ahead."

He watched as she walked to the wet bar. Or waltzed, he thought. Did he detect a little sashay in her step?

When she turned back to face him, he found his cheeks becoming red with the knowledge that he was watching her hips move. Embarrassed, he turned to face the bookshelves. His eyes immediately landed on the photograph he'd seen on his first visit to their home. It was a picture of Vincent standing next to a dead deer as he held up its head by an ample rack. An eight-pointer, Grant thought as he peered at it. He heard Meg's voice in the background but he lifted the picture from the shelf and carried it to the nearest lamp, where he studied it further. He never thought he'd see Vincent dressed in camouflage overalls. But there he was. And behind him was a log cabin, the porch tilting dangerously. He knew that porch, he thought as he stared at it. He'd walked up those steps only hours before.

"I said, do you hunt, Agent Bailey?"

Grant jerked his head toward Meg. "No. Not anymore. I used to."

She was standing only a few feet from him, sipping out of a crystal-cut glass and peering at him over its rim. She might have been a portrait from years gone by, he thought. She wore a billowing white blouse with a high neckline, its ruffles gently brushing against her neck and chin. Her dark skirt was long and pencil thin, reaching to her ankles.

She reached one hand to her hair and smoothed the sides that reached backward toward a French twist. It was blond and as becoming as a 20-year-old's. He wondered if she dyed it, and then looked at her flawless complexion and thought, probably not. All but wispy bangs were pulled away from her face into a twist that might have been tight when she arranged it, but now tendrils were escaping and framing her face and the nape of her neck.

He cleared his throat. "Your husband hunts," he said.

"Yes."

He waved the photograph. "You happen to know where he was when this picture was taken?"

She barely looked at it. "Of course I know. It's one of his properties."

"*His* properties?"

"Family money. They had a lot of holdings. Vincent, being an only child, inherited it all."

"Happen to know where it's located?"

"Not far. Down by the state line."

He glanced back at the picture. He was aware of her sipping her drink and watching him over the rim. "You ever go with him, hunting?" he asked. He hoped his voice sounded casual, as though he was just making polite conversation.

"Do I look like someone who hunts down helpless animals and kills them for sport?" Her voice was silky and smooth.

He looked at her. She was smiling at him over her glass. Her eyes were shaped like half moons when she smiled, which appeared to transform her face. But a moment later, her smile gently faded and the sadness was back—the same melancholy he'd noted on their first meeting. "No," he answered. "You don't." He waved the photograph again. "Mind if I take this?"

She shrugged. "Not at all."

"Your husband—does he go there often?"

She placed one hand on the back of the sofa. She wore a diamond ring that Grant could envision on the Queen of England. Her remaining hand was limp at the wrist and shook in a manner similar to wringing. He'd never seen a person wring their hands with one hand before, and he found himself gravitating toward it. Her drink was dangerously close to cascading over the rapidly moving wrist. "I don't know what my husband does, most of the time," she answered. But before Grant could respond, she added, "But I do know he was supposed to be there this weekend."

"Oh?"

"Yes. You've met Edward Buchanan?"

"At the bank."

"Vincent and Edward were supposed to go to the cabin this weekend. Deer season, you know."

Grant patted his hand with the small photograph. "And why didn't they?"

"I haven't a clue. Edward called here, responding to a message Vincent had left him. Seems Vincent changed his mind at the last minute."

"When was that?"

She shrugged. "Oh, maybe two days ago." She moved to the sofa and sat down. She seemed to glide, he thought as he watched her. She arranged her skirt before continuing. "Odd thing was, he asked Edward not to go, either."

"Do you know why?"

"Haven't a clue." She smiled again, very briefly. "Like I said, Agent Bailey, my husband doesn't tell me what he's doing most of the time."

Grant slid the photograph into his coat pocket.

"But certainly, you didn't come all the way out here just to talk about deer hunting."

"No," he said.

Abby wandered into the room with the housekeeper, who was folding up a leash. That would account for the dog not barking when I came to the door, Grant thought. He was grateful for the diversion as he stooped to pet the dog's beautiful light golden, silky fur. Maybe I should get a dog, he thought as he peered into her liquid brown eyes.

"You know," Meg said after a moment of silence, "Vincent is pretty upset with you. He's upset with the entire investigation, to be truthful."

"Oh?" he said, intentionally focusing on the dog.

"He doesn't like it when someone else is in control."

"I got that impression."

"He'll probably complain to the Governor about the detective at Jessie's condo, accusing him of disturbing the scene."

He straightened. "I think he took an item out of an evidence bag."

"Something like that. The detective told him he was trying to destroy evidence."

"He did, did he?" His voice sounded more monotone than he would have liked it. He couldn't pull his eyes away from hers now.

"And he wasn't happy with you at all, trying to follow him as he paid the ransom."

"Why do you think that was? Other than him wanting to be in control and all."

"Maybe he thought you'd scare away the kidnappers. If they were watching, that is."

"Did you know about the five million dollar insurance policy?"

She took another sip. For someone who seemed so focused on her drink, it was a wonder the glass wasn't empty already. He stared at her hand and that diamond ring.

"I told you, he doesn't tell me anything."

"I see."

"Do you think it's odd, Agent Bailey, that the kidnapper never called our home? That he always called Vincent's cell phone instead?"

Grant perched on the arm of the chair facing Meg. "What do you make of that?" he asked. He wished he had a drink in his hand; it would be something to keep his hands busy, something he could turn to when he needed to pull his eyes away from hers.

"Oh, probably nothing. Ever get your cell phone charged up?"

Her smile was intriguing. He honestly didn't remember if he'd charged it but he answered, "Yes."

"You should open an account with First Palmer Bank."

"Why is that?"

"They're giving away free cell phones."

"They are, are they?"

"Pre-paid minutes. You can't lose."

Grant wished he had that drink now. He watched her finish off her drink. She returned it to the wet bar, placing it on a silver tray. He imagined the housekeeper would come along after their little visit, whisk it away and replace it with a fresh one.

"It was Vincent's idea," Meg continued. "You know, he likes to be in control."

"Yes," he said, almost robotically.

"Are we finished?"

He stared at her for a long moment. He wanted to see her hair come loose from that bun; he wanted to see how far down her bodice it would cascade. She had delicate features. High cheekbones, like Jessie's. Large eyes. She was beautiful once, he thought. Still was. But her puffy eyes, though she tried to hide it with cosmetics, revealed her sadness. The sadness seemed to permeate her; the bags spoke of sleepless nights. Tossing and turning. Or befriending a bottle. Something told him she would never have been this talkative had Vincent been there. He was a bully, he thought as he stared at her. A bully who had taken this beautiful woman and squeezed the life out of her with his insatiable urge for control.

"We're finished, Agent Bailey?"

"Yes."

She stood there, smiling gently, her lips barely turned up, one eyebrow slightly lifted. He realized he was still staring at her and he cleared his throat and turned to go.

"Agent Bailey," she said as he reached the door.

"Yes?"

"I'm so glad Vincent demanded that you personally handle this case."

He stopped and looked back at her, but she had turned back to the wet bar and was pouring another drink. He waited while she recapped the decanter. She sipped it as if it was her first, but she kept her back to him. She was staring into the back yard.

After a moment, he turned and let himself out.

36

Grant stopped long enough to take an extra large bite out of his calzone. When the day just kept getting longer, there was nothing like Italian food to take the edge off. As he chewed, he read the paperwork he'd completed for the US Attorney, his mind reliving the moment he'd stood in front of the Federal Grand Jury requesting subpoenas so they could review all of Vincent Palmer's personal account records from First Palmer Bank.

He polished off the calzone and opened another container. The cheesecake had slid to one side. He was just about to reposition it when Ivory breezed through the door with an armload of documents.

"What'd you get me?" she asked, plopping the stack onto the edge of his desk.

He nodded at a plastic bag on the opposite corner. "Thai."

She grabbed her chair and wheeled it to his desk before diving into her lunch. "Instead of 'divide and conquer', you should have come with me."

"Somebody had to get us lunch."

"We could have done it together, afterward."

"What, they give you a problem at the bank when you showed them the subpoena? Did 'the little lady' need a man with her?"

"I'll deck you."

Grant snickered.

"Look at this stack," she continued. "All of this came from First Palmer Bank. Vincent's bank."

Grant glanced through it as Ivory continued talking.

"So, let's say you work at the bank. And I come in and say I want all the information on the bank's CEO. Not only am I asking for personal info on your Big Boss, but it's a powerful—and nasty—boss. One that could chew you up and spit you out before you could blink."

"Yeah?" Grant said, taking a swig of black coffee. "So the bank gave you a hard time?"

"That's just it. They didn't."

"Really?"

"Really. You'd think the Operations Manager would, at the very least, get her supervisor to approve the subpoena. Gets her off the hook, you know, when Palmer demands to know who gave what to us."

"Makes sense."

"Only she didn't. She had this kind of weird smile on her face, and she sat right down and started pulling up stuff on the computer and printing it out."

Grant threw his trash in the wastebasket. He waited for Ivory to continue, but she was concentrating on her take-out. "So, what do you think? That Vincent is such a tyrant, his own employees would like to see him put away?" he asked. Before she could swallow her food and answer, he answered his question himself. "That's not such a far stretch of the imagination, you know? I can see them hating the guy that much."

"Good thing he was in meetings all afternoon. There I was, sitting at the base of the steps, in plain view of everybody, waiting over an hour for the Ops Manager to print everything. The whole time, I kept glancing at the top of the steps where Vincent was sitting behind a closed door, just waiting for it to open and for him to lower the boom."

"But he didn't."

"Nope. Did you hear me, Grant? It took over an hour. Do you know how many transactions that is?"

Grant rifled through the papers. He always liked to get a sense of the type of information he had before him before he got down to the details. "The subpoena asked for a year's worth of activity in Vincent's and Meg's names, right?"

"You helped me word it."

"Personal accounts."

"Not his bank holdings," Ivory said. She hadn't finished her meal but she stopped with her fork just above the container. "Did they give us data on the bank, too?"

Grant pulled out a section of paper. "No, but take a look at this." He spread the paperwork on top of the others so they could study it. Ivory stood and while Grant continued talking, she finished her food in silence. "What's 'The Palmer Family Limited Partnership'?" he mused, reading from the top page. "We didn't ask for this."

"She gave it to us in error?"

"In error?" Grant repeated. "I don't think so. I think she meant to give it to us."

"Did you know about this?"

"The company? Hadn't a clue. Check it out. Vincent's the General Partner and the only one authorized to sign checks." He pointed at the documentation.

"You'd think a 'family partnership' would at least include the spouse."

"Yeah. But not only is Meg's name nowhere on this—"

"Meg?"

"Margaret. Mrs. Palmer. Whatever."

Ivory raised one brow.

"So, as I was saying," Grant said louder, "Her name's not on this. Anywhere. And look at this. All the other account statements are mailed to the home address. But this one," he said, holding up one sheet and waving it, "this one is mailed to a post office box."

"I bet you 'Meg' doesn't know a thing about it."

Grant didn't answer. His eyes were glued to the account statement like a cat stalking a mouse. "I guarantee she doesn't know," he said after a long moment of silence. "Each month, just like clockwork, Vincent's writing a check to somebody named 'Susan Jones'."

"Mistress?"

"If I had to guess… Why else would he be writing her a check for five grand each month?"

Ivory whistled. "That's a chunk of change."

"And another one for $4,289 to a mortgage company."

"It's not his mortgage. Can't be. The house has been in his family for generations."

"What do you want to bet it's for Susan Jones' house?" Grant said, looking up from the paperwork.

"Follow the money," Ivory said with a conspiratorial smile.

"How many times have we heard that?" Grant smiled back. "And wouldn't you know. Vincent even wrote the address on his payments."

"Let me see that." Ivory reached over and grabbed the paperwork from Grant's hand. "I'll be."

"You know where that is?"

"Haven't a clue."

"Handmacker Road is on the same highway that leads to the Palmer estate."

"Oh, that cute little subdivision?"

"The one with the private golf course and fitness center? Yep, that's the one."

"Well, he keeps her in style, doesn't he?"

"Looks like we have a little lady to visit."

"I'll run a check on her first."

"Of course."

"Just want to see what we're dealing with," Ivory said, handing the paperwork back to Grant. "I think I'm going to enjoy meeting this woman."

"I also want to run down this post office box."

"I'll get all the info on that."

"My guess is it's in Vincent's name only."

Ivory sat in her chair and wheeled it closer to her own desk. While she was busy on the computer, Grant continued to pour over the accounts. After a few minutes, he stood up and placed two stacks of paper side by side. "Ivory."

"Yeah?" She glanced at him but continued typing.

"So, Vincent has an individual bank account. Checking. And each month, there's a direct deposit of two hundred grand."

Ivory whistled. "I'm in the wrong business."

"And on the day the money is deposited, Vincent writes a check to his wife."

"Oh, yeah?" She leaned back in her chair.

"For two grand."

"Wait a minute," Ivory said. "I misunderstood you. I thought you just said Vincent makes two *hundred* grand a month and he gives Meg two grand."

"That's exactly what I said."

"It's got to be mad money."

Grant continued looking through the paperwork.

"Are you thinking what I'm thinking?" Ivory asked.

"That Vincent Palmer has his wife on an allowance?"

"—of twenty-four thousand a year? That's chump change for a guy worth as much as he is."

"It's also less than half what he pays his mistress."

"If," Ivory said, "she is his mistress."

"Obviously we need to find out."

Ivory rose from her desk and crossed to the printer. While she waited for information to print, Grant continued searching through the stack from the bank.

"This amount of money is mind-boggling," he said as much to himself as to Ivory. "Why," he said louder, "would someone worth so much want to have his daughter kidnapped to earn five million more? Wouldn't the risk outweigh the benefit?"

"He's a bully," Ivory said, pulling the printed documents from the tray, "but no one ever said he was smart."

37

Jessie barely heard Nick as he came up behind her and wrapped his arms around her.

"You've been staring out the window for an hour," he said.

"I know." She didn't turn around, but she placed her hand on his forearm as he tightened his hug. He rested his chin on her shoulder and peered out the window in the same direction.

"You wish you were home?"

Her hand squeezed his forearm, and it took a moment for her to answer. "I miss my condo—the way the sun peeked through the bedroom window in the morning; the little rug in the living room where Abby loved to lay; even the tiny kitchen table where I did my homework… But something's changed. Things are different."

He parted her hair at the nape of her neck and kissed her. "How so?"

"I can't explain it exactly; it's like a door has closed. It's as if I'm entering a new chapter in my life, and things will never be what they once were."

"They would have been that way, anyway. I mean, you're nearing graduation and you'd be getting a job. Who knows if you could have stayed in that condo? Or if you'd outgrow it, or it would be too far from your new job?"

"You're right." She turned and faced him. "And sooner or later, I'm going to have to walk back in there and pack up my things and move. But right now, I can't begin to imagine walking through that building's front door—seeing the foyer where I was attacked, and—and—"

"You okay, Jess?"

She nodded. "I'll be okay. I'll have to be." She sighed and rested her head against him. "I miss Abby," she said suddenly.

He wrapped his arms tighter around her. The top of her head fit perfectly beneath his chin, and he rested his head there and listened to her breathe. "Abby is okay," he said. "Your parents are taking good care of her. I'm sure of it."

"I don't like the thought of my father being there with her."

"You don't think—no, Jessie, your father wouldn't hurt your dog."

"He wouldn't? Are we talking about the same man who wouldn't have his own daughter kidnapped?" When Nick failed to answer, she continued, "Look at me. Look at these bruises. What kind of a father would do this to his own daughter? *What kind?*"

"An evil kind," he answered. He ran his finger across her cheek where the outline of a bruise was painfully visible.

"You know what I want to do, Nick? I want to get my dog. I want my friends to go to my condo and clean it out. And I want to start over, somewhere else."

Nick pulled back and tilted her chin up so she was looking into his eyes.

"I have to start over, and it can't be here," she continued. "But wherever it is—" her voice started to choke but she caught herself, "wherever it is, I want you to be there."

"I'll always be there for you, Jess," he said. "I'd follow you to the ends of the earth."

She stared into his eyes for a long time. "I think you would, Nick," she said at last.

They stood there until the room darkened with the setting sun. When they finally moved apart, Jessie sat on the sofa while Nick perched on the armrest and held her hand.

"I want to get Abby," Jessie said.

"I know you do."

"No, Nick, I want to get her now."

"Jessie, you can't. You heard what Agent Bailey said. Who would walk her? Me? How would that look if your dad was going to your condo and he saw me out walking your dog? What kind of questions do you think that would raise?"

"I don't care. I know he deserves to be in prison. Locked up for the rest of his life."

"Are you that sure it was his voice you heard?"

"I couldn't be more sure. And it's frustrating me to no end that the FBI doesn't already have him locked up."

"But they don't. And as long as he's out there, he can go to your place any time he wants. And he can look for you. Jessie, don't do anything stupid. Let the FBI do their job. Stay here with me, where you're safe. Where I can protect you."

"And who will protect Abby?"

He looked at her for a long time. When he spoke again, his voice was quieter, almost hushed. "How can I get her out of your folks' home?"

Jessie had grown up on the Palmer estate. It was the only home she'd ever had until her father purchased the condo during her first year at Vanderbilt. She knew the roads that led from Columbia to her home like the back of her hand; she'd traveled those roads as a toddler, along for the ride as her mother ran errands. As a pre-schooler on the special bus that took her to a private school. As a cheerleader in junior high and high school. Every event she'd ever gone to had taken her along those roads. But now, as she stared out the window, they seemed foreign. Different, somehow. As if her entire world had turned upside down and nothing would ever be righted again.

As Nick approached the turn-off to the Palmer estate, a black Porsche careened out of the driveway.

"Get down," Nick ordered.

Jessie crouched on the floorboard. She kept her eyes on Nick's face. He kept both hands on the wheel and stared straight ahead as if watching the road. A few seconds later, a flash of light crossed his face.

He glanced in the rear-view mirror. "He's gone."

Jessie sat back in the passenger seat. "Do you think he saw you?"

"I doubt it. It's too dark."

"What about your car?"

"I don't think he paid enough attention to it the other day to be able to recognize it again, to tell you the truth."

He turned into the driveway and they began the long, slow journey through the estate. As the car moved forward, casting the trees and brush into long shadows that seemed to leap and bend in front of the headlights, Jessie began to doubt her decision to go there. They were trapped now, trapped on an isolated road with one way in and one way out. All her father would have to do is turn around and come back home, and she would be there—like an ensnared animal.

"Do you want to stay in the car?" Nick asked as they neared the house.

"No," she said. Her voice sounded shakier than she would have preferred and the sound of it almost caused her courage to wane. "No," she said, forcing herself to sound stronger, "Mother will be there. She may not let you have Abby, but she wouldn't hesitate to give her to me."

Nick turned off the engine. "I don't think this is a good idea."

"We won't stay long. Just long enough to get Abby."

"And your mom won't have any questions?" he said with more than a hint of doubt.

Without answering, she opened the door and was halfway up the front steps before he caught up with her. She giggled nervously when they reached the door. "I don't have my keys," she said. She rang the doorbell. "I don't know where they are." Her mind flashed back to her keys spinning across the foyer at her condominium, and she squeezed her eyes to try and shut out the image.

When the door opened, Heddy, the housekeeper, exclaimed, "Ms. Palmer! It's Miss Jessie! It's Miss Jessie!"

"Shh," Jessie cautioned as she and Nick stepped into the vast marble foyer. "We're only here for a minute."

Heddy bear-hugged her with the abandonment of an aunt greeting her favorite niece. Jessie returned the hug, feeling safer with the woman's broad, capable arms around her. "Heddy," she said, "you're a jewel." Before the older woman could answer, Jessie caught sight of her mother coming down the steps. She was in stark contrast to the housekeeper's rotund, fleshy build: slender and svelte, she almost seemed to float down the stairs, her hand barely brushing the balustrade.

"Mother!" Jessie exclaimed.

"Jessie," she said as a smile swept slowly across her face. It was an awkward smile, Jessie thought, the kind of smile she'd become so accustomed to: it appeared out of place on her, as if an old tintype photograph had suddenly come to life. She reached the bottom of the steps and reached out to hug Jessie, who had extricated herself from the housekeeper's strong grasp. But unlike Heddy, Meg hugged her with the same intensity as one would hug a fragile glass ornament.

"When will Daddy be back?" Jessie asked.

A myriad of emotions appeared to cross her mother's eyes, leaving them dark and sad. "He's gone to one of his meetings," she said. "He won't be home for hours."

Jessie breathed a sigh of relief. Before she could respond, she heard Abby's frantic barking, followed by a servant's voice as she tried to keep the dog under control. The golden retriever burst through the house, surging into the foyer so rapidly that her paws slid across the marble floor until the Oriental rug in the middle of the foyer gave her enough traction to stop. Behind her was a younger but hefty servant, panting as she tried to reach Abby and restrain her. But at the sight of Jessie, she stopped.

"Miss Jessie!"

Jessie had barely responded before Abby was upon her, licking her and sniffing her as if reading her clothing to determine where she'd been. Jessie buried her face in her dog's fur and fought back the tears that threatened to explode from her. Abby was okay. She was fine. Unhurt.

"Heddy," Meg said, "get Jessie—and her friend—something to eat."

"Oh, Mother," Jessie said, crouching to hug Abby even closer to her, "you met my classmate, Nick?" Her words sounded halting and she wondered why she didn't have the courage to call him her boyfriend. Surely her mother would understand. But her father would not. And soon, soon she would be strong enough not to care.

Her eyes met Nick's as he reached past her to shake her mother's hand. "Mrs. Palmer," he said. "It's nice to see you again."

"And under such different circumstances," she said. Far from being cordial, her voice sounded distant. "I hope you are not writing an article for the newspaper about all this?"

"Oh, no, ma'am," Nick said. "No. Not at all. No." He continued shaking his head.

"Mother," Jessie said, rising to come to his rescue, "I came to take Abby."

"Where are you going?" Meg said, her voice becoming higher and reedier.

"The FBI has what they call a safe house for me."

"You're safe right here."

Jessie stole a glance at Nick. "I know. But they want me to be where they can watch me."

"They're welcome here. My goodness, they took over the house after your—" She stopped abruptly as if afraid to say the word. "Why did you leave the hospital?" she said at last.

"The FBI wanted me in the safe house," Jessie said. She was grateful for the diversion of the golden retriever, and she focused on her long, silky fur as she spoke. "Look, Mother, I want to stay but I can't. The FBI doesn't know I'm gone, and I have to hurry back. Or they'll put out an APB on me or something." She smiled as she said the last sentence, as if to lighten the mood but her mother didn't return the smile.

"Why does *he* get to know where you are, and not me?"

"I don't know," Nick said, stepping forward and looking at Jessie. "I'll take her back to the FBI office, and they'll take her to the safe house."

"I see." Meg's eyes narrowed. "But they don't know she's gone."

"Mother, I'm taking Abby with me," Jessie interjected. "You know I'll be safe with her."

"Yes," Meg said, tearing her eyes away from Nick's to look at her daughter. "Heddy," she said, "Get all of Abby's things and put them in—this young man's car?"

"Yes," Jessie said. "It's right outside."

Meg nodded. "Then you're not staying."

"No, Mother, I can't." Jessie looked up the broad staircase, at the way it wound around as it reached the second floor, resulting in a perfect circle overlooking the foyer. There was nothing she'd rather do than dash up those stairs to her own bedroom, close the door and block out the rest of the world. She felt her spine stiffen. But this was her father's house.

"I don't know what you'll tell Father about Abby being gone," Jessie said.

"He most likely won't even notice," Meg said. "He seems very preoccupied."

Jessie's eyes met her mother's. "Mother, I have to tell you something—"

"Here it is, Miss Jessie," Heddy's voice sang out. In one arm, she carried a bag of dry dog food; judging from the way she handled it, Jessie thought it must have been close to fifty pounds. In the other hand, she carried a small box with toys and Abby's leash.

"Let me help you with that," Nick said as he dove forward to grab the bag.

In an instant, the foyer came alive with Abby's barking and the commotion surrounding the transport of the items out to the car. Almost before she knew it, Jessie was standing at the car door. Abby was in the back seat but dangerously close to jumping into the front. Nick was behind the wheel. Heddy was standing at the front door, smiling and waving, and Meg stood just beyond Jessie's reach at the base of the steps.

"I wish I could tell you more, Mother," Jessie said. She felt a pull in her heart as though some unseen force was begging her to stay there, to remain in the comfort of the mansion, surrounded by all she'd grown up knowing and loving. But now, as she looked at her mother and the home her father had also grown up in, it was as if a door was slowly but methodically closing.

"I think I know," Meg said. "And I wouldn't want to be here with him, either." Before Jessie could respond, she added, "I don't have a choice."

Jessie hugged her mother once more, wrapping her arms around her and placing her head against her chest. But as she pulled away, she felt as though she'd just hugged one of the massive granite pillars that stood outside their home.

She returned to the car with a sense of almost overwhelming sadness beginning to wash over her. She settled into the passenger seat and gently pushed Abby's wet nose out of her face, banishing her to the back seat once more. But when she looked back, expecting to see her mother's face, she was gone. The lone light fixture that hung from the third floor ceiling above the porch swung with a growing breeze, casting areas of the porch in a pale yellow light before plunging it back into shadows. The enormous front door was closed. Heddy's giddy face was gone.

And so was her mother.

38

Grant stopped in front of a set of double doors and opened one side for Ivory. "After you," he said.

She opened the opposite door. "No," she said, "after you."

They stood there for a moment while another pedestrian walked through the open doors, thanking them both.

"You're insufferable," Grant said as he walked through his door and watched Ivory walk through hers.

She batted her eyelashes rapidly in a mock imitation of a silent screen star.

He adjusted his briefcase under his arm as they crossed to the stairwell. Ignoring the row of elevators directly next to the stairs, he climbed to the second floor, taking the steps two at a time. Ivory was right behind him with her own loaded briefcase.

They walked down a broad hallway that might at one time have been nice, but which was now covered in a frayed, coffee-stained carpet. The walls had fared no better; they were in deep need of repainting. Catching Grant's eyes as he studied the surroundings, Ivory said, "Let's hear it for government budgets."

He shook his head in response as they neared the U.S. Attorney's office.

When he opened the door, he was greeted by a middle-aged woman at a file cabinet, her half-glasses perched precariously at the end of her nose as she studied the files. "Agent Bailey," she said in greeting. Then as Ivory followed him inside, "Agent Lang. Is Mr. Rye expecting you?"

"Yes," Grant said. "He didn't tell you?"

She pushed her glasses higher on her nose. "He never tells me anything." She motioned for them to follow her. As they walked behind her, Grant felt as though he was walking behind a box of lit cigarettes. The woman must be a chain smoker, he thought, her whole body is permeated with this odor.

She stopped at an open door. "Agents Bailey and Lang here to see you, Boss."

"Come on in," Jim Rye greeted them. "Have a seat."

Grant shook Jim's hand, his own almost feeling as though it was being swallowed in the process. The man was at least two hundred and fifty pounds, Grant thought. Maybe more. He looked like he'd gained since the last time they saw each other—which was just a couple of weeks earlier.

"How's the wife?"

"Mean as ever," Jim responded. "She's actually heading down to my old Alma Mater."

"The University of Alabama?"

"Yep. Christmas break and all that. Our oldest son, you know Jimmy, don't you? He's coming home for the holidays."

"I hadn't realized Jimmy was attending college there."

"Wide receiver, just like his old man." He smiled but as he lowered himself into his chair, the chair groaned with his weight at the same time Jim groaned. Football had not been kind to him, and old injuries had taken their toll. "So, what have you got for me?"

"You're not gonna believe this one, Jim."

"I've seen it all. Nothing surprises me anymore."

"Well, this one might. You know about the Jessica Palmer kidnapping case."

Grant detected a flash of light in Jim's eyes before he answered. "I'd have to be living under a rock not to know." He stuck a pipe in the corner of his mouth but didn't light it. "You got a suspect?"

"And you know her father, Vincent Palmer. The third, to be exact."

"I know *of* him. That's the way I'd like to keep it."

"Well, you're actually gonna get to know him a lot better," Grant said. He felt like he was picking his words and stepping around what he really wanted to say. But now that the time had come, he was having trouble expressing himself.

"Elise has been getting to know him, that's for sure," Jim said, nodding toward the open doorway and his secretary's desk.

"Oh?"

"He's been breathing down our necks here, wanting to know if we have a suspect and when we're taking Jessica Palmer's kidnappers to trial. Elise keeps telling him as soon as we know something, he'll know something."

"You're kidding."

"I don't know why he hasn't barged in my office yet and demanded justice be served, to be honest."

"Well, Jim," Grant said, leaning closer to the desk, "I don't quite know how to tell you this, but Vincent Palmer *is* the suspect."

Jim laughed a loud guffaw that echoed down the hallway. "April Fool's isn't for four more months, Grant."

"We have reason to believe that Vincent actually planned his own daughter's kidnapping."

"Motive?"

"Money."

"The Palmers already have so much money, they probably could never spend it all. Unless," he said, pulling the pipe out of his mouth, "you're about to tell me it's a house of cards."

"No." Grant opened his briefcase and pulled out a report. "Jessica Palmer was abducted from the lobby of her condominium close to Vanderbilt, where she attends law school. Her father was called, and when he got there, he disturbed evidence."

"That's no reason to think he planned his own daughter's attack."

"Then we set up our equipment at the Palmer estate. The kidnappers always called Vincent's cell phone, never the landline."

"That doesn't prove anything."

"They demanded five million dollars—the exact amount of insurance First Palmer Bank maintains just in the event one of the employees or their family members were kidnapped."

"Okay," Jim said, leaning his forearms on the desk and tapping the pipe against it. "So far, it's looking like an inside job. Somebody has his cell phone number and somebody knows how much the bank carries in insurance. But you haven't told me anything that links Vincent Palmer to it."

"The kidnapper demanded the money be turned over in just two hours' time. That was enough time for Vincent to get to his bank, pull out the money, and get to the drop-off point. But not enough time for us to mark it."

"Again, sounds like an inside job—and a professional one. But tell me how Vincent ties in."

"He tried to lose me."

"Grant, we've known each other for what, twenty years? You know not to waste my time with conjecture. You don't have probable cause for me to request an arrest warrant. And if you're planning to arrest Vincent Palmer, you'd better have all your ducks in a row or he's likely to have you for dinner."

"Oh, I've got evidence." Grant glanced at Ivory. On cue, she pulled two photographs from her briefcase and handed them to Grant.

"This is the truck that transported Jessica Palmer from her condominium to a cabin, where the kidnappers kept her hostage while the ransom was being paid."

Jim studied the truck in silence.

"You know who that truck belongs to?" Grant continued without waiting for his reply. "Vincent Palmer."

"He report it stolen?"

"Nope. Not then, and not yet. I don't think he knows we have it." Grant slid the second photograph toward him. "Fingerprints on the visor match Palmer's. The rest of the truck had been wiped down."

Jim nodded. "This still isn't enough, Grant."

"There's more. The cabin where Jessie was taken? It belongs to Vincent Palmer."

"Wait a minute. You're telling me that Vincent Palmer had his own daughter abducted and had her brought to his own property?"

"That's exactly what I'm telling you. Property's near the state line that he uses to hunt on. I don't know if Jessie Palmer had ever seen inside it before she was captured."

"Interesting." Jim rubbed his chin for a moment. "But you know the minute Vincent Palmer is arrested, he's going to have a Dream Team of lawyers defending him. And they'll try *us* on the front pages of every newspaper in the country and on every morning news show. If you're planning on arresting Vincent Palmer, you'd better have an ironclad case. And what I'm seeing so far is nothing more than circumstantial evidence."

"Jessie—the victim—is also ready to testify that she heard her father's voice while she was in captivity."

"Tell me more."

"The first time, she was bound and gagged inside the cabin and heard Vincent and another man discussing her kidnapping outside on the front porch."

"She's sure it was her father?"

"Positive. Then after they transported her from the cabin to a cellar, she heard him again."

"I read in the newspapers that she escaped."

"Yes, she did. And during her escape, she found her father's glove."

"Is she absolutely sure it belonged to her father?"

Grant smiled. "Custom-made, just for him. Ironically, she'd bought him the gloves herself."

Jim nodded and continued to study the photographs of the truck and cabin. Ivory handed him a photograph of the glove alongside an evidence tag.

"We found three hairs on the duct tape used to bind up Jessie," Grant continued.

"And?"

"It's a DNA match."

"Vincent Palmer's?"

"Yep."

Grant's cell phone rang. "I gotta take this," he said, glancing at the caller identification. "It's one of our techs."

Jim waved his finger in an approving gesture and Grant answered the phone. "Shannon?"

"Grant," the young man said excitedly, "you're not going to believe this."

"I'm sitting here with the U.S. Attorney," Grant said, "and I think we started our conversation the same way."

"We traced those phone calls to Vincent's cell, you know, the ones made by the kidnapper demanding the ransom?"

"Yes." Grant felt a chill come over the back of his neck as if someone was breathing on him.

"It took us awhile because they're the kind that's pre-paid. You know, no contract. Just activate the phone and make the calls until the time and money runs out."

His information didn't match the enthusiasm in his voice and Grant pressed the phone closer to his ear as if it would help him understand Shannon's words more clearly.

"So we traced the pre-paid phones. It's from a whole shipment made to—get this—First Palmer Bank."

"What?"

"You heard me. Whoever made those calls got their cell phones from some kind of promotional campaign at First Palmer Bank."

"A promotional campaign that Vincent Palmer came up with," Grant said.

"Well, I don't know that—"

"I do." Grant glanced at Ivory, who furrowed her eyebrows and mouthed, *"what?"*

"Incredible," Shannon said excitedly.

"That it?"

"Yeah."

"Thanks, Shannon. That's great. Just what I needed." He hung up his phone and relayed the conversation to Jim and Ivory.

Jim leaned back in his chair, causing it to tilt so dangerously that only the wall kept the chair from tumbling over backward with his weight. "This can all be brought out in a courtroom as supporting evidence," he said slowly, his eyes locking onto Grant's. "But it isn't enough to get a conviction. A good lawyer will see to that. And if he gets off, we can kiss our jobs good-bye."

"I've saved the best for last."

"Then let's have it."

Grant reached beside his chair and pulled his briefcase onto the desk between them. He stood over it and hesitated briefly. He could feel his cheeks begin to grow warm. Jim's eyes wandered to his face, and Grant knew his friend could see the color rising in it. "We issued a subpoena to get all of Vincent's bank records."

"And?"

"He has a bank deposit box."

"You get a subpoena to search it?"

"Sure did."

Jim didn't respond but continued looking at Grant expectantly.

"The morning after his daughter was abducted—hours after he paid the ransom, he accessed the bank deposit box." He opened the briefcase with a flourish. "And this is what we found in it."

Jim whistled.

"Two point five million dollars. Cash." Grant leaned back, a contented smile creeping across his face.

"Any surveillance cameras in the bank?"

"Yep. Including one in the area of the deposit boxes."

"And?"

"All the video was removed."

Jim's eyes widened.

"So," Grant said, his smile broadening, "How's that for enough evidence to get an arrest warrant?"

39

They could have served the arrest warrant the evening it was issued. Grant knew that at the time and suspected Ivory knew it, also. But they waited until the next morning, after they'd briefed the Special Agent in Charge of the FBI Division and announced it at an impromptu meeting. The arrest would generate an avalanche of media coverage, and the FBI would have to be ready for it. As they left their office, their boss was already on the phone to FBI Headquarters in Washington.

They bypassed First Palmer Bank's parking lot, opting instead to pull directly in front of the bank's main doors. The spaces here were diagonal and were generally more difficult to back out onto the main street, but the FBI car's flashing lights in the grille and rear windows could stop the traffic in an instant. He parked in a handicapped spot, where the pavement was marked on either side to allow for the broader silhouette of a wheelchair. And, Grant thought as he exited the car, the wider perimeter would make it easier to escort Vincent Palmer to the car and deposit him in the back seat.

"Kind of conspicuous, don't you think?" Ivory said over the hood of the car.

Grant glanced at the front doors, where a security guard was peering at him through the glass. "Maybe so."

They met at the front doors, where they both grabbed the handles of the opposite doors and opened them simultaneously.

"I think it's Freudian," Ivory said under her breath.

Grant didn't respond but went directly to the first desk he saw. He flashed his credentials. "We need to see the bank president right away."

"Yes, sir." The young woman stopped midway through her bank business with a customer, who remained seated and watched the action with growing curiosity. She picked up the telephone, entered a couple of digits, and then turned her back to Grant and Ivory as she whispered into the phone. A moment later, she turned back around, replaced the phone in the cradle and stood.

She motioned for them to follow her as she walked to the base of a broad, winding staircase.

"This looks familiar," Ivory said under her breath. The woman seated at the base of the stairs looked up as they neared, and Ivory half-nodded to her in greeting. Though she attempted to respond in kind, her jaw dropped partway open. Grant was tempted to reach over, place his finger under her chin and shut it, but knew better.

"You'll find Martha at the top of the stairs. She's secretary to both Mr. Palmer and Mr. Buchanan. She'll get him for you."

"Thank you."

Grant took his time walking up the stairs. He wanted to survey the bank from above: the line of tellers off to his left, the single line of customers waiting for an available teller as they stood behind a plush burgundy rope, the variety of desks situated throughout the lobby, and the open doors around the perimeter. Just as importantly, he wanted to identify any possible escape routes.

As he climbed ever higher, he became acutely aware that all eyes were on them. The tellers had stopped their transactions and were looking expectantly upward. And now the customers were beginning to turn and face them.

"We could have waited and arrested him at home, you know," Ivory whispered.

"We could have," Grant answered in a normal tone. "But we didn't."

By the time they reached the second floor, an attractive lady in a smart, tailored suit was waiting for them. Her hands were clasped in front of her, and Grant noticed her medium blond hair with platinum temples was perfectly coifed. She did not attempt to shake their hands, but it seemed to Grant more a matter of formality than neglect.

"I understand you'd like to see Mr. Buchanan," she said as they stepped onto the plush carpet at the top of the stairs.

Before Grant could answer, Edward Buchanan appeared in the doorway of his office. Another man brushed past him, laden with a stack of paperwork. He kept his eyes downcast as he scurried past them and down the stairs.

"Mr. Buchanan," Grant said, approaching him.

"Please come in."

As he gestured to them to enter his office, Grant noticed that he didn't seem surprised to see them.

"We met a few nights ago," Grant said once they were inside and the door was closed behind them.

"Yes." He shook his hand. "I'd say it's nice to see you again, but I'm not sure that's appropriate?"

Grant forced a smile. "This is Agent Lang. Ivory, Edward Buchanan."

"Ed, please." He laughed but it sounded a bit contrived. "Or, if you run into any of my old schoolmates, it's 'Eddie.' Funny how we can grow up but never leave the childhood names behind."

"Isn't it."

Ed Buchanan was shorter than Grant and now as he looked at him, he wondered if he'd ever played football. He was built like a stout little fireplug, but there was something about him that made Grant think he could be a barracuda. His neck was so thick that beneath his tie, he could tell the top of his shirt was left unbuttoned. His eyes were dark, but they weren't brown; as Grant locked eyes with him, he realized they were almost the color of a midnight blue sky. His nose was crooked, and under the harsh office lighting, his skin was pockmarked. Grant found himself staring at his face.

"Home burned to the ground," Ed said suddenly.

"Excuse me?"

"My face. I was twelve years old. House caught fire—grease left on the stove. We all got out, but I was left—" he waved toward his own face "—with this."

"I'm sorry."

"Don't be. I survived, and that's what counts." He gestured toward an immaculate white sofa. "Please. Have a seat."

Grant surveyed the massive corner office. "No, thank you," he said. He felt like time was standing still as his eyes moved over the oversized oil paintings in antique, gilded frames. Just the way in which they were mounted with individual lights above each one shouted that they were originals. The carpet was thicker here and now as Grant looked downward, he realized he was standing on top of a plush Persian rug, which in turn was on top of a pristine white carpet.

"Is there something I can do for you?" Ed asked. His voice was polite but his breathing was labored, as though his lungs had been damaged by too much tobacco. The office reeked of it—an odd mixture of cigarette smoke and pipe tobacco.

"We're here to serve an arrest warrant."

The blood seemed to drain from his face and he leaned back against his enormous walnut desk.

"Vincent Palmer," Grant continued. He was watching the other man closely.

"You're joking," he said. His eyes moved from Grant to Ivory. "This is a joke, right?"

"I'm afraid not. We're notifying you because we're going to be escorting him out of the bank in a few minutes. Assuming he's here?"

Ed seemed to be coming out of a stupor. "Yes," he said finally. "He's—he's in his office. In a meeting."

"The U.S. Marshalls should be here soon, if they aren't already downstairs."

"What are the charges?" Ed asked. His eyes were narrowed, and he continued to remain against the desk as though it was supporting him.

"Let's go to Vincent's office," Grant said. "And I'll inform you both at the same time."

When they exited the office and walked past the balustrade to Vincent's office on the other side, Grant glanced downstairs. Three U.S. Marshalls were standing at the base of the stairs. Grant glanced out the floor-to-ceiling windows and noted their vehicles pulled across the parking spot behind his FBI car. He nodded briefly as they continued to Vincent's office.

Ed didn't knock but opened the door wide.

"I'm busy!" Vincent growled.

Grant caught a glimpse of Vincent's secretary. She was standing behind her desk, having risen as they approached. She appeared positively mortified that someone had dared open Vincent's door without proper protocol.

Grant brushed past Ed. "Meeting's over," he announced as he strolled into the office.

Grant didn't think an office could be larger than the one he'd just left, but now he realized that Ed's office was only a fraction of the size of his boss' office. It actually rested on two corners, providing a view of downtown Columbia that was more than one hundred and eighty degrees.

Three men were seated at an oblong conference table at one end. Each of them was impeccably dressed in dark suits, starched white shirts and deep red ties, almost as if they were wearing a uniform.

"We need to speak with you in private," Grant said, pointedly staring at the three men.

Vincent rose from the end of the conference table. His face was ruddy and his hands were balled into fists as they rested on the table. Without pulling his eyes away from Grant's, he said in a hoarse whisper, "We'll continue this meeting later."

The men instantly rose, gathering their paperwork and exiting the office expeditiously. Grant stepped aside as they moved into the hall, but out of the corner of his eye, he realized once they had crossed the threshold, they had stopped and were peering back as if they were children watching something of great interest unfolding on the playground.

Once they were out of Vincent's office, the marshalls entered and stopped just short of where Grant and Ivory stood.

"Did you find the kidnapper?" Vincent asked.

"We found one of them," Grant said evenly.

"Well?"

"We're here to arrest you, Mr. Palmer."

The room felt frozen in time: Grant, Ivory, Ed and the marshalls all staring at Vincent from one end of the long room. And Vincent staring back at them, his face immobile and without expression. Behind him, Grant could feel the stunned silence of the secretary and the three men who had exited the office.

When Vincent exploded, it sounded like a deafening roll of thunder. His words boomed from his mouth like a lion's roar and both hands came down hard on the table. Before Grant could blink, he was upon them and past them in a flash. "Get out!" he bellowed.

Grant whirled around. Vincent was standing outside his office now, pointing his finger toward the front doors downstairs. Everyone stood like statues: the secretary, the three men, and everyone downstairs. All faces were turned toward Vincent Palmer, the blood appearing drained from them, the eyes wide and dark, mouths open.

Grant stepped from Vincent's office into the open foyer upstairs. He was keenly aware that every eye was now upon him.

"Vincent Palmer," he said in a clear voice that was so loud he felt like an actor on a stage, "You're under arrest on charges of conspiracy to commit kidnapping, kidnapping—"

"This is preposterous!" Vincent thundered.

"—two counts of felony grand theft," Grant continued, "bank fraud and insurance fraud."

Vincent's rage exploded as he spluttered, "Get out! Somebody get Dalton Mitchell on the phone. Get the Governor on the line. Get—"

"Mr. Palmer," Ivory said, stepping forward, "You have the right to remain silent."

Grant reached into his pocket and pulled out his handcuffs. He'd hoped it wouldn't go down like this, but the expression on Vincent's face was frightening. He appeared almost like a caged animal. His movements were jerky, his face the color of a beefsteak tomato, and now specks of saliva were forming at the edges of his mouth.

"Anything you say," Ivory continued, "can and will be used against you in a court of law. You have the right to an attorney—"

"You know damn well who my attorney is!" he shouted, the saliva flinging in Ivory's direction.

Grant grabbed his hands and wrestled them behind his back.

"If you cannot afford an attorney," Ivory went on, "one will be appointed to you." As Grant snapped the handcuffs on him, she ended, "Do you understand these rights as they've been read to you?"

His head flailed around and something akin to a jumbled roar escaped his lips.

"Mr. Palmer," Ivory repeated, "do you understand these rights?"

Grant dropped the arrest warrant on the secretary's desk. Then he clasped his hand around the metal that joined the handcuffs together and led Vincent Palmer down the winding, broad staircase, past the stunned onlookers and into the bright sunshine.

40

Jessie stood at the rear bedroom window in Nick's apartment. The grounds stretched only thirty feet or so from the edge of the building before they gave way to a row of hedges that separated the apartment dwellers from a neighborhood behind them. And now as she pulled back the sheers to peer outside, she could easily look down upon Nick in a neighbor's yard as Abby played in the safety provided by a chain link fence.

Jessie had met the neighbor months before; he was perhaps eighty years old and widowed. He'd called out to them as they'd walked Abby past his house. He explained that once he'd owned a small dog, but like his wife, it had passed away, and he enjoyed watching the neighbors walk their own dogs past his home now. When they'd reached Nick's apartment, he'd remembered the gentleman and wondered if he would allow him to let Abby frolic in his back yard until they'd made other arrangements.

As she watched them, Nick glanced up at the bedroom window, grinned and half-waved. That was the answer, Jessie thought. The tall hedges that bordered the chain link fence in the neighbor's yard would shield Abby from view; but her father would have to drive down a side street, anyway, to spot the dog, since he wouldn't have the vantage point she had now.

The thought of her father made her chest feel as if someone was sitting on it, and she watched Abby without the joy she thought she would have. After a couple of minutes, she left the window and showered.

She'd just finished getting dressed when she heard the key in the door. As she started down the hallway, she could sense Abby bounding inside even before she heard her claws clacking on the hardwood floor.

"Jess?"

At the sound of Nick's voice, her heart skipped a beat. But before she reached the living room, she stopped cold. Another man's voice wafted down the hall; it was too low for her to decipher the words. Then a woman's voice chimed in.

"Jessie?" Nick called again. He stepped into the hall and their eyes met. His smile turned to concern and then to relief. "It's okay, Jess. It's Agents Bailey and Lang."

She sighed. "Whew," she said as she continued down the hall toward him.

He wrapped his arm around her shoulder as she neared, steering her into the living room. "They were just getting out of their car when Abby and I came around the building."

Before she could respond, Grant said, "I see you got your dog back."

Nick squeezed her shoulder. "Yes," Jessie said. She felt a lump in her throat like a child caught in the act. "My father wasn't home—we made sure of that."

"Did your mother know you were taking her?"

"Yes. Why? Is that a problem?"

"Nope," Grant said, moving toward the sofa in the living room. "Just wanted to plan my response if she called."

Grant sat on the sofa while Ivory moved to a hardback chair perpendicular to it.

"Have a seat," Nick said.

Jessie flashed a sideways glance at him and stifled a smile.

"We have some news for you," Grant said.

At the serious tone in his voice, she felt the all-too-familiar tightness in her chest again, and she made her way to one of the bar stools at the counter separating the kitchen from the living area.

Grant waited for her to sit before continuing, "We wanted you to hear this from us first."

"Hear what? Has something happened?"

Grant glanced at Nick.

Jessie could feel Nick moving closer to her but she didn't dare take her eyes off Grant. Nick picked up one of her hands and held it in his as they waited for Grant to continue.

"We arrested your father a short time ago."

Jessie felt as though she'd been kicked in the gut. All of her breath seemed to leave her, and she felt suddenly light-headed. The room almost appeared to tilt as she continued staring at Grant. She could feel everyone's eyes on her as if they were laser pointers, and her cheeks felt flush and hot.

"You okay?" Nick said. He reached around her and retrieved a half-empty bottle of water from the counter. "Here," he said, handing it to her.

"I'm okay," she managed to say, though she took the water and easily downed half the remaining contents.

"He's been charged with your kidnapping," Grant continued. His voice was slow and deliberate, as if he was carefully selecting each of his words.

"So," she said at last, "you got the evidence you were looking for?" Her voice sounded hushed and small, and she cleared her throat self-consciously.

"Jessie, your dad had a safe deposit box at his bank. We had it drilled, and—" he hesitated as his eyes locked onto hers "—and we found half the ransom money."

She gasped. "How—how did you know—?"

"We're going on the assumption that your dad wouldn't have had another two-point-five million that was totally unrelated to your kidnapping, or that he'd put it in a safe deposit box instead of an account."

"But, when—?"

"The morning after you were abducted. Hours after the ransom was paid."

Jessie was silent. She could hear their breathing now. Even Abby, who had lain dutifully on the rug when they'd all been seated, seemed to feel the tenseness in the air. She sat up and whimpered as she peered at her mistress.

"That's only half the ransom," she said at last.

"Yes," Ivory said. "We're going to be interrogating your father. We're still trying to develop leads on the other men."

"We think maybe the deal was for your father to get half, and the two men who kept you at the cabin would split the rest of it."

"But now one of them is dead."

"Which probably means the one you called 'Brainiac' took the rest," Grant finished. "Jessie," he said after a long pause, "I want you to understand that you're our star witness."

She felt her spine stiffen and the blood drain from her face. "I—I'll have to testify against him at the trial?" Her heart began beating wildly as her thoughts spun out of control. "There's going to be a trial, isn't there? He's not just going to be locked up?"

Nick squeezed her hand harder.

"It's not going to happen today," Grant said, his voice calm. "Or tomorrow, or next week. It won't happen for months, most likely."

"Months."

"If he confesses and pleads guilty, there will be no need for you to testify."

"And if he doesn't..." Her voice faded and she looked at Grant pleadingly.

"If he doesn't, we're going to need your testimony." His throat sounded dry now as he continued, "We're going to need you to testify about what you heard when you were bound up in the cabin. What you heard in the cellar. And how you found the glove, and how you knew it was his."

"Your star witness," she said as if in a fog.

"All you'll need to do is tell the truth."

They fell silent once again. And once again, Jessie felt their eyes on her. The weight of their stares felt stronger than someone's palms bearing down on her shoulders. "If I don't testify for months," she said, "will he be kept locked up until then?"

Grant's expression did not change as he continued to stare at her. A long time passed before he answered; so long that Jessie was tempted to repeat her question.

"I don't know," he said at last. "We're going to ask the judge to keep him incarcerated."

"But he could be let out on bail," Ivory interjected.

Jessie nodded.

"Do you feel like you'll be in danger if he's out on bail?" Grant asked.

Jessie laughed. It was a forced laugh, one that startled even her. "He had me kidnapped," she said. "What do you think?"

Grant nodded. "I understand," he said finally. His eyes met Nick's. "Jessie, what do you think about staying here until the trial? Or do you want to go back to your place? Or to your mother's?"

"Going to my mother's house is not an option," she said quickly. "It's my father's house, too. And there's no way I'd be caught dead under the same roof as him." She paused as she realized her choice of words. She glanced across the room at the window that pointed in the direction of her condominium. "And I don't want to go back to my place. I—I don't think I could."

Nick squeezed her hand once more, and wrapped his free arm around her. "She can stay here as long as she wants," he said.

"Thank you," Jessie said, choking back a sob that wanted to rise in her throat. "I'll stay here."

Grant nodded and rose to his feet. "It's going to take a few hours before your father goes before the magistrate. If you're going back to your place to pick up any of your things, I'd suggest you do it now."

Ivory joined him and they walked to the front door. Like a sleepwalker, Jessie slid off the bar stool and accompanied them to the door.

"Just one more thing," Grant said, his hand on the door knob. "The media is going to try and turn this into a circus. I'm not advising you to hide, but…" He stopped and looked at her. His eyes were sad, she thought; sad and troubled.

"I understand."

He opened the door and Ivory stepped into the hallway. He started to follow her and then stopped. He turned back around to face Jessie. Nick had joined them and had his arm wrapped around her once more.

"Jessie," Grant said, "Do you happen to know someone named Susan Jones?"

"Susan Jones," she said, studying the floor for a moment. Then she looked back at Grant. "No. Why? Should I?"

"No particular reason," Grant said. He leaned forward and, grasping the door knob once more, pulled the door closed behind him.

41

Grant slowed the car as he neared Governor's Lane. As he turned into Richland Country Club Estates, he couldn't help but notice the contrast between the sleepy, rural road and the upscale neighborhood. He noted the wide border of dark red brick lining both sides of the street, and how it also appeared horizontally roughly every fifty feet.

He drove the FBI vehicle under Victorian style lamps that no doubt kept the neighborhood brightly lit and safe, and across a small bridge that contained pedestrian walks in both directions. From the bridge's height, they could look down upon a clubhouse with windows more than two stories tall; some of them overlooking tennis courts, which were empty and stark this time of year, while others kept watch over two separate swimming pools, now covered in light gray tarps.

"You know," Ivory said, breaking the silence, "I used to work out here."

"Out here?"

"Yeah, but it wasn't a country club back then." She chuckled. "Far from it. I worked summers while I was in college at a nursery—"

"The old Richland Nursery!" Grant interjected. "I remember it now. They used to have the best honey around."

"Never got their honey," Ivory said, "but since I got an employee's discount, my mother landscaped her whole yard during my college years."

"How times change," Grant murmured as they approached a guard station. He slowed in front of a wrought iron gate with elaborate scrollwork and the letter "R" emblazoned in the middle. As a young man stepped out of the guard house, Grant reached inside his jacket and retrieved his identification.

No matter how long he'd been with the FBI, he had to admit he enjoyed the expression on a person's face when they saw his badge. The guard was no exception. His face was so smooth, Grant wondered if he was even shaving yet. Had to be about twenty years old, he thought. He was clean cut with dark hair barely visible under a starched cap. His uniform was impeccable, the stitching tailored as though he was a Marine guard. He even wore gloves, Grant noted. He was tempted to look over the side of the door to see if he was wearing patent leather shoes, but thought better of it.

"Yes, sir," the young man said as he stared at the identification. "What can I do for you, sir?"

"We're here on official business," Grant said. He waved his finger toward the closed gate.

"Did you need Management, sir?"

"No. We're visiting one of your residents."

The young man hesitated. He glanced into the empty back seat before his eyes peered past Grant at Ivory. She held her badge so he could see it. Then his eyes wandered to the menagerie of radio equipment and electronics mounted in the dash.

"Official business, sir?"

"That's what I said."

The man stepped back, reached inside the guard house and pressed a button. The gates opened without a sound, the wrought iron gliding backward as smoothly as a butterfly opening its wings.

Once they were past the gate, Ivory leaned back in her seat. "You could have told him who we were here to see, you know."

"Could have. But didn't." When she didn't respond, he added, "I like the element of surprise." He glanced at the GPS, noting their present location and Susan Jones' home as they entered a circle that wound around a massive fourteen foot tall fountain. It was as white as alabaster and rose majestically like the type of statues he'd seen in Venice on his honeymoon. At the thought of that time in his life, he felt a knot growing in his stomach.

"You know," Ivory said as they continued to the other side of the circle, "I took the liberty of checking out this development online."

"Why am I not surprised?"

"Small lots. Made for people presumably too busy to do their own yard work. Want to know what home prices start at?"

"You're gonna tell me anyway, right?"

She rolled her eyes. "Over a million. Heck, the monthly community fee is almost five hundred. Can you imagine?"

"Nope," Grant said as he turned onto a side street, "I can't."

"Life as the other side lives it," she mused. "Oh, and online—get this—the first one hundred bricks in that statue back there were shipped from the Middle East."

"Why?"

"I don't know. Maybe they have a ribbon of gold in them," she quipped.

"Or oil."

"Anyway, those first hundred bricks have the names of the first one hundred owners permanently engraved in them. Guess who one of them was?"

"Susan Jones?"

"Vincent Palmer the third." She raised her chin. "I kid you not."

The road meandered past an expansive golf course. Even in the middle of winter, the grass was green and as pristine as a freshly vacuumed carpet. Wonder how they manage that, he thought.

"Twelve hundred dollars a month for club membership," Ivory continued.

"What are you, an encyclopedia?"

"Just doing my job."

The road continued around to the clubhouse they'd spotted from the bridge. It appeared even larger as they neared it, its colossal walls casting them in shadows as they drove past. It was the type of building, Grant thought, which could totally intimidate a kid approaching it for the first time.

"That has to be over a hundred thousand square feet," he mused as they continued past it. When Ivory didn't answer, he glanced at her. "You're not going to tell me exact specs?"

"I could live here," Ivory said, ignoring his comment.

He whistled. "Not on our salary, you couldn't… Maybe you need to find a rich sugar daddy."

"Maybe you," she said, poking him in the side, "need to find a sugar momma."

"You know," Grant said, growing serious, "I've always been told you can marry in fifteen minutes more money than you can make in a lifetime."

"That so? Well, I've always heard the hardest money you'll ever earn is marrying a rich man."

"Guess we'll never know."

"How far is this place, anyway?" Ivory asked, leaning toward the GPS.

Grant was forced to slow to ten miles an hour as they travelled on a road that curved around immense, centuries-old trees. Their thick branches stretched above their vehicle like giant tentacles ready to snatch them. Soon the golf course and clubhouse were behind them. They drove three quarters around another circle before exiting on a narrower road that led across a covered bridge over a bubbling brook.

Here, the homes were stately, two-story structures with copper roofs and matching mail boxes set along extra wide sidewalks constructed entirely of brick. The road widened to allow for street parking, but there wasn't a car in sight.

"Where are all the cars?" Ivory asked. Her voice was as hushed as if she'd just entered a church sanctuary.

"In back," Grant said. He motioned between two homes. "There's an alley that runs behind them, leading to all the garages."

"That's it," she said, pointing to a brown brick home.

"How can you tell?" Grant asked. "They all look alike." Then before she could answer, he pulled to the curb and said, "I know, I know. The mail box."

As they exited the car, he couldn't help but notice the silence in the air. It was almost as though he'd entered a ghost town. As they strode along the brick walkway leading up to the house, he felt as though every window in the home and those surrounding it had turned into eyes that followed them.

He stepped onto the tiny front porch. Out of sight of the road, it contained a cozy rattan loveseat with a pale yellow print. He glanced inside an unencumbered window alongside the door to a vast hallway with shiny hardwood floors and a curved banister.

He rang the doorbell and waited for someone to appear in the hallway. A moment passed and then another.

Ivory reached past him and rang it a second time.

A lone bird took flight from a tree in the front yard, its loud caw breaking the silence of the neighborhood.

He tried the doorknob but it was locked.

"Stay here," Grant said. "I'm going to take a look around."

Ivory nodded and took his place at the door. As Grant made his way down the steps, he glanced back to see her staring into the front hallway.

The house was erected on a tall crawl space that made the ground floor windows almost too high to see within, but he found a few bricks left along the side that he used as an uneven step. They boosted him high enough to peer inside a formal living room with a baby grand piano. The dark, ornately carved furniture appeared to be antiques.

The dining room contained a table with at least ten chairs around it, he thought as he hopped up to glance inside. As he neared the ground again, he caught a glimpse of the extra high ceiling and a multi-faceted chandelier that looked to be almost six feet in circumference.

All the rooms were dark, the lights off. As he neared the back, the curtains were drawn. The wind whistled as it made its way down the alley.

He reached the opposite side of the house and nearly bumped into a buxom woman, her arms crossed in front of her. He was so astonished to see a person in the quiet neighborhood that he almost flinched at the sight of her. From the suspicion in her narrowed eyes, it was clear that she'd been watching him.

"I'm calling Security," she said, eyeing him from top to bottom.

He halted in his tracks, his hand moving automatically to his inside jacket pocket. "FBI," he said, displaying his credentials.

She leaned forward to compare his picture with his current appearance. He was tempted to comb his hair or at least run his hand across it, but he didn't. He forced himself to remain expressionless.

"I'm looking for Susan Jones," he said in his most authoritative voice. "Have you seen her?"

The woman turned and headed back toward the front of the house. She walked with a slight limp; judging from her movements, Grant thought she might have had a knee or hip injury.

"She's not here," she called over her shoulder.

As they neared the front corner, Ivory appeared at the edge of the porch.

"I can see that," Grant said, his eyes meeting Ivory's.

"Do you know when she might be back?" Ivory said, managing a slight smile.

The woman did not return it. She eyed Ivory for a brief moment before answering. "You FBI, too?"

Ivory responded by leaning over the porch railing to display her ID.

"What do you want her for?" the woman asked.

"That's none of—" Grant began.

"We just need to speak with her," Ivory interrupted. "She's not done anything wrong."

The woman sniffed. "I imagine she hasn't."

Grant's eyes met Ivory's again. He wondered if his own brows were furrowed like hers.

"What do you mean?" Ivory asked.

"Susan's the salt of the earth," the woman answered. She swayed as though being on her feet was bothering her. "Never did a bad thing to nobody. Sometimes, you have to wonder what God's plan is."

She continued to walk around the front of the house.

Grant followed. Now, he knew his brow was furrowed and as he glanced at Ivory, she was mouthing something he couldn't quite decipher.

The woman stopped abruptly and looked back at them. "Susan Jones is in Houston."

"Houston," Grant repeated.

"M.D. Anderson Cancer Center."

"What—?"

"She's got stomach cancer. She's undergoing experimental treatment. Something from Germany." She began to waddle again as she moved toward the sidewalk. "It's her last hope. I can't tell you for sure if she'll ever be back."

42

Jessie watched the second hand on the oversized wall clock. It was just after two and it already felt as though it should be midnight. She flipped the television stations with the remote. "Two hundred stations and nothing to watch," she said.

Nick stirred a mixture of berries in a bowl as he wandered around the counter and approached Jessie. "Here," he said, holding up a serving spoon filled with his latest concoction, "try this."

She dutifully tasted the blueberries, blackberries, and something similar to store-bought, ready-made vanilla pudding. "Yum," she said, managing a smile.

"Too sweet?"

"No. Just right." She leaned her head against the back of the couch and flipped off the television. "I've got to get out of here."

He sat on the edge of the coffee table and tasted his newest recipe. "Too sweet," he said.

"I've got cabin fever."

"Jess, it's not safe—"

"You heard what the FBI agents said. My father will be held for at least a few hours—at least. Come on. Let's get out of here. Get some sunshine."

At the sound of her owner's animated voice, Abby looked up from the rug beside the window and perked up her ears.

"Okay," Nick said, trudging back to the kitchen and pulling out some plastic wrap. "Where you want to go? The park? For a stroll?"

When Jessie didn't answer, he looked up.

"How about," she said, managing a mischievous grin, "we take a little drive?"

"Yeah? Where to?"

She hesitated before replying, "To the cabin."

"The cabin," Nick repeated. Then he stopped securing the plastic wrap over the bowl. "Not *the* cabin?"

She nodded.

He finished with the bowl and placed it into the refrigerator. When he turned back around, he was frowning. He placed both palms on the counter and stared at her. "Why on earth would you want to go there?"

Her grin faded. When she spoke, her voice was low and serious. "I know it sounds nuts—"

"You got that right."

She rose from the couch and walked toward him. When she reached the counter on the opposite side, she stopped and peered into his eyes. "I need to see it again."

"Why?"

She picked up a cashew from a snack bowl, looked at it, and then put it back down. "I don't know. It's something I just have to do."

"Why, Jessie?" His tone was insistent.

"If I don't go now," she said, her words coming out slow and measured, "I'm always going to have this memory of that room, of what happened there…"

"That's why it's not a good idea to go," Nick said. "The memory needs to fade, Jess, not get more vivid."

"You know, my mother's mother, my grandmother, lived in this house in Spring Hill. And I remember it sat up on a hill and it had this huge porch. In the summer evenings, they liked to sit out on that porch in rockers and watch the traffic go by. Wasn't much traffic," she laughed, "maybe a car every few hours. But I remember that porch so clearly. And I remember those tall, concrete steps coming up from the road, and those monstrously large urns that always contained plastic flowers…"

Nick listened dutifully, his eyes never wavering from hers.

"She died and the house was sold, and years went by. There I was, living just a few miles south of Spring Hill and going to school a few miles north of Spring Hill—and I just never took that turn and went down that road. Until, about a year ago. I don't know what prompted me to do it. When I saw the house, I just had to stop in the road and stare at it. It wasn't on top of a big hill. It was four steps above the road. *Four steps.*" She cocked her head as if disbelieving her own words. "The new owners had three rockers on the front porch. They were jammed in so tight, I doubt if they could've rocked in them. This incredibly large front porch that had always intimidated me—it was barely four feet deep and maybe a dozen feet long."

Nick smiled. "They still have plastic flowers in the urns?"

Jessie laughed and shook her head. "Those urns were about eight inches in diameter. They were still there, kind of cocked because of the concrete shifting and cracking—but they were empty."

He joined in her laughter but a moment later they both grew silent.

"Don't you see," Jessie said, her voice hushed now, "I have to see that cabin. I have to see it in the light of day. I have to know there's nothing there to give me nightmares the rest of my life."

He looked at her, his brows furrowed and his eyes dark, but he reached to the other end of the counter and grabbed his car keys. "What are we waiting for?"

By the time they pulled off the interstate and Jessie caught a glimpse of the ancient Gulf Oil sign rusting in front of a deserted service station, her stomach felt like it was full of rocks.

"Maybe this wasn't such a good idea," she said.

Nick gave her a sideways glance. "You having second thoughts?"

She stared straight ahead. There was the restaurant with the lights half out, and the neon signs. They'd seemed so much brighter and garish in the pitch darkness. Now they just appeared cheap. "No," she said finally.

"We can turn around any time you're ready."

She nodded her head slightly. "I know." He moved his right hand from the steering wheel to her lap, and she grasped it in both of hers. "I know," she repeated.

If she closed her eyes, she could feel the curve in the road and she could almost envision herself tied up in the back of the truck, tumbling as the vehicle took the turns. She looked for the area where she'd forced them off the road, but she never saw it. It was as if the overgrown brush had already enveloped it, as though it had never happened…

She felt her breath becoming shallow and beads of perspiration broke out across her forehead. Abby whimpered a couple of times as she spotted cows or horses in nearby pastures, and the car began to shake with the weight of her body moving from one side window to the other in an effort to spot all of the livestock. Nick was quiet, though he occasionally squeezed her hand and glanced at her with a smile that was meant to reassure her.

When, at last they stopped at a driveway, it seemed as if they were all frozen in time.

"This is it," Nick said, his voice betraying his nervousness. "You sure you want to do this?"

She nodded. "But—are you positive this is it?"

"This is my first time here, Jess," Nick said, the obviousness of his statement causing them both to laugh uneasily. "You want me to keep driving?"

"No. No, let's turn in."

He turned off the road and began the sluggish journey down a poorly maintained drive. It wasn't long before Jessie spotted yellow crime scene tape through the trees. "This is it," she stated the obvious. Her voice almost cracked as she spoke and she felt her chest begin to heave with the fight to catch her breath.

"I'd know the sound of tires anywhere," she said finally. "I was inside the cabin and I heard them coming and going…"

She rolled down the window and peered outside. "They're pine cones," she said with a touch of awe in her voice. "We're driving on old pine cones." She managed a little bit of a laugh but it sounded forced. "I thought it was gravel."

Nick stopped briefly at a gate. As he exited the car to walk around it and open the rusting, sagging livestock gate, Jessie felt winded, almost as though she'd just run a marathon. He didn't bother to close it once they'd driven past it, and she almost felt defiant as she looked in her side mirror at it growing smaller behind them.

Nick stopped the car a few yards from the cabin. The winter sun found it easily; though it was nestled amid groves of trees, most of those closest to it were oak and had lost their leaves. The branches hung like ancient, craggy fingers, almost touching one another in their effort to shelter the small structure. A family of squirrels raced from one tree to the next, sometimes flying through the air to land on a distant branch. Without a glance in their direction, they continued upward to nests that swayed in a gentle winter breeze.

The sun's muted rays stretched across the metal roof and Jessie stared at it for a long time.

"You okay?" Nick asked.

She nodded. She was in no hurry to get out and he didn't push her. He turned off the engine and they sat there silently, listening to an occasional bird. Somewhere in the distance, a dog howled and Abby pricked her ears and stuck her head between Jessie's neck and the front window.

The fireplace jutted upward from the center of the cabin. There was no smoke emanating from it, but with her window rolled down, she could smell the sweet odor of burning wood as if she was snuggled up next to a cozy fire that kept the winter chill at bay. Her eyes moved slowly to the front porch.

As if he was watching her, Nick said, "It's small."

"Yes," she whispered. "It is."

She studied the precarious tilt to it and her eyes automatically sought the underpinnings. They were shifted in the soft dirt, the wood stilts supported with chunks of concrete, but neither of them capable of holding up the porch for much longer.

Quietly, she opened her door and stepped shakily outside the car.

She didn't remember Nick opening his own door or coming around to stand beside her. She didn't remember Abby tumbling out of the back seat and running around the cabin as if she'd just found a new play yard. She just knew that with the next blink of her eyes, she was there—standing on the edge of the porch, looking upward at the rotting wood, at the crooked doorframe, at the grimy window, and wondering why this had happened to her.

The cabin was one room, just as she'd remembered it. It was smaller, though; so tiny, she wondered how her father could ever have remained there during his hunting trips. But as she looked around her at the moldy couch, the grimy bathroom sink and toilet filled with more muck than water, she realized he had never stayed there. She yearned to know who built it; whether a Palmer somewhere, generations back, before the bank, before the wealth, had built this little place and called it home. And she wondered how it had become so decrepit. She felt anger growing inside her—at Brutus, at Brainiac, at her own father. She forced herself to look at the walls, to memorize how structurally unsound they were, how the flooring was so flimsy the entire cabin seemed to shake with their footsteps. She forced herself to memorize the wood stove in the center of the room, the chain that held her now gone.

Nick stood just inside the doorway. He reached inside and flipped a switch and a lone light bulb sputtered on. She stood beneath it, looking at the dark ceiling above it; how it swayed in a lone breeze that found its way into the little cabin.

"I'm done," she said finally.

She felt exhausted, as if every ounce of blood had been drained from her.

Nick stepped aside as she wandered back onto the porch. She stood where a railing might have been, had the porch been finished off, and gazed at the ground. There was a drop of only six inches or so from the wood to the ground, not enough to warrant steps. But further down, her eyes found the crumbling, crooked steps on which Brainiac struggled to transport her from the cabin to the truck on that last fateful night. They were hand-made, she thought.

As she stared into the dirt, her eyes came to rest on two wooden matches, each snapped in the center, their heads black. "He'd stand out here," she said, "and smoke."

Nick's lips moved as if he'd planned to respond, but thought better of it. He bent down and picked one up and held it in the waning light. "Fire Chief," he said with a slight, awkward grin.

She placed her hand on his and pulled it closer to her so she could see the words emblazoned on the wood match. She'd seen those types of matches so many times before. How many times she'd attended the events at Vanderbilt University's Blackacre courtyard, watching students and faculty alike lighting cigarettes and pipes with those Fire Chief matches.

She wondered if she'd ever be able to see them again without thinking about this place and what happened here.

She nodded silently to Nick and he released the match into her hand as he stepped back to the door, reached in and turned off the light. He closed the door, and for the first time, Jessie realized it didn't even lock.

Like a sleepwalker, she climbed down from the porch and walked back to the car. Nick whistled for Abby and opened the passenger side door.

Jessie stood for a long moment, watching the cabin's windows almost as though she expected a face to appear on the other side of them. Someday, she thought as Abby bounded back to the car, jumped in and settled into the back seat, someday I will return here. And I'll burn this place to the ground.

She didn't realize until the driveway gate was closed behind her and they'd turned onto the road leading back to the highway and back to civilization, that she still held the spent match in the palm of her hand.

43

The grounds of the courthouse had turned into a media circus, Grant thought as he maneuvered his way toward a side door. He recognized every major news outlet in the country, marveling at the high-profile television hosts who had dropped everything to fly to Nashville for Vincent Palmer's appearance before the magistrate. On the courthouse steps, a collection of microphones were set up and as Grant passed by the side of the impromptu stage, he heard Vincent's attorney, Dalton Mitchell, proclaiming his client's innocence, already trying his case in the World Court of Opinion.

Grant kept his face tilted away from the stage. All he needed was for Dalton to point him out to the media and he'd be hounded every waking moment. And that was the last thing he needed.

He reached the side door and slipped inside. The security staff had their hands full with people not authorized to enter the courthouse through this particular entrance, and Grant side-stepped several reporters trying vigorously to convince Security that they should be allowed to pass. He pulled out his FBI badge and prepared to display it as he approached the x-ray machine, but the security guard recognized him and waved him onward.

He did, however, stop briefly and deposit his FBI-issued weapon on the conveyor belt before stepping through the x-ray. He stopped on the other side and retrieved it, placing it back in his holster before proceeding.

He had hoped the halls would be quieter and Vincent Palmer's appearance would be low-key, but he should have realized that nothing Vincent ever did was modest. Grant marveled at the resources in evidence throughout the building, causing his own movements to slow to a crawl.

At his first opportunity, he ducked into the hallway that ran behind the courtrooms, an area normally off-limits to everyone except law enforcement and court staff. Through a network of back staircases and secure hallways, he eventually found himself at the magistrate's courtroom.

He passed it, walking down the hallway that would be used to bring Vincent before the magistrate. He was surprised to find that he was already there in a suit and tie, his hands not cuffed but under the watchful eyes of the U.S. Marshall.

Grant caught the Marshall's eye just as Dalton burst into the area, out of breath from running the media gauntlet. As soon as Vincent saw Dalton, his face, already red with anger, became almost purple.

Grant stopped his progress and stood back, out of earshot. It was a thin line that law enforcement had to walk. If he came within earshot, he could be accused of trying to listen to a private conversation between the defendant and his attorney. He was forced to remain on the sidelines, waiting for an appropriate time to approach the Marshall about Vincent's incarceration.

Vincent talked non-stop. Several times, his voice rose to a level that caused others around him to look in their direction, their eyes wide. He punched the air several times, as if trying to drive his point home to Dalton. Once, he even jabbed his finger into Dalton's chest. As a Marshall moved forward, Dalton waved him back, indicating he was fine.

Vincent was clearly attempting to gain control of this situation, Grant thought as he watched him. He was a man accustomed to having people jump when he told them to, and he wasn't about to change his behavior in this unique set of circumstances.

In contrast, Dalton's face appeared almost immobile. He nodded as though in agreement, but he remained impassive and reserved.

"I feel like I'm at the O.J. trial," Ivory whispered.

Grant almost jumped at the sound of her voice. "Where'd you come from?"

She ignored his question. "I hope he acts like that in the courtroom," she said, nodding her head slightly in Vincent's direction. "That'll go over well with the judge."

Grant tried to chuckle, but he couldn't shake a growing concern. Here was a man who had bended the rules his entire life and gotten away with it. And for the first time, he began to realize just how important it was going to be to help the prosecutor present an iron-clad case against him.

They were called into the courtroom. It was hushed, the massive doors closing out the din of the media outside. There were no windows and the seating was limited. It wouldn't have to be large, Grant thought as he entered and stood near the prosecutor, unless Vincent had dozens of lawyers at work on this case. No spectators were allowed in, and deputies were posted at the doors to maintain order.

As the judge entered the room, everyone stood. Dalton kept a hand on Vincent's shoulder, and as Grant watched out of the corner of his eye, he wondered if he was attempting to maintain control over his client.

Then, they were instructed to be seated as the proceeding began.

The magistrate was a woman of mixed Cuban and African-American descent. Judge Isabella Strickland was known as "Judge Strict" for her humorless demeanor and exacting adherence to the rules. Her upbringing was the stuff of legends: her mother had fled Cuba, applying for citizenship and political asylum in the United States. She'd married but soon after Isabella's birth, they'd divorced. Her mother had raised Isabella on her own, working two and often three jobs, primarily as a cleaning woman.

Isabella had excelled in school, eventually winning scholarships to college and working full-time to earn enough to fill in the financial gaps, enabling her to get her law degree. She had a reputation for remaining close to her roots, showing personal disdain for ostentatious behavior. She was, Grant thought as he watched the proceedings, the perfect judge to come up against Vincent Palmer the Third.

Vincent turned slightly in his chair, peering over his shoulder at the others in attendance. Grant's eyes met his. He stared at him with unblinking eyes, narrowed, dark eyes that showed a total lack of fear. He hoped his own eyes were veiled, though every time he looked at Vincent, he wondered anew what despicable kind of human being could arrange to have his own daughter kidnapped.

He was probably wearing a three thousand dollar suit, Grant thought, judging from the impeccable fit. A custom suit, he thought as Vincent turned back to look at the judge. And, soon he'll be in a prisoner's uniform with a number emblazoned on the back.

The arrest warrant was read before the court. The prosecutor made an appeal to deny bail, but Dalton provided an impassioned argument for allowing Vincent to maintain his freedom while the trial was pending. The preliminary hearing was waived, and the judge fixed her eyes on Vincent as she rendered her decision.

"Mr. Palmer," she said in a voice that was deep and direct, "I'm setting your bail in the amount of five million dollars."

Grant felt his shoulders shift downward. A man like Vincent could easily satisfy that amount, he thought.

"Thank you, Judge," Dalton responded immediately.

"There are conditions," Judge Strickland continued. "Mr. Palmer," she said, shifting in her seat to look directly at Vincent, "you shall not violate any municipal, state, or federal laws or ordinances."

Grant moved his eyes slowly from the judge to the defense. There was no visible response from either Vincent or Dalton.

"Mr. Palmer," she continued, "you shall not have any direct or indirect contact with the victim."

The air seemed to shift as Vincent's face grew red.

"My God," Ivory whispered in Grant's ear, "his cheeks are puffing up like an adder."

Indeed, as Grant continued to stare at him, Vincent's face appeared to be swelling. Before the judge could continue, he snapped, "The victim is my daughter," he said venomously.

"Mr. Palmer—"

"No one on earth can keep me from seeing my only daughter!"

Judge Strickland rapped the gavel as Dalton whispered something to his client, placing his hand again on his shoulder and squeezing.

"Mr. Palmer," the judge repeated, "You will have no contact, direct or indirect, with your daughter, the victim, Jessica Palmer, as a direct condition of your bond. I do not need your consent. If you violate this term, I can and I will hold you without bond until your trial."

"My client agrees," Dalton said instantly. Grant noticed his hand had become so tight on Vincent's shoulder that his suit was becoming wrinkled.

"Furthermore," Judge Strickland continued, "you shall not consume any alcoholic beverages or use any illegal, controlled substances." She paused for effect, but neither Vincent nor Dalton responded.

"You have twenty-four hours in which to surrender your passport to the court."

Vincent's brows furrowed and he stared at Dalton, as if silently ordering him to contest the restrictions.

"And," Judge Strickland was saying, "you shall not travel or attempt to travel outside the state of Tennessee for any reason whatsoever."

"Ludicrous!" Vincent thundered.

Judge Strickland again used her gavel in an attempt to maintain proper decorum, but Vincent had become so furious that he was spitting in his attorney's face as he argued with him.

"Mr. Mitchell," the judge said, "Mr. Mitchell, please maintain control of your client or I will find him in contempt of court."

"My job requires travel!" Vincent boomed. "You can't force me to stay here!"

"Mr. Palmer," she continued, her gavel hitting the bench with greater frequency and velocity, "This court has the authority to stipulate the terms and conditions of your release pending trial. If you do not adhere to these conditions, you will remain in jail."

Dalton was speaking in a rapid whisper; his face coming so close to Vincent's that a Marshall stepped forward in the event of an altercation. Vincent backed away, but he brushed an imaginary speck of dust from where Dalton's hand had remained on his shoulder, and turned back to face the judge. His lips were moving now as though he was chewing on the inside of his mouth.

"You shall not travel or attempt to travel outside the state of Tennessee," Judge Strickland repeated. "For any reason," she added emphatically. "Do you understand this is a court order, Mr. Palmer?"

"My client understands," Dalton responded immediately.

Judge Strickland continued to stare at Vincent as if she was waiting for his direct response, but he continued standing silently as he faced the bench.

After a long pause, she continued, "If you violate these terms, you will be in direct violation of the bond conditions and you will be incarcerated until your trial. Do you understand?"

"My client understands," Dalton responded.

"Mr. Palmer," she said, staring directly at the defendant, "Do you understand?"

"No," he said with such disgust that Grant jerked his head back toward the bench.

Judge Strickland stared at him in disbelief. Dalton was again speaking in a rapid whisper, the tone getting louder and more insistent. Vincent's eyes narrowed as he glared in defiance at the judge. She banged the gavel. "Order in the court," she said. "Order in the court!"

When Dalton stopped speaking and all eyes were again on the judge, she glared back at Vincent Palmer from the height of the bench. "Mr. Palmer," she said at last, "your total lack of respect for this court leaves me no choice. Your bail is hereby rescinded. You will remain incarcerated pending your trial."

Vincent lunged over the heavy table that separated the defense from the bench. The courtroom inhaled in a collective gasp as the bailiffs sprung forward to stop him. Judge Strickland banged her gavel once more. As Vincent Palmer was hand-cuffed and led shouting and struggling against his bonds through the side door, the judge exited quietly through another.

44

J essie opened her eyes for the umpteenth time. The bedroom was bathed in shades of wisteria blue that transcended from deep blue to shades of purple, as though watercolors had been brushed over the room. Her eyes went immediately to Abby, who lay on her back in her dog bed by the window. She smiled sleepily as she studied her back legs sticking straight up in the air while her forelegs were thrown over her head in abandon.

She wished she could sleep with as much peace as Abby, but as her eyes roamed around the bedroom, they came to rest on the clock on the nightstand. It was already past two in the morning, and it was to be a big day. A good night's sleep was more important than ever, but she'd been tossing and turning about as restlessly as she would if she'd tried to bed down on an ant hill.

She turned onto her back and studied the ceiling fan as the blades rotated rhythmically above her. She looked toward the door, which was open part-way, revealing the source of the strange colors in the room: Nick was right down the hall with the television set still on, though she suspected he'd long ago succumbed to sleep in the recliner.

She rolled onto one side and then the other until she drifted into an uneasy slumber.

She was ten years old and sitting at the breakfast table, watching her father prepare pancakes for her. He always rose early while her mother slept. She often would wander down the stairs to find him at the table, finishing a cup of coffee while he poured over every word in *The Wall Street Journal.* He would smile, kiss her on the forehead, and inevitably mention that she was a sleepyhead or lazy because she'd slept until six thirty, her usual time to awaken. She'd sit on his lap, still trying to fully wake up for a few minutes before he would set her down in her own chair and begin to cook her breakfast.

Today it was chocolate chip pancakes, and not just any pancakes but Mickey Mouse pancakes. He poured two small circles of batter into the pan and before they were fully cooked on one side, he dropped chocolate chips below them to make the eyes and a smile. Then a larger circle of batter was poured beneath the first two, making the original two circles into ears. A moment later, he flipped all three together with an expert twist of his wrist. Sometimes the smiles would come out just right and sometimes they would be lopsided or comical, but to Jessie, they were always perfect.

"Eat your breakfast, Shadow," he said as he slid the plate in front of her. At the mention of the nickname, Jessie almost felt as if she was awakening, but she slipped into that realm between sleep and wakefulness, remembering with a twinge and a sinking heart how he had always called her "Shadow" because she was always one step behind him, following him everywhere.

"I'm taking off work early this afternoon," Vincent was saying in the dream. "How about if I pick you up from school and we go play tennis at the country club?"

She smiled as she ate her Mickey Mouse pancake, her anticipation of the afternoon with her father causing her eyes to glow. But when she looked up, her father was gone and she was standing alone on the street between Vanderbilt and her condo. She turned and looked behind her as Nick faded into the darkness.

She called out to him, begging him to return and walk her home, but he disappeared in a fog that materialized out of nowhere. It swept outward and upward like smoke from an explosion, but when it engulfed her, it was white and as odorless as a cloud. She batted at it and through it, until her fingers were bloodied.

As she stared at her hands, the fog lifted and she was sitting on a moldy couch in a dark cabin. The chill in the air caused her to tremble and shake, and she realized the fog had been the smoke from the wood-burning stove in the center of the cabin. The embers were dying back now, but the purplish glow continued to linger like phantoms sweeping outward from the corners of the room, undulating as they sped toward her.

She tried to scream, but her mouth was covered. Now a mask obstructed most of her sight and her hands were tied. She felt the duct tape squeezing her wrists together, could feel the pull of the tape on the fine hairs around her ankles. She could taste the dust in the air, dust from a decade of neglect, could smell the distinct odor of a pipe and cigarette smoke mingling with the burning embers.

She was trapped like an animal. The cabin was her cage. Brainiac was her master, and he was coming back to torment her.

Then, it was Brutus who stood before her. And the conspicuous stench of ether filled the air as he leaned toward her, a cloth soaked with the offending liquid approaching her like Death itself.

Next Brainiac was behind Brutus, and now an axe was raised high above his head. It came down on Brutus' skull with a boom that echoed through the tiny cabin. Now the axe was embedded in Brutus' cracked skull and as he laid face-down in a pool of blood, writhing and moaning, Brainiac leaned toward her.

He laughed and then walked away from her. He stepped onto the front porch and lit a pipe, closing the door behind him.

Now, the room was bathed in light as Brutus rose to his knees and then his feet. She tried to scream but her voice was so muffled that it sounded barely louder than a whisper. Blood was running down his face, pouring over his shoulders, soaking his clothes. He raised his arms straight out in front of him. And with the axe still embedded in his skull, he came toward her, his hands seeking out her neck to strangle her.

Her scream was so loud and so intense that she awoke with a start. She was bathed in sweat, and the bedcovers were strewn violently around the bed. Before she could catch her breath, Nick was beside her, pulling her to him.

"Shhh," he was saying, "it's okay. It's just a bad dream. You're okay."

Abby began barking and pacing behind Nick and he turned to allow the dog to see her mistress. "It's okay," Nick repeated. "It's okay."

"It's *not* okay," Jessie sobbed. "It will never be okay."

He pulled her head against his chest. Despite his calm reassurances, she felt his own heart beating wildly. He rested his chin on top of her head and stroked her hair. She could feel him trying to catch his breath even as she fought to catch hers.

It had all been too real, she thought as she squeezed her eyes shut to keep the tears from streaming down her cheeks. But realizing her efforts were in vain, she released them with a strangled cry.

She didn't know how long she lay there in Nick's arms, but when the tears had been spent and she pulled away from him to wipe them away, Abby was laying attentively on the bed, her furry face wrinkled with concern, a whimper escaping her as she stared at her mistress. Nick's shirt was soaked, and she noticed for the first time, the bags under his eyes and the dark circles that told of his own sleeplessness.

He gently lowered her onto the bed and drew the sheet over her. With his body beside her, he came to rest on one elbow and watched her with his own face just above hers. With his free hand, he combed her bangs with his fingers, brushing them away from her perspiring forehead.

"It's no wonder you're having nightmares," he said quietly.

"What time is it?"

He glanced at the clock on the nightstand. "Just after four." She didn't respond, and he added after a long pause, "The trial will begin in just about five hours. You need to get some sleep."

"I can't," she said, her voice sounding small, "I'm afraid to close my eyes."

"I'll keep you safe," he said. "I won't leave you alone."

"How could he do it?" she asked.

His eyes appeared dark and weary, his mouth taut with tension. Finally, he said, "I don't know, Jess."

"He loved me," she said. "He *loved* me." At the sound of the anguish in her voice, she wondered if she was trying to convince Nick or herself.

"I'm sure he did," he whispered. He rested his head on the pillow next to her and closed his eyes. His fingers moved from her forehead to her cheek, where they brushed against her skin in a drowsy embrace.

A moment later, his breathing became rhythmic and measured. Sandwiched between Nick and Abby, she lay awake, staring at the ceiling, watching the purple hues turn to muted golden sunrays, and wondering how the man who had made her Mickey Mouse pancakes could have hired cold-blooded killers to steal her innocence away from her.

45

Jessie brushed the snow from her shoulder before removing her coat. It was nearing the end of February, and the first heavy snow of the season was bearing down on the Nashville area. The warnings to remain off the roads had gone unheeded by the throngs of spectators who had gathered around the courthouse for weeks, waiting for any glimpse of the famed banker or his daughter. As Jessie took her seat in the courtroom next to Nick, she marveled at the judge proceeding with the trial on such a hazardous day. But judging from the packed courtroom and the media circus outside, she quickly concluded that Judge High wanted to get this over with as expeditiously as possible.

Judge Harden High had been assigned the case. Known as Hang 'Em High for his no nonsense demeanor, he was the male equivalent to Judge Strict. He was nearing seventy years old and his conservative, by-the-book attitude was often a throw-back to the days when a man was only as good as his word, and criminals were punished with a heavy hand. During his prime, he'd towered over others. Now, although he was stooped, he was still a force to be reckoned with, often glaring with eagle eyes that demanded respect.

"Boy, this judge knew what he was doing, picking the smallest courtroom," Jessie whispered.

"Oh, yeah?" Nick asked as his eyes took in those in attendance.

"This way, he could limit the number of folks in here—"

"Yeah, I can't believe who's trying to get in here," Nick interjected, looking back at Jessie with wide eyes. "Can you believe all the national TV news stations are here? You'd have thought they were covering the White House."

Jessie shrugged. "Dad was on the Board of the Federal Reserve Bank of Atlanta for six years. Maybe that's it?"

"Come on, Jess, look around. It's way bigger than that. The Who's Who of TV is here."

"Ugh." Jessie tilted her head back and closed her eyes.

"I know what you're thinking—"

"That they want to see me as much as my father."

He reached for her hand and squeezed it. When he spoke, his voice was softer. "It'll all be over soon, Jess. You've been through the worst of it."

"I am mentally, emotionally and physically exhausted."

"When this is all over…"

"We'll what? Take a cruise and it will make things better?"

Nick was silent. After a long moment, Jessie leaned against his shoulder. "I'm sorry, Nick. I'm just getting punchy."

He nodded but wrapped his arm around her.

"Hey," she said, "See that little bald headed guy in the gray pinstriped suit?"

He followed her gaze to the defense table. "That pipsqueak?"

She giggled but grew serious immediately as she stared at the tiny man who, despite his lack of hair, appeared more like a middle school student than a renowned adult. "Yeah. One of my law professors told me that's Dr. Eric Wunderlook."

"You're kidding me. That little guy? He's the shrink from San Francisco that specializes in jury selection, right?"

"Yep. He's the one. His fee's more than a hundred grand."

"I heard he's got a ninety percent success rate."

Jessie glanced at her watch. They were early, and the judge had started each day right on the dot. Heavy security had been placed around the courthouse and getting into the courtroom itself required running a gauntlet of spectators and media outlets, all waiting for that split second glimpse of the defense and prosecution teams. Now, the room was filling up with people who spoke in hushed tones, but the rustling of paper and the settling of people was growing to a small din.

She watched as the lead defense attorney made her way into the courtroom. As it did each day when she watched her during the trial, Jessie's stomach began to tie in knots. Kristin Cook was in her forties and had already made a name for herself that was legendary. Though she was drop-dead gorgeous with a height of nearly six feet, straight auburn hair that reached past her shoulders, and a figure that rivaled any supermodel's, Jessie knew she wasn't selected for her beauty. She'd graduated at the top of her Harvard class and was clearly enjoying her status as one of the most successful defense attorneys in the country. Early in the trial, Jessie had turned on the news to see Kristin's face splashed across the screen while commentators spoke in wonderment of her almost flawless success rate and weekly fees of half a million plus expenses.

A man made his way into the courtroom. He stopped a few rows from Jessie and bent down to speak to some of the spectators in a hushed tone. His back remained to her, but there was something about him that made her uneasy. A faint scent of tobacco permeated his body.

"That's Ed Buchanan," Nick said, following her gaze.

"Oh." Jessie thought she was going to be sick.

"He's now Chairman of the Board."

"*Interim* Chairman of the Board," she corrected.

Ed placed his hand on the back of the seating in front of him with the ease of a man who felt as if the world was his oyster. Jessie placed a hand on her stomach, absent-mindedly rubbing it and trying to keep from getting sick.

"They had to do something," Nick said. "I mean, with your dad in jail awaiting trial…"

"Who? The Board of Directors?"

"Yeah."

"I know. They had no choice but to call a special election."

"If your dad is found not guilty, he'll be back as CEO."

"Tell me something I don't know."

After a moment, Ed left the courtroom. Though her eyes followed his movements, he never turned in her direction and she was left staring at his black wool coat with melting snow across the shoulders.

As she waited for the day's testimony to begin, one absence was glaring: her mother had chosen not to attend the trial. She'd spoken to Jessie about it in the briefest of terms: the media would have a field day with her. Whose side would she take? The husband that she'd married thirty years prior, to whom by all accounts she was totally devoted? Or her only child who had been viciously attacked and kidnapped, who was expected to testify against her own father? Best that she stay away entirely, providing her support quietly and privately. Not even their friends were welcome at the Palmer estate these days, as though Meg Palmer was in mourning.

The courtroom clamor rose in unison as the side door opened and Vincent Palmer was led inside by two bailiffs. His eyes wandered around the room until they came to rest on Jessie, as he'd done every day since the trial began. At the sight of him staring at her, she looked away. He took his place beside his defense team, and they began speaking in rapid, hushed tones.

The jury was led in next: six men and six women, plus five alternates. Most of them appeared to be working class, something that hadn't escaped Jessie. If Vincent Palmer was expecting a jury of his peers, he must have been quite disappointed—despite Dr. Eric Wunderlook's expert opinions.

"All rise," the bailiff stated in a firm tone.

As the courtroom rose, Judge High entered the room. Just the appearance of the stern man dressed in the harsh black gown intimidated Jessie. A man of few words, when he spoke, people listened.

"Be seated."

He struck the bench with his gavel. "This court is now in session."

As they had done each morning, the defense and prosecution entered motions. Most of them seemed trivial. If Jessie had not been personally involved, she might have been fascinated by the maneuverings, wondering whether the additional paperwork and tedious debates were worth it for an inch of ground gained here or there.

Now, the two teams were debating the admission of a lie detector test. Vincent wanted one and the defense team was eager for the court to allow it. The prosecution argued against it, citing the unreliability of the test and their inability to cross-examine. If Vincent wanted to tell his side of the story, he should take the stand.

In the end, however, the defense had chosen not to call Vincent to the stand, a move that Jessie understood perfectly. He was unaccustomed to being questioned, much less cross-examined. All it would take was for the prosecution to get him to lose his temper—which Jessie thought could happen very quickly—and Vincent would become his own worst enemy.

Judge High ruled against the admission of the lie detector test.

Jessie's eyes wandered to the jury. She tried to read their faces but they were all blank. Perfectly expressionless, she thought, as if they'd been hypnotized just before entering the room. She would have given anything to know what they thought thus far. The burden of proof was on the prosecution. As her eyes drifted to the prosecutors, she knew they had to prove that her father was guilty beyond any reasonable doubt.

They had already presented evidence that Vincent had intentionally disturbed the crime scene. But, the defense had argued that he'd been so upset about the kidnapping, he didn't know what he was doing. Was any parent in the room taught how to respond to their only child's abduction? They'd asked.

They'd called First Palmer Bank's chief financial officer, Pam Woody, to the stand. Though she testified she'd released five million dollars to him, the defense had argued that it wasn't reasonable to wait until normal banking hours in such a tragic situation. The prosecution was left, in Jessie's opinion, neither gaining ground nor losing any with her testimony.

They'd spent almost an entire day debating Vincent's fingerprints on the truck's visor. He owned the truck, the defense argued; of course his prints would be expected to be on the truck and in the truck. Was there anyone in the courtroom who expected their own prints were not present in their own vehicles? Furthermore, they'd argued that he hadn't reported the truck was stolen because he hadn't known it was stolen. It was kept on a remote patch of real estate that, at best, was visited once a year.

The defense was clearly attempting to convince the jury that Vincent's arrest was the result of purely circumstantial evidence. Even the appearance of the money in the bank deposit box was debated; because no one at the bank knew precisely what was in each of the boxes, how did anyone know how long that money had remained there before Agent Bailey had opened the box?

The three gray hairs found in the cellar were presented as evidence that Vincent had been in the room where Jessie had been transported. But the defense team had argued that the hairs could have been on Jessie's own clothing, picked up either from the cabin that Vincent owned or even from the Palmer estate. Again, they argued, it was circumstantial evidence.

It was appearing more and more like the case would rest on Jessie's own testimony. And as the days and weeks had crept past, the weight of that testimony and the life-altering consequences of it were beginning to take on greater significance.

"Jessica Palmer."

The voice jerked her back to the present.

"Will you please take the stand?"

Jessie paused to take a quick gulp of water. She had been testifying for hours, and her lips were beginning to feel as parched as if she'd been trudging through Death Valley. Her hand shook as she raised the simple glass, and she used her other hand in an attempt to steady the first. When she set the glass back down in front of her, she raised her eyes to the prosecuting attorney.

Rudy von Heiss appeared to be in his early thirties. Jessie had been surprised to learn he was the lead prosecutor on the case; especially going head to head with her father's dream team, she would have preferred a more experienced attorney. He seemed to love the spotlight; each evening, she caught him on the nightly news, presumably providing his opinion on the day's events, though they kept the television muted to lessen the stress on her. Just this week, Nick had decided to turn it off entirely.

She presumed he was dressed to the hilt in order to impress the media. Though she usually was behind him, staring at the back of his silk suits, today she had the perfect vantage point to take in his crisp ebony suit, starched, powder blue shirt and bright turquoise silk tie. When he stood close to her, she couldn't help but notice he also wore French cufflinks.

He seemed to stand in such a way that the artist drawing the pictures—cameras were not allowed—would have the best view of his profile. And when he crossed the courtroom from the witness box to the prosecution table, he walked with a swagger.

He held up his finger now. It might have been meant to be portrayed as an after-thought, but to Jessie, it appeared too staged.

"Just one more question," he was saying. "Are you absolutely positive that you heard the voice of Vincent Palmer the Third, your father, when you were held against your will?"

Jessie didn't hesitate. "Absolutely positive. Without a doubt." Her voice sounded clear and strong as it was caught by the microphone and projected throughout the room.

"That's all," Rudy said as he took his seat. He picked up a pencil and thumped the eraser against his bottom lip as he held his chin high.

"Does the defense," Judge High said, "wish to cross-examine the witness?"

Kristin Cook rose from the defense table. "Yes, Your Honor." As she made her way toward the witness box, Jessie couldn't help but notice her stiletto alligator heels. They were reported to be her trademark; a visible sign that she could rip a witness to shreds with the heartless, cold abandon of an alligator. As she approached her, she felt herself tighten. Her hands, which had been held in her lap, now curled into fists.

Jessie reminded herself not to look into the defense attorney's eyes. With the prosecution, she was on friendly ground. She could look into the prosecutor's eyes with no fear, no apprehension. There would be no surprises.

But the defense attorney was there to tear her testimony to shreds. She could do it with a look, a smirk, a roll of the eyes—things the jury would never see from their position on the side. But things meant to unnerve her and throw her off.

As Kristin greeted her cordially, Jessie reminded herself to look not at her face but at a point just to the right of the attorney's right ear. Close enough for the jury to believe she was looking directly at her. But far enough removed for her not to see any expression in her eyes or her face.

"Congratulations, Jessie," Kristin was saying. "I understand you'll be graduating soon."

She paused as if waiting for a response. After a moment of silence, Jessie said simply, "Thank you."

Kristin turned and walked a few steps away from her. When she turned again, it was with the fluid, fast movement of a snake. "You must have been under an enormous amount of stress, emotionally and physically—"

"Objection!" Rudy called out. "Leading the witness."

"Sustained."

Kristin walked back to the witness box and placed her hand on the edge. She wore a French manicure, Jessie noted, and a tiger eye ring. "You testified that you were in the cabin overnight."

"That's right."

"How much sleep did you get?"

"Very little."

"How would you define 'very little'? A few minutes, a few hours—?"

Jessie shrugged and kept her attention on a point just beyond Kristin's ear. "I couldn't see my watch. My hands were tied."

"But certainly, you'd have had some sense of how much time had elapsed?"

"Maybe a couple of hours."

"A couple of hours."

At the sound of Kristin repeating her words, Jessie wondered if she had responded correctly. *Tell the truth,* the prosecution had advised her. Simply tell the truth.

"How much sleep do you normally get? Say, if you were in your own bed, on a normal night?"

"Six hours. Sometimes more, sometimes less."

"So, it is fair to say that you were operating on a lot less sleep than normal." It was said as a statement, but Kristin remained so silent that Jessie finally said, "Yes."

"Now, you testified earlier that the cabin had one room, correct? One room—not counting the bathroom."

"Yes."

"And you were at one end of the cabin, on the side."

"On one side, yes."

"Was there any noise in the cabin?"

Jessie almost looked into her eyes, but reminded herself not to. Her nails were beginning to dig into the palms of her hands. "Noise?"

"Well, you said you were in a cabin in the woods. I presume there are sounds in the woods?"

Jessie hesitated. "Dogs barking—occasionally. I think I might have heard a coyote or an owl. Squirrels on the roof, that kind of thing."

"Any sounds inside the room?"

"No. Just the wood stove."

"The stove made noise."

"Well, the firewood—it kind of crackled."

"Let me make sure I understand." Kristin left the side of the witness box and wandered purposefully toward the defense table. When she stopped, she was standing strategically just to the front and side of Vincent Palmer. As Jessie tried to stare at a point beyond Kristin's ear, she was acutely aware of her father staring back at her.

"You were in a cabin, deprived of sleep—"

"Objection! That's not what the witness said."

"—going on less sleep than normal—" Kristin interjected.

"Overruled."

"—and there were dogs barking—occasionally—maybe coyotes, owls, squirrels, and now the crackle of a fire. And amid all this *noise*," she emphasized this last word with her hand on her hip, "you heard your father's voice?"

Jessie felt the heat rising in her cheeks. She's trying to make a fool out of me, she thought. When she spoke, she forced her voice to remain calm and clear. "I heard my father talking to one of the men, yes."

"And was your father—" she gestured now toward Vincent "—in the room with you?"

"No."

Kristin waited. The people who filled the courtroom seemed to be sitting on the edge of their seats.

"Well, how did you know it was your father?"

"I know my father's voice."

"I want to make sure I understand," Kristin said. Her voice was smooth, even bordering on pleasant. Yet Jessie wanted to reach out and slap her. "Could you hear *clearly* with an exterior wall between you and your father?"

"Clearly…no…but I could hear."

"Well, were the voices *muffled* at all?" She tilted her head.

"Yes. To some degree. But I could hear." Jessie felt like she was stammering, and she dug her nails deeper into her flesh to keep her alert.

Kristin crossed back toward the witness box. Jessie breathed a sigh of relief as the defense attorney's body blocked her father's face from her view.

"Jessie, this must have been just horrible for you."

Jessie waited for the prosecutor to object but he didn't.

"Did they at least give you something to eat or drink?"

Jessie wanted to laugh. "I wasn't exactly invited to a party."

Some of the people in the courtroom snickered or giggled, but Kristin appeared unphased. "Is that a 'yes' or a 'no'?" She asked with a touch of sarcasm.

Jessie felt her superior smile fading. "No."

"So, there you were," she said, her voice growing softer and more empathetic, "without sleep, without any food, without any water, listening to the sound of wild creatures outside the cabin and the roar of a fire inside—"

Again, Jessie attempted to look past Kristin and waited for an objection but it didn't come.

"Were you at least, dressed properly for the extreme cold weather?"

Jessie hesitated. She'd just walked home from Vanderbilt, but now as she thought back to the night she thought she'd never forget, she couldn't remember what she was wearing. But she did remember the embers dying down, and how the cold had chilled her to the bone. "No," she said at last.

Kristin shook her head, and Jessie almost expected her to begin clucking. "You were in this one room hellhole," she said, "held against your will. Cold. Sleep deprived. Hungry. Thirsty." She hesitated while she looked pointedly at Jessie's half-emptied glass. "Coyotes howling outside. Animals on the roof. Certainly, you were hoping and praying someone would rescue you?"

"Objection. Leading the witness."

"Overruled."

Jessie stared beyond Kristin's ear.

"Were you wishing that someone would rescue you?" she asked finally.

"Yes." She wanted another sip of water but was afraid to move her clenched hands from her lap.

"Were you wishing your father would rescue you?" Her voice was silky, almost friendly.

She can fake sincerity really well, Jessie thought. "Yes."

"You were wishing your father would come to your rescue."

Jessie fought the impulse to look at him. Despite herself, she dabbed at a tear forming at the corner of her eye. "Yes."

"So, as you're fighting this need for sleep, this hunger, this thirst—" again she stopped and pointedly looked at Jessie's glass "—fighting the chill, and the fear of the animals, not knowing what these men had in store for you, waiting and hoping your father would appear and rescue you—you heard his voice."

She stepped to the side. Jessie was caught off guard as her body no longer blocked her father's face. She caught a fleeting glimpse of his expression. He appeared as if he was ready to cry, and she wanted nothing more than to rush from the witness stand right into his arms, and forget this whole ordeal had ever happened. She wanted him to whisk her out of the room, past the media, and spirit her away to a safe place, a happy place.

Kristin was in no hurry to continue. When Jessie had recovered enough to look away from Vincent's face, she caught a glimpse of Kristin's mouth pursed in victory. She quickly looked away, past her ear. But now the audience was staring at her. All of these eyes pointed directly at her, like daggers—

"Do you dream, Jessie?"

She swallowed hard. "Of course."

"Is it possible," she said, stressing each word, "that you were dreaming when you heard your father's voice?"

"I don't think so."

"You don't think it's possible?"

Jessie hesitated. "It's possible. But not probable."

"So, you agree it's possible."

She wanted to recant, but after an awkward silence, she said, "but not probable."

"Possible," Kristin repeated, "but not probable." She raised one eyebrow before Jessie quickly looked away again.

Kristin Cook walked to the jury box and appeared to make pointed eye contact with each of them. "It is possible you were dreaming," she said finally as she turned to face her.

As Jessie stared past Kristin, her eyes rested on the faces of the jurors. They seemed to be looking at her in collective sympathy, but it wasn't the compassion of people sorry for what she had endured. It was, she thought, the pity of people who thought in her moment of greatest stress, she had hallucinated.

46

Nick had fallen asleep in the recliner again. Jessie watched his chest heaving rhythmically, his face relaxed in slumber. It was, perhaps, the only time his expression was truly relaxed these days, she thought. He'd been there for her every step of the way, managing to sit through each day of the trial with her and still stay on top of his job at the newspaper. To be fair, his new employer was expecting only part-time work from him until the trial had ended, but it had to be grueling just the same. Now he slept with his laptop sitting precariously in his lap, his half-written story still on the screen.

Slowly and carefully, Jessie reached past his hands and saved his document. Then she extricated the laptop from his grasp and slid it onto the coffee table. He stirred and for a moment, she was afraid she had awakened him. But after a second or two, his chin dipped again and she knew he was still asleep.

She made her way to the kitchen and opened one cabinet door after another, barely seeing the cans and boxes on each shelf. The days were acceptable, even exciting on occasion. The time went by quickly, even when the trial bogged down with tedious details. There was activity all around her and regardless of her moods or emotions, it was never boring.

The nights were the killer. Those hours between midnight and dawn when she was completely alone with her thoughts. It was during these times that she often tossed and turned, waking to find herself drenched in perspiration, seeing things and hearing things that were not there. It was during those darkest hours that she feared closing her eyes, afraid of the dreams that would visit her, terrified of reliving those hours when she had no way of knowing whether she would live or die.

With only her father on trial and no leads on Brainiac, she often arose several times a night to check and recheck the front door, peering through the peephole, glancing out the windows to the street below, staring hours on end at her condominium, now dark and quiet, checking and rechecking the locks on the windows…

Tonight was no different. She had gone to bed fairly early, only to awaken a short time later. The tossing and turning came first, followed by the pacing, making her rounds throughout the apartment, staring outside, and eventually back to bed and a fitful few minutes of sleep before the alarm went off and it started all over again—getting ready for the trial, the trial itself, back home from the trial, pushing food around on a plate, and then another night of unrest.

Not finding anything in the cabinets that appealed to her, she stared into the refrigerator, her eyes fixed on one item after another without really seeing it. She reached toward a bottle of wine on the door. "Cakebread Napa Valley Chardonnay," she whispered to no one in particular. But at the sound of her voice, Abby raised her head from the rug in the hallway and watched her sleepily. She opened the bottle and poured herself a glass, filling the goblet to within an inch of the top. She hoped the alcohol would cause her to slip into a deep slumber, and she consciously chose to ignore the fact that if this night was like all the others, she would awaken the next morning to find half the contents still in the glass.

She tiptoed down the hall to the bedroom. After Abby dutifully followed her into the room, she softly pushed the door almost closed. She didn't know why, but ever since her ordeal, she had an aversion to completely closing the interior doors.

Perhaps she wanted to know she could escape quickly. Or perhaps it would allow someone else to come to her aid. Whatever the reason, she checked and rechecked the door to make sure it was not locked, and it could be easily opened.

She sat on the edge of the bed, the goblet in her hands, and stared at the floor. Tonight was the last night. Tomorrow, the jury would begin deliberations. Which meant tomorrow, both the defense and the prosecution teams would have to deliver their most eloquent, compelling closing arguments. And tomorrow, her father's fate would be in the hands of twelve people he had never known, twelve strangers he would never see again.

She set the wine on the night stand and climbed into bed. Still wide awake, she sat propped up against the headboard, her knees pulled to her chest. She hugged her legs close to her, almost rocking as she thought.

As the clock inched past two, she wondered what her father was doing; whether he was able to sleep or if he, like her, was sitting up, taking stock of what the next day would bring. Only he would awaken in a tiny room barely large enough to turn around in; a room with bars on the door, a room where even the toilet and sink had no privacy.

She hoped Rudy von Heiss had prepared for the argument of his life and was now getting the slumber he would need to be refreshed and at his best.

She leaned her head against the headboard, eventually closing her eyes and drifting into a fitful, restless sleep. She awakened once with the memory of her dream fresh in her mind. She was playing at the park, swinging as high as she could, with each jerk forward shouting for her father to look at her. He was sitting on a bench nearby, his lap filled with paperwork, a briefcase at his feet, his pen moving swiftly from page to page. Finally, she'd had enough and she slowed the swing to a crawl, jumping off before it had completely stopped. The wood seat swung back toward her, hitting her hard and knocking her to her knees.

Before she could manage more than a cry beginning to form on her lips, Vincent was there, lifting her up, clucking to her, and hugging her close while he wiped the dirt from her knees.

When she awakened, she realized it hadn't been a dream at all but a memory. As she remembered him taking her to the ice cream parlor afterward—because a double-dip of ice cream would cure anything, but especially bruised knees—she began to cry.

Eventually, she dosed off again, but this time she was in the cellar. She was what her grandfather would have called hog-tied: both her wrists and her ankles were securely tied before being tied to each other, making it impossible to move. Her mouth was dry with the acrid taste of an old rag stuffed into her mouth before duct tape was plastered over it. And she knew she was dying.

Though she hadn't witnessed it in her dream, she knew she'd been tortured repeatedly, and now as her head hung low and her swollen, blackened eyes closed once more, she prayed she would not open them again, that God would simply allow her to breathe her last breath.

Then, she was floating above her own body, looking down with a mixture of sadness and heartbreak. The bonds magically disappeared from her body, and she was gliding through the tiny cellar, moving toward the door like a beam of light.

Something small and black caught her eye and she stopped at the doorway and looked below her. Her feet were suspended in the air. Below them lay a single glove.

She swooped down, picking up the glove before returning to her position in the air. She bobbed there as if she were a hummingbird. She opened her palms to reveal the black glove.

But to her surprise, it did not have the letter "P" embroidered on it.

A nauseating spurt of adrenaline rushed through her, causing her eyes to fly open. She sat straight up in bed, staring ahead as though she was catatonic, her heart thundering in her chest, until she realized she was holding her breath in horror.

47

The FBI office was unusually quiet. Only one agent was there; he was speaking on the telephone in a low tone, taking notes as he went along, barely raising his head in greeting as Grant entered the office.

Grant went directly to his desk. He sat down heavily and rolled his chair so he faced the windows. Behind him, he heard the call end but as the other agent returned the receiver to the cradle, he remained with his back to him. He wanted to be alone.

He would have preferred to have gone home, where he could be assured of peace and quiet. But that wasn't an option. He needed to remain close to the courthouse. A verdict could come at any minute, or it could be days.

It had already been three days, which didn't look good for the prosecution. When the case is open-and-shut, a verdict is returned in short order. The longer the deliberations go on, the more likely the defendant will be found not guilty or the trial could end in a hung jury.

From his desk, he could see the top of the Federal Building where the case was being decided. But, as he stared at the roofline, his mind was thousands of miles away.

Eventually, he reached for his wallet and opened it, revealing a series of photographs that were worn from years of resting in his palms, from nights lined up on the kitchen table next to a bottle of wine, or taking turns stuck next to the bathroom sink, where the mirror met the vanity.

He went through the pictures now in chronological order: the 1966 Ford Mustang with its unique dark moss green metallic paint, a color that wasn't available until the middle of that year. Why he should remember that, he didn't know. But he did remember it, and he remembered the dashboard as though he'd only driven it yesterday. He remembered the leather seats, the sound of AM radio coming through the speakers, of listening to The Beach Boys singing *Sloop John B*...

And he remembered a summer evening when the humidity was low and the breeze was cool, watching the Cumberland River roll past, and slipping his arm around Linda, drawing her to him. She was beautiful then, and he wondered if she was still beautiful today and decided she would be.

He could close his eyes and remember that first kiss: the planning, the rehearsing alone in front of the mirror, the nervous beat of his heart, wondering what he would do if she rejected his advances. But she hadn't. She'd lain in his arms, her head against his chest, and he thought as he stared through that Mustang's windshield, if he lived to be a hundred, he would never forget that moment. And he never had.

He moved onto the next picture, taken at their wedding ceremony in 1972. He looked like a dork, he decided, with his hair cut similar to Paul McCartney's but looking like anybody except him; wearing a tuxedo and worn tennis shoes because the tuxedo rental had supplied the wrong size shoes, a fact he didn't discover until it was too late. But Linda—Linda was ravishing. Her raven hair was full, ending with a flip up at her shoulders, her eyes smoldering beneath full bangs, her white dress stopping inches above her knees to reveal slender, shapely legs that ended in platform shoes. She was the most beautiful creature he'd ever laid eyes on—until Julia.

He flipped to the next picture, of Linda in the hospital room with Julia in her arms: a petite newborn of just five pounds, her eyes so dark and enormous, they seemed to take up half her tiny face. Of Linda smiling so broadly, it was clearly the happiest day of her life, despite the pain and exhaustion. And then there was Grant himself, holding Julia, his hands so large they seemed to dwarf his small daughter, and he smiled as he remembered how frightened he was to hold her, afraid he would drop her or break her…

He squeezed his eyes and tried to shut out the pain. Where was she, after all these years? Had Julia lived after her abduction? Had she been made a slave, forced into a harem? Had she degenerated into a drug addict, forced to remain high or numb, just to deal with the overwhelming pain of her circumstances? Had she waited and prayed and cried for her father to rescue her, night after night, wondering why he never came?

He couldn't find her. He was powerless. But for the first time since Julia's abduction, he thought he could make a difference. Jessie was now safe. Her physical ordeal had lasted only a couple of days—not even that, actually—though he knew the emotional ordeal would last a lifetime.

If the jury found Vincent guilty, perhaps Jessie could pick up the pieces and move ahead with her life. She had Nick's love; that was obvious. And it was more than Grant had. At his lowest point, at the very moment he needed Linda the most, she hated him. He could still remember the day he entered their home to find her gone. Of sitting on a folding chair in the living room, staring at the empty room, of the spot where their sofa once sat, the television once blared, the games Julia once played. All gone in a heartbeat, and his family along with them.

Grant opened his eyes and tried to force himself back to the present. It was Jessie's case he needed to resolve, not Julia's. Julia's memory would come later, as it always did, in the middle of the night between two a.m. and three, the hour he'd come to think of as the arsenic hour…

No, Vincent's trial might be over and only the verdict remaining, but the case was far from solved. He still had no clues to identify the man Jessie had referred to as Brainiac, Vincent's partner. And they still had not found Brutus' body with an axe wound in his skull.

Until they found them both, Jessie would always be looking over her shoulder, always peering at each and every stranger, wondering if the man who changed the oil in her car or mowed the lawn at the condo or performed a handyman's job was the man who had brutally abducted her. She would be haunted, as he was haunted.

The door to the office flew open and Grant felt more than saw Ivory's presence as she breezed through the office.

Before he could turn around, Ivory was saying, "You'll need to catch up on your beauty sleep later, Dear. I'm hungry."

He spun around as she plopped a bag down on his desk. "I'm not—"

"Yes, you are. Who knows when the verdict will come in? And if I know you, you haven't had a bite to eat all day. Huh? Am I right?"

He leaned back in his chair as she pulled out two Styrofoam lunch plates.

"I'm right," she said without missing a beat. "Here." She set one of the lunch plates in front of him. "Exercise those fingers and open it yourself."

Despite himself, he leaned forward and began opening it. "What'd you bring me?"

"Piggly Wiggly fried chicken."

"Fried?" he groaned.

"Leave the skin for me. You know how I love it. And fried okra and fried tator cakes."

Grant stared at the food. "Do they fry everything?"

"*Do they fry everything?*" she mimicked. "Show some gratitude."

He grudgingly began to peel off the skin, depositing it on Ivory's plate.

"So," Ivory said, "this is a working lunch."

"Oh?" The chicken wasn't half-bad, he thought.

"So, let's talk about Susan Jones."

"What about her?"

"Is she of no use to us at all?"

He stabbed one of the tator cakes. All this grease was going to come back to haunt him. He just knew it. "You're asking me this, now that the trial is over?"

"Just curious. We still have two suspects yet to account for."

"But Brutus and Brainiac were both men."

"I know that… But you don't think Susan Jones factors into this at all?"

"What are you getting at?"

"I've been thinking. How could Vincent have been leading a double life like that, without Meg knowing?"

"I don't know that she didn't know," Grant said. "But here's the news flash: it has nothing to do with Jessie's abduction. So the man is a Class One jerk. We knew that already. He has a sense of entitlement. He thinks the rules don't apply to him. So that carries forward to his sex life. You shouldn't be surprised."

Ivory popped a piece of chicken skin into her mouth and chewed in silence.

"But because he's boinking the woman, doesn't mean she had anything to do with his daughter's kidnapping," Grant continued. "Susan Jones is fighting for her life. You think she has the energy—or the inclination—to help her sugar daddy commit a crime?"

"I guess you're right."

"I'm always right."

"Yeah. Sure."

They chewed in silence for awhile. Grant didn't like okra. After a couple of bites, he unloaded the rest of it onto Ivory's plate.

"So, here's the other thing I don't get," Ivory said. "You made Vincent the deal of a lifetime."

"Identify his accomplices for the possibility of a reduced sentence."

"And see, if I was a rich man and I was facing a ten by ten cell for the rest of my life, I'd be turning evidence faster than Jimi Hendrix could play."

"Jimi Hendrix died before you were born."

"His music lives on. Anyway, my point being that not only did Vincent Palmer not try to make a deal, but he became infuriated when it was even brought up."

"I told you. He has a sense of entitlement. Men like him think money will buy them everything. So he'll hire the best dream team money can buy, and he'll be acquitted."

"You'd better hope he's not acquitted."

"He'll never admit guilt," Grant continued, "no matter what happens."

"You think he's really got a dream team?"

"I think he's betting that beauty queen from Atlanta has the jury thinking 'not guilty'."

"No way!"

"Maybe. Or maybe he thinks he'll get a hung jury."

Grant's cell phone rang and he answered. "Court," he mouthed. Then louder, "We'll be right there." As he hung up the phone, he pushed back his chair. "Well, pardner, we're about to find out. Verdict's in."

48

On a hunch, Grant decided to walk the short blocks to the Federal Building and now as they drew closer, he was glad they did. If he thought the trial had been a media circus, it was nothing compared to the swarm of press and spectators gathering around the front of the building. Security had been reinforced and now ropes had been strung to keep the throngs of people from completely overtaking the courthouse steps. Traffic had come to a complete halt, and even the parking lot entrance reserved for law enforcement was blocked.

Grant and Ivory quickened their pace, avoiding most of the crowd by ducking through a back alley and taking a circuitous route to the side entrance. As they made their way through security, he glanced behind him.

"Miss Atlanta is behind us," he whispered to Ivory.

"Oh?"

They paused to watch Kristin Cook rushing across the parking lot. A swarm of reporters were running down the sidewalk, catching up with her before she could reach the side entrance. As they watched, she became completely surrounded.

"Good," Grant said. "They won't give the verdict without her there. We've got time."

Grabbing his Glock from the security tray, he returned it to his holster as they rushed down the hallway. Spotting the crowd waiting for the elevators, they ducked into the stairwell and made their way upstairs.

When Grant opened the ten foot high, double doors leading into the courtroom, the room was almost completely full. Unlike the previous days when people spoke in a hushed tone, the room was abuzz.

Vincent Palmer was already seated at the defense table, flanked by Dalton and Dr. Eric Wunderlook. At the sound of the door opening, Vincent turned and looked.

"He's expecting his attorney," Ivory whispered.

"Think we should tell him she's been delayed?" Grant asked with a wry smile.

Vincent half-smiled at him before immediately turning back around. As Grant made his way toward the front of the room, he felt haunted by that smile. It wasn't a good sign. Vincent appeared too self-assured, even smug.

As he and Ivory took their seats directly behind the U.S. Attorney, he noticed Vincent was even chuckling with Dalton. He was wearing an expensive dark blue, pin-striped suit, a white shirt and a yellow and blue striped tie. He figured his attire must have set him back at least a couple of thousand dollars, and he fought the quickening beat of his heart as Vincent caught him out of the corner of his eye and smugly wiped a non-existent speck from his pricey suit jacket.

Rudy von Heiss was seated at the prosecution table. In contrast with the defense team, he rapped his pen absent-mindedly against the table while speaking glumly to his assistant. On the other side of him was Jim Rye, looking every bit as nervous. Grant knew what they were both thinking: if Vincent Palmer was acquitted, their careers were over.

Grant continued searching through the room for familiar faces. He located Jessie and Nick a few rows back. She looked pale and there were dark circles under her eyes, as if she hadn't slept in days. He thought everyone would have understood if she'd decided not to attend the reading of the verdict; she'd been through so much already. He watched her for a few minutes, hoping with his eyes locked on her, she would notice and turn toward him so he could give her a reassuring smile. But her eyes were focused straight ahead, as if she didn't even notice the others converging in the room.

Nick held her hand in his, but he was also solemn and kept his gaze focused ahead of them.

"The missus isn't here," Ivory whispered.

"Can you blame her?" Grant asked. He envisioned Meg sitting in the dark den under the dim lights, the heavy draperies drawn to shut out the winter sun, sipping on a straight gin as she watched the breaking news unfold on television. He could only imagine her conflicting emotions as the man she married was convicted of kidnapping, while the daughter she gave birth to received justice.

At least he hoped she'd receive it, but the longer they waited, the worse he felt. He just couldn't shake this feeling that something wasn't right.

Kristin Cook finally made it into the courtroom, her stiletto heels rushing down the aisle to join the defense. She set her briefcase on the floor beside the table as Dalton hurried to help her get her coat off. They had barely succeeded when the bailiff called out, "All rise."

Judge High made his way into the courtroom with the same staunch demeanor he'd maintained throughout the proceedings. He took his seat, banged his gavel and called the court to order.

After a brief pause as he made certain the prosecution and defense teams were in place, he called for the jury.

Grant watched as the men and women filed into the room. None of them looked at Vincent. His heart began to beat faster and for the first time since entering the courtroom, he began to feel hopeful of the verdict. It was always a good sign when the jurors wouldn't look at the defendant. If they looked him in the eye or if any of them gave so much as a half-smile, he knew they'd just found the defendant not guilty. He'd seen too many cases, too many verdicts, and he knew the tell-tale signs.

And when they avoided looking at the defendant, as they were doing now, it often meant they had just convicted him. Perhaps it was that they themselves felt guilty for participating in throwing a man behind bars. Or perhaps they simply didn't want to lock eyes with a man they believed to be a criminal.

He could feel the surge of emotions around him, the anxiousness to hear the verdict read.

"The jury has been deliberating on three counts," Judge High said. "Have you reached the verdicts?"

The jury foreman rose. Grant figured he was in his mid-thirties. He was tall and reed-thin, tanned though it was winter. But although he was across the room, Grant noticed as he held the precious piece of paper in his hand that his fingers were bent. His clothes were neat and clean but simple, the clothes of a man who earned his living on the land. A farmer, perhaps; maybe even a carpenter. But most definitely not a banker.

"Yes, Your Honor." His voice was clear and solid.

"Bailiff." With that simple word, the bailiff took the Verdict Sheet from the jury foreman and carried it to the judge. He put on a pair of reading glasses. He opened it and studied it silently for what seemed to be an eternity. Grant had hoped for some sign, some spark, that would reveal the verdict, but even as he watched for it, he knew he would not find it with Judge High. He was too much of a professional.

He peered over his reading glasses and said, "Would the defendant please rise?"

Dutifully, he rose. His entire defense team rose with him.

Grant could feel the entire courtroom holding its breath. Everyone seemed to be leaning forward, listening to every sound lest they miss the verdict.

Everyone except Vincent.

He stood tall and calm. From Grant's location, he had a clear view of his profile. He appeared to have a slight grin on his face. Grant thought if he could see him straight-on, he'd consider his expression more of a Cheshire grin, and he felt his heart begin to sink. *He knows he's going to be found not guilty,* Grant thought. *But how can he know?*

Vincent clasped his hands in front of him. Dalton leaned over and whispered something to him, and Vincent smiled more broadly.

Finally, the judge announced the findings of the jury:

"As to Count I of the indictment," he read, "We the jury find the defendant guilty of violation of Title 18 U.S.C. Section 1344 by bank fraud."

A collective gasp rose from the audience.

The judge waited a few seconds and then banged his gavel. "As to Count II of the indictment," he continued, "we the jury find the defendant guilty of violation of Title 18 U.S.C. Section 1033 by insurance fraud."

Again, a gasp rose from the audience. Grant leaned forward to catch a glimpse of Vincent's expression, but Kristin and Dalton were speaking to him in rapid voices.

Judge High banged the gavel. His eyes were not wavering from Vincent.

Grant saw the bailiff step forward. This was not a good sign, he thought. It was an indication that the judge detected something in Vincent that could "break bad," a term they used to describe everything from a defendant lunging toward the bench to pulling a weapon or letting loose with a vicious tirade. Grant caught Ivory's eye. Without speaking, they both perched near the edge of their seats, ready at a second's notice to lunge toward Vincent and help the bailiff restrain him.

Judge High continued banging the gavel until the buzz in the courtroom subsided.

"As to Count III of the indictment," he said, his eyes locked on Vincent's, "we the jury find the defendant guilty of violation of Title 18 U.S.C. Section 371 by conspiracy to commit kidnapping."

Now the courtroom was erupting in a collective murmur. Grant caught sight of Vincent's profile. His face was so red it almost appeared purple. As Grant stared at him, he saw a vessel beginning to protrude in his neck, and the skin next to his collar seemed to swell right before his eyes.

Someone screamed in the audience. The double doors to the courtroom immediately flew open as the press who had been allowed inside the room rushed to announce to the world that Vincent Palmer had been found guilty on all counts. The audience exploded in a simultaneous roar, as everyone began chattering at once.

Judge High banged his gavel repeatedly but the audience was out of control. "Order in the court!" he shouted. "Order in the court!"

Then one voice was heard above the others.

Grant turned to face the rows of onlookers behind him.

"No!" the voice screamed again. It was a female voice, young and forceful.

As his eyes raked the audience for its source, he saw the onlookers sitting back down, stunned. All eyes were on the young woman standing near the center of the room: Jessica Palmer.

They were still now, their words frozen on their lips, their faces riveted to her.

"No!" she shouted again, her voice drowning out the judge's gavel. "He's innocent! My Daddy is innocent!"

49

The agents in the FBI office were popping open a bottle of Vandalia Cabernet Sauvignon, a non-alcoholic wine, but Grant would have much preferred one of his bottles of Chilean wine with all the alcohol they could manage to bottle. He didn't think he'd ever been so stunned in his entire career, and judging from Ivory's expression, she was feeling that same kicked-in-the-gut feeling.

"Justice served!" Tom Bradley said as he offered Grant and Ivory drinks in plastic wine glasses.

Grant took the glass and set it on his desk before slowly lowering himself into his chair. He watched Tom as he continued to pour glasses of the red liquid for everyone in the office. He'd worked with Tom for more than ten years. A straight-shooter and hard working agent, Tom had worked high profile cases himself and knew the dangers of going up against powerful figures.

"A toast," he said now, holding his glass high, "to Grant and Ivory, who showed us today that the law can prevail over wealth and power."

Grant sipped the wine as he watched Ivory over the rim of his glass. She was doing the same, and their eyes met in a speechless gaze.

She rolled her chair close to his desk.

"You okay?" she asked.

He took another sip. "We sent a criminal to prison," he said. "Right about now, Vincent Palmer should be changing from that expensive suit to an orange jumpsuit."

"You know he'll appeal."

"No doubt about it. And Miss Atlanta will attempt to get him released on appeal."

"Think that'll happen?"

"Not if Judge High has anything to do with it."

They sat in silence for awhile. The other agents, having finished their toasts, were back at their desks, working the phones or tackling their own caseloads. Finally, Ivory broke the silence.

"What the hell?" she said.

"My thoughts exactly."

"What could Jessie have been thinking?"

Grant shook his head. "Vincent obviously has enormous power over her."

"Like a svengali."

"She needs counseling."

"You think?"

Grant swirled the liquid in his glass. "She's obviously got Stockholm syndrome."

"I don't know," Ivory said, reaching for the bottle and refilling her glass. "Stockholm syndrome is when the hostage learns to identify with their captors somehow, having positive feelings toward them instead of fearing them or hating them."

"Your point?"

"Well, Vincent's her father. She started out with those feelings—trusting him as a little girl, loving him—maybe her mind just can't grasp that her own father was capable of such a horrendous crime."

"I'm not a shrink," Grant said, taking Ivory's lead and refilling his own glass, "but call it what you will—Stockholm syndrome, post-traumatic stress disorder, whatever—the girl's obviously not thinking rationally."

"Did you see Judge High's face?"

"Did I ever." He chuckled. "You know, in all the years I've been in his courtroom, I've never seen but one expression on his face. Regardless of the verdict, the stupidity, the outrageousness. But, man, oh man, today his eyes were as big as saucers."

"And his jaw dropped." Ivory laughed. "It actually dropped."

Grant guzzled the wine now. After all, he told himself, it was non-alcoholic.

"Patty Hearst had Stockholm syndrome," Ivory said suddenly.

"I remember that case," he said, leaning back in his chair. "She was kidnapped and kept in a closet, wasn't she?"

"For months. Then she pops up with a machine gun or something, committing a bank robbery with the Symbionese Liberation Army."

"Yeah, yeah, that's right. She claimed the SLA brainwashed her."

"Didn't work," Ivory said. "They convicted her for the bank robbery, anyway."

"I don't think Jessie had Stockholm syndrome."

"You just said she did."

Grant gazed out the window toward the top of the courthouse. Had it been just an hour before that they were waiting for that important call to come in? Now it was over: the trial, the media circus, waiting for the verdict...

"Wonder if Vincent wishes he'd copped that plea agreement now," Ivory said.

"I've been thinking about that." He drummed his fingers on his desk. "I have a theory."

"Well, let's hear it."

"I don't think Vincent knew the two men who kidnapped Jessie."

"Have you lost your mind?"

"Hear me out. I think he hired them, alright. I think he masterminded the whole thing. But you know what? I think he went into some seedy part of town and picked up two loners. Petty criminals, maybe. Maybe he couldn't cop a plea because he didn't even know who they were."

"Then how would he get hold of them? Communicate with them? Plan the crime?"

"He had it all planned out already. So when he finds these two perps, he tells them what he wants them to do, when to do it, how to do it."

"But the money—"

"You know that bag he dropped at the water that was picked up by the boat?"

"Yeah."

"I don't think all the money was in it. I think he was emptying the bag while he was driving."

"What, like tossing money out of it?"

"It could happen. So when he gets to the water, he drops the bag with only half the money in it. The kidnappers pick it up and they're gone."

"And the other half—"

"I never looked in his car. Didn't feel like I had a reason to, at that point. So he hops in his car, goes back home, stashes the money somewhere overnight—could even have been under the seat in the car, for all I know. Then the next morning, he puts it in a bag or a briefcase or something, goes to his own bank, and puts it in a safe deposit box. Never dreaming we would look there."

"Interesting theory."

"Then the two kidnappers argue over the money, and one kills the other."

"So, we're still looking for a corpse and a kidnapper."

"That's right."

Ivory finished off the bottle. "And if I was that kidnapper, I'd be long gone by now."

"He could be anywhere. West Coast. Canada. Europe. Anywhere but Tennessee."

"He'd be too afraid of Jessie seeing him and recognizing him."

"Yep."

"He's probably as afraid of Jessie now as she once was of him."

"Maybe."

"Meanwhile," Ivory said, putting her feet up on Grant's desk, "Vincent Palmer never suspected he would actually be convicted."

"He lived in a different world. A world of entitlement. Of power."

"And corruption."

"He never thought we'd get as far as a warrant for his arrest." Grant looked at his watch. Now that the content of the bottle was depleted, he was craving that Chilean wine again. "Wonder how long it'll take for him to lose that arrogance in prison?"

"About as long as it takes for Bubba to meet him."

"You can be so crude."

"I just have this thing about men who think rules don't apply to them. Who think they're above the law."

"Well, he's learned a lesson today, hasn't he?" Grant stood up.

"Where're you going?"

"Home. It's been a long day."

"You ought to sleep well tonight."

"Oh, yeah?"

"Yeah. It's over. It's all over."

Grant walked to the door but stopped with his hand on the doorknob. He turned to face Ivory, who was still swirling the last remnant of the liquid around the plastic wine glass, her feet still propped up on his desk. "I don't think it's over," he said. "I've got a bad feeling about this."

But before Ivory could respond, he was out the door and down the hall. As he stepped onto the elevator and waited for it to whisk him downward, he had a sinking feeling that it was far from over—and that something else had just been put in motion.

50

Jessie stood at the window in her condominium. It felt strange to be looking at Nick's apartment windows, after the weeks she'd spent staring over here. The rooms, which had once felt so comfortable and cozy, felt cold now. Detached. Or maybe it was just she who was detached.

She turned back to the living room as Nick finished packing the last box. He sat down in the rocker, pulling the day's newspaper into his lap.

"I'm beat," he said, catching her gaze.

"Thanks for helping me pack everything."

"I'd say 'my pleasure', but..."

"Yeah. I know." She caught a glimpse of Abby, sleeping soundly in the hallway, seemingly oblivious about the turmoil going on around her. As her eyes wandered around the room, they stopped at the front door where Abby's claw marks were the only clues to the crime that had taken place downstairs. The back of the door and the doorframe were almost in splinters.

She had to force herself to look away; it was almost like a train wreck—she didn't want to remind herself of that horrible day that changed her life, but she couldn't look away.

When she finally did, all of the boxes piled high in the living room caught her attention. Nick, in typical student fashion, had gone to the neighborhood liquor store and asked for packing boxes. They were ideal, especially for glasses, small enough to carry easily but large enough to make packing them worthwhile. But along with the free boxes came labels such as Jim Beam, Jack Daniels, Wild Turkey, Old Grand Dad, and Early Times. And for some reason, they brought a flood of bad memories back to her. Memories she thought had been gone forever.

As she stared at a box marked with the Smirnoff vodka logo, she remembered all those days, all those years, of watching her mother pour tall glasses of it, "sipping" on it throughout the day. When she was much younger, she never saw her pour it. She just knew she drank "water" from her glass, water that Jessie was never to drink herself. It was only when she was older that she realized it wasn't water at all, but gin or vodka. And by the time Jessie left for Vanderbilt, Meg was no longer hiding her consumption of alcohol.

Perhaps it was a hangover that had kept Meg in bed all those mornings when Vincent made Jessie breakfast. Perhaps it was the drinking that kept her from all of Jessie's school plays, ballet recitals and sports activities. She hadn't really missed her then; Vincent had always been there. He never missed an event.

She turned back to the window. "Where are those movers?" she asked.

"They'll be here," Nick said, a bit absent-mindedly.

She glanced back at him. He was engrossed in *The Tennessean*.

She sighed. It was time to move on. The *For Sale* sign was already posted in the window, already listed in the weekend newspaper, and her realtor, Kay Kay Williams, already had a student's parents lined up to look at it.

In a few hours, after the movers had arrived and all of her belongings were securely on the truck, Jessie would be whisked away from Nashville, and she hoped it would be a long time before she laid eyes on this neighborhood again. She still had a few weeks left at Vanderbilt Law School, but she already knew where she'd park to avoid even looking toward her old condo.

She glanced back at Nick, still reading the newspaper. They were moving in together. After her belongings were delivered to their new place in Franklin, the movers would return to his apartment to get his possessions.

She tapped her foot. "Which company did you hire?"

"Starving Students," Nick answered, not bothering to look up.

"The three business students at Lipscomb U?"

"Yeah."

She turned back to the window. Okay, she thought. I'll give them a break, since they're trying to work their way through college.

Nick finished the newspaper and tossed it into the last box. His eyes locked on Jessie's as he rose and joined her at the window. Wrapping his arms around her, he stood behind her, his chin resting on her head.

"Hey," he said, parting her hair to plant a kiss at the base of her neck. "It just occurred to me, I'll never be spending the night over here anymore."

"Cut it out," she giggled. "The movers will be here any minute."

"Maybe they're late for a reason."

They stood at the window in silence. Jessie placed her hands on Nick's arms as they wrapped around her, and squeezed them.

"Anything interesting in the news?" she asked, more to break the silence than out of any interest.

"Same old stuff," he shrugged. He leaned down and brushed his face against hers. His cheek was soft, she thought. "Bad economy. Record unemployment. Forty percent of all banks are losing money…"

"Thanks for cheering me up."

"There is one interesting article," he added, "about your dad's bank."

"Oh?" She felt her heart quicken.

"The day after the verdict, Edward Buchanan fired the CFO, Pam Woody, and the Chief Auditor, Bill Farris."

"Really?"

"It did give your dad credit for his leadership at the bank, though…"

"His *past* leadership."

"Yeah."

"There's the movers."

As Jessie tried to turn around, she felt Nick's arms tighten around her once more before he reluctantly let her go. She caught a glimpse of the truck out of the corner of her eye, maneuvering into place in front of the building, before she crossed the room with a renewed sense of urgency. As she propped open the door, she saw Nick returning to the last box, sealing it shut, along with the final memories of her home.

51

Jessie sat in the driver's seat with the engine running. She felt conspicuous in the parking lot of the prison; her shiny Mercedes stood out like a sore thumb among the dusty pickups and economical cars.

As she peered through the windshield, she noted the high fence with razor wire rolled around the top. At one corner stood a brick, two-story guardhouse. A guard stood motionless, watching her. The brick had once been painted white but was now peeling and mottled, a sad reminder of the lives that languished inside.

With the eyes of the guard still upon her, she felt compelled to step outside. She turned off the engine, and though her mouth was as dry as cotton, she couldn't bring herself to take a quick swig of the soft drink that rested in the cup holder. She removed her driver's license from her purse and slid the purse to the seat behind her. Watching the video cameras on the building pan the parking lot and surrounding area, she came to the conclusion that this just might be the safest place to leave it.

She opened the door and stepped outside, pausing only long enough to grab her briefcase from the front seat.

It was a beautiful day. More than a month had passed since her father's sentencing. More than a month since she'd seen him. She hadn't been able to attend the sentencing itself; she had been too distraught and too afraid she would be unable to control herself when he was led away. In the days that followed, winter had turned to an early spring. And now as she crossed the parking lot to the sidewalk, she could see green blades of grass beginning to crop up in the narrow stretches of lawn between the parking lot and the nearest building.

As she neared the gatehouse, she caught sight of crocus in brilliant yellow erupting from a miniscule planter, but as her eyes moved past it, she peered through the chain link into the dreary confines. The overwhelming colors were shades of gray: gray sidewalks, once-white buildings now dingy and dull, the ground between them nothing more than drab gray dirt that drifted away like miniature dust bowls as the wind caught it.

There were no trees. No birds singing, no squirrels chattering. Just an eerie silence.

She reached the window at the gatehouse. The guard was standing there, watching her, as she suspected he'd been doing since she exited her car. His eyes raked over her, making her self-conscious of the dark navy suit she'd purchased during a Jos. A. Banks' sale, the crisp white blouse and feminine gold cuff links. By the time his eyes reached her new shoes, stiletto alligator heels, she was wishing she'd dressed in her diamond gusset blue jeans that hid her legs, and an oversized blouse that could hide her figure.

"Jessica Palmer," she said. "I called earlier."

"Identification?"

She handed him the driver's license through the window and a moment later, he slid it back to her, along with a logbook.

"Sign in," he directed.

After she signed in, the door buzzed open and he directed her inside. She was led to a small, plain table that looked like it had seen better days, where he instructed her to place the briefcase. She dutifully opened it and watched as he inspected the contents.

The leather briefcase was a recent purchase in anticipation of her new job as a junior level attorney. It had been purchased from Col. Littleton of Lynnville, and she'd been very proud of it when she came home and showed it to Nick. But now it felt woefully sparse; its only contents, clippings from *The Tennessean* about the trial. She'd hoped she'd appear like a confident lawyer walking through the prison to confer with her client, but now she felt small and vulnerable and over-dressed. As the guard closed the case and handed it back to her, his eyes narrowed and veiled, she knew that he was aware she was not there to see a client. She was there to see her father.

Another guard appeared at the door. "Follow me," he said brusquely, without introduction. He walked with a purposeful step that Jessie had a hard time keeping up with. But as they left the gatehouse and made their way through a sparse courtyard and into another building, she was glad he was moving so quickly.

They passed several inmates in their distinct orange and white striped jumpsuits, sweeping the floors and emptying wastebaskets. They looked up as she walked past, their eyes taking in her attire in the same manner the guard had.

The guard passed through a doorway and Jessie followed, finding herself in a room about the size of a classroom. There was a row of steel chairs running lengthwise down the middle of the room, neatly arranged in front of a table barely deeper than a shelf. Behind the table was a sheet of Plexiglas that Jessie suspected was bullet-proof. It was anchored to the floor and the ceiling, effectively cutting the room in half. On the other side was another set of steel chairs.

The guard motioned toward one of the chairs. "Have a seat."

She removed the suit jacket and placed it over the back of the chair. Her desire to look professional simply made her feel conspicuous now. She sat down and waited for her father.

The time slowed to a crawl. A large clock on the opposite wall ticked down the minutes. The room was so still that she could hear the second hand as it moved. Even the guard stood completely silent at the door from which she'd entered, his hands clasped in front of him and his eyes straight ahead, discouraging any conversation.

A heavy door on the opposite side opened and a man was led in. Jessie was tempted to rise from her chair and shout through the Plexiglas that this was not the man she was waiting for, when the man looked upward and saw her.

Her jaw dropped and a few seconds passed before she consciously closed it.

Vincent Palmer made his way to the table across from hers. He kept his head down, peering out of the corner of his eye at the guard as he pulled the chair back from the table; almost as if he was afraid the guard would admonish him for doing so. His frame was gaunt. In place of the expensive, tailor-made suits with his name embroidered on the inside pockets, was the distinctive one-piece, orange and white striped jumpsuit, colors he detested as a Vanderbilt alumni. The squared shoulders she remembered so well were now rounded and hunched forward and downward.

She started to speak, but he motioned for her to pick up the phone on the divider that separated the long table into separate visiting areas.

"Daddy," she said. She'd rehearsed what she would say to him; rehearsed it and revised it a thousand times. Once she'd decided to visit him here, she'd lain awake night after night, envisioning their conversation, seeing him as he'd looked the last time he'd visited her at Vanderbilt. But now she was at a total loss for words.

All she seemed to be able to do was stare at him through the thick glass, at his sunken eyes, now lifeless, the outer edges turned down; at the dark bags that had formed underneath them; at the permanent crease between his brows as if he spent every waking moment worrying.

A light bulb crackled overhead as it sputtered and died, and he jumped with the apprehension of a man staring into the barrel of a gun.

"Daddy," she said again.

He didn't answer her but stared through the glass at her. His eyes didn't waver from her own, and she doubted if he even saw the white blouse or the gold cuff links that she was now embarrassed to be wearing.

"Are you okay?" she asked.

His eyes shifted toward the guard at the door and then to the guard that stood behind her at the opposite door. They moved slowly, almost imperceptibly. "I'm fine," he said. His voice was no longer strong. It was no longer filled with the tone that some thought was arrogance and others considered confidence; it was weak and small and resigned.

"I'm sorry," was all she could manage to say.

A spark of light seemed to flitter across his eyes before they became dull once more. "You did what you felt you had to do," he said finally.

The sense of guilt she felt as she stared at him was enough to overwhelm her, and she fought the impulse to break down and cry like a blubbering idiot. Instead, she asked, "Are they feeding you okay?"

She thought she almost detected a smile. "It's not my cooking," he answered.

"Are you healthy?"

He shrugged. "As good as can be expected."

"Daddy—"

"I didn't do it," he blurted.

"I know," she said. But even as the words passed her lips, she knew they sounded false. There were just too many unanswered questions.

"Daddy, what happened that night?"

He looked at her for a long time, his eyes occasionally beginning to dart as if he was trying to remember. When he began to speak, the words came haltingly but as he continued, his pace quickened. He told of the call he received from the Nashville Police Department, the urgency he felt as he sped toward her condominium, of the trooper who pulled him over and who eventually escorted him there. He spoke of immediately notifying Grant Bailey, of his and Meg's confidence in his abilities, never realizing that he himself would become Grant's prime suspect.

He spoke of the hours of waiting, of the kidnapper's phone calls, of the demand for money. And of his rush to get the ransom in the short amount of time demanded; of trying to follow the kidnapper's instructions as he repeatedly phoned him, changing the route. Of reaching the water's edge, hoping and expecting to see her there, ready to be exchanged for the duffle bag filled with cash.

When he finished, he ended with seeing her for the first time at the farmhouse, of the wretched feeling as she slapped him, of the despondency that had crept in as he realized that his own daughter thought he had orchestrated her kidnapping.

"But I heard your voice," she said.

At the sight of his face, his eyes wide, his cheeks drained of color, she wished she hadn't spoken.

"I don't know why you thought you heard me," he stammered. "I've thought about it a hundred times—a thousand times." His eyes wandered toward the closest guard. "It's about all I can do in here is think."

"I don't understand. It was your voice—"

"Could the kidnapper giving me directions have had me on a speakerphone? Was that the voice you heard?"

She leaned back in the chair. It was hard and cold. "No. It was a conversation. And it wasn't him giving you directions."

"I swear to you," he said, leaning toward the glass, "I swear to God Himself: I never, *ever*, not once spoke to the kidnappers except to get directions from them."

"But—"

"Directions on how much money, how fast I was to get it, and where I was to go. I swear to you."

"You were never at the cabin?"

"Not while you were there, no. I've been there dozens of times—you know that—but I wasn't there after your kidnapping."

"When was the last time you *were* there?"

He looked downward at the table while he thought. She realized as she watched him that his hair was turning from gray to white. It was cut short, shorter than she'd ever seen it before; the haircut of a man who'd been plopped into a chair and an electric trimmer run over his skull. She longed to have her father back; to see his vibrant, dark locks; to look into his eyes as he laughed, to see his shoulders squared once more—

"Sixteen months ago," he said abruptly. "The day after Thanksgiving, year before last. A group of guys from the bank went deer hunting… We didn't stay in the cabin; just went for the day."

The guard on Vincent's side of the room stepped forward. "Time's up."

Vincent stood robotically.

"Daddy!" Jessie exclaimed, standing also and placing her hand against the Plexiglas that separated them.

"I love you," he said simply.

"I love you, too, Daddy! Daddy—is there anything you want? Anything you need?"

He hesitated. "Keep an eye on your mother. Make sure she's taken care of. That nobody takes advantage of her…"

"I will. I promise."

"Someone was fooling around with the cars—"

"The antique cars?"

"Yes. Driving them. The odometers—" He stopped and a strange smile came over his face, as though now that he was voicing it, the problem seemed so trivial. "It's nothing," he said. "I had installed cameras to see if I could catch whoever it was." His eyes locked onto hers and seemed even sadder than before. "It doesn't matter anymore."

Without saying good-bye, he returned his phone to the cradle. With his head bowed, he walked toward the door.

"I'll be back!" she shouted, but he didn't acknowledge her. "Daddy, I'll be back!"

He didn't turn around. Instead, he walked through the door and out of her sight. It wasn't until he was gone that she realized she was crying.

52

As Jessie turned off the main road onto the long, winding drive that led to the Palmer estate, she felt as if the hands of time had turned back.

Springtime was in abundance here. The pansies that had been planted late the previous fall had taken root and were proliferating on either side of the driveway. Their yellow and purple blooms were a testament to something that appeared so delicate, and yet they had survived the harshest ice and snow, emerging on the other side stronger and more vibrant than ever. It was an omen Jessie hoped would mirror her own life and that of her father's.

The trees were full now, their light green foliage sheltering an abundance of bird nests. As she rolled down her window to key in the code that opened the massive gates, she heard the sound of a woodpecker busy on a nearby tree. She kept the window down, enjoying the sounds of robins singing, until she rounded the last corner that separated her from her old home.

She parked the car in the circle in front of the house and sat there for a long time, watching the landscapers busily spreading fresh mulch. She wished now that she'd never heard her father's voice. If she hadn't been the star witness against him, she was convinced he would never have been convicted. It had all been circumstantial evidence, she thought—everything except her own incriminating testimony.

When she finally exited the car and made her way up the wide steps to the front door, her mind registered the bright red tulips set in pots on each step, as they had appeared every spring ever since she could remember. Yet something was different, something she couldn't quite put her finger on. She stopped before opening the front door, turning back to look at the expanse of lawn in front of the house, the fountain flowing amid cherubic statues, the tops of the trees bending gracefully with the slightest breeze, the butterflies and hummingbirds nestling among the year's earliest blooms.

It was in stark contrast to the gray confines of the prison. She wanted to remember her father, but not that way—not with his head bowed, his wrists grasped in front of him, his spirit broken.

She swallowed hard and opened the door, stepping into the broad foyer. It was as empty as a tomb, and she wandered from room to room, searching for her mother. She called out several times, but no one answered. She made her way up the stairs, stopping briefly in the doorway of her mother's bedroom. She was coming to the conclusion that Meg was not home when Heddy's voice echoed through the upstairs hallway.

"Lawdy mercy, Jessie!" she exclaimed.

Jessie turned to watch the housekeeper waddle down the spacious hallway, a basket of clean and folded clothes on one hip.

"Why didn't you tell me you were comin'? I'd have had lunch ready for you!"

"I didn't know I was coming," Jessie answered, hugging the big woman. "I'm looking for Mother."

The older woman's eyes darted to the stairs as one eyebrow shot up. "Last time I seen her, she was in the sun room," she said, "polishing off a pitcher of *iced tea*."

The emphasis on the words caused Jessie to stop and peer into Heddy's mahogany eyes. "Long Island iced tea?"

"You didn't hear it from me."

"No. No, I didn't." Jessie pulled herself from the woman's grasp and started toward the stairs. "It's good to see you again, Heddy."

"Oh, Lawdy, it's so good to see you, Jessie. It's been so lonesome here with you and your Daddy—"

She stopped abruptly. Jessie thought of telling her not to worry; that she wasn't her father's enemy and there was no reason to keep his memory from sneaking into the conversation, but when she turned back around, Heddy was gone, disappeared into one of the rooms off the broad hallway.

Jessie watched as her mother finished the last drop of amber liquid in her tall glass. The pitcher sat empty on a woven tray, surrounded by remnants of popcorn drizzled with dark chocolate. It might have appeared to the casual onlooker that they were finishing a fresh pitcher of sweet iced tea, complete with sprigs of mint on the glasses' edge. Or that they were enjoying a sunny afternoon on rattan chairs with extra thick cushions, soaking up the sun's rays as they filtered through the open French doors.

But a closer look would find Meg slurring her words, Jessie's glass filled with ice water, and an air of friction growing between them.

"I don't know whose voice I heard," Jessie was saying, her impatience apparent.

"But Jessie, you testified. Under oath. Why would you have done that, if you hadn't been convinced it was your father you heard?"

"I was convinced. Then. But I'm not now."

"This isn't one of those times you think you want Chinese food and then decide you'd rather have Italian," Meg said hotly. "Lives are at stake here. Futures are at stake. And they're all riding on your sworn testimony."

"Mother, I thought you'd be happy to know this."

"Happy to know what? That my daughter's emotions are all over the place?"

"That Daddy's innocent."

"*That Daddy's innocent,*" she mimicked. "If your daddy is innocent, what's he doing serving time in prison?" Before Jessie could respond, she continued, "Do you understand your father destroyed the Palmer name? The Palmer reputation? Possibly the Palmer fortune?" She reached toward the tray and pulled out newspaper articles and hand-written note cards, scattering them on the floor between them, as if to make her point.

Jessie laughed. "The Palmer reputation? Please, Mother. The family's name has been synonymous with 'scandal' for generations."

"Well, there you have it. One more generation and a scandal to top all the others."

"Mother, I came here to tell you that I want to recant my testimony."

"Do you understand what you're saying?"

Jessie watched her mother's hands. They were limp, as they always were when they weren't holding a glass, but they were shaking like a woman coming awake only to discover her hands were still asleep. She didn't think she had a single memory of her mother when she either wasn't holding a glass or wasn't shaking her wrists.

"We just put you through law school," Meg continued. "Your whole future is before you. If you recant your testimony, you can kiss your legal career good-bye."

"I don't think—"

"Who would want to hire a lawyer who doesn't even know what she heard? Or what she thought she heard? You'd be deemed unreliable. A laughingstock."

"I don't care. It's the right thing to do."

"The right thing to do? And what happens next week or next month or next year, when you change your mind again?"

"Mother, I need money to pay for Daddy's appeal."

Meg chortled. "So that's what you're here for, money?"

Jessie swallowed. "It's Daddy's money."

"Yeah, that's right, 'it's Daddy's money.' Well, news flash for you, Honey, Daddy's money is all tied up."

Out of the corner of her eye, Jessie caught a glimpse of Heddy as she moved into the doorway. Upon hearing the heated conversation, she tried to duck back out but Meg stopped her.

"Bring me another pitcher," she ordered.

"Yes, ma'am," Heddy said, her eyes meeting Jessie's before she turned around.

Jessie waited until the housekeeper was out of earshot. "What do you mean, the money's all tied up?"

"Your father," she said, wringing her hands, "was so paranoid that some woman was going to pilfer his fortune that he placed it beyond my control."

"But—"

"That's right. Your precious Daddy," she spit, "put me on an allowance. He paid all the bills. Now that he's in prison, I don't have the money to keep the electricity on."

Heddy returned and replaced the empty pitcher with a full one. Her downcast eyes and ashen skin told Jessie that she'd heard every word. She watched in silence as the older woman placed ice cubes in a clean glass and poured a drink for Meg.

"Oh, don't you worry, Heddy," Meg said, "We'll find the money to pay you. I've asked my attorney to petition the court and place me in charge of Mr. Palmer's accounts."

Instead of her words sounding accommodating, Jessie thought, they sounded insensitive. As she glanced at Heddy, handing the fresh drink to Meg, she realized that as much as the housekeeper attempted to veil her emotions, she had to have been thinking the same thing.

"Miss Jessie?" Heddy asked, motioning toward the tray.

"No, thank you. I have my water."

"Then let me get you a fresh sandwich. I have some—"

"Didn't you hear her?" Meg interrupted. "She doesn't want anything. Now leave us alone."

"Yes, ma'am."

As Heddy picked up the dirty glass and spent pitcher and made her way out of the room, Jessie stared at her mother.

"You're having trouble coming to terms with your father's evil ways," Meg said.

"He's not evil—"

"And you don't need another trial. He doesn't need another trial. He's where he belongs. And you, young lady, need counseling."

"What?" Jessie felt her cheeks begin to burn.

"Face it. You're a daddy's girl. You've always been a daddy's girl. And now that your testimony has helped put him behind bars, you're consumed with guilt."

Jessie leaned back in the rattan chair. She set her water glass on the end table and crossed her arms.

"You need to come to grips with the fact that your father had you kidnapped. And if he's rotting in prison now, it's because he's not as smart as he thought he was. He left clues behind. And if your testimony hadn't put him behind bars, the other evidence would have."

There was a long silence before Jessie spoke. "Maybe you're right."

"Of course I'm right."

"But what if you're not?"

Meg jumped up with a force that stunned Jessie. Her hand was shaking so violently that some of her drink spilled onto the expensive Oriental rug. "Wake up!" she shouted. "Stop chasing dreams like some preschooler fantasizing about Peter Pan." She stopped and stared at the glass, her hand covered in alcohol, and the ruined rug. "Now, look what you made me do," she snarled. "You just ruined a perfectly good drink."

With that, she tossed the remainder of the liquid in Jessie's face. Before Jessie could recover from the shock, Meg was gone—and so was the pitcher.

She came shakily to her feet. She grabbed some napkins from the tray and hurriedly mopped her face, hands and arms. Her blouse was soaked and now she reeked of alcohol. She's drunk, Jessie thought as she prepared to leave. She's drunk and she doesn't mean it.

53

Jessie opened the refrigerator door and sighed with relief when she spotted her favorite banana yogurt. Nick hadn't failed her. He'd gone to the grocery and had stocked both the refrigerator and the cabinets. He'd even set the coffee maker to come on automatically, and now as she hunted through the kitchen drawers for a spoon, she could detect the unique aroma of Godiva Chocolate Crème Coffee.

She found a dark blue coffee cup with *First Palmer Bank* emblazoned in white on the side. She stared at it for a long moment, debating whether to trash it, and decided once everything was unpacked she would go through the new apartment and purge it of anything that smacked of the bank carrying her family's name. The memories were just too painful.

Abby joined her in the kitchen. Jessie located the pantry where Nick had neatly placed Abby's canned dog food and treats. She found two bowls sitting on a placemat on the floor near the sink; one empty and the other filled with water. She replaced the water with fresh tap, and emptied the contents of one of the cans in the other one.

As Abby ate, Jessie poured a cup of coffee and then meandered through the kitchen and into what should have been the dining area. She could spot the table and at least one chair, but moving boxes littered every inch between them. She ended up eating the yogurt while she stood in the doorway of the kitchen.

There was no feeling that came close to the one she had now as her eyes took in the disaster in the apartment. The furniture all appeared to be in place, from what she could see. But if there was a spot to sit in, it was hidden by boxes in every direction.

In her old condominium, she knew where everything was located. She could still remember the day she moved in, and the days following: of the excitement as she unpacked each box, of the pride she had in living independently for the first time in her life, of her self-sufficient mood as she placed every item, no matter how small or trivial, in the exact spot where she wanted it.

She didn't feel that way now. She felt discombobulated, as if her life was falling apart and the new apartment and all the boxes lying helter-skelter were an external symbol of her turmoil within. She felt somewhat like those boxes: she had a home once, a place she called her own, and now she was picked up and misplaced.

Somewhere in the back of her mind, she knew she needed to open a box and begin to unpack. But she couldn't bring herself to cut the tape on that first box. It felt too overwhelming, almost sickening, when she thought of it.

She was standing in the doorway with her coffee cup in her hand when she heard a thump in the bedroom, followed by Nick cursing. A few seconds later, he emerged, his dark hair tousled.

"What happened?" she asked.

"Tripped over a box."

"You weren't here when I got home yesterday," she said as she watched him climb over the boxes to reach the dining room chair.

"I think I broke my toe."

"On a box?" When he didn't answer, she continued, "You had a late night."

He sat down and inspected his foot. "Worked late. They have me covering the crime beat. Today's gonna be another long day."

"Cup of coffee?"

"Love one."

She disappeared into the kitchen and located another First Palmer Bank cup. She poured the coffee and reemerged in the doorway a moment later. "How'd you get over there?" she asked.

He stopped rubbing his foot and peered around him. There was about a two-foot-square space that was cleared on the dining room table, enough for a plate and a cup if one didn't need elbow room. Jessie came to the edge of one of the boxes and examined the fortress mounded around him.

"I don't know," he said. "I think I climbed over."

She managed to squeeze between two boxes and held out the cup for him. He stood on top of one box as he leaned in to get it. When the cup passed hands, some of the coffee spilled, and he cursed again.

"It burned me!" he wailed as he retreated to the table.

"Looks like you're not having a good day," she muttered.

"Jess," he said, setting the cup on the table and rubbing his affected hand against his pajama pants, "when are you going to unpack this stuff?"

"Well, some of it's yours."

"Jess." He waited until she looked him in the eyes before continuing. "My stuff has been unpacked for two days. This is all yours."

"Oh."

"How do you think everything got into the cabinets and drawers in the kitchen? That was all from my place. The closet's filled with my clothes. I'm using my bowls to feed Abby, 'cause I don't have a clue where her dog dishes are."

"I'll get to it," Jessie said, feeling her cheeks burning.

"Today?"

"I don't know. I've got stuff to do."

"I've got stuff to do, too. I started a new job, Jessie, in case you don't remember. I'm working long hours, and I still made the time to unpack. Where have you been?"

"What is this, an inquisition? We move in together, and you think you can dictate to me?"

He clinched his teeth as if he was trying to prevent words from spilling out. When he spoke, his voice was low and his words came slowly. "No, Jessie, I'm not trying to dictate to you. I don't want to control you. I just want to live in a nice place."

"Well, then, make it a nice place." As she took in the scene before her, she pointed at some pictures stacked against the wall. "Hang your pictures. Make it homey."

"Are you crazy? Do you not see all this crap everywhere?"

"You have no idea what I've been doing."

"No, Jessie, I don't." They stared at each other for a long time. "Did you start your new job?"

"Not yet."

"So you're not working. You've finished with school, right?"

"Right."

He waved his arm over the boxes nearest him. "So?"

"So, I'll get to it." Her words were more venomous than she'd intended, but once she said them, it was too late to take them back.

"When?"

She continued staring at him.

"Jessie, I can't live this way. I was fine in my old place—"

"Then why didn't you stay there?"

His jaw dropped. "Because *you* didn't want to go home."

"Oh, so now it's all my fault?"

He spread his hands out. "I'm not trying to find fault. I just want you—I need you—to take care of all this stuff. I can't live this way."

"Are you giving me ultimatums?"

"Did it sound like an ultimatum, Jessie?"

Abby whimpered and pawed at the door.

"She needs to go out," Nick said.

"I know when she needs to go out. She's my dog." Jessie walked to the door of the apartment. "She needs to go out."

"Well, are you gonna take her out? 'Cause I've been taking her out. I don't know where you've been, but I've been taking care of *your* dog—"

"I can take care of my own dog, thank you very much." Jessie looked around the living room. "Where's her leash?"

"I don't know where her leash is, Jess," Nick called from the dining room. "Take your pick. Look in any of those boxes in there! Maybe you'll find it! Oh—oh, and if you don't, maybe she can use the kitchen floor like she did yesterday—But you wouldn't know that, would you, because *I* cleaned it up—"

"Because I cleaned it up," she mimicked as she opened the apartment door. She stepped outside with Abby beside her and then slammed the door behind her. She was halfway down the stairs before she realized she'd left her keys somewhere in the apartment. But it was too late now. She wasn't going back. Not until after *he* left.

54

By the time Jessie heard the key in the lock, she was too tired to be tense. After a short walk with Abby to a neighborhood park, she'd returned to the apartment, only to have to wait until the management office opened to get someone to let her back in. By that time, Nick was gone.

She spent the day unpacking. Or rather, moving boxes around. She opened one box after another, rummaged through it, and more often than not, shoved it against a wall. There were some that she kicked and shoved down the hallway to be placed in one of the three bedrooms, until she had removed all of the boxes in the middle of the floor. Now almost all of them were stacked against the walls.

But she had found Abby's leash, along with her dog dishes and toys. And she'd located her toiletries and some clothing that she'd hung up in the bedroom closet beside Nick's or placed in her dresser drawers.

Now she was arranging the rest of her sweaters in a drawer that seemed larger when they'd resided there before. Finally, she got the last one in and managed to close it. When she turned around, she bumped right into Nick.

"Jessie," he said, scooping her into his arms.

She rested her head against his chest. With his hands combing through her hair and massaging her scalp, all of the resentment she'd harbored against him all day began to disappear.

"Jess," he said, his lips close to her ear, "I'm sorry."

"Shh," she said, pulling slightly away from him and placing a finger on his lips.

He took her hand in his and pulled it away from his mouth. "I love you."

She moved back to the comfort of his chest. His arms closed around her once more. His cologne smelled of smoky sandalwood and clear water, an aroma that permeated his sweater and made her want to sink her face into it. His chest was firm and as she pressed against him, she could feel his muscles even through the thickness of his clothing. "I love you, too," she whispered.

They stood there for a long moment before he kissed her hair.

"I thought you were working late," she said, hoping he would not tell her he had just dropped in and would be leaving immediately.

"I was. But I couldn't work. Not tonight."

She hugged him tighter. "I'm glad you're home."

"I see you've been unpacking."

She felt herself begin to tense.

"Thank you," he said before she could answer.

They stood for a long moment. She felt so tired that her eyelashes hurt just trying to keep her eyes open.

"Have you had dinner yet?" he whispered against her ear.

The question surprised her, and as she thought about it, she realized the only food she'd had all day had been the banana yogurt for breakfast. "No."

"Pick a place," he said, pulling her away from him and sweeping her hair off to the side of her forehead. "Any place. My treat."

"Oh, I don't know," she said reluctantly. "I don't really feel like—"

"You have to eat something," he urged. "It doesn't have to be fancy. It can be a burger. Or pizza. Just, let's get out for a little bit. Get some fresh air."

She brushed her lips across his. "Give me fifteen minutes."

As she began to pull away from him, he drew her back and before she had a chance to close her eyes, he had her in his arms once more, his lips finding hers and lingering there. After a long moment that she didn't want to end, she pulled slightly away. "You want me for dinner, or real food?"

.

The Italian restaurant was dark inside, the bulbs muted by stained glass fixtures in shades of red, green and white. It took a moment for Jessie's eyes to adjust as the hostess led them to a booth near the back corner. They were barely settled in before their waiter appeared.

"Can I get you something to drink?" he asked as he placed some coasters on the table.

"White Merlot?" Nick asked, grasping her hand across the table.

"I don't know…"

"It'll relax you. And it goes with anything."

"Okay," she said reluctantly.

"A bottle?" the waiter asked pleasantly.

"No, just a glass for me," Jessie answered.

Nick nodded. "Same."

But as the waiter began to leave, Jessie called after him. "On second thought, make it a bottle."

When she looked back at Nick, one brow was raised. "It's been a tough week," she said.

The sound of Dean Martin crooning *"That's Amore"* drifted lazily through the tiny restaurant. Before long, the fragrant smell of freshly baked bread and olive oil with cracked black pepper and basil teased her, and soon she felt her inhibitions melting away as she downed one glass of wine and started on another one, interrupted only by the soft bread that only a true Italian could bake. By the time she was halfway through her spaghetti with tomatoes and mushrooms, Nick was finished with his beef lasagna and was leaning back, watching her as he swirled the wine in his glass.

"You've almost finished the bottle," he observed.

"Have we?" she giggled.

"*You* have," he corrected with a sly smile. "I'm driving. I've had half a glass."

"You're a stick-in-the-mud."

He laughed. "Go ahead. Enjoy yourself. I don't care if you're half lit."

She joined him, her laughter sounding like bells ringing. Oh, it had been so long since she'd laughed. But even as she did so, there was a sadness inside her, a melancholy she'd never felt before the events of the last few months, and she found herself staring uneasily at the others in the restaurant.

"What is it?" Nick whispered.

She shook her head. She watched a rotund lady polish off a tall slice of tiramisu and a young couple dive into a family-sized appetizer of tomato and feta bruschetta. "Nothing," she said. "Just tired."

"It's the alcohol," he noted.

She watched a young girl sitting with her parents. She was perhaps five years old, Jessie thought. She had long blond hair that was unsuccessfully swept behind her ears; as the little girl tried to swirl her spaghetti, it kept falling across her face. She looked up once and caught Jessie's eyes with huge, sky-blue eyes, and Jessie smiled at her. She returned the smile, her eyes so wide and innocent and her smile so ready, that Jessie felt like protecting the little girl from harm.

Now Tony Bennett was singing *"I Left My Heart in San Francisco."* Jessie leaned against the back of the leather booth and closed her eyes. She felt Nick's eyes on her, vaguely felt the waiter return to whisk away the remnants of their dinner, and listened to the clink of glasses and the murmur of voices. When she finally opened her eyes, the little girl was leaving a plate of spaghetti that appeared to have been barely touched. She wiped her face with a large cloth napkin and slid out of the booth.

Jessie followed her with her eyes as the little girl made her way across the restaurant toward the rest rooms. As she walked along, she ran her tiny hand across the backs of chairs. Jessie noticed for the first time that the restaurant contained a diminutive bar, and she watched as the brave little girl passed the men lined up at the counter, their eyes locked on a ball game being played out on a small set above the bar.

One man removed his black nylon jacket and hung it on the back of his chair, but he kept a knitted winter cap on his head. It had always annoyed her father when a man didn't have the manners to remove his cap inside a building, and now as Jessie watched the back of the man's head, she found herself becoming aggravated.

The man wore a red and black plaid shirt that appeared at this distance to be flannel. It was tucked unceremoniously into ragged jeans with no belt, as if he'd been in a hurry to leave the house and hadn't taken the time to properly dress. As she stared at him, she noticed his hair was long and unkempt, the straggly brown locks protruding from under his cap in all directions.

"What is it?" Nick asked.

She couldn't pull her eyes away from him. "I—I just have this feeling."

"Are you okay?"

She felt Nick's eyes on her, could see in her peripheral vision how he held his hand across the table, expecting to take hers, but her hands were frozen in her lap.

"I—I know that man."

"Which man?"

She nodded toward the bar.

"Jess, there's ten men over there. Which one?"

"He's getting up," she said. Her heart was pounding in her chest so loudly that she had difficulty breathing. The little girl was still in the bathroom, and for some inexplicable reason she couldn't quite understand, she was petrified the girl would emerge and would have to walk past that horrible man.

"Jess, let's go."

She didn't respond and Nick remained on the edge of the seat, not completely in it but perched ready to depart at a second's notice.

The man turned toward her, and she caught a glimpse of his unshaven face and his sunken, dark eyes set wide apart.

"Oh, my God."

"What's wrong?" Nick demanded, reaching across the table for her arm.

"It's him."

"It's *who*?"

"It's him. The man I told you about, the one I called Brutus. It's him."

"*What?*"

"Oh, my God, oh, my God," she said, scrambling for her purse.

"What are you doing? Are you sure it's him?"

One of the men said something that caused the others to break out in loud laughter. The man closest to Brutus grabbed his cap and pulled it off his head, tussling his hair as if it was part of a joke. As Brutus snatched his cap from the other's hand, Jessie found herself staring at the back of his head. In the middle of his head like the Red Sea parting, was a swath of shaven skull with a jagged scar that almost divided his head in half.

55

The night sky was ablaze with flashing lights from a myriad of FBI vehicles and local law enforcement. They had descended on the tiny Italian restaurant in droves after Grant notified the dispatcher to put out the call. As Grant stood beside his own bureau car, parked sideways across the street to cordon it off, he thought every officer who heard Jessica Palmer's name had responded, each either fantasizing that he would be the one to snare the infamous kidnapper, or he would be a witness to the event.

A block away, the press was descending, also. They were being kept back by local police, but Grant knew it was only a matter of time before their cameras would be picking up the action. And with the newest telephoto lenses, his face could be plastered across television sets even as he stood in the middle of the street.

He turned his back to the media and pressed his cell phone closer to his ear. He'd called the restaurant owner as soon as he'd disconnected from Jessie's call. He knew there were two exits—the front door that he was facing now and a back door off the kitchen, which led to a back alley and through which deliveries were made.

"We have police officers at your back door," he said now to the owner, Raul Crocetti. "We have the back alley covered. How many are in your kitchen?"

"Five," Raul answered. "And three servers."

"I need you to listen very closely. Are you on a cordless phone?"

"Yes, yes, a cordless."

"Go to your back door now."

A moment later, Raul responded that he was there.

Grant radioed to the other officers. "Back door will be opening and the kitchen staff will be leaving. We're looking for a man with a scar on the back of his head. You won't be able to miss it." After he received the acknowledgement from the officer in charge in the alley, he said to Raul, "Open the door to the alley very slowly. Tell me when you have it open."

"It's open."

"Listen for the officer's orders. One at a time, have your kitchen staff leave the restaurant and walk with their hands up toward the officers."

"But—we have stoves on; food is cooking."

"Leave one person to turn everything off."

"But these are commercial—"

"Leave one person. And I want to know who that person is, and what they look like. Do you have a female chef?"

"Yes."

"Leave a female there."

The minutes ticked by slowly. The restaurant was an intimate little place, an eatery he'd been to many times in the past. Now he tried to remember the layout of the tables and the bar. Because it was a favorite among romantics, it did not have any windows looking onto the street. It relied instead on inside mood lighting. Now the coziness of the place was working to his advantage; the kidnapper Jessie had called Brutus would have to physically exit the building before he would spot them surrounding him.

Almost four minutes went by. Grant kept the cell phone to one ear while he listened to the officers identifying each person as they exited and were confirmed not to have matched the description of the suspect.

Grant peered out of the corner of his eye at Ivory, who was also listening intently. She'd been on a date with a man she'd described as a "gorgeous hunk" when the call came through, and she hadn't been too thrilled about leaving her date behind to rush to the scene. In fact, Grant thought, she'd been downright miffed and her attitude had only gotten worse as the minutes ticked past.

"Sorry," Grant said as he waited for the last of the kitchen help to exit the building.

"My first date with him," she said. "Do you have any idea how long I've been waiting for this night?" Grant didn't answer and she continued, "I have had this major league crush on him *forever*. I'm just hoping this doesn't spell the end of things before they even get started."

"Couldn't be helped."

"If he tells me he never wants to see me again because of this, you will pay, Grant Bailey."

The radio crackled, notifying Grant that all of the kitchen help except one had left the building and were secured at the end of the alley.

"Mr. Crocetti?" he said into the cell phone.

"Yes?"

"Who is left in the kitchen?"

"A cook, my daughter, Rosalie."

"Tell her to stay in the kitchen."

"Yes."

"How many patrons are there?"

There was a pause on the other end of the line.

"Mr. Crocetti, have one of your wait staff count the number of customers. We need an exact count."

Another two and then three minutes passed. Grant looked at his watch and then peered down the street toward the media. The crowd had grown and now onlookers had gathered. It wasn't every day they barricaded a street in downtown Franklin, and he suspected it would be one of the lead stories on television news.

"Twenty-eight."

"Okay. Now, Mr. Crocetti, I need for you to listen very carefully to me. There's a young woman there with her date. She told me she's wearing a royal blue sweater, a turtleneck, and jeans. She's also wearing black leather boots. Do you see her?"

A moment passed. "Yes."

"I am going to be just outside the front door to your restaurant. I want you to tell her and her boyfriend to come out of the restaurant very calmly, as if nothing is happening."

"Okay."

Grant looked at Ivory. "Cover me."

Then he made his way from his FBI car to the front door of the restaurant. He stood just off to the side, where anyone exiting the establishment would not be likely to see him until they were in full view of the officers. He glanced behind him. Ivory had moved into position behind the opened door to the vehicle. He started to count the number of other law enforcement vehicles there, but stopped when he reached six. The door to the restaurant was opening.

It opened slowly at first, as if the person on the other side was unsure. Then Jessie spotted him, and a mixture of relief and anxiety crossed her face.

"Keep moving," Grant said.

Nick followed her outside. Grant caught a glimpse of an older gentleman with a cordless phone plastered against his ear, watching nervously.

"Stop there."

Jessie and Nick stopped at the edge of the curb.

"Over here, behind me."

He waited until both of them had moved behind him so his body was between them and the door to the restaurant.

"Where is he?" Grant asked.

"He went to the rest room."

"How long ago?"

"Maybe ten minutes ago."

"And he didn't come out yet?"

"No. We've been watching."

"Did he spot you?"

"No; I don't think so." Jessie eyes were wide.

Grant nodded. Then he raised the cell phone to his ear. "Mr. Crocetti?"

"Yes."

"Ask the party closest to the front door to come out of the restaurant. I need for you to keep me informed how many are in the party, male or female, approximate age..."

After a minute or two during which Grant could hear the owner fretfully describe a vague "situation", asking his patrons to exit the building, the first group emerged. His eyes swept past the children and women and honed in on the males. If the kidnapper was smart, he would attempt to blend in with a group or family, hoping he would make his escape simply by walking away. But each man that emerged did not elicit any recognition from Jessie. Each one had a full head of hair or was naturally balding. There was no man with a scar running down the length of his skull.

One by one, Raul Crocetti was directed to escort a group to the door. One by one, they emerged—some appearing perplexed, others red with fury, still others with fear in their eyes. But once they emerged from the restaurant and caught sight of the law enforcement vehicles and personnel assembled outside, their faces all turned to shock. One by one they were directed across the street, where police officers whisked them out of the line of danger.

Grant didn't know what they were being told, if anything. He knew they would be detained until the entire restaurant was empty, and they had their man in custody.

Finally, Raul came back on the line. "Everyone is gone."

"Everyone?"

"I have three wait staff, myself, and my daughter who is in the kitchen."

"Did you check the restrooms?"

"No. I can do that now."

"No." Grant hesitated. "Send out the wait staff. Then you come out."

One by one, the wait staff exited. One by one, they were led across the street to join the others. When Raul Crocetti exited, he still held the cordless phone in his hands.

"You can hang up now," Grant said with a slight smile. He folded his cell phone and slipped it into his pocket. "You did very well."

He waited until the owner had united with his staff before motioning to Ivory. She emerged from behind the door of the vehicle, joining him at the door.

A moment later, they were inside.

The restaurant lighting was low. Too low, Grant thought as his eyes raced over the walls nearest the door, hoping to find a set of light switches. Not finding any, he pulled his gun and watched as Ivory followed suit.

Wordlessly, they crept down the center aisle. There were no sounds, no voices, no footsteps. He looked ahead, his eyes searching the floor around each table, but he saw no feet and no signs the restaurant was inhabited. The bar was empty; the only sounds coming from the muffled television set, where a sports game was just ending.

They rounded the bar and stopped abruptly in the hallway outside the rest rooms.

The hallway was perhaps thirty feet long, he decided. There were two doors, both on the same side of the hall. The one closest to him was marked "Ladies" and the other one, "Gentlemen." The hall ended in a wall. There was no escape except past him and Ivory.

He glanced at Ivory. With a slight nod, he positioned himself on one side of the men's room door. Ivory positioned herself on the opposite side. They stood there for only a second or two before Grant kicked in the door. It swung back and hit the wall behind it, but when it began to move back in place, he was there with his back against it, keeping it pinned to the wall. His gun was extended, his eyes moving swiftly over the room, ready to fire.

There was no one there.

He waited until Ivory had moved in beside him. There were three urinals and two stalls. They moved on either side of the stall doors. At precisely the same time, they kicked in the two doors. They both swung open to reveal empty toilet seats.

Grant's eyes met Ivory's. He knew what she was thinking, and he could feel his own cheeks beginning to turn hot. "Ladies' room," he mouthed.

They made their way to the men's room door. He made a final sweep over the room with his eyes. There was no window. No means of escape.

The ladies' room was empty as well.

They made their way back through the restaurant and down to the kitchen.

"Anybody come through here?" he asked when he spotted Rosalie Crocetti.

She shook her head, her mouth slightly parted as if she was speechless.

"How do you turn on the lights in this place?" he asked.

She hurried to the hallway and opened a cabinet door, behind which was a set of switches. She began turning them on, flooding the restaurant with light.

An hour later, Grant stood just inside the front door. The restaurant was teeming with people—but they were all law enforcement. They had swept every inch of the place. No one— not even a mouse or a cockroach—could have successfully hidden from them.

Raul Crocetti's demeanor had turned from eagerly assisting the FBI to one of complete disgust. He had lost an entire night's revenue. Not one of the patrons had been able to pay for their meals before they'd been ordered out of the restaurant. And the swarm of policemen had kept any others from coming within a block of his establishment.

There was no way he could have exited unseen. Grant knew that. And he'd confirmed it again and again with those positioned outside the front door and those in the alley. There were no windows. Only those two doors, and they had been covered. No one else had acknowledged seeing the man with the black cap, a man with straggly hair who sported a jagged scar that split his hair in two. How could they miss a freak show? Grant wondered. Unless the freak was never there.

He glanced at his watch. Two hours had passed. Two hours of clearing out the restaurant and searching every inch. Two hours and nothing to show for it.

He avoided looking at Ivory, though he could sense her biting her lip and could see out of the corner of his eye, her foot tapping impatiently. He just wanted to go home and pour a drink.

He opened the restaurant door and stepped outside, into a cluster of cameras popping, their lights blinding him, as he found himself surrounded by the media.

56

Grant closed the door to the conference room, shutting out the gawking FBI agents who had wasted the previous evening on a phantom. When he turned around, he stopped for a long moment and stared at Jessie and Nick.

He'd summoned them both to his office this morning like a principal assembling a couple of misbehaving students. Now, as he looked at Nick, he could feel his discomfort. The young man was sitting very solemnly, his hands in his lap, his cheeks almost burgundy. When Grant looked him in the eye, he looked away in discomfort—first glancing at Jessie, and then at his hands.

But Jessie returned Grant's stare. Her chin was high and squared, even defiant. Her eyes didn't blink but remained steely. There was no doubt she was convinced her kidnapper had been there and had somehow mysteriously disappeared into thin air. And she'd no doubt try to place the burden on him to pick up Brutus' trail.

And it would fall to him this morning to set her straight.

He dropped a folder filled with paperwork on the table with a resounding bang that echoed in the small room. Ivory sat at the opposite side of the table, expressionless. The folder was filled with a mishmash of documents, most of which he probably needed to trash, but it looked good to come in with a thick folder, as if he'd amassed a great deal of information on this case. But he knew, and Ivory knew, he hadn't. The fact was the trail had grown cold. He had no leads on Jessie's kidnappers, and Vincent Palmer, as miserable as he was in prison, wasn't talking.

He pulled out a heavy metal chair and sat down. He didn't say anything at first, but simply sat there, staring at Nick for a brief moment and then shifting his attention to Jessie. Nick was along for the ride, Grant thought, even though he had summoned him himself. But it was Jessie he needed to talk to.

"So," he said at last.

No one answered. Jessie continued to return his stare. Nick remained uncomfortable, and Ivory leaned back in her chair.

"Do you know what you've done?"

"I did what I was supposed to do," Jessie answered without hesitation.

He waited a long moment before talking. When silence elapsed, it almost always resulted in the person he was interrogating trying to fill the air with their own voice—and most of the time, talking themselves into deeper trouble. But Jessie didn't take the bait.

"Why don't you tell me what you thought you were 'supposed' to do?" Grant said.

"I saw one of my kidnappers. So, I called you. Certainly, you didn't expect me to apprehend him myself."

He glanced at Ivory, who was trying to suppress a smile. The kid's got gumption, I'll give her that, he thought.

"Let's go back a bit," he said. "You told me—and you testified under oath—that you saw one kidnapper, the one you called Brainiac, kill the other one. The one you called Brutus."

"Yes."

"So which man did you think you saw last night?"

"Brutus."

"The man who died in front of you."

"The man I *thought* died in front of me."

"Well, let's just revisit that scene, because I'm a bit confused," Grant began. Nick shifted in his seat. "You were on the sofa. Chained to it, as I recall."

"Chained, but not to the sofa. To the wood stove in the middle of the room."

"Ah-ha. And I think you had duct tape around your ankles and wrists—"

Jessie motioned toward her arms where the duct tape had been placed. "Here."

"And, as I recall, they had a cap over your head. Like a ski cap."

"That's right."

"But you testified that it was turned backward, so the eyeholes were in the back of your head."

She nodded.

"And there was duct tape keeping the cap on you."

"Yes."

"So, you had a hole in the cap that prevented you from smothering. But the cap acted like a blindfold."

"Kind of."

"Kind of," he repeated.

"Well, the fibers weren't that close together. I could actually see through the cap, and I'd even torn it so I could see even more."

"But you testified under oath that they kept this on you, even after moving you to the second location."

"That's right."

Grant clasped his hands in front of him on the table. "Okay, so I'm a little confused," he continued after a long pause. He looked up to catch Ivory rolling her eyes. He quickly looked away from her. She knew the drill, and that was her way of letting him know he was overdoing it. Maybe, he thought. Maybe not.

"So. You were on the sofa. Chained. Arms and legs tied up—with duct tape. You were wearing a cap turned around backward. But you managed to see through it because the fabric was loosely knit. Have I got all of that right?"

"Yes." Her eyes were locked onto his.

"And now, two men approach you."

"One man."

"One man."

"Brutus."

"So, Brutus approaches you with—I think you testified—ether in his hands?"

"On cotton balls."

"And he's just about ready to knock you out when the other guy—"

"Brainiac."

"—comes up from behind. And what does he do to him, again?"

"He hits him in the back of the head."

"With an axe," Grant finished pointedly.

Jessie nodded.

"Now, as I recall, he didn't hit him with the handle of the axe."

Jessie continued staring at him.

"Or with the side of the blade."

Her expression had not changed.

He stood up and held both hands up, as if he had an axe handle held in them. "He took the axe," he said, holding his hands above his head, "and he came down on the back of Brutus' skull—" he dropped his hands down quickly, banging them against the table and causing Nick to jump.

Jessie continued staring at him.

"And, if I recall correctly, you testified the axe was embedded in his skull. I think that was the word you used, isn't it, Jessie?" His voice was fluid and smooth.

"Yes. I think so."

"Now, the man—Brutus—has just been struck from behind with the blade of an axe. He falls—" Grant pushed his chair out of the way. "And he lands on you. Blood is everywhere."

"That's right."

"And the axe—it's still in his skull. He's actually lying there across you, with an axe *embedded in the bone.*"

"Look," Jessie said, her eyes still locked on his but her face reddening in anger, "I know what you're getting at. How could a man be lying there with an axe in his skull, dying, and then get up and recover and find his way to a bar like nothing happened?"

"Is that what I'm thinking, Jessie? Or is that what you'd be wondering if you were standing here in my shoes?"

She bit her lip.

After a long moment, he sat back down. Nick continued looking at his hands in his lap. Grant glanced at the other end of the table, where Ivory was studying Jessie's expression.

"Jessie," Grant said finally. His voice was a bit softer but remained firm. "There are all sorts of reasons why someone could have a scar. Let's say you really did see a man at the bar last night. And maybe he had a scar. But maybe—just maybe—he'd been in an auto accident. Did that ever occur to you?" Before she could respond, he continued, "Or maybe he'd just had surgery. Maybe he had brain cancer. And maybe what you saw was a man with an incision."

"I know what I saw. And what I saw was Brutus. I am absolutely, positively sure of it."

Grant allowed the silence to become oppressive before he continued. "And what if you are absolutely, positively wrong?"

"I'm not." Each word was emphasized with a visible frustration.

"Okay. Let's say that while you were eating dinner, Brutus walked into the restaurant, sidled up to the bar and ordered a drink. How long did you wait before you called me?"

"A minute. If it took that long."

"A minute. Now, I happen to have the exact time you called me. And I have the exact time the police cars arrived at the scene and covered the two exits. Three minutes. Three."

"Now that deserves a pat on the back," Jessie responded. Grant looked at her for a long moment, but he wasn't able to determine from either her expression or her tone of voice whether her comment had been meant as sarcasm.

"So, you told me last evening that you never took your eyes off this man—"

"Well, I didn't go into the bathroom with him."

"But you saw him go to the rest room."

"Yes."

"Ah-ha. But there's no exit from the rest room."

"Your point?"

"My point," he said, stressing each word, "is there are two ways out of that restaurant. The front door and the back door. You told me last night he did not exit the restaurant before we arrived. That means he disappeared into thin air."

Jessie crossed her arms and raised one eyebrow. "It's not my fault that you lost him."

Grant slammed the palm of his hand down on the table in front of him. "I didn't lose him," he growled, "because I never found him!"

Jessie stared at him coolly. After a long pause, she said, "Your emotions are getting a bit out of control, don't you think?"

Grant bit his lip. If there ever was a female version of Vincent Palmer, Jessie was it. No doubt about it, she was a Palmer, through and through. He stared at her for so long, her image began to blur in front of him. And still, she did not blink and she didn't look away.

"Jessie," he said finally, "you need help."

"That's why I called you."

"No, Jessie, you need professional help. Mental help. Counseling."

She tilted her head. "Do you really think if I get counseling, it will help you locate Brutus?"

He exhaled sharply. "I've never met anybody as exasperating as you." From the corner of his eye, he could see Ivory hiding her mouth behind her hand, suppressing a laugh. "Jessie, I'm going to tell you like it is. You might not like it—you probably won't like it—but you'd better listen up.

"We didn't find Brutus in that restaurant last night because Brutus was never there."

"Yes, he was—"

"Did *you* see him, Nick?" Grant turned to the young man.

Nick hesitated, glancing first at Jessie and then at Grant. "No."

"No?" Jessie almost screamed. "No?!"

"The post was in my way," he said apologetically. "I never got a good look at him."

"Jessie," Grant said, his voice loud and commanding, "do you have any idea—any idea at all—how much you cost us last night? How many police officers and FBI agents were taken off other cases to rush to your aid? How much money that poor man lost because we shut down his business?"

She leaned back in her seat. "I hadn't thought about it."

"Well, maybe you need to think about it, young lady," Grant said, emphasizing the last two words.

She clenched her teeth as she glared at him.

"Because here's the deal. You can do that sort of thing one time and one time only. And you've just used up your free ticket."

She kept her arms crossed in front of her and her face began to redden.

"If you call me again—if you ever call me again—you'd better have Brutus or Brainiac or whatever you want to call them, bound and gagged and ready for me to pick up and cart away. You got that?"

"Are you giving me the authority to arrest someone on my own?"

"No," Ivory said, leaning across the table. All eyes turned toward her. "What he's telling you is: you can't use the FBI like we're your own personal servants. We're not. We have other cases to solve and we can't spend all our time chasing after people you think you see when you're drunk."

"I was not drunk!"

"You smelled like alcohol last night," Grant interjected.

"I had one drink. Maybe two."

Grant stood up. "Jessie, do yourself a favor. Get help. You've gone through a lot. And now you're seeing things—seeing people—that aren't there."

With that, he picked up his stack of papers and walked purposefully to the door. Without turning around, he opened the door and walked out, leaving it hanging open for the other FBI agents to continue gawking.

57

The tension in the car was thick enough to slice it with a knife, Jessie thought as Nick turned onto their street. He had barely parked the car before she threw open the door. When she closed it, she purposefully slammed it so hard that the small Volkswagen shook.

She had her key in the door before she heard his footsteps on the stairs below, just beginning to ascend to their floor. She left the door partially open as she stormed into the apartment.

Abby followed her to the living room, her large brown eyes searching Jessie's for the cause of her bad mood.

A moment later, Nick walked through the door and closed it silently behind him. As Abby walked over to him, he paused to stroke her muzzle and under her chin.

Traitor, Jessie thought as she watched. "We need to talk."

"Yes," Nick said, rising from Abby's side. "We do."

Jessie stood in front of the sofa and glared at him. "I'm going to be honest with you," she said. "You let me down."

"What?" Nick's jaw dropped.

Jessie continued frowning at him.

"What?" he repeated. When she didn't answer, he moved toward her, his brows furrowing. "Just how do you figure that *I* let you down?"

"Don't play innocent with me."

"Don't play—?"

"You know exactly what I'm talking about. You made me look like a fool."

"I—*I* made you look like a fool?" His face reddened. "From where I was sitting, it looked like you were doing a pretty good job of that all by yourself!"

"Ah!!"

"Don't tell me I made Jessica Palmer *speechless*?"

"Don't you dare change the subject. Don't you dare." Jessie felt tears beginning to well up in the corners of her eyes. "Why did you tell them you didn't see Brutus? Why?"

"Because I didn't, Jessie!"

"Yes, you did! You were right there!"

"I didn't. Don't you remember, Jessie? You told me not to turn around."

"But—but—"

"I did exactly—" he pointed his finger at her "—*exactly* what you told me to do. And now I'm catching hell for it? You're attacking *me* because of something you think *you* saw?"

"You always told me you're a good reporter. The best!"

"What does that have to do with anything?"

"Good reporters don't miss a thing."

"Oh, oh, that's low, Jessie. That is low."

"I know you saw him! Why didn't you tell Grant?"

Nick bit his lip and held it for so long that Jessie was afraid it would begin bleeding. When he spoke, his voice was low and his face was beginning to turn an odd shade of blue. "Jessie, I have a brand new job."

"This isn't about you."

"Well, for once, Jessie, it's not all about you."

She crossed her arms in front of her and tapped her foot.

"My new boss thinks his employees should be working half a day. You know what that is to him, Jess? Do you know?"

She continued to glare at him in defiance.

"That's twelve hours a day. Seven days a week."

Jessie rolled her eyes. Why was he changing the subject? Was he not able to see how much she needed him right now?

"You have no idea what it took for me to be off during your trial. No idea. Now it's all over—it's *supposed* to be all over. How am I ever going to explain why I'm still taking off?"

"Well, what do you expect me to do about it?"

He pointed his finger at her again. "You're going to make me lose my job."

"If your precious job means more to you than I do, then leave. Just leave!"

He glowered at her, his dark brows knit together. He's kind of cute when he's mad, she thought in a perverse sort of way. He started toward the door.

"Don't you leave me!" she ordered.

He stopped with his hand on the doorknob and looked back at her with his head cocked. Then without a word, he opened the door and walked out.

"Don't you walk out on me!" she screamed, rushing out the door behind him. She stopped and leaned over the railing and watched him as he continued down the stairs. She lost sight of him as he reached the ground floor and rounded the corner behind the stairwell.

Jessie sat on the living room couch. The television set blared in front of her, but the images that flashed across the screen could have been a ball game or a sitcom, for all the attention she paid to it. Abby was sprawled across the chair beside the couch, her head lolling over the arm, occasionally fretting in her sleep as if she was chasing a rabbit.

Jessie continued to hold the glass of wine in her hand, although it had been empty for more than an hour. The wine bottle on the coffee table was also empty.

My life sucks, she thought. Everybody is victimizing me. It's like I have a sign on my back.

She stared at the boxes lining the walls. They moved here to start a brand new life and all they seemed to do anymore was fight. This was supposed to be a place of joy. Happiness. A place where she could forget everything that had happened.

As she stared at the boxes, the empty walls, and the chaotic environment caused by the recent move, she felt instead like she was in a crypt. Or worse, she thought. At least in death there's peace. I'm somewhere in between, like purgatory.

Maybe Nick was right. Grant was right. Maybe she did need a shrink. Maybe she didn't see him at all. She felt the blood rising in her cheeks. How embarrassing, she thought, if I really saw somebody else and my mind turned him into Brutus.

She began to count the boxes. Nineteen, just in this room alone.

With a heavy sigh, she rose unsteadily from the couch. May as well start unpacking. Nick would be home in a few hours. Maybe, if the place looked neater, more like a home, he'd forget their little tiff.

Abby opened one eye and barely raised her head as Jessie approached the first box. With a little effort, she peeled the tape off the top and opened it.

The contents were covered with *The Tennessean* to keep them from shifting in the move, and now Jessie picked up the top sheet. The headline caught her attention. *First Palmer Bank Enters New Era.* This was the article Nick had been reading the day she was waiting at the window for the movers to arrive, she thought. God, that day seemed so long ago.

She sat back down and skimmed the article. It made her ill just to think about First Palmer Bank—the very bank that bore their name—in the hands of someone else. The end of an era, the newspaper called it, the end of the Palmer family control.

The article was continued on the next page, and she came close to wadding it up and tossing it in the trash without reading it. But something prodded her to continue, something deep inside. Maybe it was a yearning to know what was happening there so Daddy would know what he'd have to do when he changed things back. When he was out of prison, that is. Out of prison, vindicated, and back in control.

She took a deep breath and tried to push away the uneasiness she felt. She folded back the page and continued reading.

At the bottom of the article was a picture of a man, and she found herself staring at him with her heart in her throat. The events of that horrible December evening came rushing back to her—of grabbing the man as he steered the truck, trying to throw them into the ditch along the side of the road, trying to escape—of the man who walked up behind Brutus, the axe raised high. The man who tried to carry her out to the truck by himself, who deposited her in the cellar to die.

She closed her eyes. She was going crazy.

When she reopened her eyes, she expected to see a different face staring back at her from the newspaper. A man with a beard, perhaps. Of an Asian man. Or a black man.

But it was a white man, a clean-shaven man. A man with an odd face, as though one side had been affected by a stroke, or disfigured by an accident.

The newspaper began to swim in front of her, and she found herself clutching the arm of the couch in an attempt to steady herself. The caption below the picture read Edward Buchanan.

58

Jessie stood in front of the full-length mirror in the master bedroom and studied herself closely. Her hair was normally worn straight, its light brown shoulder length tresses gently skirting her shoulders. Now it was pulled up and back into a no-nonsense bun. Her eyes appeared greener and more vivid with the addition of a smoldering eyeliner, and her lips were perfectly outlined in a down-to-earth, tawny color that was neither too blatantly feminine nor too harsh.

Her eyes moved downward from her ears, the lobes outfitted with brilliantly underplayed pearls, to her navy pin-striped suit. The blouse was visible with its fresh white, buttoned-down collar and coordinating navy pin stripes. The skirt was just the right length, ending right at the knee.

If she was going to confront Edward Buchanan, she was going to look the part of an aggressive prosecuting attorney.

She slipped on a pair of alligator stilettos, remembering vividly how expertly Kristin Cook had played the role of successful lawyer. As she made her way through the apartment, she traded her normal scrunched denim bag for a deep brown leather briefcase that was just compact enough to tuck under one arm.

She stopped in the kitchen to give Abby a treat and to rub her soft golden muzzle under her chin, where she liked it most. Then she straightened. With one final inhale, she stepped toward the door of the apartment.

She was ready to meet Brainiac now, on her terms.

As Jessie maneuvered her shiny Mercedes into the parking space next to her father's reserved spot, she couldn't help but notice a brand new, polished Lincoln Navigator Limited Edition in tuxedo black parked there. It was hard to see his spot usurped, and she swallowed hard and looked away, lest she begin to lose her resolve.

As Jessie entered the side door into the bank lobby, she came to a dead stop. The last time she'd entered this lobby, she realized, was seven years ago, just prior to beginning her undergraduate studies at Vandy. And now as she peered around her, she became conscious of the fact that everything had changed.

The walls had been wallpapered in an ornate pattern that looked suited for the Oval Office. As her eyes moved down the wall past the polished walnut chair rails, they came to rest on the plush Oriental carpet beneath her feet. The entire lobby had sparkling new marble floors and one lavish carpet after another had been spread atop it, effectively dividing the massive room into a variety of smaller work areas.

She continued into the lobby, moving more slowly now as the changes began to sink in. The row of teller windows, once a long metal counter with deep blue accents, had been replaced with a granite counter in an earth-tone color, a dark walnut countertop accent with matching chair rail accentuating its richness. The furniture was new; the austere business desks replaced with flamboyantly carved walnut in front of opulently plush gold chairs.

"Jessie!"

The use of her name in an urgent stage whisper startled her, and she turned quickly in the direction of the voice. But as she opened her mouth to speak, he hurriedly grabbed her elbow and ushered her into a conference room, closing the door rapidly behind him.

"What are you doing here?" he asked. Though they were now alone, his voice remained a whisper and as Jessie stared at him, his eyes darted from her face to the door behind her as though he was afraid it would open at any minute.

She didn't remember the first time she'd met Paul Buttrey. She supposed she might have been in diapers at the time, perhaps even still at the hospital after her mother had given birth to her. She'd always known him as Uncle Paul, and was stunned to learn in her pre-teen years that he wasn't even related to them. He had grown up with Vincent as Paul Buttrey, Sr. had grown up with her grandfather. All four of them had made banking their business and now as Jessie stared at him, she wondered why he had not been made the chief executive officer in her father's absence.

He looked thinner than he had the last time she'd seen him, almost wiry. His hair, once shoe-black, was now gray and sparse. Heavy bags formed under his eyes and he appeared as if he was tired, worn-out.

"Uncle Paul," was all she could manage to say.

"You shouldn't be here," he whispered. He moved around so his back was against the door.

She swallowed. "I came to see Edward Buchanan."

His eyes widened, emphasizing the red veins in the whites of his eyes. "Why?"

She stepped back and squared her shoulders. "I don't think I owe you an explanation." There was an odor in the room that made her begin to feel uneasy, but she couldn't quite put her finger on it.

He exhaled as if he was trying to rid himself of every breath in his body. "I'm sorry, Jessie," he said, mopping his forehead with his handkerchief. "Mr. Buchanan isn't here."

"Where is he?"

"Nashville. He won't be back for several hours."

She narrowed her eyes. For some reason, she didn't believe him.

"Jessie," he continued, his voice low, "if Mr. Buchanan finds out we've talked, he'd fire me on the spot."

"Why?"

"You know my loyalty is with your father. I'm sorry, I know you testified against him, but I won't—I can't—believe he had you kidnapped."

She squeezed his arm. "I know. I don't believe it anymore myself."

His jaw dropped and for a moment, he moved his mouth back and forth like a fish.

"But—why would you get fired for talking to me? Am I that hated here?"

"No. No, it has nothing to do with you. Or your testimony. It's just—"

She waited for him to continue. When he didn't, she blurted, "Just what?"

"Your father had a reputation for being hard-nosed. Some might have said at one time or another that he was a bully. But he was honest. And he made this bank successful."

"What are you getting at?"

"As soon as your father was—convicted…"

"It's okay. Go on."

"Buchanan fired the chief financial officer, Pam Woody."

"I know Pam. I've known her for years. She's one of the best—if not *the* best."

"And Bill Farris."

"The chief auditor?"

He nodded.

"But why?"

"I don't know. They'd both been here almost as long as I have."

Jessie dropped her eyes, staring at her alligator shoes and the rug beneath them. "My father rewarded loyalty." She looked back at Paul. "And hard work."

"I know."

"He'd be furious." She dropped her hand from his arm and crossed to the table, where she set her briefcase on the polished burled wood. As she turned around, her eyes rested on a row of photographs in ornate frames along the wall. It began with her grandfather's photograph as the founder of the bank, progressing to her father. But now there was another picture and she began to feel as though she'd been punched in the gut. It was Edward Buchanan, sitting as regally as a king. And as she stared at it, her eyes came to rest on the distinct chin with the pointed jawline.

"What happened to his face?" she asked softly.

"Whose?"

She pointed toward the picture.

Paul shook his head, as if her question had been trivial. "House fire. Killed his sister. He was on the second floor. Rumor was he tried to save her—but he was on fire himself. Jumped out of the second floor window. What the fire didn't burn, the fall broke."

She turned back to Paul, who was watching her curiously. "What reason did he give for firing them?" she said at last. Her voice sounded strange to her; muffled and almost piercing, all at the same time.

"Officially, no reason. He's in charge now. He doesn't have to explain himself to his subordinates. But unofficially, behind closed doors, he said their performance was substandard."

"That can't be."

"He replaced them with two kids right out of college. No offense, Jessie, I know you just graduated—"

"None taken."

"It's just that—these are executive positions. A person works for years to make it to that level."

She lifted her chin and studied him. He'd been loyal to her father; and in her opinion, he should have been the one to step into her father's position. But there was something in his expression that made her think he wasn't telling her all of this just because he'd been passed over for a promotion. She looked at the lines around his mouth: tired, tense lines. And then she looked back at his eyes. "Why did he put two newcomers in those positions?"

"I don't have any proof. But… the only reason I can figure it is, you put kids in high level positions if you want somebody there who doesn't know what they're doing."

"You're saying, he'd purposefully put people in these positions not for their experience, but precisely for their lack of experience?"

He nodded.

"What reason could he possibly have for doing that?"

Paul cocked his head as if listening through the door. After a long moment, he said, "Because with new kids as the CFO and Chief Auditor, Buchanan can intimidate them. Instead of those kids watching over him as quality control, he's got them thinking his job is to look over them instead."

"But—the Board—"

"Three days after your father's conviction, the Board called an emergency meeting. They made Edward Buchanan the Chairman of the Board and CEO."

Jessie pulled out a chair and sat down heavily. A polished ash tray rested in the middle of the table with a box of Fire Chief wooden matches beside it. After a moment, she said, "So that's why his picture is on the wall."

Paul looked briefly at the picture. "Yes."

"Who called the meeting?"

"Mr. Buchanan himself."

A soft knock on the door interrupted them and as Jessie peered at Paul, she thought he would faint. But before either of them could respond, the door opened a crack.

"Martha!" Jessie exclaimed.

Her father's secretary burst into the room. Her arms were full and it took her a moment to set the items down. As Jessie rose to hug her, Paul slipped out the door, closing it behind him.

"Am I interrupting something?" Martha said, realizing Paul was gone.

"Oh, Martha. Daddy was right when he nicknamed you Radar."

Martha chuckled. She'd been Vincent Palmer's executive assistant for longer than Jessie could remember. She was extremely dedicated, both to the bank and to her father. Jessie remembered visiting on Saturdays and finding her hard at work, even though she was supposed to be off, and she couldn't begin to count all the long nights her father had worked with Martha by his side. He nicknamed her 'Radar' because he said she'd always have documents and agendas typed and ready before he would even ask for them.

Now, she stood back and grabbed Jessie's hands, admiring her clothing. Jessie didn't think she'd ever seen Martha in anything other than a smart tailored suit, even when she'd run into her at local stores. Now she wore a hot pink blouse with a flowered jacket of hot pink, yellow and orange; sunny colors, Jessie thought, that always countered her father's brusque demeanor. Martha adjusted her glasses.

"What are you doing here?" she asked. Though she was smiling, her brows began to furrow.

"I came to see Edward Buchanan."

"The King?"

Jessie felt nauseated, and she dropped Martha's hands and reached for the back of the chair. As she did so, she realized what the older woman had brought into the room was a set of golf clubs and a cap.

"Honey, are you okay?" Martha asked.

"Whose cap is that?" Jessie asked. She reached toward it but couldn't bring herself to touch it. On the front of the cap was a shark logo.

"Edward Buchanan's. You don't look so good, Honey."

"I'm fine."

Martha's eyes rested on the golf clubs. "He's in Nashville," she said by way of explanation. "He called and asked me to put his clubs in here. When he returns, he's got a tee time."

"I see. I—have some unpleasant business with him."

"You and everybody else."

Jessie looked up sharply. "What do you mean?"

"Child, if he was on fire, the folks around here would not even spit on him. That's what we think of him." Jessie was taken aback by her sudden change in demeanor.

"Why?"

"People are either givers or takers. And he's a taker. What a greedy man he is. And no loyalty to this bank, whatsoever."

"Then, how can he remain in charge?"

"Oh, he's got half the board thinking he's holy."

"And the other half?"

"They don't trust him. If you ask me, the board has given him too much authority. Especially with his lending limits."

"How much power does he have?"

"Too much. You know who the board members are; who you can trust. Go talk to them. Let them know things aren't right here. But that didn't come from me. I might not want to work for him, but I *have* to work."

"I understand."

Jessie pulled out her cell phone and took a picture of the golf cap.

"What are you doing?" Martha asked.

"For my scrap book," Jessie answered. She whirled around and snapped a picture of Edward's picture before returning to the table and taking a picture of the matches.

"Child, you need to get out of here before he comes back and finds you here. He'll have you escorted off the property."

"I'm still a shareholder," Jessie said. "And I'd just *love* to see him try to throw me out." As Martha's face dropped, she added, "But I won't make trouble for you. I'll get up with him later." She moved past Martha and quietly opened the door. "And you'll know it when I do." With that, she was gone, making her way to the side door before anyone else recognized her.

59

Jessie sat in the driver's seat of her Mercedes. Though she stared straight ahead, she wasn't focused on the parking lot or the side of the bank building. Instead, her mind was focused on Paul and Martha and First Palmer Bank.

She'd been sitting in this position for more than half an hour. It was hotter than usual on this spring day, and the Mercedes was stifling. Somewhere in the back of her mind, she began to register the odor of stale perfume and shortly after that the first beads of perspiration began to form on her forehead.

It was stupid to come here, she thought. If Edward Buchanan—Brainiac—had been here, she didn't know now whether she would have had the chutzpah to confront him. And with the warnings from her old friends—more importantly, perhaps, her father's old friends—she realized she was quickly getting in over her head.

She pulled out her cell phone and held it in the palm of her hand as if she was weighing it. She needed to notify Grant Bailey; he needed to know Brainiac was here, running First Palmer Bank. She would forward the pictures to him as evidence. He would know exactly what to do.

As she stared at the bank building, the back door started to open and then held its position as if the person leaving was speaking to someone else. Her father had brought her through that door many times as she was growing up. It was used primarily by the caterers, as it led first to a commercial kitchen before providing ready access to a set of conference rooms. He liked it, he teased, because he could sneak in and out of the building without being detected by too many people—the kind of people, he said, who shouldn't know his business.

His words now took on greater significance, and she continued staring at the door.

When it opened fully and the person emerged, she felt the blood drain from her face.

It was Nick.

She ducked. What in the world would she tell him if he detected her there, crouched across the front seat of the SUV? She wondered. She slipped her briefcase to the floorboard. If he happened to walk past her window and noticed her there, she would claim she was getting something out of her briefcase. She even dropped the cell phone to the floor beside it, as an additional excuse.

What am I doing? She thought frantically. I should be asking him what he's doing here, not the other way around!

She eased higher and peered over the dash. He was gone. As she began to rise to a seated position, she heard an engine start in the row behind her. Peeking around the headrest, she spotted his yellow Volkswagen Bug pulling out of a parking spot.

She waited until he'd pulled onto West 8th Street before she started her own engine and pulled out behind him.

She kept a respectable distance from him. He knows my vehicle, she thought. This is insane! She thought of phoning him, telling him she was a block behind him, but something deep inside her stopped her. He wasn't only at First Palmer Bank, where she knew for a fact he didn't have an account, but he was exiting the back door—a door not available to bank customers. That meant someone had escorted him through the maze of hallways where only seasoned bank employees would ever have a reason to venture.

He turned onto Interstate 65 heading north and she followed behind him. She maintained a comfortable gap between them, which was quickly filled by other vehicles. At least her SUV was black, and if she stayed far enough behind him, he might not know whether it was a Mercedes or a Ford. Or he might not care.

He stayed on the interstate for forty miles, long enough for Jessie's curiosity to turn to irritation. She *lived* with him, she reasoned, he had every opportunity in the world to tell her he was going to First Palmer Bank—unless he didn't want her to know he was there. She felt her face begin to burn with a growing anger. By the time he pulled off the highway onto Broadway, she was seething.

He drove into a permit-only parking lot, parking in a spot near the door. She pulled to the side of the road and watched him gather paperwork from the front seat. How dare he go there when he knew what that bank meant to her—meant to her father! She slammed her foot on the gas pedal and pulled out, barely missing a passing car.

She would confront him right now, right here, and he'd be forced to explain himself.

She swerved into the parking lot as he was nearing the building. She'd barely put her foot on the brake before she'd thrown the gear into park. But by the time she hurled open the car door, he was in the building.

She kept the car door wide open and the engine running as she rushed after him. Flinging open the door, heated words on her lips, she was stunned to find herself in an empty hallway.

More slowly now, she continued down the hall until she reached a row of elevators. One was moving upward from the lobby, and she watched as the indicator displayed each floor, stopping at the third.

She pressed the elevator button, impatiently summoning it back down. While she waited, she alternated between pacing and pushing the button again and again, her rage growing with each punch. She stopped at the directory and tried to see past her anger to the words printed there.

She was in the headquarters building of *The Tennessean* newspaper. His job. She thought of turning around and heading back home, perhaps waiting for him to arrive later that evening and asking sweetly, "Where have you been this afternoon, Sweetheart?" And he would no doubt tell her he'd been at work. He'd never mention that he'd been at the bank.

That liar, she thought as she marched back to the elevator button and punched it again with renewed vigor. That liar!

Finally, the elevator doors opened and she stepped inside, striking the third floor button with enough force to hurt her finger. How dare him! She thought, staring at her finger. If it hadn't been for him, I wouldn't have just hurt myself!

The elevator was agonizingly slow. By the time it reached the third floor and the doors opened, her face was burning hot and her fists were doubled.

A receptionist in front of the elevators started to smile but it froze on her face, leaving her with a silly grin. "May I—?" she began.

"Nick Rhodes," Jessie snapped. "Where is he?"

The receptionist picked up the phone. "I'll call the newsroom for you," she said nervously.

"The newsroom? The newsroom?" Jessie said, her voice becoming louder with each word. "This way's the newsroom?"

"Oh my God," the receptionist breathed into the phone.

Jessie marched through the lobby and past a wall, finding herself in a large room where activity appeared at a fever pitch. There must have been dozens of desks crammed in the room, separated by partitions that were so low, she could see dozens of heads bobbing up and down—some on the phone, others staring into computer screens, their fingers rushing frantically over the keyboards. Phones were ringing in every direction, filling the air with a constant chorus.

"Ma'am," the receptionist called, "you can't go in there!"

"I just did," she retorted.

She marched down the center aisle, peering at each cubicle as she went. They were all the same size, perhaps eight feet square.

Maybe even smaller, she thought. Paper was everywhere—newspapers stacked, copy paper, paper spitting out of the printers…

Somewhere in the back of her mind, she could hear the receptionist calling out to her, trying to stop her, but she strode onward with renewed purpose.

She found Nick in the middle of the long aisle, setting down his paperwork beside a computer.

"Jessie, what are you—?"

"What were you doing there?" she demanded.

The young woman on the other side of the partition looked up, her brows furrowed.

"Doing where?"

"Doing where?" she mimicked. "Don't play innocent with me. I saw you!"

"Calm down, Jess." His eyes quickly roamed through his cubicle and realizing he had but one chair, he slid his toward her. "Have a seat. Let's talk about it."

"I don't want to have a seat. You can't make me have a seat!"

"Okay," he said, prolonging the last syllable. He started to pull the chair back but she grabbed it.

"Give me that seat," she snarled. She held onto the back of it with both hands until her knuckles turned bright white.

"What's going on, Jessie?" he said in a measured voice.

Without looking to either side, Jessie knew the newsroom was coming to a screeching halt. Though the phones still rang incessantly, no one appeared to be answering them. There were no more keyboards clacking or voices filling the air. Like a carnival game, heads were popping up all over the newsroom, and all eyes were on her.

"You know what's going on," she said through gritted teeth. "I saw you sneaking out the back door of First Palmer Bank." She lifted her chin high, as if she'd just caught him red-handed.

"What?" he said.

"Don't pretend like you weren't there, either," she continued. "I have proof. I—I took pictures of you with my cell phone!"

His lips parted and for a moment, he simply stared at her. When he finally spoke, his words had an edge. "You came all the way here, to my new job, to ask me that?"

She lifted her chin higher. Out of the corner of her eye, she glimpsed a man entering the newsroom from an office at the far end. His most distinguishing feature was a bald head, which ended in folds at his neckline. He pointed a thick finger at the person closest to him. "Answer the damn phone!" he barked.

Then, his eyes locked on Jessie. As she turned her attention away from Nick, the bald-headed man moved up the aisle with his chin almost resting on his chest and his eyes staring straight ahead, fixed on her. He looked, she thought with growing alarm, like a charging bull.

"Rhodes!" he growled, not taking his eyes off her.

"Yes, sir." Nick's voice was quiet, but Jessie detected an anger boiling just beneath the surface.

Maybe she should have waited until he'd gotten home to confront him.

"You got that story on community banks yet?"

"I just got back from interviewing folks at First Palmer Bank," he said, pointedly staring at Jessie. "They gave me some great information on how they're managing to remain profitable during this recession." As he spoke, his words became more pronounced, each one louder than the last.

The man didn't answer but stood there in the aisle, his wide physique almost touching the partitions on either side of it, as he peered back and forth from Jessie to Nick, his eyes narrowing. Finally, he punched his wristwatch and snarled, "Deadlines, Rhodes! Deadlines!"

"Yes, sir!"

"Fifteen minutes," he continued. "The article had better be on my desk." His words hung in the air, the ultimatum clear.

After a few agonizing seconds that seemed more like minutes, he turned around. The heads that had popped up to watch the action just as quickly disappeared into paperwork or computer screens.

"You need help, Jessie," Nick said. His eyes were narrowed, his lips moving as if he was chewing on the inside of them. For the first time, Jessie realized his hands were balled into fists and now as she watched, he appeared to be clenching them more tightly.

"Look, I made a mistake," she said, keeping her voice low so the others wouldn't hear her.

He yanked the chair out of her hands. "You heard my boss," he said. "Fifteen minutes. You're wasting my time."

60

Jessie sat on the couch with the photograph album opened in her lap. The light was waning as the sun dipped below the horizon, but she didn't feel motivated enough to get up, walk across the room, and turn on a light.

Nick should have been home by now, but as she stared at the closed door to their apartment, she felt an emptiness in the pit of her stomach. He hadn't telephoned either their home phone or her cell phone, and she frankly didn't blame him.

She turned back to the photograph album. As she'd continued to open more boxes, she'd run across one that contained all of her photographs. She'd opened a bottle of Chardonnay and plopped down on the couch, and here she'd sat for hours, simply staring at the pictures.

She studied a picture of herself standing in front of the first school she'd ever attended. Her hair was halfway down her back and as straight as an Indian's, as Daddy used to say. It was pulled off her face in the photograph with pastel pink ribbons, ribbons he had placed in her hair that morning before driving her to school. She'd hated them then; she'd thought they were too childish and she was starting kindergarten and was too old for that kind of foolishness. But now, as she stared at those large green eyes, the long light brown hair, the pink dress and matching ribbons, and the patent leather shoes her father had tied, she wished she was there again.

She flipped the page and looked intently at another picture of her on a swing set. Her feet didn't even touch the ground beneath her. This time, she wore pink and white sneakers, again, neatly tied by Daddy, a hot pink pair of leggings and a pink plaid blouse. She'd forgotten how much Daddy loved the color pink on her when she was a child. He'd already told her how thrilled he'd been to learn that he was the father of a baby daughter. He'd never wanted a son, he insisted; just her.

Now she stared at a shadow in the photograph: a shadow of Daddy snapping the picture. And behind him, a sign to Maury County Park and the Kid's Playground that Daddy helped to build when he was a young man.

Jessie leaned against the sofa and closed her eyes tightly in an attempt to keep back the tears. How had her life gone so completely off track?

At the age of fourteen, she knew what her future would be as clearly as if she'd laid out a blueprint. She'd go to Vanderbilt University for her undergraduate degree and a law degree. And upon being admitted to the Bar, she'd become President of First Palmer Bank. When Daddy retired, she'd be ready to step into the position of Chief Executive Officer. And by so doing, she'd become the third generation Palmer to be in control of the bank that bore their family name.

All of those plans had gone badly awry with one incident. But as the shadows grew longer in the room and she continued contemplating how drastically her life's direction had changed, she realized that to allow that change would also allow Brainiac and Brutus to be successful.

She sucked in her breath. It hadn't been enough to get five million dollars' ransom for her. That had only been the tip of the proverbial iceberg. No; what Brainiac—Edward Buchanan—had really wanted was control of the bank.

And, now he had it.

She didn't have the experience to fight him on the bank's turf. Only her father could do that. As she recalled the conversations with Paul and Martha, she realized they also wanted him to return, to snatch the bank out of Edward's hands, and regain control.

The only way for her to do that was to prove his innocence.

A tear escaped and then another. What she needed right now, at this very moment, was for Nick to rush through the front door, pull her into his strong arms, and tell her how much he loved her.

She leaned forward and picked up her cell phone from the coffee table. She checked for messages, knowing even as she did so, that he hadn't tried to call her. She had no idea where he was, or if he even intended to return to her. She'd pushed him beyond the brink. As she thought of how she'd embarrassed him in front of his co-workers and the trouble she'd probably caused with his boss, her skin grew hot and clammy. He was right, if he hated her. She deserved it.

Daddy was the only one who had always been there for her. And now even he was gone, locked away behind steel bars and razor wire.

She closed the photograph album and placed it on the coffee table, resting her cell phone on top of it. She looked around the apartment: at Nick's furniture, his knick-knacks, the pictures he intended to hang on the walls. She stared at the boxes arranged around the walls. And she felt overwhelmed.

It had been a mistake to move here. She should have packed up her things in her old condominium and gone home.

She thought of the last time she'd seen her mother, the hurtful words she'd said and the way she'd felt when she'd tossed the alcohol in her face. But she'd been drunk. And she probably didn't even remember it now; didn't remember Jessie ever having been there that afternoon, or what had been said or done.

Maybe she needed to pack some bags and go home. Her old bedroom was still as it was the day she'd left for college; her father had seen to that. Nothing had been touched. She could move back in and work on proving her father's innocence—and Edward Buchanan's guilt.

She couldn't call Grant Bailey. Not yet. He'd thought she was either crazy or hallucinating when she reported Brutus at the restaurant. If she were to call him now and report to him that

Brainiac was right there in Columbia and running the family's bank, he'd probably hang up on her.

No. If she was to find Brutus and bring him to justice, and also expose Brainiac, she would have to do it herself. It was the only way.

From out of the shadows, Abby emerged and pawed at her. Jessie glanced at her watch. It was well past the time she should have been taken for her walk.

Jessie knelt down to her, wrapping her arms around the dog's silky neck, running her fingers through her long, sleek golden fur. She still remembered the day Daddy had surprised her with the golden retriever. That was more than eleven years ago. And now, Abby was so much more than a dog. She was her constant companion. Her protector. She loved her when no one else did.

She pulled back from Abby and wiped the tears from her eyes.

"Come on, Girl," she said, managing a weak smile. "Let's go home."

A few minutes later, Jessie stood at the front door and looked back at the apartment. It looked forlorn. Empty. Dark.

She opened the door and slid two rolling suitcases into the hallway. As she stood there with one foot in the apartment and one foot out, she thought she was going to be ill. She stared at the plastic bag tied to one of the suitcases that contained Abby's food bowls. And then she turned back to the apartment and glanced at the table beside the door. When Nick came in, she decided, whenever that might be—the note would be waiting for him.

She'd thought about the words long and hard before she'd written them:

Nick,

I'm sorry. I'll always love you, but we both know you are better off without me.

Please don't try to reach me.

Jess

She took a deep breath and held the door open for Abby. "Come on girl," she said, hoping her voice sounded stronger than she felt. "We're going home."

61

J essie reclined on the plush lounge and sipped a glass of chardonnay. It had been dark when she arrived at the Palmer estate; prematurely dark, she thought as she watched the sapphire clouds begin to roil and tumble. A storm was brewing and as she scrutinized the horizon, she knew within another hour—maybe less—they would get a torrential rainfall.

After settling into her old bedroom and feeding Abby, she'd uncorked the bottle and wandered to the middle veranda behind the house. She loved these terraces. The topmost veranda was completely covered and contained more than half a dozen patio tables and chairs, enough for an intimate party. By taking one of the sets of marble steps that branched off from the center and both ends, she wandered to the middle terrace, which consisted of an Olympic-sized swimming pool and lounge chairs. Now as she stared at the pool, she reflected on the years past when she used to soak up the sun's rays without a care in the world. How she longed for those days again!

She swished the wine around the round glass and looked below her to the third terrace. It was distinctly different from the other two because it contained an Old English maze in the center. Remembering years past, she knew when the weather grew warmer and the breezes blew, she would be able to detect the boxwood's sweet perfume.

At each side of the maze was a set of elaborate gardens. When Jessie was younger, she remembered her grandmother toiling there among the variety of rose bushes, day lilies, and iris. Her grandfather used to admonish her for doing such menial labor when there were landscapers paid to maintain the gardens, but Granna Palmer loved it. She always said when in full bloom, the garden glowed with all the bright colors any artist would need for a watercolor of the beautiful hills of Tennessee.

Abby stirred, sitting up and perking her ears as she watched the terrace below. Jessie followed the dog's intent gaze until she caught sight of her mother wandering through the garden. Instead of enjoying the last of the spring bounty of jonquils, winter aconites and checkered lilies, she seemed agitated. She held a cell phone against her ear while her other hand was jerking wildly.

Jessie shook her head. Her mother was the only woman she'd ever known who could wring her hands with just one wrist.

She continued up the gently curving walk toward Jessie, seemingly unaware that her daughter was there. She kept her eyes downward and now as she grew closer, Jessie began to catch bits and pieces of her conversation.

"That's ridiculous!" she was saying, her voice reaching a fever pitch. "I don't have access to that kind of money!"

She paused as if listening to the person on the other end of the line. "Impossible!"

Jessie caught herself leaning forward to catch more of the conversation. Her mother stopped and turned her back to her, still so engrossed in her conversation that she didn't appear to have noticed her daughter sitting just above her.

"I don't care who you call. You have no proof!"

After another pause, she continued, "It'll be your word against mine. And, who do you think they'll believe—?" She turned around and stopped, her mouth open, her words left hanging in mid-air.

With Jessie's eyes upon her, Meg abruptly closed the cell phone and stuck it in her pocket. She stood for a brief moment, ogling her as if Jessie had grown two heads. Then, she continued up the walkway toward her.

"You should never sneak up on a person like that," Meg snipped as she neared.

"I didn't 'sneak up' on you. I was sitting right here."

"It's rude to eavesdrop."

"I didn't hear a thing."

"What are you doing here?" Meg asked, staring back at the house. It was coming alive now with internal lights as the sky grew darker.

"I'm home for a visit. Just a short one."

Meg's eyes wandered around the property, as if she could see through the house to the front lawn and winding driveway. "Where's your car?"

"In the garage," Jessie said, waving toward the detached garage about five minutes' walk from the house. It had once been a carriage house containing at least a dozen horses at one end and several carriages in the middle, but had since been converted to a garage that could house eight cars. "Where I always used to park."

Meg nodded.

She didn't seem drunk, Jessie thought, which in itself seemed odd. After a moment and without another word, she marched across the terrace and up the stairs to the house. Jessie watched her, perplexed by her behavior.

Then the first droplet of rain fell on her and she jumped up and grabbed her wine glass and the half-empty bottle. "Come on, Abby!" she called out as she raced toward the house.

62

Jessie watched the lightning on the horizon but the flashes barely registered on her mind. She was sitting in her room overlooking the front of the estate. The bottle of wine and half-empty glass sat on the petite glass table beside her as she stared out the open window. She could feel the air thicken as the rain rushed in, but the roof's overhang kept it from sweeping in through the tall window. The sheer curtains rose like puffs of smoke as the wind caught them, tumbling back into the room, only to rise and brush forward again like angel wings.

Abby lay quietly at her feet on a plush Oriental rug, her head resting on her paw but her eyes shifting with Jessie's movements.

Jessie grasped the stuffed arms of her chair as she stared outside, over a second roof that protected the portico below.

After several minutes, she reached for her cell phone. She scrolled through the pictures she'd taken at the bank, peering at Edward Buchanan's face, studying the matches and the cap before forwarding them to Grant Bailey's cell phone. Then she telephoned him. When he answered, she was relieved to hear his voice.

"This is Jessie—" she began.

"Jessie," he interjected. "How are you?"

She hesitated. "Not good."

There was a brief moment of silence on the other end. "What's up?"

"I know who the kidnapper is."

He sighed. It was a heavy sigh, the kind that revealed a long, hard day. If he'd worn glasses, Jessie thought she'd envision him taking them off and pinching the bridge of his nose. "You saw Brutus again?" he asked tiredly.

"Not Brutus. Brainiac."

"Jessie."

"Hear me out." When he didn't respond, she continued, "I know who he is."

"Oh?" She could hear the rustle of paperwork and wondered if he was only half-listening to her.

"It's Edward Buchanan."

"Edward Buchanan." Jessie thought she detected a hint of sarcasm. "The banker," he said after a moment's pause.

"Yes."

"The one who took over First Palmer Bank."

"Yes. I forwarded you his picture."

"I know what he looks like. Jessie, do you have any idea who you're accusing? Edward Buchanan is a respectable citizen. A prominent citizen."

"Like my daddy?"

He sighed again, but this time it sounded more resigned. "Just what makes you think that Edward Buchanan is Brainiac?"

"I was at the bank yesterday."

"First Palmer Bank?"

"Yes."

"Why?"

"It doesn't matter. Look, two bank officers told me he's firing valuable employees."

"That's not exactly evidence, Jessie."

"Yes, but—"

"A new CEO has every right to surround himself with the people he wants."

"He also doesn't have the respect of the employees."

p.m.terrell & T. Randy Stevens

"Obviously, he's got somebody's respect or he wouldn't have been made CEO. Jessie, did you get the help I urged you to get?"

"This isn't all in my head," Jessie retorted, her voice sharp.

"So you didn't." She didn't answer, and Grant continued, "I think you're way off base here…"

"You're not even hearing me out."

"Then give me evidence. Nothing you've told me so far makes me think Edward Buchanan was involved."

"Okay, then listen to this. He owns a golf cap."

Grant chuckled. "So?"

"The cap has a shark logo. I forwarded that picture to you, too."

"You're kidding me, right? Jessie, I'm a busy man."

"It's the same cap the kidnapper was wearing. The exact same cap."

"Are you a golfer?" Grant asked abruptly.

"No."

"Well, if you were, you'd know there are probably a million people who wear a golf cap with a shark on it. They're fans of Greg Norman, one of the best golfers in the world." She didn't answer, and after a moment, he continued, "You're going to have to give me something better'n that to go on."

"The same kind of matches were in the bank's conference room—"

"Fire Chief, right?"

"How did—?"

"We picked up evidence at the cabin. It's being tested for DNA. Please don't tell me you sent me a picture of them, too." When she didn't respond, he added, "Jessie, do you have any idea how common those matches are?"

"My father was framed!"

"Jessie, I am not a shrink. But it's sounding more and more like you're feeling a whole lot of guilt. Are you sorry you testified against your father?"

"I don't know—yes."

"Even without your testimony, he would have been convicted. There was too much evidence. He disturbed the crime scene.

He destroyed evidence. He was behind the five million dollar insurance policy—"

"That was my grandfather's idea!"

"I could go on and on," he continued, "including the fact that we found half the ransom money in your father's safe deposit box. You remember that, right?"

"But I'm trying to tell you, my father was framed!"

"What makes you think a kidnapper would be willing to give away more than two million dollars just to frame an innocent man?"

"A man who has much more to gain than a measly two million."

There was a long pause on the other end of the line, but this time Jessie didn't hear a heavy sigh or the sound of paper rustling. "Go on," he said finally.

"I went into the conference room yesterday. It reeked with tobacco smoke, the exact same brand I smelled at the cabin—and on Brainiac's clothing."

"You're a tobacco connoisseur now?"

"There's a picture of Edward Buchanan in the conference room," she continued. "Remember I told you Brainiac's chin was strange, like it had been reconstructed?"

"Yeah."

"Well, it's the same chin. I asked Paul Buttrey about it and he said Edward had been in a fire as a child. His skin was disfigured, and I think a jump from an upper window shattered the bone in his jaw. How many people have that characteristic?"

"It doesn't mean…" he said slowly.

"How many people do you know who've had facial reconstructive surgery?"

There was a sound on the other end of the phone as if he was shifting the receiver from one hand to the other. "Does this have anything to do with the fact that an outsider is now the CEO of your family's bank?"

"What?"

"Weren't you supposed to follow in your father's footsteps?" he asked. His voice was calm, almost silky.

"How did you know that?"

"I know a lot of things I haven't shared with you," Grant said. "And I know that your life is now upside down because you were supposed to become the CEO of First Palmer Bank someday. Weren't you?"

"Yes, but that doesn't have anything to do with—"

"Doesn't it, though?" he interrupted. "Now that you're through the trial, you're starting to put your life back together, aren't you? Only the biggest piece of your life was going to be a guaranteed-for-life job as the head of your family's bank. Now, that's looking pretty impossible, isn't it?"

"I can't believe I called you for help, and you're talking to me this way."

"You need help, Jessie, but not the kind of help I can provide. You need a good psychiatrist. Somebody to help you get your life back together. Somebody who can help you get inside your own head."

Jessie slammed the cell phone shut. She hadn't realized until now that she'd come to her feet as they'd been talking. The rain was coming in through the window now, brushing the curtains and her clothing with fine drops. Her palm wrapped around the small phone like a shark grabbing prey, and as she continued to stand there, her hand began to shake in anger.

She felt the heat rising in her cheeks and she gritted her teeth. In a final fit of fury, she tossed the phone out the window. It clattered across the roof before disappearing over the ledge onto the circular driveway below.

She immediately regretted her action. But before she could make another move, a strong gust of wind pelted her with a sheet of rain, and she hurried to close the window as her curtains swirled around her.

63

The knock at the door almost caused Jessie to jump out of her skin. Whirling around, she watched Abby rise from the rug at her feet and trot to the bedroom door. The dog sniffed at the threshold and then pawed at the door, glancing back at her mistress with a silly grin.

When Jessie answered the door, she was surprised to see Heddy standing there, panting.

"I'm too old to be climbin' these steps, Child," she puffed as she walked into the room.

"What's wrong?"

"Ain't nothin' wrong. That friend of yours—Nick—he's called twice now, wantin' to talk to you. I tried callin' up those stairs but you didn't answer."

"Oh."

Heddy sat on the edge of Jessie's bed and peered at her. "This Nick is more than a friend, ain't he?"

"Yes. No. He was."

The older woman tossed a cordless phone onto the bed. "Well, the next time the phone rings and it's him, whoever he is to you, I'm callin' you on the intercom. Got that?"

"Why not ignore it?"

"You think every call here is for you? There's other people livin' and workin' in this house."

"I don't want to talk to him, Heddy," Jessie said, sitting beside her.

They both stared out the window for a long moment, watching the storm rage outside.

"I got to go soon," Heddy said.

"You're not driving in this bad weather?"

"It's your momma that worries me. When she starts drinkin' them spirits, it's like the Devil hisself is takin' o'er her."

"She just goes to her bedroom, doesn't she? And drinks alone?"

"She gets plumb mean when the sun goes down. And ever since your daddy was arrested, folks just dropped her like she was a hot potato. I think it made her even meaner."

Jessie stood and walked to the window. The massive hanging light on the front porch was now casting fingers of muted illumination across the grounds below. The lights shifted as the winds blew, making it appear as though shadowy figures were making their way around the estate.

When Jessie had been a little girl, she'd been terrified of the lights. Other lamps at the edges of the house came on automatically from dusk to dawn, while the outlying buildings had motion-sensor lighting. The family cemetery at the edge of the circular driveway appeared to come alive with the lights. Often a bird or an animal would cause them to turn on, and the effect would be one in which the tombstones appeared to light up on their own, as if the ground beneath them was coming alive.

There were two carriage houses on this side of the property. The one in which she'd parked her car had been converted to a garage that routinely housed a half dozen vehicles, including her father's 1936 light green Stout Scarab, of which only six were left in the country, and his 1948 blue Davis, of which only thirteen still existed. She had a fleeting thought of someone driving her father's antique cars without his permission, but the notion of her father living each day in a cell now, powerless to protect what was his, was too painful.

Her thoughts turned to the other carriage house, which had been transformed into a magnificent guesthouse by none other than the famous architect from Savannah, Georgia, Jackson Evers. As the lightning continued to flash across the sky, both carriage houses were illuminated for brief intervals.

"Do you remember Uncle John?" Jessie asked suddenly.

"Colonel Alderson?" Heddy asked. "Why, Lord, yes. I still miss that man."

"I remember when I was just a little girl, running down that path to the guesthouse to visit with him. He was always painting."

"You know," Heddy said, her voice growing soft, "though he wasn't really your uncle—by blood, that is—we all sort of adopted him here, and loved him like he was our own."

Jessie half-turned toward her. "He'd been in the Army, hadn't he?"

"Twenty-five years, I think... Had a medal on display in that guesthouse. Don't know whatever happened to it after he died." She was silent for a long moment before adding, "He was famous for those paintin's. One year, he was even made Artist of the Year by Ducks Unlimited."

"I remember that," Jessie said. "And I remember how proud we all were of him. And when he died," her voice became almost a whisper, "we kept all his paintings—those he hadn't already sold or had been commissioned—right there in that guesthouse."

Heddy joined Jessie at the window.

"Is there a light on inside?" Jessie asked.

"Most likely, it's your mother."

"Really?"

"She goes there some nights. She says she likes to look at them paintin's."

"Funny. I never knew she appreciated art. Not like Daddy and me."

"She gets her a bottle or has me bring a tray down there for her, and she sits there sometimes for hours on end. Many a night, she's down there when I leave."

The phone rang and both of them jumped.

"It's that boy," Heddy said, moving back toward the bed. "I know it is. I can feel it."

"I can't talk to him. Not now."

Heddy let the phone continue ringing.

"Aren't you going to answer it?"

Heddy shrugged her shoulders. "I'll go downstairs in a minute and check the answerin' machine."

"What about all the other people living and working in this house?" Jessie giggled.

"Well, there's you and you ain't wantin' to talk to him. There's me, and I ain't expectin' no calls. And there's your momma," she half-nodded toward the other building, "and she's down there."

"Nobody else is here?"

"Maybe the groundskeeper is all. But he'll be leavin' soon if he ain't left already."

The phone stopped ringing and Jessie stared at it.

"Child, you know I half raised you. I can read you like a book. You tell me you don't want to talk to this man. But your heart is sayin' you want him. So which is it?"

"I don't know, Heddy. He wants—or wanted, at one time—to marry me."

Heddy whistled. "Lordy, lordy. Does your folks know?"

"No. And I don't want them to."

"Is he a good man?"

Jessie stared at her for a long moment before answering. "Yes. I'd say he's a good man."

"Well, then?"

"I don't know. I see what's happened to my parents, and I don't want that to happen to me."

Heddy nodded. "Your mama wasn't always like this."

Jessie half-laughed. "It's all I remember."

"I reckon it is, Child."

"Did she marry him for financial stability, you think?"

"Who? Your mama?" Heddy cocked her head. "I suppose that had somethin' to do with it. Your daddy gave her a good life here."

Jessie stared at the guesthouse as a shadow moved in front of the window. It was too far away for her to see details, but she imagined her mother moving about with a drink in her hand. And with the storm raging, she was likely to remain there until it passed.

"I know one thing," Jessie said. "I'm keeping the Palmer name. Even after I get married."

"You are, are you?"

"I'm proud of it. No matter what others might say."

"Well, I gots to get downstairs," Heddy said with a heavy sigh. "There's more I gots to do before I can take off."

"Don't leave in this weather," Jessie begged. "Promise me you won't."

"I'll wait 'til it dies down a bit," she said as she made her way to the door. "As long as it don't take its own sweet time movin' through."

Jessie heard the door open and then close softly. Abby returned to the Oriental rug by the table and lay down with a tired moan. Jessie returned to her thoughts and to watching the lightning flash across the sky, casting the grounds into various shades of goldenrod and purple.

The minutes ticked past and the thunderclaps began to sound more distant and less frequent. She was staring at the trees bending and swaying in the wind, often appearing violent as the gusts whipped them around, when a movement caught her eye.

She thought at first her eyes were playing tricks on her, as they had when she was a small girl. Perhaps an animal had moved through the thicket of trees just beyond the circular driveway. Or a large bird had flown past. She leaned closer to the window as she watched for the lights scattered throughout the estate.

The movement came again and with it, one of the motion sensors kicked on, causing a light to flicker and come on. There was someone out there, she thought as her heart began to race.

She was afraid to blink for fear she'd miss the next movement. Convinced now it was larger than a bird, she waited and watched for it to continue. After several excruciatingly long minutes, the light turned itself off.

Momentarily, the figure moved again, but it was further from the house, just out of range of the motion sensors. As she strained to watch, she realized it was a man.

He traveled around the house, always facing it as though he was watching it, and suddenly self-conscious of her own presence, she backed away from the window and turned off the light in her bedroom. As she made her way back to the window, she could hear her own breath coming fast and shallow.

It took a few seconds for her eyes to adjust to the darkness, but then she saw him again, moving toward the end of the house where he would soon be out of her line of vision. He was moving between the carriage house and the main house.

A wicked burst of thunder erupted overhead at the same moment as a blaze of lightning threatened to rip the sky in half. Jessie gasped as the entire house shook. She grappled for the sheers or the window ledge—anything to keep her bearings in that split second. Then, she caught sight of the figure down below, staring up at the house.

It was Brutus.

She struggled for her breath, throwing herself against the wall beside the window.

She would have known him anywhere. His face was forever emblazoned on her mind, and in that moment, it had been fully, grotesquely illuminated.

She struggled to grab her cell phone in her pants pocket, and then stopped cold. Her phone was outside on the driveway, probably broken into smithereens.

She lunged for the bed, tripping over Abby as she grabbed the cordless phone on the bed. Dialing 911, she waited for the dispatcher to answer. Grant Bailey would know what to do, she thought frantically.

But the dispatcher never answered. The phone never rang. And as she stood there in the darkness, she realized the lines were dead.

64

The rain hit Jessie full force as she raced toward the carriage house. Though she'd run through the house at breakneck speed, calling for Heddy, the woman hadn't answered. She had no recourse now but to get to her mother before it was too late.

She found herself fighting against the wind, which was gusting so violently now that the rain was pummeling her in sheets, raking across her bare cheeks and stinging her eyes. She held one arm above her brows in an attempt to push on, but her vision was impacted so dramatically that she wasn't sure anymore where the carriage house was located.

Her clothes now hung in wet folds about her body, her slacks clinging to her with such ferocity that she seemed to be fighting against them with every step. What had seemed so clear to her from the safety and height of her second-story room now felt like the English maze at the rear of the estate.

Abby bounded ahead of her, stopping every few steps to look back at her. Though her mouth moved, her barks disappeared with the howling of the wind before they reached Jessie's ears.

She no longer knew where Brutus had gone. The last she'd seen of him, he was sprinting past the trees toward the carriage house. Now those trees were surrounding her, their branches whipping wildly like a school of octopi striking out. She heard the sound of wood cracking and a split second later, the earth shook with the thud of a giant branch or tree, but she was hard pressed to figure out which direction it was in. She continued onward, blind now to all but the torrential rain and pellets of hail that began to pelt her.

Abby moved away from the path and toward the cemetery, stopping to make certain her mistress was following her. Jessie hesitated. If she remained on the path, as long as her feet were able to find it in the darkness, she knew eventually it would lead her toward the carriage house.

But Abby was right, she realized. The cemetery was faster. Abby knew where she was going—or she knew danger lurked ahead if they stayed on the path.

She began to slide as her foot struck the grass, and she threw her arms outward in an awkward attempt to regain her balance. The lawn was quickly turning to mud and as she skated along the gently rolling terrain as it descended to the cemetery, the water began to rise over her ankles.

She reached the outskirts of the cemetery breathless, her ribs aching with her exertions. She stopped at the first headstone and tried to catch her breath, leaning over it for support but her feet sank in the soft dirt beneath her.

Frantically, she glanced around her. Through a break in the clouds, she could barely see the lights in the carriage house. She looked back toward the main house, standing tall and imposing against the tumultuous sky. She realized she was past the point of no return; it was faster to try and reach the carriage house than it was to turn around and go back.

Abby was barking just up ahead, her cries sounding muffled and faint against the rain. Then the wind kicked up once more, and Jessie sprinted away from the headstone and tried to run after the golden retriever. Her legs now felt as though she was running in water, and more than once, the wind caught her and pushed her backward, taking back the ground she'd fought so hard to conquer.

A tree branch in front of her suddenly whipped upward as a barn owl shrieked and flew past her, alarmed at her presence.

The cemetery didn't seem so large when she looked at it from the safety of her bedroom window. But now as she tried to move through it, it felt as though it had taken on a life of its own. Each headstone no longer marked the location of a decaying body, but rather of a spirit alive, and she felt both terrified and oddly comforted to know the Palmers were there with her. But while half of her mind tried to draw on their strength, the other half just as quickly reduced them to haunting apparitions that could ensnare her in their grasp.

The ground itself was uneven, the older graves sunk so deep that they threatened to submerge her. She found herself clawing at the ground, her nails raking over exposed tree limbs that felt now like the bones of her ancestors.

Abby was at the edge of the cemetery, her mouth moving as if she was barking once more. The wind was so brutal that Jessie could only focus on the golden fur that fell in wet drapes at the cemetery's lip, and hope she could reach her.

When at last she clambered up the slope, Abby was gone once more, racing toward the carriage house.

The seconds turned to minutes as Jessie was caught in the maelstrom and by the time she'd reached the edge of the building, she threw herself against it, her chest heaving as she fought to breathe.

She pressed her back against the wall. Her legs felt like rubber under her; soft rubber that was about to give way and leave her collapsed on the ground beneath her. She ran her hands down her torso until they reached her legs, but she didn't know which was shaking the worst. It had been a mistake to come out here, she thought frantically. Now, she would have to ride out the rest of this storm out here.

She tried to focus on the terrain around her. In her struggle to reach the carriage house, she had no idea where Brutus had gone. He could be watching her now, she thought with rising alarm.

The trunks of the trees bent and swayed in the storm, their branches coiling and twisting as though they were struggling to free the roots from the ground and walk toward her. A man could be hidden in the thickets and blend in with those trunks, even as he moved ever more swiftly toward her.

She moved to the corner of the house and peered around it. A yellowed stream of light washed outward through a window, the glow marked with the shadows of raindrops against the glass and the partially drawn curtains that were gently dancing inside from an overhead fan.

She moved ever closer to it, keeping her back to the wall, until she had come upon the window itself. She stopped and peered within, expecting to see her mother reclining with a drink in her hand.

But the room was empty.

She continued to the door and quietly, slowly, tried the knob. It was locked.

Taking a deep breath, she moved around the small building, trying to remember the rooms each window represented. All of the drapes were partially open, and some of the rooms were darker than the others. But unless her mother was hiding in the shadows or in a closet, the tiny house was empty.

She would have to break in. The storm was too vicious to try and make it back to the main house. And Brutus was out there somewhere. If she could get inside, perhaps the phone would be back in working order and she could call for help. If it wasn't, she could certainly find a tool that could be used for self defense.

She was debating breaking a window when two swaths of light blanketed the carriage house. Jessie gasped and instinctively lunged toward the shadows.

They were headlights.

She watched as a vehicle crept up the long, winding driveway. But rather than continue around the circular drive and stop in front of the main house, it came to a standstill just beyond a thicket of tall evergreens. The headlights were turned off. A few seconds later, she saw the faintest light flicker as the door opened and a figure emerged.

It was a man; she was sure of it, even though a hat shielded his face. He was dressed in a long black slicker; the rain glistened as it raced across his torso and arms. He marched purposefully toward the two carriage houses with an obvious familiarity.

Jessie crouched toward the corner of the building, wrapping her fingers in Abby's golden fur. The dog was barking despite her efforts to keep her quiet, but the gale-force winds carried the sound away.

Just as she thought she would have to run for her life, the figure turned. Instead of continuing toward the carriage house, he took the other path, toward the garage.

Jessie peered back at the main house, where lights illuminated the large structure. Where Heddy was, she thought. And safety.

The house would protect her, if she could reach it.

Then, she turned in the opposite direction and watched as the tall figure continued toward the garage. With one final, deep breath like a swimmer diving into the pool, she raced after him.

65

The winds grew louder, the rain pelting her in a sideways rush that threatened at any moment to hurl her off her feet. Abby was a short distance in front of her, leading the way. Her lower profile tolerated the elements more effectively than Jessie's taller body. She stopped frequently to look back at her mistress, moving her mouth as though she was barking encouragement, but the winds were howling so ferociously that Jessie couldn't hear her at all.

Two men were meeting at the garage: Brutus and this man in the black slicker. Her mind raced through the people who worked on the Palmer estate. Remembering Heddy had mentioned the landscaper was still on the property, she wondered if he had played a part in her kidnapping.

It made sense for the conspirators to meet there, she realized, since the back of the garage stored items needed to maintain the estate—mowers, trimmers, and yard implements. And now the landscaper was meeting Brutus on his own turf.

The thought of the two men converging at the Palmer estate was enough to take her breath away. But, despite her inner urgings to go back and call for help, she continued moving forward toward the outbuilding.

When she heard the first tree cracking, she thought the world around her was collapsing. It happened suddenly, in the blink of an eye: an oak almost two hundred feet tall falling over like a cheap plastic bowling ball pin. It took down the tree next to it, and the one next to it, until the entire wood line appeared to be caving in like a row of dominoes.

The wind tossed her off her feet, throwing her into the side of the garage, where her breath was knocked out of her. It might have continued to hurl her had the side of the building not stopped it; but in the process, she was pinned against it and unable to move.

Her heart began beating wildly as she realized she was experiencing straight line winds, that weather phenomenon that could strike terror in the hearts of those living in middle Tennessee. The winds were almost like tornadoes; but while a tornado could spin debris around, tossing it in every direction at once, straight line winds—though just as vicious—came in one direction, annihilating everything in its path.

She could no longer watch as the rains moved in, blinding her to everything more than an arm's length away. She tried to call for Abby, but her voice disappeared into the wind so quickly that she couldn't hear her own voice. She could only remain pinned against the wall and listen as the trees crashed around her, each trunk sending shockwaves across the ground. Shingles from the building began to fly above her like great wings, bending and extending as though they'd been brought to life.

She struggled to breathe as the winds whipped against her. When they subsided as quickly as they had materialized, she was astonished to find that she'd sunk to her knees and her feet were unnaturally buckled up behind her. She gasped for breath and peered around her, trying to catch sight of her dog.

Her blood went as cold as if ice had been poured into her veins. There, only a few yards away, was the man in the black slicker. And it wasn't the landscaper. It was Edward Buchanan.

The front of the garage contained an awning smaller than a carport that, in days gone by, had been used to attach the horses to the carriages. Now she watched in horror as he stood underneath the roof, his clothing soaked and raincoat shining, yelling at the top of his lungs, unaware of her presence.

Her only hope was to remain perfectly still.

She became as motionless as a statue. Her eyes barely veered away from him as she wondered where Abby had gone. She breathed a quick prayer that she wouldn't come running to her now, bringing Edward's attention and wrath down upon her.

"Don't you ever call my office again, do you understand me?" he was shouting. As the winds suddenly abated, his voice echoed through the estate.

Jessie's eyes roamed closer to the building. He was speaking to someone standing just outside the door to the garage, but she was unable to see the second person. Brutus? She wondered. But why would they choose this place to meet?

"Do you realize how many red flags that can raise? Are you an idiot?"

He paused as if listening but as much as Jessie strained to hear the other person she couldn't even detect a murmur. But judging from Edward's face, he was becoming more irate with the words he was hearing. His thick neck began to bulge and turn red and then purple and a single broad vein began to throb.

"How could he have contacted you?" he demanded with such anger that he was almost stammering. "I killed him myself. It's somebody else; somebody who knows what we've done and they're blackmailing you."

He took a step closer to the building. "Think! Think who it could be! Who have you told? Who?"

He raised his hand in a fist as though he was about to pummel the other person.

I've got to get out of here, Jessie thought frantically. She'd gone against her gut instinct yet again, and now she was exposed, too far from the house for anyone to hear her, even if she were to scream at the top of her lungs.

But he didn't know she was there. He was focused on someone standing at the door, unaware that she was only yards away. Keeping her head immobile, she rolled her eyes toward the main house. The lights were still on, the tall structure unscathed by the storm. It seemed so far away, she thought with a sinking heart. And yet her only hope was to get back there and somehow call for help.

Suddenly, through the darkness, she heard Abby barking. She almost fainted at the sound of it; it couldn't be coming at a worse moment.

But, as she looked back at Edward, she realized Abby was on the other side of him. She was at least fifty feet away from him, and she was snarling now at this unwanted intruder. He turned his head away from Jessie to look at the dog.

Jessie took a deep breath. Abby was giving her the moment she needed to rush to the back of the building and try to disappear once more into the woods in a circuitous route back to the house and to safety.

Without warning, in the split second before she was ready to plunge away from him, the other figure stepped forward.

Jessie stopped in mid-step. The building blocked the other's identity but as Jessie stared at the edge of the building, she managed to see the person from the elbows to the slender, delicate hands.

Jessie's mouth went dry and her knees threatened to buckle from under her as she recognized the limp wrists wringing uncontrollably.

66

The side door to the main house was within a hundred feet of Jessie, but it may as well have been a mile.

She was covered in muddy water from head to foot and she felt as though her entire body had been hammered relentlessly. Another storm wave had come through, even more vicious than the last. The combination of the rain and wind had whipped her off her feet more than once, catapulting her onto the asphalt path, skinning her shins and her forearms. She knew she'd have bruises from head to toe.

She may as well have been running through knee-deep snow as she fought her way against the torrent. Branches from nearby trees were flying through the sky as if they had wings. A shingle flew off the roof, hitting her across the face and knocking her backward. She flailed outward, trying to stop herself from falling, but she was no match against this monster storm. She hit the ground on her back, the brutal landing blowing the wind out of her.

She screamed with the pain but her voice was carried off on the wind. Her sight was blurry now, and she raised the back of her hand to wipe the rain from her eyes, only to find that her face was cut just above the brow and her own blood was mixing with the rain.

With a groan, she came to her knees and fought against the rising wind as she tried to get back on her feet. Once upright, she held her arms outstretched like a mummy; limping forward, she attempted to shield herself from the storm's onslaught. She had only three more feet before her hands could touch the side door. Then two feet. And then one.

The sky erupted in a thunderous explosion that shook the ground, knocking Jessie back off her feet. At the same moment, a flash of lightning bolted so close to her that her hair felt the static, piercing into an eighty foot oak tree just beyond the house. The tree erupted in flames that shot above the canopy of the other trees, even as the rain pelted down upon it.

Then, the rain stopped so abruptly that it felt as if someone had turned off a plumbing valve. There was complete silence. The air was still. The thunder and lightning had stopped. The silence was more frightening than the storm. Jessie peered upward. The sky was the color of pitch, a hundred times blacker than ink. It was the most terrifying sight she'd ever witnessed. Her heart felt caught in her throat as she realized a tornado was headed toward her. With every ounce of strength left in her, she leapt to her feet and bolted for the door.

Inside, the house was warm and quiet. The kitchen's goldenrod walls cast a glow across the room and the sweet aroma of cinnamon bread wafted beneath her nostrils. She stood for a moment as the water washed off her and formed a pool at her feet. She felt as if she'd entered another world.

Her shoes squished as she walked, threatening to slide her unceremoniously across the slick ceramic tile, until she stopped and removed them. When she reached the door into the hallway, she glanced back to find a swath of muddy water following her across the floor like a river cutting through the desert.

"Heddy!" she screamed.

Her voice sounded foreign to her. It resonated in her ears, sounding rude and harsh in the clean, neat house.

She continued through the downstairs, calling out for Heddy and then Abby.

She'd started to climb the stairs when Heddy emerged in the upstairs hallway.

"Child!" the older woman shrieked. "Where have you been? I've been lookin' all over for you!"

Jessie slipped and slid up the stairs, feeling like an oiled pig with every step. Heddy disappeared, only to reappear at the top of the stairs with an oversized towel.

"Child, where have you been?" she demanded.

"A tornado—" Jessie gasped. "We're in the path of a tornado."

"Now, jest calm down, child. This house has been here for two hundred years and it'll be here for two hundred more. You're safe here."

She slipped the towel around Jessie's shoulders and helped her down the hall to her room. "What have you been doin' outside in this storm?" Her eyes were so wide that a circle of white was visible around the irises.

"Heddy, listen to me," she begged. "My daddy didn't kidnap me. He had nothing to do with it—"

She patted her as one would pat a fretting child. "I know, Child. I know."

"It's my mother," she blurted. "And Edward Buchanan, from the bank. They're both here now—"

"Lord!" Heddy said, straightening her back. "What are you sayin'?"

"Jessie."

The voice was strong and abrupt. Though Jessie couldn't see her mother, she let go of Heddy's arms and stepped back.

Meg stepped into the bedroom. She was soaked from head to toe and for once, her hands were perfectly calm. Her eyes were narrowed and one eyebrow raised, her lips thin and motionless.

Jessie looked at Heddy, imploring her silently, but the older woman's eyes were veiled, her head tilted backward as if she was peering at her through non-existent bifocal lenses.

"What are you doing, Jessie?" Meg's voice was deliberate and calm.

Jessie felt her blood run cold.

"Tryin' to find that blessed dog," Heddy said in disgust. "That dog is goin' to be the death of you, Child. Don't you got more sense than to be runnin' around in the storm like this? Now, you just get yourself right in that bathroom and get them clothes off. Lord have mercy," she clucked as she marched to Jessie's closet and flung the doors open.

Jessie looked at her mother. Meg stood completely immobile, her eyes so narrow they were mere slits. Before her mother could say another word, Jessie scurried toward the bathroom.

67

Grant leaned back, the chair's protesting groan the only sound in the deserted FBI office. All of the lights had long ago been turned off, leaving the room in shades of sapphire that were broken only by the reflection of the pounding rain against the windows. He rotated his chair until he could reach his desk lamp. He switched it on and stared at the daunting pile of work spotlighted by the bright yellow glow, knowing even as he looked at it that he hadn't the motivation to work on yet another case.

He turned back to the windows and watched the water running down the glass in torrents. Somewhere out there was Linda. He wondered if she ever thought about him, ever wished she hadn't blamed him for what happened to Julia.

He could find Linda easily enough. Though it was against agency policy, he could easily pinpoint her latest address in their vast database, and could just as easily appear on her doorstep. But as he continued watching the storm gather in intensity, a knot began to grow in his stomach and he wondered, after all these years, what he could say to her that could possibly ease her pain—and his own.

When the phone rang rudely in the quiet office, his first inclination was to let it ring. He wasn't supposed to be at work, and he wouldn't still be there, had he had anyplace else to go. He listened to it ring three times, knowing on the fourth it would switch to the answering service. But before it rang again, he lunged for it.

"FBI. Agent Bailey speaking."

There was silence on the other end of the line, and he wondered if he'd grabbed it too late and the caller had already passed to the service. As he started to hang up, he detected breathing.

"Can I help you?" he asked, pressing the receiver closer to his ear.

"Agent Bailey?" The voice was female, small and hesitant.

"Yes. This is Agent Bailey." He sat upright, the ancient chair creaking as he moved.

"This is Martha Maguire."

"Yes?"

"Martha Maguire, from First Palmer Bank."

"Oh, yes," Grant said, leaning forward. "Vincent Palmer's assistant."

"Mr. Bailey, this is very awkward for me."

Grant waited for her to continue. He turned back to the window, where he watched the water overflowing the sidewalks from storm drains overwhelmed by the storm.

After an uncomfortable silence, she continued. "I was filing a signature card today for Victoria Palmisano, when I came across the signature card for Vincent Palmer."

"Go on."

"Well, I don't know quite how to say this, but—the signature isn't his."

Grant turned back to his desk. "Which signature?"

"All of them."

"*All* of them?"

"I know this sounds crazy, but I've worked for Mr. Palmer for years. I know his signature. I know it better than my own. And the card used to open the safe deposit box—the one where the money was found—that's not his signature."

"Are you saying someone forged his signature?"

She hesitated. "I guess I am. I mean, when you look at the card, all the way down the line, from the time it was opened to the last time it was used—it's the same signature. But it's not his."

"Do you have possession of the card? Can I drop by in the morning to look at it?"

"Well, I guess you could. But there's more."

Grant pressed the phone to his ear. Her breathing had grown faster. "Go on."

"Ever since the FBI requested the surveillance tapes and we discovered them missing, we've been looking for them.."

"And?"

"I--I'm not supposed to access Mr. Palmer's personal safe in his office... I mean, it's Mr. Buchanan's safe now..."

"Go on."

"It was there."

Grant felt the heat rising in his cheeks.

"The time stamp on the video matches the time on the card. It wasn't Mr. Palmer. It was his wife."

"Are you telling me Vincent Palmer's wife has access to the vault where the safe deposit boxes are kept?"

"No, sir. I'm not saying that at all. She has to go through the same security protocol as anybody else. It takes two keys to access the box—one used by a bank employee, and another by the customer."

"Then how—?"

"Not *how*, Mr. Bailey. *Who*. It was Edward Buchanan who helped her get in."

68

Jessie leaned forward in the bed as Heddy plumped up the pillows behind her back. Neither had mentioned Meg's disheveled appearance, but Jessie had been scolded continuously for wandering the estate in a storm.

She was dry now and clean, having washed the mud off herself in a shower that felt surreal. She'd almost expected Meg to walk in and calmly shoot or knife her, and she'd had to use every ounce of self-control to stop herself from shaking.

As she'd walked from the bathroom to her bedroom under the two women's watchful eyes, she'd peered around her, even managing to glance downstairs. She knew Edward Buchanan was in the house. She could feel him.

Heddy had brought her a fresh pair of pajamas and a robe, despite Jessie's insistence that she find Abby. The woman would hear none of it as she muscled Jessie into bed.

"I'll go downstairs," she was grumbling now, "and I'll call for that dog. I bet she's sittin' on the front porch right now. Bet she's been there the whole time you was out runnin' around like you had no sense in that head o' yours."

Meg stood in the corner of the room. She hadn't breathed another word. It was her silence and her stillness now that threatened to bring Jessie to the brink of hysteria.

Jessie's entire body began to tremble.

Meg stepped forward. Heddy moved to the side and continued tucking Jessie in as if she was ten years old.

"Mother," Jessie said, her lower lip quivering, "Brutus—the man who I thought was killed with an axe—he's here."

Meg's eyes narrowed. "You don't know what you're saying."

"I saw him," Jessie continued, the words spilling out of her. She glanced toward the bedroom window. The rain was coming down now in solid sheets that blocked the view. "I was standing over there, and he was running across the lawn—"

"You testified that man was killed right in front of your eyes." Meg's voice was chilling.

Jessie glanced at Heddy, but the woman's face was immobile.

"He didn't die," Jessie's words tumbled out. "I thought he was dead, but he wasn't. I don't know how he managed to survive, but he did. And he's here."

They continued staring at her in complete silence.

"Don't you understand?" she cried out, "we're all in danger!"

"You don't know what you're saying," Meg said flatly. Her arms were folded now in front of her. Though her hands were tucked beneath her slender biceps, Jessie could still see them shaking.

"You have to listen to me!" Jessie screamed. "While we're up here debating this, he could be right outside that door, right now!" She pointed toward the doorway but neither woman looked. They both continued to stare at her as if she'd lost her mind.

"You're unbalanced," Meg said, her voice detached. "Your kidnapping was solved, don't you remember? I asked for FBI Special Agent Grant Bailey myself."

"*You* asked for him?"

"He did such a wonderful job of solving his own child's abduction."

She had asked for him, Jessie thought, her cheeks growing cold as if all her blood were being drained from her.

"You need a good night's sleep," Meg was saying.

"No."

"You're going to take a sleeping pill," Meg continued. "Just like you had to do as a child. Because you're acting like a child now." She calmly slid the drawer to the nightstand open and dug out a bottle of prescription sleeping pills.

"They're too old," Jessie stammered. "They've been in there for years—since before I left for college."

"Then we'll just have to give you double the dose."

"No!" Jessie screamed, trying to toss the covers off her. Meg reached for her and with surprising strength, pushed her back into the bed, managing to keep her immobile.

"Lordy, lordy," Heddy said, stepping forward. "Doesn't this bring back memories?" She took the bottle of pills from Meg. "We're gonna have to do this just like we did when you was a child. 'Cause just like your mama said, you's actin' like a child now."

"Heddy!" Jessie screamed.

"Ms. Palmer," Heddy said, calmly tucking Jessie back underneath the bed covers, "You jest leave this to me. You know how we used to do it."

Jessie stared at Heddy, her mouth open.

Meg hesitated briefly. Then her hands began to wring again. "Yes," she said finally. "Just like we used to do it." Her eyes were so narrow Jessie could no longer see them. There were just two folds in her skin where the eyes should have been.

"You remember those milkshakes I used to make for you," Heddy said in a tone one would use with a preschooler. "I'm gonna make your favorite one. Chocolate peppermint. With a straw. And it's gonna taste real good, and it'll help you sleep."

Meg took a step toward the door before turning back to face Heddy. "Give her double the dose."

"Yes, ma'am."

"Just like she said, it's been in there for years," Meg said, "and it's weak. And we don't want her waking up during the night, now do we?"

69

When Heddy sat on the edge of the bed, the springs creaked with her weight. Jessie felt almost as if she was sliding toward the older woman. Before she could steel herself, Heddy turned to her with wide mahogany eyes.

"I flushed them sleepin' pills," she whispered, "just as I always done."

"Thank you, Heddy," Jessie said, reaching across the bedcovers to squeeze her hand. "You're the best friend I've got."

"You gots lots of friends." Her eyes moved slowly in the direction of the open door. Jessie knew she didn't dare close it. "Your mama ought to be goin' in her room soon and beddin' down with a bottle of liquor. And when she does, you need to be comin' with me."

"I don't think she's going to drink tonight," Jessie whispered, her voice strained and hoarse. "Heddy, I know you think I'm crazy."

"No," she answered slowly. Her eyes shifted downward. "I don't think you's crazy. But I do think you's a mite confused."

"Heddy, I need you to listen to me."

"I's list'nen'."

"I need your help. You know I've never lied to you. Not ever."

The older woman looked in her eyes for a long moment. She had dark circles beneath them, and red veins in the whites of her eyes that spoke of a constant battle with her health. "No," she said with a heavy sigh, "I've seen you through a lot. But you's never lied to me."

"And I'm not lying to you now." She waited for Heddy to respond, but she only looked at her with tired eyes.

"Heddy, I know who kidnapped me."

"You said—" she cut her eyes back to the open doorway "—your mama did?"

"Yes. It wasn't Daddy. It was never Daddy."

"Child, I knew your daddy didn't have it in him to hurt you. In his eyes, the sun rose and set in you."

Jessie swallowed. "I don't understand why Mother is doing this. But she's working with Edward Buchanan, the man that took over the bank when Daddy went to prison."

Heddy nodded. "I know him."

"You do?"

"He's been over to the house. Never whilst your daddy was here. He was always seein' your mama."

"He's here now."

"Tonight?"

"Yes. When I was out in that storm, I overheard him and Mother down at the garage. I think the third person who was in on my kidnapping is trying to blackmail them."

Heddy sucked in her breath. "You gots to leave with me, Child."

"Heddy, do you have a cell phone?"

The woman attempted to chuckle, but her mood was too somber. "I don't have no cell phone, Jessie. You should know that."

"Then I need for you to get to a phone. Ours is out here. I don't know if the lines have been cut. I need for you to call the FBI and tell them what I just told you."

"You's goin' with me, and you's gonna call the FBI man."

The lights flickered and Jessie held her breath. A brief moment later, they came back on.

Heddy used her hands to push her heavy body from the bed. "Come on, Child. Time's a wastin'."

"I can't."

"Why not?"

Jessie swallowed hard. "Mother will be coming back to check on me. I know it. I can feel it. If I'm not here, she'll know something's not right. But you—you can leave and get help."

"You leave with me right now, right this minute. I can take care of your mama."

"Maybe. But you can't take care of Edward Buchanan—and Brutus. And I have a hunch one or both of them's got a gun."

"If they got a gun, you ain't safe. And I ain't leavin' you."

"You've got to leave. Our only hope is for you to get to Grant, the FBI agent."

"That's his name? Grant?"

"Yes. Ask for him. Tell him who you are, and tell him I'm in trouble."

Heddy nodded unconvincingly.

"You can remember that name, Heddy?"

"I can remember it. U. S. Grant. Our eighteenth president."

"That's right."

"You ain't got me callin' in no false alarm, do you, Jessie?"

"No. You have to trust me."

"I don't want to get arrested for lyin' to the police."

"You won't be lying, and you won't get arrested. I promise."

Heddy leaned down and kissed Jessie on her forehead. "What will you do when I leave?"

"I'm staying right here in this bed. I'm going to appear like I'm asleep, just like I did when I was growing up."

The older woman smiled wearily. "You gots plenty of practice."

"Yes. I do." Jessie pushed her gently away. "Now go."

The lights flickered again and went out.

"Hurry!" Jessie hissed through the darkness.

She heard Heddy feeling her way through the room toward the door, and caught a glimpse of her as she headed into the hallway. She waited until she heard the woman's heavy feet descending the stairs, counting with each one as she did when she was a child. Once she counted the number of steps to the first floor, Jessie tossed off the bedcovers.

She had a lot to do. But first, she needed to get out of these pajamas.

70

The room was as black as pitch as Jessie felt her way to the other side of her bedroom. Once there, she grappled with an antique Italian music box that rested on top of her dresser. She knew from years of experience that when she opened the lid, she had at most two seconds before a Josquin Des Prez melody would begin to play. She tried to steady her fingers. Holding her breath, she snapped open the music box, grabbed the key she kept on top, and slammed it shut before the music could begin.

She felt for the wall and continued feeling her way around the room until she reached her bedroom door. She paused for a long moment, her head cocked, while she listened for any sound of movement.

On the second floor, there was no real hallway, but the massive hardwood stairs ended in the middle of the floor. The opening was surrounded by a railing, one which Jessie had leaned over countless times to view activities on the floor below. Four bedroom doors faced the open stairway, as well as one bathroom. The second bathroom was attached to the master bedroom.

Now she peered through the darkness toward her mother's bedroom door, but she was unable to determine whether the door was open or closed. On any normal night, it would be closed; her mother barricaded inside with a bottle of liquor.

But this was no normal night.

Jessie grabbed the door on either side and gently, slowly began to close it. It creaked as it swung, and she held her breath as if she could will it to be silent. Finally, it clicked shut.

She fumbled with the six inch square bronze lock until she located the keyhole above the enamel doorknob. Painstakingly, she rotated the key in her hand until it was situated properly. Fumbling in the darkness, she finally managed to lock the door.

It wasn't foolproof, and at best it would buy her only a little time. When she was only six years old, she'd locked herself in this bedroom and stubbornly would not allow anyone to enter, though her parents, Heddy and even a handyman tried to cajole her into opening the door. Meg had become so infuriated that she commissioned a local craftsman to create a replica key. Jessie never knew where she kept it; though she'd ravaged her mother's bedroom trying to find it during her difficult teen years, she was never able to locate it.

She had no doubt that Meg knew exactly where it was, and she could get her hands on it in seconds.

She had to work quickly.

The clouds were beginning to part just enough to allow a full moon to peak through them, casting a muted light upon rain that blew sideways, pounding the windows as if they were trying to enter. Now shadows played out on the walls, appearing like streaks of water running from ceiling to floor.

She moved back to the nightstand, where she slid open the top drawer and removed a candle and matches. Her fingers were shaking, and it took several attempts before she managed to light a match and then the candle. A weak aroma of aging lavender wafted upwards from the candle. She closed her eyes briefly and tried to compose her nerves.

The candle's light was woefully inadequate but it was all she had to augment the dim light from the moon amid the shifting cloud cover.

Had she been in her apartment, she might have looked out the window to determine if her neighbors' lights were off as well, indicating a power outage. But here, secluded in the country, there were no other homes. She could only wonder if the storm had knocked out the electricity, or if Brutus or Brainiac had intentionally plunged her into darkness.

As she found her way to the chest of drawers, she knew she had to assume the worst. They were coming for her, and it would be only a matter of time before they found her.

But what she couldn't tell Heddy for fear she wouldn't understand was simple: she needed evidence.

She'd reported Brutus to Grant, and they hadn't been able to find him. When she'd reported Edward Buchanan was Brainiac, he'd scoffed at her. Her only hope was to lead them back to the garage, where her father had installed closed circuit cameras in the hopes of catching an unauthorized driver—and hope she could get confessions on tape. It was risky; perhaps impossible. But, if it could be done, she was the only one left who could do it.

Her hands trembled as she placed the candle on top of the chest and rummaged through the drawers until she located a pair of blue jeans and a water resistant sport shirt. Quickly stripping off her pajamas, she donned the fresh clothes, followed by a pair of running socks and Gore-Tex walking shoes. Then she made her way to the closet and removed a hooded squall jacket. Grabbing her car keys from the top of the chest of drawers, she slipped them into her jacket pocket. She didn't know how she was going to do it, but once she'd gotten them to confess, she had to be ready to drive her car off the estate, past the security gate, and to safety.

She moved back to the door and pulled out her key once more. She had the key in the lock and was about to turn it when she heard a creak and a pop.

She froze. Instinctively holding her breath, she tried to listen to sounds in the hallway outside her door, but there was only silence.

She reached back to the key and then heard it again.

A creak and a pop.

Someone was coming up the stairs.

The hardwood floors were the original ones installed in the house in 1806. She knew they often made sounds of their own, as if ghosts were stepping upon them; Vincent often told her it was only the house settling.

And now as she stood there listening through the thick wood door, she tried to determine whether it was only her imagination, and her best recourse was to open the door and flee down the stairs—or if someone was lurking there, waiting for her to rush right into their grasp.

The next crack and pop made up her mind.

Someone was definitely moving upward one step at a time toward her room. The sounds were too heavy to be her mother's light step. This was a man.

Brutus or Brainiac, or both.

With her heart pounding in her ears, she rushed to the opposite side of the room. Perhaps hearing the noise made by her own footsteps, the sound on the stairwell increased tenfold, the constant cracking and popping indicating that whoever was there was now running up the stairs.

She fumbled with the window lock as the door knob rattled impatiently behind her.

Then, the door thudded violently as someone on the other side tried to kick it open.

She threw open the window and a rush of wind and rain pelted her, flooding the floor and causing the curtains to float toward the ceiling as if they were attempting to fly away.

The door shook with a growing fury as the man on the other side continued to kick it, and as she slipped through the open window, she heard the sound of wood splintering.

Dropping to the porch roof below was too easy; they would be upon her in an instant. Instead, just as the door was kicked in, slamming against the side wall, she scrambled upward to the roof above.

When she was younger, the roof had consisted of cedar shingles. Never one to be afraid of heights, she would play on the roof, much to her parent's agonized objections. After Jessie had gone off to college, they had the aged shingles torn out and replaced with a metal roof.

Now, she found herself slipping backward on the slick metal as if she was on a conveyor belt and it was pulling her downward, toward the people below. She heard the shouts of a man and a woman—Edward Buchanan, she thought, and definitely her mother—as she scrambled to remain on the roof just above them.

She clambered over the peak just as she saw Edward's head pop out of the window, peering below at the porch roof and pointing downward.

She tried to stand as she straddled the peak, but the winds were too fierce. She found herself holding onto the ridge with both hands, one foot on either side of it, running like a monkey on all fours as she tried desperately to reach the opposite end of the house furthest from the porch.

As she heard the front door opening below, she scrambled to the other side, dropping onto the roof of the one-story sunroom. She was now only eight feet to the ground.

With hands so wet the rain was running off them in sheets, Jessie grabbed onto the gutter and swung herself around, intending to slide down the gutter to the ground. But the metal was too slippery and her palms too slick. She found herself tumbling outward from the house, flying through the air before landing with a thud in the mud below, the breath knocked out of her.

She rolled away from the house and down an embankment before she came to a stop against a grove of trees.

71

Jessie hobbled into the shadows of the trees, the pain in her ankle growing in intensity. If she'd sprained her ankle, she thought, there was nothing that could be done about it now, except suck it up and keep moving.

She could hear voices from the vicinity of the house. It would only be a matter of time before they discovered her prints in the mud, and followed a trail that couldn't have been more obvious if Lewis & Clark had blazed it themselves.

She tried to stay close to the tree lines, but it was almost impossible to do as the woods wound their way further from the garage. So at the last moment, she sprinted across the open lawn.

Where was Grant? She wondered frantically, hoping Heddy had been able to reach a phone and convince him that this was not a false alarm.

The side door of the garage was hanging open. She slipped inside, leaving the wind and the rain behind her. A rumble began near the back of the garage and she realized a backup generator had kicked on. She wondered if the house's generator had also activated, and whether this meant the estate now had at least some limited power.

Besides her own car, there were a half dozen vehicles housed here. The 1936 light green Stout Scarab, with its moustache-like louvered grille mounted between the headlights, was front and center staring at her like a small post-war airplane on wheels. Ahead of her in the murky darkness closest to the wide garage doors were the black Porsche Cayenne her father had driven before his incarceration, her mother's ruby red Swedish Koenigsegg Agera, and her own Mercedes-Benz SLR McLaren Roadster.

In the calm of the garage with its odorous blend of oil, carnauba wax and gasoline, her heart rate almost began to slow to normal.

She was not alone.

She stopped beside a 1906 Rolls-Royce Silver Ghost and cocked her head. Hoping to hear Abby's claws on the garage door, scratching to get in, she was met by only silence. Through the distant windows, she could see the wind had abated and even the lightning and thunder appeared to have moved out of the area. Inside, there was only calm.

Yet, she couldn't shake the feeling that eyes were upon her. Slowly, deliberately, she turned around.

No one was there.

She waited several more seconds. The only sound was her own breathing.

She had only taken two steps away from the vehicle when a figure appeared from behind the 1948 blue Davis.

"Remember me?" The voice was low and even, frightening Jessie with its sinister lack of emotion. She wanted to turn away and rush for the open door, yet even as she tried to force her legs to move, she remained transfixed as Brutus walked around the three wheel vintage automobile.

Out of the corner of her eye, Jessie spotted a twelve inch long heavy duty wrench on the bumper of the Rolls-Royce. It would have sparked fury from her father, had he seen it left in such a careless manner.

She wanted to search the ceiling's perimeter for the tell-tale signs of a camera, but was afraid to pull her eyes away from the man inching toward her.

"Well, well," Brutus was saying as he moved around the vehicle between them, "this is an added bonus. I came for the money but I get you, too."

"Stay away from me," she warned. Her voice was higher and less sure than she would have liked for it to sound.

Brutus chuckled. "I've been wantin' to do this to you since I first laid eyes on you. But Eddie wouldn't let me. Now he's not here to protect you, is he?"

"I'm warning you," she said, pressing her body against the car. Without allowing her eyes to stray from his, her fingers locked themselves around the wrench.

"I'm gonna enjoy every second of this."

As he moved around the vehicle, she stepped backward in the opposite direction. Just as she neared the corner of the car where she had a clear shot at the door, he flung himself toward her, his long, hairy arm outstretched.

She gasped as she raised the wrench high above her head.

He sniggered as his eyes moved upward, following the arc of her arm as she raised it even higher. As he took a quick step toward her, lunging for the wrench, she slammed her heel into his groin.

He bellowed in anguish, falling backward onto his knees.

But as she turned to flee, he swung his arm outward, catching her ankles. As she tumbled backward, the wrench sailed out of her hands and through the back window of the Rolls-Royce. Instantly, the car alarm began howling, the sound reverberating in the enclosed garage.

Frantically, she clawed against him, kicking him in the face as she moved her torso further away. She grabbed hold of the back tire and hoisted herself to her feet as he came to his.

She could see the wrench inside the back window frame, but she knew it was beyond her reach.

He was on his feet now and coming after her with a renewed ferociousness; no longer attempting to encircle her in slow, measured steps, he now rushed forward in quick, jerky movements. As he slipped his long arm into the back window frame, she raced toward the Scarab.

Desperately, her eyes raked her surroundings, searching for another tool. But there were none.

She hesitated, trying to locate her position relative to the door, when he stepped in front of her, blocking off her means of escape. He held the heavy wrench in one hand while patting it menacingly in the palm of his other hand.

"I don't mind if we do this while you're unconscious," he growled, displaying yellowed, jagged teeth.

She was hemmed between two cars. As he approached, she could smell his putrid breath. She glanced upward, spotting a cable that ran the length of the garage. She had no idea what it was, though she suspected it was an air hose. It would have to do.

Brutus was barely an arm's length away from her. Now he gripped the wrench in his palm and pulled it back, his lip curling as he got ready to swing it.

As the wrench sailed through the air, she jumped as high and fast as she could, managing to grab the hose. The tool missed her head but hit her with a resounding crack in her thigh and for an excruciating moment, she thought the bone was broken. She screamed in pain, flailing for the hose as she began falling clumsily through the air.

The metal fitting at the end of the hose swung outward, striking Brutus across the nose. Everything was turning red and then black around her, and as she grabbed for her offended thigh, she landed unceremoniously on the hood of the Rolls, tumbling over it. The wrench continued sailing as though it had gained a life of its own, toppling first onto the hood of the Scarab, leaving a scratch the length of the hood in the pristine paint, before bouncing against the front windshield.

She had barely caught her breath from her hard landing when she felt her jaw exploding in pain as Brutus backhanded her. Before she could recover from the blow, he punched her in the mouth, sending her skidding across the Rolls. She might have landed on the floor beside it, but her fall was caught by the Davis. Her head bounced off the passenger side door before she slid down its side, leaving a swath of blood.

Brutus swore as he wiped the back of his hand against his grimy mouth.

She felt as if everything was moving in slow motion, almost as though she was watching everything happen to someone else. She tried to raise herself up, but before she could get to her feet, Brutus had pulled back his right hand, doubling it into a beefy fist.

As his fist came toward her like a locomotive, she whirled out of the line of fire, and his hand crushed into the aluminum side door. The sound was overwhelming, coming just inches from her face, and in her panic, she didn't know if the worst of it was the sound of the aluminum crumpling or his bones breaking. Instantly, he let out a furious, excruciating howl.

They were both bleeding now. Somewhere deep inside her, she knew she had only seconds to react. With every ounce of strength she had left in her body, she lunged for him, desperately sinking both sets of fingers into his eyes as though she was trying to remove the eyeballs. He wailed in pain, his voice sounding more like a wounded animal than a human being.

She staggered to her feet, slipping and sliding on the blood-soaked floor. It sounded like every car alarm in the garage was going off. It was enough to wake the dead, she thought, realizing with a renewed sense of urgency that the noise alone would bring Edward and Meg to the garage.

She had to make it to her own car. She felt the keys in her pocket, weighing it down, and now she limped toward it, trying to extract the keys so she could throw herself inside, hit the garage door opener, and get away from all three of them.

She was only a few feet away, and then her hands were touching the back bumper, using it to steady herself as her knees wobbled so unsteadily that they threatened to topple from under her. She barely realized she was keying the car as she moved to the side, so intent was she in reaching the door.

Her hand was on the door handle now.

Just as she began to open it, a hand wrapped itself around her ankle, smearing it with blood, and causing her to fall backward onto the hard garage floor. The room began spinning around her, and she now found herself in a struggle to maintain consciousness. She began kicking him indiscriminately, over and over, like a madwoman, until a voice from somewhere deep inside her reminded her to kick the groin. And somehow in the melee, she was able to target her heel and she kicked him again and again until he lay groaning on the concrete floor.

She managed to throw open the door to her Mercedes, leapt inside and hit the garage door opener, only to discover that the door would not automatically open. She groaned, wondering whether the generator was not hooked up to the doors—or if someone had intentionally jammed them. Her only hope was to try to open it manually.

There was a ten foot ladder propped against the side wall. Feeling like a zombie, she struggled to pull it into place with one eye on Brutus. But once she climbed it, she realized the ceilings were so high that the pull chain was just out of reach. She continued to the uppermost step, where she wobbled directly over the instructions that read "do not stand on this step" while she lunged forward, trying to grab hold of the chain. Finally, she managed to reach the orange pull chain.

She had it in her hand when the ladder was pushed from under her. She let out a scream as she fell, switching the chain from automatic to manual in the process, before landing with a violent thud against the grille of her father's Porsche.

Brutus had her in his grasp like a madman. She felt herself yanked to her feet, only to be doubled over backwards on the hood of the Porsche. Both his hands were around her slender neck, crushing her windpipe.

She tried to breathe but couldn't even manage a gasp. Though she struggled against him, trying desperately to free herself, she found her strength ebbing as her body was deprived of oxygen. The garage ceiling began to look surreal, the orange pull chain dangling above her as though a gentle summer breeze had brought it to life.

Her hands loosened on his and blackness began to set in around her. So, this is how it will end, she thought as she stared into Brutus' maniacal eyes, the white completely surrounding the iris as though they were about to pop out of his head.

She closed her eyes, knowing she had no more strength with which to fight him, when the image of her grandfather Palmer loomed before her. *Don't give up*, he seemed to be saying. *Never give up.*

Her eyes flew open as she rammed her fingers into Brutus' eyes. But unlike the last time, she twisted them and gritted her teeth as she literally tried to rip them out of his head. It's him or me, she heard the refrain in her head, and it's not going to be me.

With a blood-curdling howl, he loosened his grip on her and stumbled back. With his head just inches from her feet, she kicked him. And as he staggered backward, she braced herself against the vehicle and continued to kick him, again and again. Her entire body felt like a hammer as she pummeled him relentlessly.

She didn't know when she'd gotten off the hood of the car. Or how she'd managed to come after Brutus like an enraged attack dog. But, when she began to come to her senses, she realized he was lying on the floor in front of the Porsche, his head bloody, while she continued to kick him with blood-soaked shoes.

It was as if all the hours of captivity, all the weeks of her father's trial, and the days of realizing her father had not participated in her kidnapping, had come together in a tsunami of emotions.

When at last she stopped, he laid still, blood gushing from his head and winding its way across the once spotless floor. Realizing how painful her own throat was now, she rubbed it as she moved toward the doors. Exhausted, she managed to raise the door.

The wind from the storm caught her by surprise and she stood there, teetering on her feet as she breathed in the rich oxygen. Even the rain felt welcome as it poured across her face, and she opened her mouth to try and catch some of the water. Her lips were parched and every muscle in her body hurt.

She returned to her car. Wearily, she climbed into the driver's seat and tried to insert her key in the ignition.

It didn't fit.

Puzzled, she wiped the rain, blood and perspiration from her brow and tried to focus on the key. It was the familiar Mercedes-Benz key ring with her name engraved on the back. But the key had been switched.

"Mother," she whispered, hatred beginning to surge through her body. No one else had access to it. But, why would her mother want to prevent her from leaving?

She opened the glove compartment, but didn't find a spare key. Frantically, she searched through the other compartments. Finally, she leaned her head against the back of the seat and fought the tears that threatened to overwhelm her.

Never give up.

The words reverberated through her brain as though they'd been spoken just next to her ear.

She was surrounded by cars. Some were smashed now, windshield glass littering the floor, huge dents in others, and paint jobs that were miserably keyed.

Her father had been particular about their upkeep, which necessitated a mechanic who cared for them like they were winning racehorses. There had to be keys to them here, in this garage.

Feeling like her limbs weighed a thousand pounds she forced herself out of the Mercedes and toward the back of the garage, where a series of cabinets and toolboxes neatly lined the wall. She rummaged through one drawer after another, sending receipts flying and scattering tools. Her fingers locked onto something soft and smooth, and she pulled out the object, staring at it in horror. It was the mate to her father's glove, the large monogram seeming to stare back at her in the semi-darkness.

She closed her eyes and tried to concentrate on the keys. They wouldn't have been kept at the house, she reasoned—it would have required too much time and energy to go to the main house every time they were needed. But where were they?

She opened her eyes and stood back from the cabinets. Out of the corner of her eye, she spotted a metal box mounted on the side wall. Hurriedly, she rushed toward it, tearing the door open as quickly as she could.

It was a key cabinet.

But, in every position neatly marked with the model and year of the vehicle, the key was missing. The entire cabinet was empty.

She stood there, too tired to wonder whether Heddy had reached the FBI, where Grant was now, or how she was going to get off this estate.

She began to feel the hair on the back of her neck grow cool, as if someone was blowing on it. She held her breath in an attempt to listen, but the thudding of her heart was so loud, she could hear nothing else.

Someone was staring at her. She could feel their eyes boring into the back of her skull. Slowly, she half-turned. She could see Brutus' feet sticking out from in front of the Porsche, the pool of blood so wide now that it was encompassing his entire body.

She continued to turn around. And as she faced the open garage door head-on, she saw two figures move into place, side by side. They stood there now, motionless, silent. Two gray-black shadows, staring back at her.

Then, one of the sets of hands began to twitch and wring uncontrollably.

72

They stood like apparitions at the garage door, their figures still, their features obscured by the shadows. Without a sound, they moved forward like one body.

Their clothing was soaked. Meg's blond hair was plastered against her skull, but she seemed not to notice. Her expression was blank, her eyes staring toward Jessie but without any sign of recognition.

Jessie almost flew to her car, throwing open the door and hurling herself inside as they continued toward her, their own movements measured and deliberate.

Her breath fogged the windows as she hit the electronic door lock. With a sinking heart, it occurred to her that if the garage doors hadn't been on the generator, the chances were slim that the cameras would be. And she knew even if she was on film, it might be too late.

Meg stopped dead center of the car grille, her eyes unblinking, her wrists shaking. Edward continued in a measured, confident step that caused Jessie's heart to begin pounding so strongly that her chest felt constricted. With her eyes locked on Edward's, she slid her hand to the glove compartment and quietly opened it. She moved her hand around, touching papers and other innocuous items before her hand clenched a hard plastic device with a sharp, serrated edge. As Edward approached the driver's side door, she pulled the item from the glove compartment.

She glanced downward. In the split second she removed her focus from Edward, she realized what she held in her hand was a windshield scraper. "OxyChem" was stamped in bright red letters near the five inch edge. Ironic, she thought, since the ransom money was dropped off on Occidental's property.

She heard a sound behind her at the same moment that Edward's eyes moved abruptly from Jessie ensnared by her own car, to something just beyond it. She peered into the side mirror to see Abby standing just inside the garage, having entered it through the open side door. She was soaking wet but still large and formidable. And her lips were curled back in a vicious snarl.

Edward stopped beside the driver's window. Without a word, he pulled a LifeHammer from a deep pocket in his overcoat.

Jessie felt the adrenaline surge through her. Vincent had insisted that each of his cars carry a LifeHammer. In the event of an emergency, it could cut through the heavy seat belts like a knife through butter. And it could break a car window with minimal effort. As Jessie stared at it, she realized there should have been one in her own glove compartment. As Edward raised his hand above the window, she knew he had taken hers, in the event he had to face a situation exactly like this.

She was trapped.

She moved so quickly that she didn't even know how her legs managed to clear the console between the driver's seat and the passenger's. But, in the instant Edward's fist surged downward and the LifeHammer shattered the window into a hundred pieces, her fingers were frantically working to unlock the opposite side door.

She scrambled out, only to be stopped by her mother.

"Why?" Jessie screamed.

"You're nothing to me," Meg said. Her eyes did not meet Jessie's but stared beyond her just as Jessie had stared at the defense attorney's ear at that trial that seemed so long ago.

"I'm your daughter!" Jessie stammered, choking on her own words.

Meg's lip curled. "The day you were born is the day you became *his* child, not mine."

Jessie grabbed her mother's shoulders and flung her around, wrapping her arms around her torso. They both faced Edward, but now Meg's body was shielding Jessie. Between Edward and Meg lay Brutus in a congealing puddle of blood.

Edward didn't appear phased. He glanced quickly at Brutus' still body before snarling, "I should never have sent a boy to do a man's job." With that, he looked at Jessie, her face peering over Meg's shoulder, and smiled.

The sight of his sneer, so calm and deliberate, caused Jessie's blood to boil. As he stepped toward her, she threw her mother into his arms. But as she turned to run, Edward's voice erupted in a screech that sounded like a wounded animal. Despite herself, she turned around in shock to see Abby's powerful jaws locked onto Edward's right hand. The dog rumbled like a locomotive as she shook her head back and forth in an alligator grip, as if trying to rip his hand from his body. As she watched, her feet frozen to the floor, blood gushed from him, revealing torn tendons and muscle.

Cursing, Edward rammed the LifeHammer against Abby's head and the dog dropped to the floor in a lifeless heap.

Jessie screamed and rushed toward her dog as Edward began kicking the animal. She was coming after him like a lioness protecting her cubs. If she had to rip him apart limb by limb, she would.

As she neared Edward, Meg stepped between them. She seemed larger than ever before as she faced Jessie, her fists doubled, specs of saliva on her lips and chin, and her eyes bulging.

Edward's back was to her as he drew back and kicked Abby again with so much force that Jessie felt her heart sinking inside her. Instinctively, her own fists doubled. Surprised, she realized she still held the heavy scraper in her hand.

Meg stood in front of her, her eyes narrowed, the irises seeming to look right through her to something beyond Jessie. And in that instant, Jessie threw back her hand. When she drove it forward, it was with the anger, the pain, and the sheer torment she had suffered since that fateful night at her condominium.

It hit her mother with such force that the plastic broke in half. As her mother reeled backward, her eyes rolling into the back of her head, her jaw spun outward in a grotesque, unnatural position, no longer appearing attached to the upper half of her face.

Meg fell against Edward, pushing both of them into Vincent's Porsche, setting off the car alarm once more as they tumbled to the ground.

Jessie lunged toward Abby, but Edward threw his foot outward, tripping her and forcing her into the Davis to keep from falling.

A constant, low moan echoed through the garage. It grew in intensity as though it was gaining strength. Jessie's eyes met Edward's. His were wide as if he, too, had no idea what was making the noise.

In the corner of her eye, Jessie saw Abby's long, golden fur as the dog came to her feet. She was bloodied but she was standing, her head low, her lips pulled backward, revealing long, sharp teeth. As she continued the otherworldly sound, her eyes so large that Jessie could see the whites of her eyes reddened and wild, she looked like a rabid animal.

But, Edward was no longer looking at Abby. Nor was he looking at Jessie. He was looking beyond her, as her mother had. And now Meg's eyes followed his.

Jessie felt the hairs begin to stand along the nape of her neck. Every muscle in her body ached with a tiredness she could never have imagined. As she watched Meg and Edward's expressions and their motionless bodies, she knew her ordeal was far from over.

Turning slowly around, she saw the gun first. It was only six feet away from her. It had been pointed at Edward and Meg but as Jessie continued to turn, the gun rotated slowly in her direction.

The barrel seemed huge, and Jessie couldn't quite force herself to stop staring into the vast, black hole. But as she followed the line of the gun to the blood-soaked hand and upward to the elbow, she felt her own blood freezing inside her.

She knew her mouth was agape, but she couldn't find the control needed to close it.

Just feet from her with the gun now pointed at her head was Brutus.

It was as if he wasn't human. As if he could not be killed.

"Her first," he said, his mouth spewing blood as he talked. "Then you two. Thought you could double-cross me, did you?"

Jessie watched helplessly as his finger squeezed the trigger. The shot rang out, echoing through the garage. But as Jessie watched, expecting to feel the bullet penetrate her body at any second, Brutus' arm flew upward and his body wavered as though he'd been dealt a fatal body blow. He fell over backward, crashing through a car window, the gun hitting the floor and firing before sliding across the slick floor away from them.

Suddenly, Abby charged forward like a freight train, her teeth sinking into Edward's throat as she tossed her head from side to side. Meg opened her mouth to scream, but the sound remained on her lips as blood oozed out from her side.

Jessie felt frozen to the floor, her mind trying to grasp the situation unfolding around her. Then, her eyes fell upon three figures in the doorway of the garage.

Grant was pulling his gun back toward his body. Jessie realized as her knees sank that he had fired his gun before Brutus could fire his.

And, as Brutus' gun had hit the floor and fired, the stray bullet had penetrated Meg's torso. She now lay in a spreading pool of blood, her eyes barely focusing.

As Grant moved toward Edward and Abby, the other two figures followed behind him. With the danger over, Heddy and Nick rushed to Jessie's side. Somewhere in the back of her mind as if she was seeing through a growing fog, Jessie realized Grant was checking the pulse on the side of Meg's neck and then radioing for an ambulance and backup.

Abby released her grip on Edward, allowing him to drop to the floor, his throat resembling raw hamburger. Finally, the golden retriever moved toward Jessie with all the calm and love of a devoted dog, coming to rest in her lap as Jessie sank to the floor.

She held her there, with the dog's head cradled in her arms, as Nick wrapped his arms around them both.

73

Jessie heard a chorus of sirens in the distance, growing louder and more insistent as they neared the Palmer estate. Ivory had arrived and now Jessie watched as she and Grant handcuffed Meg and Edward.

"Are you okay?" Nick asked, helping Jessie to her feet.

"Just a little banged up," she said. Now that her ordeal was over, she felt bone-tired. It was as if it had taken every ounce of energy to fight Brutus, Edward and Meg, and now that it was over, she had no strength left—even to stand. She felt herself teetering, and Nick caught her and held her.

"When you left," he said, "I realized I was lost without you."

"I'm so sorry—"

He placed a finger on her lips, silencing her. "Shhh," he said. "It's over now. I don't ever want to be apart from you again."

An ambulance arrived, flooding the garage with its rotating red light, followed by several sheriffs' vehicles.

"I think this one's dead," Grant said, kneeling beside Brutus and feeling for a pulse in his neck.

A paramedic squatted beside him, feeling his wrist. "Yep," he said. "But we'll have to take him in anyway and have a doctor declare it."

"You'll want to take this guy first," Grant said, pointing at Edward.

He had come to a seated position but was leaning against the Porsche, groaning. Jessie watched his blood gushing out onto her father's once-pristine car, and wondered if he'd be furious that his car was getting trashed or relieved that the real kidnappers had been caught. Now, she thought suddenly, he'll be coming home.

"What happened to him?" the paramedic asked, moving from Brutus to Edward.

"Dog attack," Grant said, glancing at Abby. "Self defense."

Abby wagged her tail and laid down at Jessie's feet as if they were reclining by the fireplace on a relaxing winter evening.

While the paramedic worked on stopping the blood flowing from Edward's throat, Grant began reading Edward his Miranda rights. When he finished, he said, "We'll be posting a police officer at your hospital room door, and you'll be cuffed to your hospital bed. As soon as the doctor clears you for discharge, you're headed to the county jail."

Edward moaned and avoided Grant's eyes.

"Why?" Grant asked. "Last year's annual report showed you earned more than six hundred grand. That wasn't enough for you?"

Edward rolled his eyes. "I want a lawyer."

Grant nodded. "You'll get one."

"You'll need one," Jessie interjected. As Grant and Ivory looked toward her, she pointed to a half-moon object in the corner of the garage. "Closed circuit cameras. Smile," she added, hoping the generators had powered the camera, "you're on Candid Camera."

Jessie turned to her mother. Meg appeared pale and thin, and her hands jerked against the handcuffs as she pathetically tried to wring them. "What I want to know," Jessie said, fighting back tears, "is why you did it?"

"You think," she said, holding her bound hands against her aching jaw as she spoke, "it was easy living here, with everything in your father's name? Living on a paltry allowance? Knowing he was sending a small fortune to another woman? Then when

Edward and I began our affair, I knew we'd have not only the Palmer fortune but the power—"

"Shut up," Edward gurgled.

"Don't talk," the paramedic admonished as he began wrapping his throat with a bandage.

"Tell her not to talk," he grumbled.

Ivory stepped forward and hoisted Meg to her feet. As she did, she began reading her Miranda rights and walking her toward the FBI car.

"Am I going to the hospital?" Meg whined. "I'm hurt, I'm bleeding."

"That little bit of blood?" Ivory retorted. "The doc at the jail can take care of that. After you've met Big Berta."

Jessie watched as Ivory led her past the others descending upon the Palmer estate, ready to process the garage as a crime scene. Another ambulance arrived and two paramedics began readying Brutus' body for transport. Her eyes fell on Heddy, who was soaked from the strong rains and looking haggard.

Grant moved closer to Jessie. His eyes roamed from Jessie's hands, firmly in Nick's clasp, to her eyes. "You okay?" he asked.

"What took you so long?" she asked. Though she attempted a smile, it was beginning to sink in just how close she had come to being killed.

Grant pointed at Heddy. "You've got a good friend there," he said.

Heddy moved toward Jessie, extending her arms, and Jessie gratefully allowed the older woman to embrace her tightly.

"She's not just a friend," she whispered. "She's my mom. She might not have given birth to me, but she's my mom, in every other way."

Tears flowed down Heddy's cheeks. "Lord 've mercy, child. You've been through a lot. More than any soul ought to."

Jessie pulled back a bit and wiped the tears from the older woman's cheeks. Turning to Grant, she said, half-joking, "So, you believed her but not me?"

"I was already on my way," Grant said, eying Edward as the paramedic continued to bandage him.

"What made you change your mind?"

"Got a call from a bank employee. It'll all come out at Meg's trial." He glanced toward Ivory, who was securing Meg in the back seat of the FBI car. "Turned out, it wasn't Vincent who put that money in the bank's lockbox."

"Oh?" Jessie's eyes cut over to Edward.

Grant waved toward Meg. "It was your mother. She forged your father's signature."

Nick wrapped his arm around Jessie's shoulder, leaning closer to look into her eyes. "You okay?" he asked quietly.

Jessie nodded, though she felt far from okay. Her stomach felt as if it was turning somersaults inside her, and she was beginning to worry that she was going to be sick.

The paramedic finished bandaging Edward and helped him to his feet. Only a yard away, a stretcher awaited him to whisk him to the ambulance.

"You all don't think I'm crazy anymore?" Jessie asked. She wasn't quite sure who she was asking—Nick or Grant—but Nick responded.

"I showed up at Grant's office," he said. "Told him about our—" he seemed to be searching for the right word "—little spat. I had to work late, and when I got home, I found your note. I tried calling you, but couldn't get through."

"He knew where you were," Grant said. "And by that point, I knew we needed to talk."

"So—you were already on your way here?"

"We were on the highway when Heddy called," Grant continued. "When she said your life was in danger, we radioed for backup and sped up."

"I'll say we sped up," Nick added. "Lights flashing, siren blaring, people were pulling off the road to let us pass."

"Heddy was at the entrance to the estate when we arrived. And she got us through that security gate. Otherwise, we'd have been—a little late."

Jessie thought of Brutus pointing the gun at her and began to feel sick again. "I don't want to think about it."

"Where'd you call from?" Grant asked. "My caller ID said 'Vincent Palmer'."

Heddy grinned. "I ain't never used no cell phone before. But I 'membered Mr. Palmer, he weren't allowed to take his phone with him. So I grabbed it, drove to the main road, out of sight of anybody at the big house, and called this FBI man."

Jessie leaned against Nick. Just the musky scent of his cologne and the feel of his strong arms around her comforted her. He was there for her when she needed him most, she thought. As she watched Grant escort the stretcher carrying Edward Buchanan to the ambulance, she realized everyone had rallied to her aid. Not a moment too soon, she thought, but they'd been there for her.

She glanced at Abby, who had closed her eyes. Even with the buzz of activity increasing around them as crime scene technicians descended on the garage, Abby was taking a nap. She'd had one stressful evening, Jessie thought.

"I'd like to get Abby to an emergency vet," she said abruptly. At the sound of her name, Abby opened one eye. "Just to make sure she doesn't have any broken ribs—or anything. She took a bit of a beating."

"Come on, Ab," Nick said, patting his thigh.

Abby sprang to her feet.

"Come on, Jess," he said, planting a kiss on her forehead. "We'll get Abby to the vet. And then both my girls are coming home with me, where they belong."

74

Jessie sat in the brown leather chair at the conference table as First Palmer Bank's board meeting dragged on, but she felt her eyes drawn to the window that encompassed the entire wall opposite her. Outside, the maple trees were turning a brilliant red, heralding the arrival of the autumn season. Already, the farmers were selling a bumper crop of fleshy pumpkins, turning vacant lots into a bright orange tribute to the approach of Halloween and Thanksgiving. The mornings greeted her now with a crisp chill, and her summer wardrobe had been replaced with wool skirts and coordinating blazers.

She watched as a brisk wind caught the branches of nearby trees, tossing their yellow, orange and red leaves into the air before floating gently to the sidewalk. Reluctantly, she turned back to the room and allowed her eyes to wander around the table.

At its head was Vincent, who was clearly relishing his role as Chairman of the Board. There was a different air at the bank these days, an excitement and a renewed loyalty to him, as well as relief that Edward Buchanan's days as Chairman and CEO were over. Jessie tapped her pen on the desk as she thought of him now in a jail cell, awaiting a trial that was expected to begin in just a few days.

As Vincent continued speaking about the future of First Palmer Bank and upcoming sales campaigns, her eyes wandered to Pam Woody, who caught her gaze and smiled. One of Vincent's first orders of business had been to reinstate her as Chief Financial Officer, replacing the recent college graduate whom Edward thought he could manipulate. Pam, in a particularly generous gesture, had decided to keep the young man as her assistant, teaching him how First Palmer Bank was expected to operate.

Across from Pam was Bill Farris, reinstated as Chief Auditor, good-naturedly sparring with Vincent on the various campaigns scheduled.

Jessie took a deep breath. She sat at the opposite end from Vincent, frequently catching his eye. His eyes had a sparkle in them now. The sadness was gone, and he was more his old self, though the arrogance he once portrayed was muted now.

She had been named as Chief Executive Officer and the Board's newest member, also making history as the bank's youngest board member. It was a role she cherished, even if she did work 'half days' as Nick called it, which meant arriving just before 7:00 a.m. and turning out the lights at precisely 7:00 p.m. Her days had flown by in a flurry of activity as she unfolded fraudulent transactions that Edward had made in his brief stint as CEO to financially benefit himself.

A movement just outside the window caught her eye. She followed the dark four-door sedan as it parked on the street. She glanced at Vincent, who followed the nod of her head, and they both watched as Ivory and Grant left the FBI vehicle and headed toward the bank's front doors.

Vincent adjourned the meeting. The others had noticed the FBI agents as well, and departed the conference room quickly.

Vincent met Jessie at the door of the conference room, placing his hand on her lower back. They shared a closeness now that was stronger than ever, and though Jessie tried to downplay her role in his release, Vincent made it clear that he considered his release from prison and the official news that he was not guilty after all, to be his daughter's accomplishment.

"Mr. Palmer," Martha said, approaching the conference room door, "Mr. Bailey is here to see you."

Vincent stepped into the hallway, shook Grant's and Ivory's hands, and invited them into the conference room.

Jessie smiled at them as they entered, exchanging pleasantries. They both appeared relaxed, she thought.

"Thought I'd give you a bit of a status report," Grant said as he seated himself.

The others followed suit and waited for him to continue.

"As you know, the defense attorneys have requested separate trials for Meg and Edward," he continued after everyone was situated. "And Edward's trial is coming up first."

"Will separate trials make the cases stronger—or weaker?" Vincent asked.

"Definitely stronger. Meg is determined to redeem her reputation by testifying against Edward. She swears it was all his idea."

"And Edward?" Vincent said the name as if he had trouble saying it.

"Oh, he's ready to testify against Meg. He swears it was all *her* idea." Grant chuckled.

"Who do *you* think was the mastermind?" Jessie asked. The words felt odd, as though she was speaking of total strangers, but the fact that her mother had been so callous had left an undeniable mark on her. She wondered some nights whether she would ever manage to move past the pain.

"We may never know exactly who gave birth to the plan," Grant said quietly, "but my theory is that Edward was obsessed with power and money. Did you know he broke the security codes and accessed your bank records before Jessie's kidnapping?"

"I know," Jessie said. "It's one of the things I'm working with now—how to make the security codes more secure." She chuckled at the irony of her statement. "But what I really don't understand," she continued in a softer, more somber tone, "is how my mother ever got involved. And why she did it. I guess," she added, "we may never know."

"Well, I'm not so sure about that," Grant said, glancing sideways at Vincent.

"Do you two know something I don't know?"

"Maybe I said too much," Grant said.

"No," Vincent interjected, "you didn't. I have no secrets from my daughter."

"You sure about that?"

"Positive." Vincent cocked his head and narrowed his eyes. "Why would you think I do?"

"Well, in interrogations—and keep in mind, suspects will say just about anything, whether it's true or not—"

"What did Meg tell you?"

"What we've pieced together," Grant said slowly, as though he was carefully selecting his words, "is when Edward cracked the security codes and got into your accounts, Vincent, he discovered you'd been writing pretty substantial checks to…" He stopped and looked at Vincent as if unsure whether to continue.

"To Susan Jones." Vincent's eyes grew wide as though a light bulb had just come on.

"Susan Jones," Jessie said. "You asked me about her once, Grant. But I didn't know—" she interrupted herself and stared at her father, her mouth half-open. "Daddy, you haven't—have you?"

Vincent waved his hand. "It isn't what you think. It's one of those things the family just doesn't talk about."

"Don't leave me hanging, Daddy."

"Just between the four of us," Vincent said, looking pointedly at Ivory and Grant before his eyes came to rest on Jessie. After each of them nodded, he continued, "My father wasn't exactly the stellar citizen folks thought he was."

Grant laughed loudly. "Hate to break this to you, but he wasn't known in the community as an angel."

"Okay, you're right. He could be mean, he could be ornery. But, he had a reputation for being faithful."

"Faithful," Jessie said, "you mean—in terms of—"

"Your grandmother."

"He wasn't?"

"Not exactly. He had a—relationship—with another woman. Lasted more than forty years."

"Did Granna know?"

Vincent shrugged. "She never said a word to me, if she did. But before your grandfather died, he asked me to watch over Susan—my half-sister."

Jessie sucked in her breath. "Are you serious?"

"She's a lovely woman, Jessie. Sweet, smart—and tough. A whole lot like you, come to think of it."

"Wow," Grant said. "Was Edward ever wrong."

"He thought *I* was having an affair?"

"Not only did he think that, but he brought 'evidence' to Meg. From what we were able to piece together, that started the ball rolling with their—relationship. And their kidnapping scheme."

"But—they planned my kidnapping because they thought Daddy was having an affair?"

Grant touched Jessie's shoulder lightly. "I don't think Meg ever intended for you to get hurt," he said softly. "The plan was for you to be taken somewhere overnight, plant evidence that Vincent was behind the kidnapping, and when Vincent went to prison, Edward would take control of the bank, Meg would take over the Palmer finances—which might have been questionable, whether a judge would ever have granted her those rights—and they'd split the ransom money."

"And Brutus?" Jessie asked. "How did he come into the picture?"

"Ah, yes. Brutus. Name's Harry Loney. Two bit criminal with a record this long—" he placed his hands about two feet apart. "Mostly petty crimes, breaking into homes, cars, stealing out of mailboxes. That kind of thing."

"How could Mother have known such a man?"

"She didn't, according to her. Edward met him at some honky-tonk when he was looking for somebody to help him carry out the kidnapping. He was the brains behind it, but not the brawn. He needed somebody for the dirty work."

Jessie nodded silently.

"We tried to contact next-of-kin," Ivory interjected, "but couldn't locate anyone."

"So, what will happen to the body?"

"Pauper's field."

Jessie's cell phone rang. "It's Nick," she said. "Will you excuse me?"

Vincent nodded, and Jessie moved toward the window as she spoke to him. When she turned back around, Grant and Ivory appeared to be leaving. "Wait!" she called out.

They stopped in the doorway.

"Can you join us for lunch?" she asked. "Nick is parking the car now. He'll be here any second."

Grant looked at Vincent. "I guess we're not in a hurry—"

"A gal's gotta eat," Ivory chimed in.

"It'll be a celebratory lunch," Vincent said, "on me."

They started into the hallway and Grant stopped suddenly. "Oh, I almost forgot."

"There's more?" Vincent teased.

"Your mechanic's son."

"What about him?"

"He's the one who was driving your antique vehicles. The reason you installed the closed circuit cameras. You'll need to contact the sheriff if you want to pursue charges against him; that's a local matter... But he kind of did you a favor."

"Oh?" Vincent said, the color rising in his cheeks.

"If you hadn't installed the cameras, we would never have gotten the evidence on tape." He chuckled. "Of all the places where Meg and Edward could have decided to make their plans..."

"So, it's all on tape?"

"Right down to the doctored audiotape of you. You see, Edward was taping your conversations at the bank. He must have hired someone to splice them together into conversations he could play to make Jessie think you were there and you were part of her kidnapping."

"He didn't actually splice them in the garage?"

"No. And he's not talking. But he did play them for Meg."

"In the garage." Vincent laughed. "On tape. How ironic."

* * * * *

The Greek café smelled of olives, fresh-baked bread and pungent cheeses. Vincent wanted to order a bottle of wine to celebrate a new chapter in their lives, but Ivory and Grant were on duty. So they settled on a round of non-alcoholic, sparkling Ariel Brut Cuvée.

"To all of us," Vincent said, standing. He raised his wine glass in a toast. "To quote an old Irish blessing: May the road rise up to meet you; May the wind be always at your back; May the warm rays of sun fall upon your home; And may the hand of a friend always be near."

They started to raise their glasses to join in the toast when Nick interrupted. "Wait."

Jessie turned toward him, astonished.

He stood beside Vincent. "And," he added, continuing the Irish blessing, "May green be the grass you walk on; May blue be the skies above you; May pure be the joys that surround you." He paused before kneeling on the floor beside Jessie. "And May true be the hearts that love you."

A bit embarrassed, Jessie looked around the table to see everyone beaming. Even the owner of the Greek café and his staff were grinning from the sidelines, and it seemed as if every eye was upon her.

Nick opened his palm to reveal a small black box. With his eyes locked on hers, he opened it to reveal a cushion-cut diamond surrounded by bead-set diamonds that stretched along a white gold band.

"Oh, my God," Jessie said. She didn't know whether to stare at the ring or the box with "Tiffany & Co." elegantly displayed, along with a card that read "Tiffany Legacy." The diamond had to be over a carat, she thought, and perhaps two. It was stunning. It took her breath away.

Nick set his wine glass on the table, his hand trembling. "Jessie," he said, "You are the best thing that's ever happened to me. I love you with all my heart. Will you marry me?"

"Yes!" she said, melting into Nick's arms. "Yes!"

The restaurant erupted into applause.

"Toast!" Ivory said, laughing. "All that Irish stuff times two!"

As Grant, Ivory and Vincent clinked their glasses, Jessie and Nick remained in a tight embrace. When she finally, gently pulled herself away, Nick removed the ring from the box and reached for her hand.

"But—not with that ring," she said hesitantly.

"You don't like it?" Nick whispered.

"I love it," she responded. "But—you can't afford something like this. Not on your salary. Not from Tiffany's."

Vincent stepped forward and clasped her shoulder. "It's a wedding gift," he said, "from me."

Jessie's jaw dropped. "You knew?"

He laughed. "He stopped by yesterday," he said, his eyes glistening as he glanced at Nick before looking back at Jessie. "And he asked for my blessing. Which I gave," he added, "instantly!"

"Why do you think we showed up when we did?" Grant added, smiling.

"You all knew?"

Grant laughed. "If you hadn't invited us to lunch, we'd have invited ourselves!"

"Well, you sneaky thing!" She looked back at Nick. "All of you!"

Nick slid the ring onto her finger as the onlookers erupted in applause once more.

Jessie didn't know whether she was crying due to happiness or the bittersweet emotion she had as she bid farewell to Grant and Ivory. They'd been with her through the most painful time in her life, and though she was happy her ordeal was over, she didn't want to lose contact with them.

"There's a reason for everything," Grant said quietly, hugging her good-bye. "And there was a reason I was in the right place, at the right time, to help you." He swept her bang away from her brow. "Maybe—if Vincent will share you—you'll be the daughter—" he started to choke and turned away.

"Yes," Jessie said, pulling him back. She kissed him on the

cheek and wiped away a lone tear, "There's enough trouble in this body to share with the both of you."

Grant laughed and dabbed at his eye.

Then he was gone, striding away with Ivory toward the dark sedan Jessie had come to recognize so well. Nick, Jessie and Vincent continued walking to the bank but before they reached the corner, Vincent stopped them.

"You two lovebirds need some time to yourselves," he said, kissing Jessie on her forehead. "But before I leave you, I've got another gift for you ." He reached into his jacket's inside pocket and pulled out a thick envelope.

"No, Daddy," Jessie objected. "You've done too much already."

He pressed the envelope into her hand.

Despite her objections, she opened it. Inside was a bank savings register. She opened it to the first page, where one thousand dollars had been deposited on the day she was born. Flipping through it, she noted one deposit after another, the amounts increasing with each year. She was hesitant to turn to the last page. "Daddy—how much is here?"

"Two million," he whispered.

"What?" She turned to the last page, where the final deposit was made the day before her kidnapping. "So, is this—?"

"The money Brutus never got? No. This was made the old-fashioned way."

She held the envelope in her hand as though she was thoughtfully weighing it.

"My work," Vincent said, "isn't about the money. It's about doing something I love." He squeezed her shoulder. "And one of the benefits of an honest day's work is I can give it to someone I love."

"All those years that Edward Buchanan had worked for you," Jessie said, wiping a tear from the corner of her eye, "yet there was one lesson he didn't learn."

The light turned and they began to cross the intersection.

"Oh?" Vincent said. "And what's that?"

"That nothing good can come from the banker's greed."

* * * * *

ABOUT T. RANDY STEVENS

T. Randy Stevens is Chairman of the Board and Chief Executive Officer of First Farmers and Merchants Bank. First Farmers operates seventeen banking locations in a seven county area in Middle Tennessee. He has been employed by this bank for over 38 years. His philosophy is to put your faith first, your family second, your friends third, and your career fourth in order to have a successful life.

T. Randy Stevens is very active in his community and has received the following awards: Jaycee Distinguished Service Award, Boy Scouts of America Long Rifle Award, Boy Scouts of America Silver Beaver Award, Rotary Club of Columbia Service Award, Rotary International Paul Harris Fellow Award, Boys & Girls Clubs of America National Service to Youth Award, and Tennessee Bankers Association Leader in Banking Excellence Award.

Visit www.trandystevens.com for more information.

ABOUT P.M. TERRELL

P. M. Terrell

p.m.terrell is the pen name for Patricia McClelland Terrell. She is the award-winning, internationally acclaimed author of eleven books, including four suspense/thrillers (*Exit 22, Ricochet, The China Conspiracy,* and *Kickback*); two historical adventure/suspense (*River Passage, Songbirds are Free*); a how-to book for authors (*Take the Mystery out of Promoting Your Book*); and four computer books (*Creating the Perfect Database, The Dynamics of WordPerfect, The Dynamics of Reflex,* and *Mememto WordPerfect.*)

Ms. Terrell is a co-founder of The Book 'Em Foundation, a partnership between authors and law enforcement agencies dedicated to raising public awareness of the correlation between high crime rates and high illiteracy rates, increasing literacy, and reducing crime.

Ms. Terrell also serves on the Robeson County Friends of the Library Board of Directors and initiated the *Writers Rally in Robeson Visiting Author Series*; and she serves on the Robeson County Arts Council. Both organizations are committed to supporting the arts, science, history and heritage of Robeson County, North Carolina. She served as the first female President of the Chesterfield County/ Colonial Heights (Virginia) Crime Solvers Board of Directors and as the Treasurer for the Virginia Crime Stoppers Association. She began the *New Leash on Life* program in Robeson County (North Carolina) in which dogs scheduled for euthanasia are rescued and paired with prisoners, who are taught how to care for and train the animals.

Visit her website at www.pmterrell.com for more information.

ABOUT ABBY

Abby, Jessie's golden retriever, belonged in real life to Marion and Tommy Thompson of Lumberton, North Carolina. She was adopted by the Thompsons when she was approximately five and a half years old, when her previous owner became ill and had to give her up.

Abby had a sixth sense—she could tell when someone was ill, depressed, or having a bad day, and she always tried to cheer them. Regardless of the situation, she always wanted to please. And she liked nothing better than being close to her owners.

She always acted like a lady, except when she sensed danger. She would sit under the table at outdoor restaurants. She loved nursing homes, and because her previous owner was wheelchair bound, she was always gentle. She helped children get over their fear of dogs with her loving and sweet ways. Intelligent, outgoing, she loved riding in the front passenger seat of the car as though she was a person. When she sensed danger, she was instantly ready to protect and defend.

Sadly, Abby passed away in May of 2008 from a hemangiosarcoma. She was twelve years old.

Abby's owners, Marion and Tommy Thompson, won a silent bid to have Abby memorialized in this book. The proceeds from that bid were donated to the Robeson County Humane Society of Lumberton, North Carolina, to be used to rescue and care for homeless animals.